KINGS OF
BRIGHTON BEACH

D. B. SHUSTER

CRIME BYTES MEDIA

NEW YORK

D1502840

ALSO BY D.B. SHUSTER

A Bundle of Neurotica: Eight Neurotica Short Stories

DEDICATION

For Gene, my favorite Ruski.

ACKNOWLEDGMENTS

I have been the fortunate recipient of a number of blessings in the process of creating this series.

Dina Fischbein and Lisa Shiroff, comrades in the writing trenches, critique partners, and most importantly friends—these incomparable women push me to bring out the best in myself and my writing. My life and my work are both infinitely better as a result. I trust we will celebrate many books, theirs and mine, together.

Producing these first episodes has been a team effort. I am immensely grateful for the beautiful work of editors Denise Vitola and Lynne Cannon Menges and of cover designer Asha Hossain. I also thank the brave beta readers who shared their impressions and critiques of early drafts.

Steve Bennett appeared in my life at exactly the right moment with his wisdom and enthusiasm, joining me on this adventure and convincing me to follow my vision for publishing this series in episodes instead of novels. I am ever so grateful that he has taken me under his wing. I also thank him and his talented team at AuthorBytes for creating a website home for my series and opening the world of social media to me.

Joseph Pascarella, retired Captain of the Brooklyn Police Department, has been another unexpected and wonderful blessing. His guidance on police procedure, jargon, and "mobbed up" crime scenes has been invaluable. Any mistakes are, of course, my own.

Thank you to my friends and family for believing in me and loving me, my neurotic obsession with my fictional characters notwithstanding. I gratefully acknowledge the first readers of this work, especially those at my day job, who didn't laugh when I told them what I was doing and eagerly demanded to see more. Thank you for being my first fans. I especially thank my mother, who taught me that every blade of grass has its own angel telling it to grow and that I should listen to that special voice.

Finally, I thank my husband and children—for your love and support, for the beauty and meaning you bring to my life, and for your humor and caution in entering my dangerous writing lair where I am prone to bite your heads off.

EPISODE #1

D. B. Shuster

INNA

INNA LAY ON something cold and hard, and a steady beat thumped beneath her. Far away, she heard the din of voices and the rhythmic swell of techno music. Closer, there was quiet, save for an intermittent drip drop, drip drop, like a faucet with a slow leak when water has pooled in the sink basin.

Where was she? Why was she so wet and cold? Her heart beat sluggishly, and she strained for consciousness. Behind her eyelids, she sensed light. She shivered with cold, felt a strange wetness under her shoulder. She struggled to open her eyes, but the effort seemed so great. Lethargy sucked at her, and she sank down into a quiet haze before again trying to fight her way to the surface.

Drip. Drop. Drip… drop.

Familiar scents teased her nose. She tried to inhale, but something large and heavy crushed her ribcage. What was it? She smelled laundry detergent and men's cologne. These scents mingled with others, familiar, but not pleasant—the stench of sweat and fear and something else, something distinct and metallic.

Her limbs seemed far away, her head fuzzy. She tried to move her legs, her hands, but, like her eyelids, they didn't quite obey. What was wrong with her? Why couldn't she move?

Drip. Drop. Drip… drop.

Her thoughts tangled and drifted. Unfocused images played behind her eyes. The lacy hem of a short red dress against her thighs. A sparkling drink with a wedge of lime. The dizzying glitter of the chandeliers at Troika.

Troika. She remembered accepting a drink from the bartender at her brother's nightclub. Then what? Her memory was blank.

Drip… drop… drip… drop.

She recognized the coppery smell now. Blood. It was blood. And the scent was all around her.

Panic knifed through her stupor. She opened her eyes. She was on the floor. Light from a chandelier stabbed at her eyes, and she turned her head away.

Near her shoulder, she saw a long-fingered hand with wisps of black hair over olive skin, palm spread against the familiar tiles of the nightclub she had decorated. A man's hand.

Dread jolted her system, coursed through her limbs. He was on top of her, his groin against hers, his leg thrown over hers. She thrashed underneath him, trying to heave him off, but he didn't budge.

He didn't resist her efforts. He didn't move at all.

Drip… drop… drip… drop.

Who was he? She craned her neck, felt slick, sticky wetness under her cheek and the skin of her bare shoulder. She angled her head to look at him, but couldn't see his face. His chin was cradled against her shoulder, and his arm had pinioned hers. All she could see was the blood pooled on the floor.

Something was in her hand. She managed to wiggle and flex her fingers. They curled around something hard and cold and heavy. A gun.

There was a gun in her hand! Her body started to shake uncontrollably. Had she killed him?

Inna squeezed her eyes closed, prayed she was hallucinating. When she opened them again, the horror was still there. Someone started screaming, a shrill keening.

Only when she felt the raw pain in her throat did she realize the screams were hers.

VLAD

MUSCLES TENSED, VLAD watched the Georgian representative, Dato Dzhugashvili, push an oiled black curl off of his face with the barrel of his gun then place it on the table in front of him. The weapon was too close within Dato's reach for Vlad's taste, especially when Vlad's palms itched with the sure knowledge of an impending skirmish.

Artur did not speak. He crossed his arms, leaned his trim body back in his chair, and frowned. With high cheekbones and a full head of silver hair that swept back from his forehead, he looked like a displeased monarch.

All Artur had told Vlad about tonight's meeting with the Georgians was, "Come. I want your reflexes. Shoot at the slightest provocation." Vlad's presence tonight as Artur's bodyguard could be a testament to how far he had advanced in Artur's inner circle. Or it could be a test.

Pass or die.

Artur had strategically set up tonight's meeting here on the third floor of Troika, where no one was likely to hear them or interrupt. The area was secluded from the rest of the nightclub with rooms for private parties, although oddly there were none tonight, even though it was Friday. Artur had selected a small, intimate room with rich wood paneling and framed mirrors—the better, Vlad thought, to watch every move and feint.

With a sheepish shrug, Dato hiked up his pant leg and pulled a long knife out of his silver-toed boot. He held it up, let the sharp blade catch the light, sliced the air with it as if to show how dangerous he could be. He cradled the knife in both hands and placed it on the white tablecloth with a flourish and a bow. The bravado and staged capitulation only made Vlad suspicious and twitchy. He flexed his fingers, ready to draw his own weapon.

No doubt the bodyguard Dato had brought was packing, just like Vlad. So why the show? The leathery man at Dato's shoulder, Goga, was unfamiliar, not the "associate" that Vlad had met previously, and he wondered where Zviad was tonight and why he wasn't here.

Vlad sized up Goga. The man was wiry and slight, tough but small, no match in a test of brawn. Hopefully not in a test of brains either.

Anxiety pinched Vlad's nerves, cut his edgy anticipation with an undercurrent of pain. He hadn't been honest with Artur about his purpose or motives. He had traded on history and goodwill from more than two decades ago. He had blended the lies so seamlessly with the truth that he couldn't tell which was which, who he was, where his allegiances truly lay if—no, when—the situation got bloody.

He liked Artur, respected him, perhaps more than anyone he had ever met. But men like Vlad were supposed to be cold-hearted bastards. Do the job and move on to the next one. Never get attached.

As Dato placed the knife on the table, his sharkskin suit jacket pulled back at the wrists to reveal blue tattoos, the kind Vlad's father had all over his body, the sign of a Thief in Law, *vor v zakone*, the old-time Soviet mafia. The Thieves' Law had guided his father's life, had provided a marker of who could be trusted and who could not, who would help and who might hinder. Vlad sometimes wished his own life were so simple.

In his head, Vlad could hear his father, Ivan, cursing. *Fucking Georgians. They buy their way in to the Vory. They don't earn it in the prisons. I spit on them all. Useless fucking bastards.* Vlad wasn't sure whether his father's decades-old warning or his own finely honed instincts put his guard up, but his gut rippled with an intense dislike.

Dzhugashvili was likely not Dato's real name but an attempt at self-importance, likening himself to Stalin by adopting his surname. Dato was known to have a hair-trigger temper and a disregard for discretion.

He and his crew preferred to broadcast their violence as a warning to others and prided themselves on their brutality. In Vlad's opinion, their methods made them no better than dirt beneath Artur's shoe. Artur was everything Dato and his crew were not—smart, subtle, patient, refined. People didn't cross to the other side of the street if they saw Artur coming, but this fact only made him infinitely more dangerous.

Even now, poor Dato imagined he had the upper hand. His smug smile flashed with gold teeth, but they were on Artur's turf.

"You're a gentleman, Artur, and so I come to speak to you as a gentleman," Dato said. He smoothed his shiny suit and flicked at the lapel. He tugged at his cuffs in a motion that served, no doubt intentionally, to showcase his ink.

Artur bestowed on him the mildest of smiles.

"I hear things," Dato said. "I hear Troika is the place to come for drugs. And women. And this doesn't make me happy." There was more than a hint of challenge in his words.

Artur steepled his hands. "I don't know what you've heard or who you're talking to. I'm a businessman," Artur said. "Not a dealer or a pimp." The unspoken words, "Like you," hung in the air.

Goading and evasive, Artur toyed with Dato. Was he hoping for a gunfight? Artur didn't even own the club. His son, Aleksei, did. Friday night, prime time, and the party rooms on the third floor were all empty. Dato's information had to be right. Business couldn't be nearly as good as Aleksei boasted. Aleksei's ostentatious signs of success had to come from other, less legitimate, sources of income. Like father, like son. Nothing on Brighton Beach was ever what it appeared at first glance.

The vein at Dato's temple pulsed. Vlad flexed his fingers. He was attuned to the man's every breath and twitch. He only wished he had his gun in his hand instead of in its holster.

Vlad didn't intend to let himself get shot, and he sure as hell hadn't spent the past few months reuniting with Artur and earning his way into his good graces so that he could lose either the man or his hard-won trust in a shootout with trigger-happy thugs. Vlad decided he would take out the bodyguard first, then bull's-eye his soft-bellied boss. He had a full clip of ammo, but he'd only need one bullet for each. Vlad never missed.

"I'm a businessman, too," Dato said with a defensive sniff. "And you're stepping on my turf."

His words were lost in the sound of a blood-curdling shriek. The terrible screams had Vlad reaching for his gun. Artur sprang to his feet.

"It's coming from the next room," Vlad said, and Artur gave him the signal to go.

Gun drawn, Vlad rushed across the hall to the room with the screams. He jiggled the handle of one of the wide, gilded double doors. Locked.

The screams grew shriller, a chilling sound of distress and terror, of imminent danger. Vlad didn't hesitate. He kicked the doors open.

The sight before him stopped him in his tracks.

Artur's daughter, Inna, lay on the floor, screaming hysterically. Her short red dress was rucked up around her waist. A man, bare-assed, powerfully built, and far larger than she, lay on top of her, his pants around his ankles, his hands spread on the floor by her head, and a pool of blood collecting under his forehead. She had a gun in her hand.

Her slender limbs flailed wildly, but to no avail. Inna had killed her attacker, but she was still trapped beneath him, helpless and terrified.

Vlad had seen plenty of ugly scenes before, but this one broke something inside him, stole the last tiny shred of faith he harbored in humanity, and made him want to drop to his knees and weep.

He rolled the dead man off of her and spoke to her in soothing tones, but she was still screaming, beyond hearing or comfort. Looking her over for injuries, he pulled out his cell phone to call for an ambulance. Gun in one hand, phone in the other, he hesitated.

Artur might prefer to keep this all quiet, cover it up. If Vlad made the wrong choice now, there would be serious repercussions.

Pass or die.

He slipped the phone back into his pocket, just as Artur and the Georgians appeared in the doorway. Vlad pulled the hem of Inna's dress down over her thighs, protecting her dignity. His eyes locked with Artur's, and the man's pain was palpable, even greater and deeper than Vlad's.

Vlad remembered Inna as a young girl. More than twenty years ago, she had been about five or six, with a red smudge on her cheek. She had climbed up on the sofa, stuffed bunny in hand, to sit beside him in Artur's living room, where he, fourteen years old, had sat dejected and betrayed by his entire world, waiting for Artur to send him away. Aleksei, her brother, had worshiped Vlad and chided Inna for bothering them, but she hadn't been a bother. She had curled up close to him, her chubby body warm against his arm, a welcome presence when no one had held or comforted him, when, perhaps because of his tough-guy act, no one had thought he would accept a soft touch or sympathy. She hadn't wanted anything from him, other than to be close. "Don't be lonely," she had said. She had smelled of strawberry jam and wax crayons, and she had stared up at him with solemn eyes. "You can take Zayats on your trip, and he'll keep you company." With that, she had handed him her prized doll, a scraggly, gray bunny with plastic eyes and long, floppy ears. He had tried to give it back, but she wouldn't take it. She had said Zayats wanted to be with him to be his friend, and Vlad had accepted the enormity of her gift, the only one like it he had ever received—given freely with no expectation of something in return.

Little Inna might have been the only exposure Vlad had ever had to innocence. And now she was broken and violated by the evil all around them. His rage exploded to an intolerable level. The violent fire burned so hot it might incinerate him and everyone around him.

Artur fell to his knees by Inna's side. He tenderly cradled her head in his arms. Sirens wailed in the background, growing closer. Perhaps someone else had heard Inna's screams and called the cops.

Dato shouted over Inna's blind hysteria and the wail of the emergency vehicles. "Zviad's dead! What the hell happened?"

"Your man raped her and got exactly what he deserved," Artur said.

"You can't rape a whore," Goga said, and Vlad's rage burned hotter. It would feel so good to smoke these assholes.

Goga's eyes darted toward Inna, and in a flash he pulled his gun and targeted her. Vlad's reflexes were faster. He grabbed his second gun from his shoulder holster and now had one in each hand, one trained on Dato and the other on the bodyguard. He fingered the triggers, ready for any excuse to discharge some of his smoldering fury.

ARTUR

"DON'T SHOOT, YOU idiot! She's my daughter!" Artur screamed at Goga. Inna sobbed in his arms, insensible to him or the idiot Georgian who wanted to kill her. Her eyes were fixed on the dead man with black hair who lay only inches away.

Artur touched her cheek, sticky with blood, to turn her face toward him, but her eyes stayed unfocused, her hysteria unabated. His shy, intelligent girl seemed so far beyond his reach, trapped in an endless loop of horror.

He had sold his soul, committed countless crimes, all in the name of keeping her safe, only to fail her. Each cry hit like a lash against raw skin, the deep cuts only strengthening his resolve to get them both free.

"I don't care if she's the Queen of Fucking England," Goga said, his accent guttural and heavy, his words brave for a man looking down the barrel of Vlad's gun. "She killed Zviad."

"Blood for blood," Dato said, intent, it seemed, on goading Goga to violence.

Artur crouched protectively over Inna. He heard the wails of sirens outside, growing nearer, the police in full force. For once, he welcomed their approach. But he didn't dare trust they would arrive fast enough to protect Inna from the bloodthirsty Georgians.

There would be no reasoning with Dato and Goga. The only language they understood was power. Power and money. A newer gang, their ranks swelled with recent immigrants, the Georgians aspired to rule Brighton Beach. They imagined the game here was played with guns and knives and showy displays of brute force, the way it had been in the

1990s, back when Ivan had been Artur's partner. Artur had no yearning for the old days, but he missed having Ivan fighting at his back.

"Put your gun away. Or I promise you more blood," Vlad said, voice low. He was built like a tank, big-muscled just like his father. Despite his neatly tailored shirt and slacks, his broad build and the dark scruff on his face gave him a savage look. He had Ivan's cold, flinty eyes, a killer's eyes, but Artur doubted Vlad would shoot unless Goga made a move.

If Ivan were here, Dato and Goga would already be dead, if for nothing else than the mere folly of challenging him and thinking they held the power to make demands. Ivan never shrank from stark, savage displays of power, but his blatant barbarity had earned him a lifetime prison sentence.

Goga did not lower his weapon, but he shifted his sights to Vlad with his guns, the more obvious threat. Artur acted the moment Dato and Goga's gazes shifted away from him and Inna. He reached into his pocket for his favored weapon, a dart gun camouflaged as a retractable pen. With a flick of his thumb, Artur rotated the chrome casing a quarter turn counterclockwise to load the dart and then primed it with three silent clicks of the pen. Another quarter turn and he was ready to shoot.

Artur's gut churned with the raw burn of hatred. He despised these mobsters. The Georgians, the Chechens, the Russians, the Chinese, the Mexicans, the Italians, it didn't matter. He loathed their violence and posturing, their egos and entitlement. Artur had been forced to make his life here in Brighton Beach's Little Odessa, coerced into becoming one of their leaders. It was never what he had wanted. The deals and the deceit, the secrets and favors, the evasions and maneuvers—all so that money could flow from one dirty hand to the other. Now Inna had paid a terrible price.

His deal with the Devil was only supposed to cost his soul, but not Inna's; never Inna's. She had been the prize for the trade he had made, the freedom he had sacrificed.

Now the contract had been breached. The deal was null and void. There would be no more stealthy diplomacy, no more sly bargaining, no more quietly manipulative tactics.

There was only one deal now: Anyone who threatened Inna died.

Artur surreptitiously drew the pen from his pocket, pointed the tip at Goga, and clicked the end to shoot. The dart was smaller than a mosquito, and its sting had a similar bite. If Goga felt the sharp, little projectile penetrate his skin, he showed no sign, but Artur had aimed true. In moments, the pellet would dissolve and Goga would have a heart attack. A flick of his thumb, a clockwise rotation, and the dart gun was a regular ballpoint again. Artur slipped it back into his pocket. Sleek, stealthy, and deadly.

Now to stall.

"You came here on my invitation and did this! This! In the next room. While you made your show with your knife and gun." Artur yelled at both of them, distracting them with their own farcical script of honor and justice, while he waited for the poison to take hold. "Is this how you treat my hospitality?"

"Hospitality!" Dato spat. "We came here to meet you on your turf. On your terms. And our man is dead."

Dato pretended as if they hadn't come to tonight's meeting with the sole intention of making threats and demanding Artur pay *krysha*, protection money, for whatever operation was taking place at Troika. The Georgian gang would be diminished if Artur had bested them the way they claimed, killing one of their men while they conferred—unless they struck back twice as hard.

Inna continued to cry, and Artur feared they had broken her. Worry squeezed his chest as if he were the one having the heart attack.

"Drop your weapons! Hands where we can see them."

Four officers burst into the room. About time! Goga winced, the pain hitting. Artur noticed the slight shaking of his arm. Twenty seconds, he thought. Still, too much time.

Artur shielded Inna's head and torso with his body. Anything could happen in twenty seconds. Vlad could be disarmed before Goga or, only seconds before his heart stopped, Goga could make good on his threat to claim Inna's life in reparation for his comrade's.

Over his shoulder, Artur watched Goga and Vlad match each other inch for inch as they bent to put their guns on the floor, neither willing to disarm before the other. No one dared interrupt the slow-motion mirror game. Artur anxiously counted the seconds. Fifteen. Ten. Five.

Then Goga made a sudden jerk. With the onset of gripping chest pain, he spasmed and fired a wild shot. The officers responded with a hail of bullets, and Goga crumpled to the ground.

Dato also fell to the floor, howling with pain. Goga's final shot had hit him in the leg.

"I said drop your weapons!" one of the officers shouted again.

With Goga down, Vlad quickly dropped both guns to the floor and stepped back, both hands open and up in the air.

"Hands up!" one of the officers shouted at Artur, but Artur couldn't bring himself to let go of Inna. "Up!" the asshole demanded, pointing his drawn weapon at Artur.

"We need an ambulance. She needs help." Artur's voice cracked on the words, and Inna suddenly stopped sobbing, only to turn catatonic. As the EMTs rushed her and Dato, she slipped into a trancelike state. Artur waved his hand in front of her eyes, but her pupils didn't even track his movements. She was slipping away. How far? Would he be able to get her back? He couldn't lose her, wouldn't lose her. Not like Sofia.

The EMTs bundled Inna onto a stretcher, but an officer restrained Artur when he stayed by her side as they moved into the hallway. "She's my daughter. She needs me," Artur protested.

"This is a crime scene. You have to stay and answer a few questions." The officer in charge, Tony Marano, a thickset man with a grizzled moustache, was unmoved by Artur's pleas, despite his being on Artur's payroll. He blocked Artur with his bulky body, making a good show for his fellow officers, pretending to run things by the book.

"You don't understand," Artur said as the EMTs rolled Dato's stretcher into the elevator beside Inna, his intended kill. Artur pulled away from the officer, but Marano grabbed him by the jacket and shoved him against the wall in the hallway. Artur fought him off and shouted his objections. "He tried to kill her! You can't take them to the same hospital. In the same ambulance."

"Calm down, Koslovsky. Don't make me arrest you," Marano warned. He threw his body weight into pinning Artur against the wall. "You're coming with me to the precinct detective squad. An officer will accompany her to Coney Island Hospital. A female detective will meet them there and stay with her."

As if that were enough to save his daughter from a man intent on spilling her blood.

Artur knew he could fight Marano off, but he slumped against the wall as if he had crumpled under Marano's threats. Getting arrested would solve nothing. He couldn't protect Inna from inside a jail cell.

NICK

KATYA AND NICK were supposed to have been on their way to Aleksei's club more than an hour ago. If they had taken the subway as Nick had advocated, they would already be there, seated and having drinks with Inna. But no.

Aleksei had insisted on picking Katya up at the office. Not so bad. Nick might even have given him points for chivalry had he not been a full hour late. Even Katya, with her usually sunny demeanor, had exhausted her arsenal of ready excuses and sunk into glumness. She checked her watch repeatedly and tried to raise him on his cell. No answer. "Frankly, I'm not sure whether to be irritated or worried," she said.

When Aleksei pulled up in his gleaming silver Ferrari FF and slid out of the car as if he were the star of the hour, Nick was officially irritated.

Aleksei left his silver sports car double-parked across the street and started toward them. With a wave to the guard in the lobby, Nick pushed open the heavy door to the glass-front building where his law firm occupied the seventh floor. He held the door for Katya. The fall night was crisp and cool, and a breeze off the Hudson ruffled Katya's golden curls. She paused on the sidewalk and turned to him, her bright green eyes filled with apology and apprehension.

"No worries," Nick preempted, lest she offer him an out. He had too much riding on tonight's double date. For good measure, he added, "I'm looking forward to meeting Inna."

The words were the right ones. The tension in Katya's face eased, but before she could respond, Aleksei caught her in an embrace.

"Hi, Babe," Aleksei greeted Katya and dipped her back into a showy kiss.

For his own part, Nick stood riveted. Seeing Aleksei was like stepping back into the past. He had seen pictures, knew that Aleksei strongly resembled his father, Artur, sculpted and attractive. But seeing Aleksei in person, he remembered Artur's magnetism, the flair for romance. With little more than a longing glance, Artur had made Nick's mother's cheeks flush and had lured her into sin.

"You're late," Katya chided, but quietly, as if she were dazzled by her own husband.

"Traffic," Aleksei said—no apology, as if the one word explained everything.

Nick bit his tongue. Yes, there was traffic. It was Friday night in New York City. Of course, there was traffic. What idiot didn't plan and leave extra time for traffic?

"You didn't answer your cell. I was getting worried."

"Dead battery. I forgot to charge it," Aleksei said with a nonchalant shrug.

Seriously?

Aleksei snaked an arm possessively around Katya's shoulders and then shook Nick's hand. He reeked of Drakkar Noir, as if he had bathed in the stuff, and his platinum hair was stiff with spikes. In his tight leather pants and white silk shirt, he looked more rock star than business owner, although Nick grudgingly supposed the look worked for the owner of a trendy nightclub.

"Good to finally meet the other man," Aleksei said with a touch of humor, but Katya elbowed him in the ribs. "What?" Aleksei protested and dropped a kiss into her hair. "You spend more time with him than you do with me."

"It's called work," Katya said with uncharacteristic irritation. Nick supposed Katya's hours were a point of contention in the marriage. Likely Aleksei wanted a worshipful woman at his beck and call, but

Katya was an attorney in Manhattan, where an eighty-hour-minimum workweek was industry standard for young associates.

Aleksei shrugged. "Enjoy her while you can," he said to Nick. "She's got baby fever."

Katya bit her lip, clearly uncomfortable with her husband's lack of tact, but said nothing, while Nick's opinion of Katya's husband dropped even lower. He already disliked Aleksei, by simple virtue of his resemblance to the villain of Nick's childhood. Artur, whose last name had been Gregorovich in the Soviet Union, must have been even younger than Aleksei was now when Nick had known him, but Aleksei looked exactly as Nick remembered the man.

Artur. The man his mother had loved. The man who had destroyed Nick's family. The man Nick had vowed would pay for what he had done.

Katya's silence, a confirmation in Nick's mind that she hoped to start a family and likely planned to leave the law firm, made Nick even more determined to get on with the date with Artur's daughter. He had a time-limited window to make his move. He needed to leverage his connection with Katya to get close to Artur.

"Ready to get this party started?" Nick asked and squeezed himself into the backseat of the Ferrari. Granted the car was beautiful, sleek on the outside and appointed inside with wood trim and rich leather, and did actually have four seats, but it could barely accommodate Nick's long legs. Why had Aleksei insisted on picking them up if the fit were going to be so tight?

Aleksei pulled easily into the slow-moving traffic of midtown Manhattan. He drove aggressively, dodged between cars whenever there was an opening and gunned the motor for short sprints from one lane to the other.

They made little progress despite Aleksei's jolting zigs and zags. At a red light, Aleksei sighed dramatically. "I'm almost out of gas. We need to find a gas station before we head over to Brighton Beach."

"There's a station on 47th," Nick said and leaned his head back against the headrest. He despised being late and resented this newest delay. Worse, he hated losing control of a situation, and he had a feeling Aleksei bred chaos, whether by accident or design.

What was Katya doing with Aleksei anyway? She was so cheerful and empathetic, and he was so... entitled and inconsiderate, as if life owed him something and had defaulted. As far as Nick could tell, Aleksei wanted for nothing. He certainly hadn't struggled the way Nick had.

Nick supposed he should be grateful for Katya's poor taste. The wedding announcement, in the Jewish newspaper of all places, had reinvigorated a hunt he had thought had reached a dead end. With Aleksei a ringer for his father, Nick had immediately recognized the family connection and figured out that Artur Gregorovich, the notorious KGB agent who had persecuted Jewish families in the Soviet Union, had changed his name to Koslovsky and, irony of ironies, become an upstanding member of the Russian Jewish community in Brighton Beach. Artur had even donated a wing to the local synagogue, complete with a foundation stone naming it in his and his wife's honor.

Another man might have dared believe that Artur had changed, but Nick didn't believe in happy endings or redemption. He had been in the legal world long enough, prosecuted and defended enough criminals. Rotten was rotten. People didn't change. They stayed true to their natures. Artur, no matter how honorable and good he appeared now, would always be callous and opportunistic, a murderer or a politician, a lover or a philanthropist as the situation demanded, but always a dangerous liar.

Katya regularly told Nick he was too cynical—although she had no inkling of Nick's secret obsession with her father-in-law. Nick always countered that she was too optimistic, too soft-hearted and willing to believe the best, to extend a second chance, to imagine that the next encounter would be better, different—no matter how many times she was disappointed. Sometimes he wasn't sure whether to pity or envy her.

One thing was certain: he hadn't expected someone like her to be connected to Artur Koslovsky.

He had never expected to like her, but he found he couldn't help himself. And he also found himself worrying. How much was Aleksei like his father, and how would Katya handle the truth when she learned the true nature of her husband's family—a truth that had destroyed Nick's mother?

Aside from the delay inherent in detouring to the gas station and t andhen crawling back into traffic, filling Aleksei's tank didn't take long. After a few more minutes, Aleksei had them on the Williamsburg Bridge, and traffic cleared as they left Manhattan for Brooklyn.

Just as Nick began to relax in his cramped position in the backseat, thinking the evening was back on track, the car started to list. Aleksei pulled onto the shoulder of the highway. "I think we've got a flat."

The three of them spilled out of the car to inspect. Aleksei ran his hand over his face as if confronting a tragedy. "This could take a while."

"You have a spare, don't you?" Nick asked, no longer able to hide his impatience with Katya's husband. Part of him wondered if Aleksei had caused the flat himself. Maybe Aleksei didn't want Nick to go on a date with his sister. Maybe his late arrival, his empty gas tank, and now this flat tire were all passive-aggressive attempts to thwart Katya's matchmaking. But why?

"There should be one in the trunk," Katya said.

Nick ducked around Aleksei, reached into the driver's side of the zippy silver sports car, and popped the trunk. Then he marched to the back to inspect what resources he had at his disposal.

A flat tire and Aleksei's seeming ineptitude were the only things standing between Nick and the revenge he had plotted for so long. Neither would stop him.

He would woo Inna, worm his way into the Koslovsky family, learn their secrets—and he had no doubt there were vicious, ugly secrets—and bring Artur down from the inside.

Despite the trunk's small size, he half expected to find a dead body decomposing as he peered inside, if only because he had had more than twenty-five years to weave stories about what kind of monster Artur was. What he found was the spare tire and flat kit, exactly what he needed.

"Should I call for roadside assistance?" Katya asked.

"No," Nick said, stripping off his suit jacket and folding it into the trunk, "I can do it." Grabbing the kit in one hand, he hoisted the spare tire out of the trunk then rolled it toward the rear driver's side. He knelt in the damp gravel on the roadside to switch out the flat. Aleksei, in his tight leather pants and silk shirt, only watched, arms folded. He didn't offer to help. Afraid he might get himself dirty?

"Can you see?" Katya asked. Before Nick answered, she opened the door beside him and scrambled into the car, gracing Nick with a flash of leg and a view of her skirt clinging tightly to her enticingly round bottom. Nick yanked his gaze away.

He focused on cranking the jack as Katya, on hands and knees, rummaged in the car and opened and shut various compartments. "Sweetheart, where's the flashlight?" she called.

Aleksei answered on a yawn. "Try the middle console."

"Aha!" She backed out, triumphant, flashlight in hand, and shone it on the tire. "Look, there's a slash," she said, and leaned close enough that Nick could smell her perfume, light and clean, a blend of citrus and flowers that suited her. "What do you think caused it?"

"It's New York. Anything could cause it," Aleksei said. "Maybe someone thought it would be funny to knife my car while I waited for you," he said, but Aleksei presented the night's events incorrectly. They hadn't kept him waiting. They had waited for him.

"Maybe," Katya said. She didn't correct him, and Nick wondered why not. Katya was no pushover, at least not at the negotiating table or in the courtroom. She sighed. "Well, at least Nick will have us on the road again soon."

Nick grunted with the exertion of loosening the lug nuts. The last one was stuck, screwed in tight, and he leaned into the wrench, using his weight to free it. When the nut started spinning easily he said, "Just a few more minutes."

He slid the flat off the bolts before lifting the spare into place. Katya moved closer and shone the flashlight so that he could see the bolts as he replaced the nuts. Behind them, Aleksei shifted restlessly.

"It's getting late," Aleksei said. "Maybe we should try this again another time."

"Don't be silly," Katya said. "I texted Inna and told her we'd be late. She said she'd wait for us at the bar."

Aleksei kicked at the gravel with his pointy, Euro-chic loafers. Katya moved to his side and stroked his arm, while Nick loaded the flat into the trunk. "Oh, come on, Aleksei. I know you think of her as your annoying little sister, but she's not a little kid anymore. You'll see. We'll have fun together, the four of us."

Aleksei bent to kiss Katya on the head. "Whatever you want," he said, but he sounded a bit distracted. Nick couldn't shake the feeling that, despite the jewelry he showered on her, Aleksei didn't fully appreciate what he had in his wife.

"All done," Nick said as he shut the trunk.

Katya turned to him with a determined smile. "You'll like Inna. I'm sure," she said. "She's really delightful. Sensitive. Funny. I absolutely adore her."

"I trust you," Nick said. "The date will be great—once we finally get there. Ready?" Without waiting for Aleksei's next excuse, Nick contorted himself into the backseat.

They pulled back onto the highway, and Nick's thoughts shifted to Inna. Katya had been all sunshine and love whenever she discussed Artur's daughter. Nick got the impression she genuinely liked Inna. But then Katya had also married Aleksei, and so her judgment on this matter was more than slightly suspect, despite Nick's declaration that he trusted her.

What would Inna be like? Was she also an innocent dupe, like Katya, taken in by Artur's immigrant persona, a good person who might be hurt?

He found he didn't care all that much. Truth was truth, and avenging his family had been the driving purpose in his life for as long as he could remember. A niggling conscience wasn't enough to make him deviate from his long-decided course. Justice, after all, was blind.

KATYA

THE NIGHT WAS off to a rocky start, and Katya could feel all of her good intentions buckling under the weight of Aleksei's reluctance and Nick's growing hostility. Maybe the double date wasn't such a good idea.

She had hoped that Nick and Aleksei would connect. Nick was a good, solid man, responsible and smart, professional and educated. He offered a far better choice for a friend than Aleksei's questionable crowd. Aleksei liked to be the life of the party. He enjoyed having everyone's admiration. Lately, Katya had been thinking that Aleksei was attending the wrong party, seeking the wrong people's admiration. She especially disliked his friend, Mikhail, who always seemed to be present when Aleksei dipped his foot into trouble, always behind the moments when Aleksei withdrew from her. Secretly, Katya hoped that Nick would be a good influence on Aleksei.

Katya suspected that her husband was a chameleon, the type of person who camouflaged his true self to fit into his surroundings. Sometimes she wasn't sure she knew who he really was herself. But she loved the man who joined her family for Sunday brunch, played on the floor with his niece and nephew, helped her brother-in-law fix his sports car, and stepped in quietly to help with her parents' financial worries. She loved the man who remembered his mother's birthday and brought her gifts and could be sweet and loving. She even loved the man who wore leather pants and strutted through Brighton Beach like he ruled the place.

But there was another Aleksei, a darker man, who drank too much, played games with high stakes, and grew dangerously angry if Katya asked too many questions about where he had been or what he had been doing—Mikhail's Aleksei.

Katya glanced over at Aleksei. He usually exulted in his fancy sports car. In his peacock way, he loved to see and be seen, to show off to the world that he could afford this car and could afford to go fast. Tonight, there was none of the joy or fun. He gripped the wheel with a grim determination and practically puttered along the parkway at the speed limit.

Inna wasn't her husband's favorite person, and Aleksei didn't favor Katya's efforts to befriend her. Nor was he all that excited about the prospect of getting to know Nick—or relating with anything that had to do with her work, for that matter. In a manic burst of desperate optimism, Katya had convinced herself that her attempt at matchmaking would pay royal dividends. Now she wasn't so sure.

Aleksei was doing as she had asked tonight, albeit reluctantly, but at least he was trying, she told herself, clutching tightly to thin hope. He had made some effort, had shown up, even if late, had taken a stab at conversation with Nick. Right? The evening could be salvaged. Her plan could work. *Please let it work.*

Maybe matchmaking wasn't the best strategy for trying to save her marriage, but she was running out of options. The chances of a love match between Inna and Nick were slim if she were honest. Inna was very sweet, but she was also a little shy and aloof, especially around men. She tended to hang back in the crowd, to watch but not participate. Katya had worked hard to draw her out, and she wasn't completely convinced, for all of her wishful thinking, that Inna would rise to tonight's occasion and put on the full coy charm of her heritage.

Inna, though pretty, hardly played up her looks. At parties, she seemed to work at blending into the background when most Russian women dressed for events and for men. Bright colors. Dazzle and shine. High heels. Dramatic makeup. Katya's family had survived when they first got to America by catering to the vanity that even poor immigrants saw not as luxury, but as necessity, building their American dream in Brighton Beach on the promise of Russian beauty.

A junior partner at the law firm, Nick was handsome enough, trim and tall with broad shoulders and a full head of dark wavy hair, to have his pick of women if he were actively looking. Nick worked too much to have much time to play the field and was at the right age and stage of his career to be serious about settling down. He was ready to be lured and caught.

Katya hoped her sister-in-law would dress to impress, just this once.

They exited the parkway and threaded their way through the busy lanes of traffic toward the colorful neighborhood of shops and apartments where Aleksei had his nightclub. At a stop light only a few blocks from the club, Katya reached over and placed her hand on Aleksei's knee, a small show of solidarity and affection.

He jumped and cast her a reproving glance. She withdrew quickly, and her eyes stung at the clear rejection of her advance. She closed her hands into tight fists, but holding on didn't help. Her slim sprig of hope withered and shriveled. Her chest ached with heartburn, and she rubbed at the soreness to no avail.

"Are you okay?" Nick asked from the backseat.

"She's fine," Aleksei grumbled.

"Fine," she echoed quietly. The men's mutual irritation filled the car like smoky fumes that threatened to choke her. She turned her head away from them both, opened the window slightly, and leaned her forehead against the cool glass. The salty air was tinged with car fumes and the smell of cooking meats from the restaurants, most of which served some form of shish kebab. The cool night air felt good against her skin, but the smells made her stomach roil. She closed the window again.

As Aleksei pulled into the parking lot behind Troika, an ambulance shot past them in a sudden shriek of sirens and streak of lights. Katya straightened in her seat and peered at the chaos in the parking lot. Four police cars clustered near the back entrance to the club. This had to be more than a patron having a health emergency. "What happened?"

"*Blyad!*" Aleksei swore viciously under his breath and smacked his hands on the wheel. He didn't seem surprised by the commotion, only riled. "Mikhail said he had everything under control," Aleksei muttered.

Mikhail? Katya's heart started to race. Something was very wrong.

"He doesn't even work here. What was he handling? Where's Jack? What's going on?" She battered Aleksei with questions, but he shrugged her off.

He shot out of the car and jogged across the small parking lot. She was quick to follow. Her heels clicked across the asphalt as she struggled to keep up.

Her father-in-law, Artur, and his associate, a younger, tall, brawny man, appeared at the back door, flanked by policemen. Artur spotted Aleksei and pointed an accusing finger at him. "You! Where the hell were you? You were supposed to be with her," he said.

"What do you mean? What are you talking about?" There was alarm and an almost pleading tone in Aleksei's voice.

"They're taking your sister to the hospital," Artur said as a cop hustled him into a patrol car. "She's been raped."

"Raped?" Katya gasped. A cold sensation tingled up Katya's spine. She took a step back in shock and bumped against Nick, who was right behind her. He grasped her upper arms, as if to steady her, and she pulled out of his hold, wishing to be close to Aleksei instead, wishing her intuition wasn't pinging with alarms.

"Who did it?" Aleksei demanded. The cop slammed the door before Artur could answer.

Another officer turned to them. "Mr. Koslovsky, are you the owner of this nightclub?"

"I am."

"Stick around. We'd like to ask you a few questions."

"Can we do this later?" Aleksei said. "I should be at the hospital—with my sister."

"No, I'm sorry. This is officially a murder investigation."

"Murder? Who was killed?" Nick asked.

Katya noticed that Aleksei hardly seemed surprised. Her stomach swirled with nausea.

Aleksei had seemed deliberately to delay their arrival at the club. It was as if he had known something bad might happen and had wanted to avoid arriving in time for it. And Mikhail was somehow involved.

INNA

INNA HAD A terrifying taste of déjà vu. This was not the first time she had awakened with no memory of the preceding hours. Not the first time she had awakened sore from hard sex with no recollection of who or how or where or when.

Inna took in her surroundings. She was propped up in a hospital bed. An ugly green curtain, checkered with blue and pink squares, had been pulled around her bed and an empty, utilitarian chair in pink vinyl. She had an IV in her left arm. No monitors. No bandages. No telephone for calling anyone. No windows. The overhead lights were dimmed, and she had no idea what time of day it was. Or what day it was.

She remembered having one drink. Only one.

She remembered blood and screaming. The image of the dead man and the gun made her whole body shake.

Calm. Stay calm. Keep breathing. Deep breaths. Count to ten. She practiced the techniques Dr. Shiffman had taught her for managing her anxiety. What she wouldn't do to have a conversation with her therapist now, but Dr. Shiffman had abruptly abandoned her practice to retire to Florida. Maybe she would accept a long distance call. Circumstances certainly warranted calling in the cavalry.

In the background she could hear the beeping of monitors, the announcements on the speakers for this or that doctor, and the squeak of soft shoes against industrial linoleum. She supposed she was in one of the observation beds in an emergency room. Not the first time for that either.

The distance between past and present melted away, and she was young and scared again—a teenager, away at college, who learned her first fraternity party had ended, not in finding a boyfriend or even in an exciting hookup, but in gang rape.

She had been so careful tonight. She'd had one drink, watched the bartender pour it for her. She'd been at her brother's nightclub, surrounded by people who knew her. She had been waiting for Katya, her sister-in-law, to arrive with her friend, a lawyer, a nice man she had said, whom she wanted Inna to meet. No pressure. Just see what happens. Inna hadn't wanted to be hobbled by her past. Seven years later—seven years of therapy and medication, of emotional pain, and hard work—she was finally putting it behind her.

And now this. The misery of it all bore down on her, and she started to weep. Hot, fat tears rolled down her cheeks.

She wore a faded hospital gown, white criss-crossed in blue, and the droplets collected and soaked the fabric in her lap. Where were her clothes—the red dress and strappy shoes that had made her feel attractive?

"You're going out like that?" her mother had criticized. "You look like a tart. Mark my words, walking into a nightclub like that will only bring you trouble."

Inna had discarded her mother's sharp words. Her dress was hardly scandalous for Brighton Beach, even if it was a bold departure from her usual, and she had secretly been hoping for trouble, the good kind, a little bit of it anyway. She had been feeling empowered, in charge of her destiny, in touch with her actual age. She was twenty-six, successful, and fairly pretty. Why shouldn't a romance be in her future—especially with a guy Katya had identified as one of the good ones?

Was wearing a little red dress and hoping for love such a crime that the universe would punish her again? Her mother's warnings had a way of being eerily prophetic. She should have listened.

Her sobs deepened. Deep down, she knew the fault was hers. She had reached too far, only to be smacked down by her own failings. She had been careful, but not careful enough. Had she met Katya's friend? Had he done this to her?

The only man she could trust was her father.

The curtain around her swung open. The rings securing it at the top scratched metal against metal. A man in a white coat approached. She scrambled to sit up. He clasped her shoulder with a warm hand, and she flinched.

"Easy now. Take it easy," he said.

She couldn't catch her breath, couldn't stop crying. He rubbed his hand on her shoulder, likely to soothe her. She shrugged away from him.

"Please don't touch me."

He held up both hands, one empty and the other with a clipboard, as if in surrender. She drew her knees into her chest. He was only trying to be kind, she told herself.

She was relieved when he took a step away from her. Her breaths started to slow, the sobs diminishing to hiccups. "How long have I been here?"

"Several hours," he said. "We examined you. The police investigators came from the Special Victims Unit. Do you remember?"

She nodded. She recalled the tests and prodding, the tide of panic that hadn't receded, the female detective who had been stationed at her side.

"You fell asleep after the initial exams and tests, and we thought it best to let you rest. You were pretty distraught, and we didn't feel we could release you until we knew you were stable."

"You mean until after the shrinks clear me," Inna said.

The doctor smiled, a professional, non-committal smile. He was her brother's age, in his mid-thirties, with fine lines starting to feather around his eyes. His white lab coat hung neatly over wide shoulders and a lanky frame. In another life, she might have found him attractive. His voice was soft and low, and she sensed a gentleness in him, though she didn't trust it. "How do you feel?" he asked.

"I don't know how to answer that question," Inna said, and he nodded as if her answer was perfectly acceptable.

"Do you remember what happened last night?"

"No," she said.

Again he nodded. This time he scribbled something on his clipboard. "What's the last thing you remember?"

"I was at Troika. I was waiting for my brother and sister-in-law. They were fixing me up on a blind date, but they texted that they were running late. Flat tire. I was pretty nervous, and I decided to order a drink. To take the edge off. I don't remember anything after the bartender put the drink in my hand," Inna said. "Not until I woke up screaming and then found myself here."

"That's consistent with the blood test results," he said. "You tested positive for Rohypnol."

"You mean Roofies? Someone drugged me?" Who would have done that to her?

"Unless you took them yourself? You know, to take the edge off. Some people …"

"No," Inna said. "No, I don't do drugs." He made another note in his chart.

"What else do you know about what happened to me?" she asked.

"You have bruises on your thighs, and your internal exam showed vaginal tearing. The Special Victims Unit took DNA samples for their evidence kit, but nothing's back yet. Did you have sex before you blacked out?"

"No."

He nodded as if she had confirmed what he suspected. "Your injuries were consistent with rape," he said. The doctor's confirmation made her body jolt with a nasty shock of electricity.

Rape. The ugly word reverberated in her brain. Nausea engulfed her. Dark spots danced in front of her eyes, and she thought she might pass out. Almost wished she would. She forced herself to keep breathing.

How could this have happened to her again? "Who? Who did it?"
The doctor shook his head. "I'm sorry. I don't know."

She squeezed her eyes shut, strained to remember, but all she saw
was blackness. The only detail she could recall was the heavy scent of his
cologne, mingled with the metallic odor of blood. "I can't remember. I
can't remember anything!" She sobbed as the full horror of what had
happened wracked her. "Will I ever remember?"

"Probably not," he said. "Maybe a few flashbacks. But the memory
doesn't usually come back completely in these cases."

She pulled herself into the smallest, tightest ball she could, tried to
shut out the harrowing reality. Then a hideous thought invaded. Her
heart fluttered crazily. Revulsion rocked her. She lifted her eyes to the
doctor. "Am I pregnant?"

"At least that's one thing you don't have to worry about," he said.

Thank God! She dropped her head again. The tears flowed freely.
Anguish and relief coursed through her. "Diseases?"

"We're still waiting for a few more test results, but it doesn't seem
so."

"Is she ready to answer a few questions?" Another man, this one with
a gruff voice, invaded her nightmare. She blinked wet eyes to bring him
into focus, tried unsuccessfully to catch her hitching breaths. He wore a
police uniform. Her eyes cut to the gun at his hip. She shrank back
against the pillow. "Easy there," he said. "No one's gonna hurt you."

She had been holding a gun in her hand. Had she shot her rapist?
Her stomach and chest knotted tight, so tight it hurt to cry. It hurt to
breathe. It hurt to be. She rocked herself in the bed.

"She's not ready," the doctor said. "And she won't be until she's had
a psych referral." He was firm with the officer, protective of her. Because
he thought she was going crazy?

"No, you're not going crazy," the doctor said, and Inna realized she
must have said the words aloud. "You've been through a traumatic
experience. Your response is perfectly normal."

"Did I shoot him?" she asked, frantic with terror. She was going to prison. Her life was over. Because she had dared to hope. Because she had gone out in a sexy dress. Because she had imagined a future with love and marriage and children. Because she was a terrible person who didn't deserve to be happy.

Maybe everyone would be better off if they locked her up. Her thoughts repeated in an endless loop of self-recrimination and sadness. Inna wrapped her arms around her stomach. She had tried so hard not to be a victim. And now what had she become?

"It's going to be okay," the doctor said.

"How can it be okay? I killed him, didn't I?" The words were a garble of tears and desperation. This doctor was a liar. Nothing would ever be okay again. The image of the man's blood pooling all around her burned behind her eyes. No amount of tears would ever wash it away. She was a killer. She had shot him.

The doctor pressed his lips together as if in sympathy. "If it's any consolation, I'd say it's not likely you shot anyone. Roofies tend to incapacitate people, almost paralyze them."

"Tend to, but not always?"

"No, not always," he said and stripped her of any reassurance.

VLAD

"I TOLD YOU, I didn't kill him," Vlad said. He tried to stay calm, but he was getting impatient with Detective Sharp's endless repetition of the same question: "Why'd you kill him?" Either this was some kind of advanced interrogation technique, akin to water boarding, or Sharp was not the sharpest knife in the drawer.

Vlad wondered what time it was. He felt as if he had been in the interrogation room for days. He couldn't waste time here. He needed to get out, regroup with Artur. Brighton Beach was on the brink of a mafia war, and Inna was in imminent danger.

"Zviad was already dead when I came in," Vlad said.

"Don't lie to me." Sharp threw his pen on the table and jumped to his feet as if ready to smash in Vlad's nose. The cop smelled like stale coffee and really needed a breath mint. His eyes were bloodshot with thick, dark bags underneath. "It'll go worse for you."

Vlad didn't expect a friendly chat over coffee and donuts tonight, not when he had been two-fisting guns in a room where a man had taken a bullet to the brain, but his handler was a little too intense, a hungry shark that had caught the scent of chum.

Vlad's nerves stretched taut. He remembered other visits to the station, other lengthy interrogations. Then he had been defiant, maybe even unrepentant. Vlad hadn't done anything arrest-worthy tonight, hadn't even fired his gun, but he still felt like a no-good kid with guilt itching to be confessed and threatening to show on his skin like an angry rash. If he wasn't careful, he would give himself away.

"I'm telling the truth." *About this, anyway.* "The door was locked. I kicked it in. She was trapped under him, and he was dead."

"You said they were having sex."

"I said he raped her," Vlad said.

His handler cast a frustrated look at the mirrored wall, where his fellow officers were likely monitoring the questioning, as if Vlad were obstructing justice. "You said you weren't in the room. How do you know what the hell happened?"

Vlad reminded himself that the cops hadn't seen what he had seen: Inna half-naked, trapped under Zviad, and screaming her lungs out.

"He was lying on top of her. His leg was over hers like he was holding her down. His pants were pulled down around his ankles, and her dress was torn," Vlad said. "What the fuck do you think happened?"

"Maybe she liked it rough. Maybe she wanted it," Sharp said.

Vlad's temper threatened to explode like a grenade, and he tightened his fists under the table to hold it in check.

"Maybe you got jealous and shot him. Did you know him? Were you friends? We can easily find that one out, so just tell us."

"I told you, I didn't kill him." He squeezed his fists tighter, but his hold was slipping. "And, no. I didn't know him personally. We've met a couple of times on business."

"What is it you do for the Koslovskys?" his handler asked in an obvious attempt to try a new tack.

"I'm in charge of surveillance and security for Koslovsky Industries," Vlad said. "And before you ask, yes, I'm licensed to carry guns in New York." There was nothing illegal in the job he did, part of the brilliance of Artur's scheme. Problem was, the scheme was almost too brilliant.

Vlad still had so much to learn from Artur about his business enterprise. The buyers and suppliers. The "products." The relationships with the other small businesses in Brighton Beach and in the New York metropolitan area, never mind the connections overseas. He still didn't know how it all worked, where all the money came from. Artur provided only crumbs of information, a faint trail that hinted at the larger enterprise. Sometimes Vlad felt certain Artur knew his angle and was baiting and teasing him: *I have everything you want. Come and get it.*

The door slammed open and Detective Saul Hersh stalked in. "I don't fucking believe it," Vlad blurted as one of the few men who could blow all of his plans to hell strutted into the room.

"Believe it," Saul said. He was short and on the slight side for a cop, but his threat wasn't in his physical strength. The man was clever, sneaky. He used to have a reputation as a hardcore interrogator, the kind who always got his answers. Sharp was only the warm up. The real deal had just arrived.

Another test, Vlad thought, as dangerous as the others. Artur had eyes and ears on the police force.

Saul placed scarred hands on his narrow hips, and the circular marks drew Vlad's eyes, just as they had the first time he had met Saul. Ivan's abuse hadn't left visible scars on Vlad, other than the cleft in his eyebrow from where his head had hit the corner of a coffee table. Saul had told him his own father used to burn cigarettes on his hands. "I had a choice," Saul had said, "to be like him, or go another way. You have that choice too. What will you choose?"

"Never thought I'd see you here again. On that side of the table," Saul said now. "Thought I'd scared some religion into you. Guess I was wrong 'cause here you are. Playing your father's favorite role—gangster with guns."

"Stuff it, Hershey. We both know you're the one who tried to play my father's role," Vlad said. "You thought if you saved Nadia from Ivan she'd shower you with … gratitude."

"Does your mother know you're here? That you're gunslinging for Koslovsky—just like your old man?"

"I don't talk to Nadia. The worthless whore," Vlad said. He made a spitting sound for extra effect.

Saul got up in his face, grabbed him by the collar. "Don't talk about your mother that way."

"You're defending her?" Vlad couldn't hold back a mirthless laugh. The poor fucking sap, sucker punched by love for a woman who would never love him back, who would never love anyone save Ivan, even her own son. Ivan had beaten Nadia so hard she couldn't stand and then turned his rage on Vlad, who had been too small to defend himself or his mother, and still she had professed her love. Sickening.

"She's practically signed your death warrant," Vlad said with a shake of his head.

"You want to talk about death warrants?" Saul tightened his grip on Vlad's collar as if to prevent any sympathy from leaking out of him. "Let's talk about what you were doing armed to the teeth at Troika."

"My job," Vlad said.

"Get a new job," Saul said.

"Did they send you in to play good cop or bad cop, Hershey?" Vlad taunted, and Saul winced at the jibe. "It's amazing they kept you on the force after what you did."

"We all make mistakes, son, and that was a long time ago," Saul said.

"I'm not your son."

"I'm willing to help you—for your mother's sake. Is there something you want to tell us?"

"Why don't you speed things up and write my statement for me?" Vlad said.

Ivan had been guilty of plenty of murders, just not the one for which Saul had arrested him. If anyone deserved a life sentence, Ivan did, but Nadia had turned on Saul the moment the truth of what he had done came to light, despite the fact that his actions may have saved her life and Vlad's. She had taken the story to the papers and spent every moment since lobbying to get Ivan's case appealed, to have him freed, even knowing that the first thing Ivan would do once he got out was kill Saul Hersh.

Saul cuffed him on the ear. "That's the way you want to play it? Fine by me." He pulled a metal chair back from the table and sat down.

"Maybe your statement goes like this. You and Artur walked in on Inna doing the horizontal tango in the nightclub."

Vlad interrupted. "Say you're right. Why would I bring out the heat? Not like I give a damn who she screws."

"But Artur does. Heard he doesn't want his little princess dating a gangster."

"So Artur kills Romeo to keep him away from Juliet? In his son's nightclub. In the middle of prime time when he might get caught. When he would bring the cops breathing down his neck. Are you out of your fucking mind? Artur Koslovsky doesn't even carry a gun."

"But you do. Two of them," Saul's partner interjected. He tapped his pen against his notepad.

"Thanks, Einstein. And we've already established that neither of them fired tonight," Vlad said.

"All right," Saul agreed. "Let's say you and Artur weren't the shooters. Inna fired the gun."

"Because Zviad was raping her," Vlad said, again imposing his favored theory. Sharp raised his eyebrows at Saul, sending him some secret communication.

Saul cleared his throat. "Because of what he knew," Saul said quietly.

The statement wasn't a question, and it caught Vlad off guard. There was something else going on here, some part of the story Vlad didn't know. He was missing something. He needed to focus. He sat up a little straighter, alert now to whatever clue Saul or Sharp might cast in his direction.

"You think he was blackmailing her?" Vlad asked. The detectives exchanged another glance. They didn't like this theory any more than the one about the rape. Why didn't they want to see Inna as a victim?

"While we're playing this game of hypotheticals, tell me this," Vlad said. "Inna's in her little dress, hot and heavy with her Romeo. I didn't see a purse or a holster on her. Where exactly did she hide the gun if she was planning all along to seduce and kill him? Even strapped to her thigh, the Glock would have been conspicuous."

"Maybe the gun was his," Saul said.

"Sure. Okay. So why don't you think he might have held her at gunpoint? That there could have been a struggle, and she won?"

"We're asking the questions," Sharp said.

This time the defensiveness was unmistakable. Another shifty look from Sharp to Saul, and realization hit. The detectives couldn't stomach the idea of Inna as a victim because they didn't want Zviad to be guilty—of anything. It was as if they were protecting one of their own.

One of their own. Vlad's mind started to race with the possibility. What if Zviad was an undercover cop? He would have been investigating the Georgians. What could he have found out about Inna? Was she involved with whatever was happening at Troika—the drugs and women Dato had mentioned?

People did stupid things, sure. Supposing Zviad had something on Inna, Vlad still didn't buy that she would off him like that at the club where they were sure to be found. If silence were her game, she had nothing to gain from a messy murder that would lead to so many questions. And why at Troika?

A nasty suspicion took hold and stoked the rage inside Vlad even higher. The Georgians would surely benefit from killing the cop who was spying on them and framing someone else for the deed. Even better to have the murder at Troika, have the cops swarm the place, and shut down their supposed competition.

But why involve Inna?

Vlad silently kicked himself. He should have paid more attention to Inna these last few months. She worked closely with Artur. She pointedly avoided Vlad. Come to think of it, Artur actively kept Vlad away from her. He always sent Vlad on an errand when she was in the office. Vlad had assumed Artur had been giving him a signal, well within his rights, that his daughter—his much younger daughter—was off limits. Vlad had done his best to dampen his natural interest in her long legs and inky hair and the smoky quality of her voice that made his thoughts wander. *Not for me. Not for me.*

Now he wondered whether there was more to Artur's separation of them. Perhaps Inna was central to Artur's plots and schemes and Artur still didn't trust Vlad enough for him to know. Or perhaps Artur wanted to keep her clear of the intrigue.

She might be innocent. Or she might be another spider at the center of an elaborate web. She wouldn't escape Vlad's notice now. He would learn all of her secrets. First, he needed to stop the Georgians from killing her.

"Dato and Goga were eager to blow her brains out," Vlad said. "Said they wanted retribution. But maybe it was a smoke screen. Maybe one of their crew killed Zviad—because he had something on them. And now they want to make sure Inna stays silent about the murder."

Saul shook his head with sad wonder. "You're in the wrong profession. With a mind like yours, you should have been a detective."

"Yeah? Would that help you sleep at night? You could say it was all worth it, all the lies, as long as Ivan's son turned into one of the good guys?"

"It was worth it," Saul said solemnly. "Whatever happens—to me, to you—it was worth it." Saul's intense gaze, the fatherly worry etched in the strained lines around his eyes, unsettled Vlad. He looked away.

Saul clutched Vlad's forearm, squeezed, made him meet his eyes. "I would make the same choices all over again."

Detective Sharp coughed, and Vlad was aware once more of the awkwardness of his predicament, the need for the utmost discretion. "You're a piece of work, Hershey. You know that?" Vlad shrugged him off. "Let me tell you the real difference between us. We both tell lies when it suits us, but at least I don't lie to myself. And just for the record, I tried my hand at law enforcement. It fucking sucked."

Saul blew out a heavy breath and pushed back from the table. "You're free to go."

ARTUR

AS SOON AS the police finished questioning Artur, he headed straight to Coney Island Hospital, where the ambulance had taken Inna. Maya was already there when he arrived. As soon as she spotted him in the hall outside the Emergency Room, she rushed for him, ran into his arms, and clung to him tightly.

"They won't let me see her," Maya cried against his shoulder. "I'm her mother, and they won't let me see her."

"Hush," he whispered and rubbed her back.

"I told Inna not to go out like that. But did she listen? No, she never listens to me," Maya complained.

The familiar chill washed over Artur and doused any tenderness he might feel toward her. "This isn't the time for I-told-you-so's."

Inside he pulled away, while outside he continued dutifully to hold her. His wife was very beautiful, tall and supple, innately elegant. Her white-blonde hair, blue eyes, and delicate features made her a classic Russian beauty, a rarity among the Jews, Georgians, and other former Soviets in Little Odessa. Her beauty had attracted him, but it hadn't been enough to hold his love.

For Inna's sake, he had been pretending for the past twenty-six years.

"No? Then when is the time? She doesn't respect me. Doesn't take anything I say seriously."

"You know that's not true." Artur stepped out of the embrace and maneuvered Maya back into the waiting room.

"Then why is she refusing to see me? Shouldn't she want her mother at a time like this?"

"She's had a very difficult night." Artur had tried to broker peace between mother and daughter, but he found he couldn't fault Inna for distancing herself. He would have left Maya himself if her father didn't have so much power over him, even from so far away.

"You're always making excuses for her," Maya said.

"And you're always criticizing."

"I don't criticize," Maya said. "I tell her what she needs to hear—out of love. Is it such a crime for a mother to want help her daughter be a better person?"

This was the beginning of an old argument, one that had long plagued their marriage, and Artur was not about to engage, not tonight. Maya was prickly and critical when it came to Inna, always chastising and correcting in the name of love, claiming she needed to balance Artur's favoritism, while the feckless Aleksei could do no wrong. No matter how hard Inna tried, she could never please Maya, who doled out her love generously to Aleksei, never making him earn it. Again, she would say, to balance Artur's favoritism toward Inna.

"I don't want to fight with you," Artur said.

She drew back as if affronted. "Why would we fight? I hate it when we disagree." Her blue eyes were wide and round, wet with ready tears, and she looked up at him with a guileless innocence, another familiar, almost predictable move in her usual pattern of stab and parry. Yet, he supposed her responses were genuine, born of deep wounds rather than calculated attempts at emotional blackmail.

Few in this world lived the kind of duplicitous life he did. He was a rare creature, he knew. Sometimes the complexity of his own machinations made it hard to remember that others were exactly as they appeared. He reminded himself Maya was the fragile woman, almost scorned, who had managed to hold onto the man she loved, who had taken him back after his affair had ended in devastation and disaster. She wasn't the spymaster her father was. She didn't know about the Directorate and its constant greedy demands.

Maya was hungry, especially now in this moment of stress and worry over Inna, for signs of his love and affection. It wouldn't hurt to throw her a few crumbs. Her loyalty all these years certainly merited the small effort, the emotional white lies. He clasped her delicate hand in his. "I hate it, too," he said. "You know I love you."

"Inna might not need me, but I know you do," Maya said, but her tenderness was lost on Artur as a swarthy, dark-haired man in a trench coat stalked to the triage desk.

"Where is she? I demand to see her," the man said. He had a thick accent, perhaps Georgian. He might be a member of Dato's crew, or he might not. He might be carrying a gun under his trench coat, or he might be a regular civilian.

Artur had no way to tell from his vantage point in the last row of chairs, and he wasn't about to take any chances, not when his daughter waited just beyond the emergency room doors. In less than a heartbeat, Artur was on his feet. "Stay here," he hissed at Maya.

"What's going on?"

"Trouble," he said. "Keep your head down." He pushed her low in her chair and walked nonchalantly around the perimeter of the rows of chairs, casually approaching the desk, hoping to get close enough before he caught the man's attention.

The nurse, a stout, gray-haired woman in her early fifties, murmured a response to the would-be mobster and gestured toward the chairs in the waiting area.

"You have to let me see her! She's my wife." The man's voice was louder now. He hit his fist against the desk for emphasis, and the nurse hopped back.

"Sir, sit down now, or I'll have security escort you out," the nurse warned and nodded in the direction of a burly guard.

The man looked up and caught Artur watching him. His eyes darted from Artur to the security guard and back. With an evil glare in Artur's direction, the man raised both hands and backed himself toward the first row of seats in the waiting room. "I don't want any trouble."

Artur returned to stand by Maya, not taking his eyes off of the man in the trench coat. Pensively, almost obsessively, he fingered the special pen in his pocket. Stroking the warm, sleek, deadly metal soothed him, restored a semblance of a sense of control.

"What's wrong?" Maya asked.

"I don't like the look of him," Artur whispered. "I thought he might have a gun."

"Don't be silly," she scolded, matching his quiet tone. "This is an urban hospital. Everyone goes through the metal detectors when they come in. Didn't you notice them?"

Artur had noticed them, but he also knew there were plenty of ways to sneak deadly weapons past the detectors. He should know. He was carrying his own. "I guess this whole thing with Inna has me shaken up. You're right. I'm not thinking rationally," Artur said. He sat down next to Maya as if he were a regular man, a worried father, not a master spy trained to see artifice and threat in everyone and everything around him.

"Just tell me when I can see my wife," the man said to the nurse, a quiet demand, but not as threatening.

"The doctors will let us know," the nurse answered.

"I'll be back in an hour," the man said, rising. Artur's suspicions spiked as he headed in the opposite direction away from the doors. He didn't turn his head, didn't look at Artur. Was he what he claimed, a concerned husband? Or had the Georgians sent him? Or perhaps the Directorate?

Whatever the case, the man would be back again later. Artur wasn't about to chance that he would get to Inna. He slipped his cell phone from his pocket.

"What are you doing?" Maya demanded, on the alert as ever for any offense.

"Calling Victor," he said.

"You can't be serious! You can't plan to work tonight."

"I need to check in. I had a business meeting earlier that got interrupted by … events."

"I see," she said coldly. She snatched a magazine from the table beside her. Angrily, she snapped the pages as she opened and turned them, but Artur had no patience for her pique. He needed to call in reinforcements.

NICK

AFTER HIS VERY brief and uninformative interview with the cops, Nick had taken up a seat at the bar at Troika and nursed a beer. He didn't need to hang around, but he wanted to see how the night's drama played out. He couldn't help feeling that Aleksei was guilty of something. Nick hoped if he waited around long enough, he would find a clue as to what.

From his perch, Nick watched the comings and goings, the various parties, the games of flirtation. Troika attracted a mixed crowd of older, Russian glitterati in their furs and jewels, and younger, upwardly mobile professionals, like Aleksei and Katya, all looking to show off their success or hook up. Troika, Nick decided, was a scene for the wealthy of Brighton Beach, and the clientele seemed to party hard, downing a lot of liquor.

Nick supposed the alcohol may have flowed a little more generously than usual tonight. In order to prevent a mass panic and stampede out when rumors of a violent crime and police presence had started to spread, Aleksei had announced that there had been an "incident," that everything was now under control, and that drinks for the rest of the night were on the house. Even if they had come to flaunt their wealth, the patrons were happy to be cheap. They ordered extravagantly and, Nick noticed, tipped little.

The waitstaff looked more than a little morose. He couldn't blame them. For the bad tips and the prospect of a police investigation into their immigration status, they had his sympathy. He remembered well waking up with nightmares that the Americans would change their minds and send him and his aunt back to Russia, where the rest of his family had been murdered.

Their blood was on Artur's hands. For that, Nick would have his revenge.

"Long night." Aleksei slid onto the stool beside him. He made an exaggerated yawn.

"Did you talk to the police yet?" Nick asked.

"Not yet," Aleksei said.

Nick stuffed his hands in his pockets and for the hundredth time that evening tried to hide his irritation with Katya's husband. As far as Nick could tell, Aleksei had done everything possible, short of calling a lawyer—something he could never justify when he had both Katya and Nick immediately on hand—to delay responding to the investigators' questions.

First he had to do damage control and see to the patrons, Aleksei had said. Then he had to close and lock up the club. And then he had to dismiss the staff. Hours later, he still had not closed the club nor dismissed the staff.

He had, of course, been faultlessly polite to the officers and provided them with a bottomless carafe of coffee and cookies, a quiet room, and opportunity to talk to the various waitresses and cooks, most of whom barely spoke English.

"I'm sure I won't have anything useful to say. I wasn't here when everything went down," Aleksei said, as if excusing his tardy response to the police. "I don't know why this can't wait until tomorrow. I'm beat." He tapped on the counter, and the leggy bartender hurried over in her skimpy uniform. An eye-catching brunette in her early forties, she poured Aleksei a shot of vodka, which he downed in a single swallow. He slapped the glass back down on the counter, and she immediately poured him another while Nick watched with disgust and burgeoning dislike. Was Aleksei trying to get drunk before he went to talk to the police?

"I'm sure they need to cover all of their bases. What happened here wasn't exactly your average night." Nick tried to sound sympathetic, friendly, when what he truly wanted was to throttle Aleksei and thunk his head a few times against the bar. A normal man would be concerned for his sister, might be calling the hospital for news, would certainly want to get to the bottom of what had happened to her—or to any patron for that matter—especially when a crime had been committed in his place of business.

Aleksei's recent delays, coupled with his earlier obstruction of their arrival, only made Nick certain that Aleksei had some inkling of what had happened and an investment in covering it up. *Like father, like son.*

"You might be able to help them in other ways, you know," Nick said.

"What do you mean?" Aleksei asked, and Nick noticed not even the slightest hint of a slur in his words, although he reeked of alcohol. Nick guessed the two shots Aleksei had just tossed back were not his first. He motioned to the bartender for yet another, and Nick suspected Katya's husband—to add to all of his other prize attributes—might also have a drinking problem.

"Have you given them access to the surveillance video?" Nick asked.

"No, they didn't ask for it. They don't have a warrant."

"If they don't have a warrant yet, it's only a matter of time. This is a murder investigation. Sooner or later, they'll ask to see what was caught on camera."

"Not much," Aleksei said. "We don't have any cameras in the private rooms upstairs."

How convenient. "What about the back stairs or hallway?"

"Nope."

"That seems unusual."

Aleksei only shrugged. "I guess I'll give it to them now. What can it hurt?"

Nick took a swig of beer and regarded Aleksei. What was he hiding? What did he know? Was Aleksei in this on his own, or was Artur also involved?

"Heard anything yet about your sister?"

"The doctors won't tell us anything, and they won't let anyone see her, or else she doesn't want them to. She's an odd duck."

"How do you mean?" How could Aleksei be so callous toward his own sister?

"Never mind," Aleksei said.

Nick couldn't shut off the stream of questions that came to him about Inna Koslovsky. He didn't know if she would consider dating him after what had happened to her tonight, and he found himself feeling sorry for her in so many ways—for what had happened, for her brother's lack of empathy. But what did Aleksei mean she was odd? Was there something Nick was missing, perhaps something Katya in her glow of optimism had neglected to tell him? Had Inna also inherited her father's legacy of betrayal and deceit?

"You can't throw a comment like that out there and not follow up," Nick said. "Not after Katya has been singing your sister's praises for weeks." Nick motioned to the bartender for a shot.

"Pour me another one, too," Aleksei said. This time his words ran together ever so slightly.

The bartender shook her head. "Your wife wouldn't like it."

"But I'm your boss," Aleksei said with a winsome smile that had the woman smiling back.

"That you are," she said and filled his glass.

"Svetlana, you're a gem," Aleksei said.

The bartender clucked her tongue. "Now you sound exactly like my ex—right before he traded me in for a younger model."

"Sveta, sweetheart, you know I'd never do that to you."

"You mean 'never' as long as I look good in bootie shorts," she said, "and keep the vodka flowing."

Aleksei raised his glass to her wit and then knocked back the shot. "Leave the bottle," he instructed her as she moved on to serve the other patrons.

"Look, here's the thing," Aleksei said, leaning closer, confiding, as he poured Nick a finger of vodka and refilled his shot glass. Aleksei's hand wobbled. "Inna seems okay. All put together on the outside," he said. "She puts on a good show. But inside she's a mess."

"Aren't we all?" Nick asked.

Aleksei raised his shot glass as if in agreement or salute before tossing it back. Without pause, he poured himself yet another finger, this time sloppily. Vodka sloshed over the rim of his glass and left a small pool on the bar. Nick figured he merely had to wait Aleksei out if he wanted information. With any luck, the Stoli would loosen his tongue.

"This is different. She's also a little…" Aleksei whistled and waved his finger in a circle by his temple. "Unstable. Came back from her fancy college and had a breakdown. Hallucinations or something. Panic attacks. The works."

Nick sipped from his glass, and the vodka burned his throat going down. "What happened to her?"

"No idea. Maybe nothing. Maybe the pressure of working with Papa."

What exactly did Inna do for dear Papa? Nick's resolve to meet her grew.

"Inna was seeing a shrink. Taking meds. Getting better. But this new crisis will set her back. Poor, poor Inna," Aleksei said with drunken tenderness, even as he smiled with quiet revel. "Guess Papa won't hand her the business now."

"He should give it to you. You're the oldest," Nick said, testing for Aleksei's reaction.

"He should!" Aleksei nodded his head with vigor. He clasped Nick's forearm in a gesture of solidarity, then shook his head and pulled his hand away. "But he won't. He thinks I'm a fuckup." Aleksei hiccupped.

"Can't be trusted with anything. Only thing I ever did right, s'far as he's concerned, was marry Katya. But I'll show him. He'll see."

"See what?"

"See my success!" Aleksei pounded his chest with his fist as if making a pledge. "I don't need his business. I have plans he doesn't know about." He raised his index finger to make a point then brought it to his lips. "I'm going to make a killing in Brighton Beach."

"How?" Nick asked.

"Shhh," Aleksei said. "It's a secret."

More secrets in a family that must be brimming with them. What was Artur's true "business," and how involved was Inna? He hadn't considered that she might be privy to her father's secrets.

"Aleksei! There you are!" Katya headed toward the bar, slightly breathless, her curls bouncing with each step. "The police are waiting to talk with you."

Aleksei slid off the stool. As he moved toward Katya, she wrinkled her nose and frowned. "You've been drinking," she accused. "Aleksei, how could you? On tonight of all nights."

"Tonight of all nights required a drink," Aleksei said. "Right, Nick?"

Nick gave an abashed smile. He had a beer bottle and a shot glass standing in front of him, and he had certainly done his share to encourage Aleksei to drink more—even if Aleksei had required very little nudging.

"He hasn't talked to the police yet. We can't let them interview him in this state." Katya shot Nick a reproving glance, and he hunched his shoulders, feeling vaguely guilty for disappointing her. "Sveta, do you have coffee?"

"Yes, coffee," Aleksei agreed. He plunked back down on his barstool, dropped his head into his hand, and passed out. Sveta swiftly poured a mug and brought it over. The coffee spilled onto the saucer as she placed it in front of him.

"Aleksei, wake up." Katya gently slapped at his cheek. "*Bozhe moy*, what am I going to tell the police?"

"The truth," Sveta said quietly.

Katya brought her head up abruptly. "The truth?"

Sveta clicked her tongue. "Katya, you're not naïve. You're a lawyer. In Manhattan. A smart woman. You know the truth about your own husband."

"I don't know what you're talking about." Katya sank onto the nearest barstool. She looked vaguely ill, and Nick wondered what she knew or suspected. She wouldn't meet his eye.

KATYA

THE TRUTH ABOUT her husband, Katya thought. What was the truth? Sometimes she felt she hardly knew him.

The truth was that their marriage was a hollow shell, but it had taken her a year to figure it out and another year to decide what to do.

She hadn't asked the right questions when they got married. From the beginning, she had been too dazzled—by his looks, his success, and most importantly his seeming devotion to her. Their wedding day had seemed like a dream come true. She, Katya Gendler, had been chosen by the handsomest, wealthiest man she had ever met, a man who willingly and ostentatiously showed everyone how much he absolutely adored her.

A man who, when drunk on their honeymoon, had told her that she made his life... tolerable. *In vino veritas.*

Her marriage, likely the best thing that had ever happened in her life, had been slowly falling apart, the cracked pieces slipping through her fingers from the very beginning—no matter how hard she worked to hold him.

Her mother had predicted this. From the moment Aleksei had stepped into Katya's life, Mama had taken the stance that Katya had won the love lottery and had damn well better clutch her winning ticket with a death grip. Her mother warned her constantly that Aleksei was such a catch that another woman would steal him away from her if she wasn't careful to be a good wife to him, if she didn't stop working so much, if she didn't start spending more time with him.

But Katya wasn't ready to give up her work or cut back. She needed it, needed the escape, the sense of competence. She loved working with legal contracts, where everything was set out in black and white, all the rules and expectations, so unlike her life where whatever she did was never enough.

She wasn't a good enough daughter. Or a good enough wife. Or a good enough lover. Or a good enough sister.

Katya wished she could have a stiff drink, but she needed to stay lucid. Somebody had to. What her mother didn't understand was that Katya had never had a hold on Aleksei, despite his declarations.

She had no proof, but she suspected he might be having an affair. Or considering one. He had been cagey and secretive lately, staying out late more and more, purportedly with Mikhail. He claimed he was playing cards with his buddies, and Katya wasn't sure what she feared more—the prospect of another woman or of his gambling away their future.

Work filled the hollowness, sort of. She lived for the scraps of praise, the little victories, but law was a chew-you-up-and-spit-you-out profession. She was a good lawyer, but not a star, and the work—mostly close examination of clauses and loopholes—wasn't going to change the world or make it better. She slaved hundred-hour weeks for the chance to become a partner, something that lately she wasn't sure was all that important to her anymore, even if the money she socked away with every paycheck made her feel more secure.

There was more to life than working. She wanted more than what she had.

She eyed Aleksei. He slumped on the barstool near her, his head pillowed by his forearms on the bar. He had started drinking the moment they had entered Troika and found the chaos of a full-blown murder investigation, and had only stopped now, when he had passed out.

The truth was Aleksei had a drinking problem. The truth was Aleksei might have a gambling problem, too. The truth was Aleksei wasn't really grown up or responsible enough to own a business, although he owned the nightclub and several small pharmacies in

Brighton Beach. The truth was Katya had spent the last few months agonizing over how to win back and keep his love.

Katya could feel Nick watching her, and she wanted to sink into the floor. He was the junior partner at her law firm, not quite her boss, but not her peer either, despite his friendliness toward her. She imagined she must have fallen several rungs in his estimation tonight. Her husband was showing himself to be the irresponsible drunk he was, exposing the secret that Katya's perfect storybook life wasn't quite so perfect.

Her natural inclination would be to smile, to pretend everything was fine, to hide the cracks in her marriage. But she couldn't. Not now with the police buzzing around and a terrible crime hanging over her family.

Here were the facts: a man was dead; Aleksei's sister had been harmed; all of this had happened at Aleksei's club; and he was now falling down drunk. He looked guilty, even if only by association. The police would think so, too. They already did.

She had no reason to suspect Aleksei's guilt, but deep down she didn't quite trust him. At heart, he was still a little boy, spoiled and delighted with his own mischief, quick to blame others when things didn't go his way.

What was it Mikhail was supposed to have handled tonight? Had Aleksei deliberately dragged his feet getting to the club? Was he using her as an unwitting alibi? What had Aleksei done? He and Mikhail, his partner in crime.

The police had asked a lot of questions about drugs. Was Aleksei dealing? The pharmacies he owned would give him access to prescription medications that could capture a high price on the black market, dirty money that could explain his own success when the club did so little business.

Katya's brother-in-law, Jack, complained he was barely making ends meet as Aleksei's partner at Troika. Yet Aleksei was rolling in money. He claimed the cash was from his other ventures—his pharmacies and his investments. Maybe it was legitimate. But maybe it wasn't.

Katya needed to face the truths, whatever they were, about her husband and her marriage.

"Here, Aleksei." She tapped him on the shoulder to rouse him and lifted the coffee cup to his lips. "Come on, baby. You need to wake up. You need to talk to the police."

Unaware of his own strength, he pushed her away with enough force that she slipped from the stool, lost her balance, and hit the floor. Her tailbone smarted, and her lovely ivory blouse dripped with coffee, but the damage was nothing to the emotional stab. She scrambled to her feet, indignant.

"What's wrong with you?" she demanded.

"Nothing's wrong with me," he said. He made a dismissive wave in her direction, and her temper, fueled by hurt, ignited.

"Your sister's in the hospital, and you're here passed out drunk. Don't you care what happened to her? Don't you feel responsible?"

Aleksei stood up to his full height. He grabbed her by both shoulders. She expected he would embrace her, say the words that would make everything better. Instead, he shook her hard. "Stop asking so many damn questions!"

She gasped with shock and swatted at him with her hands. "Stop that! You're hurting me."

He abruptly let go of her shoulders and took a faltering step back. He swung his arm, as if trying to balance himself, but he clipped her with a backhand across her nose.

She felt dizzy, and the salty taste of blood filled her throat. He hadn't hit her hard, but her nose was bleeding. She grabbed a stack of napkins from the bar and crushed them to her face.

"Katya, I'm sorry," Aleksei said, as if surprised by his own actions.

Nick reached his hand toward her, but Aleksei rallied. He pushed Nick out of the way. "Keep your hands off her," he said, but Nick turned around and decked him. Aleksei stumbled back.

"What's going on here?" The officer who had been conducting the interviews appeared at the bar.

"Nothing," Katya said quickly.

"He hit her," Nick said.

"He didn't mean it," Katya said. The officer gave her a suspicious look, as if he had heard that line before.

"He's had too much to drink," she said, and then wished she could take back the words. She sounded like the worst sort of cliché, the woman who stood by her man and made excuses for him no matter how he abused her. She grabbed another stack of napkins and blotted herself as if nothing had happened.

Nick moved closer and hissed in her ear. "There's no excuse. He hit you. And if he ever does it again, I will finish him."

"It was an accident," she said, wishing she fully believed it was true. "He's too drunk to know what he's doing."

She wouldn't blindly defend Aleksei or let him abuse her, but she wouldn't walk away either. Not yet. Not until she had done everything she could to fix what was broken in their relationship. She had more than herself to consider.

Ready or not, good idea or not, Aleksei was going to be a father. He just didn't know it yet.

VLAD

VLAD LEFT THE precinct with a vaguely empty feeling in his gut. He hadn't expected to come face to face with Saul or to confront how much his life seemed to have come full circle. He had escaped Brighton Beach twenty years ago, had run away and tried not to look back, had tried to make himself into one of the good guys, only to return to where it all started.

He made his way down Brighton Beach Avenue, the collar of his leather jacket turned up against the night chill. The distance from the precinct back to Troika was only about a mile, and he covered the first few blocks with long, determined strides. After tonight's events, the opening was there to move in, gain Artur's trust, secure his position on Artur's crew before slowly taking over.

The shop fronts were all dark, most with metal grates locked over their front doors and windows. Some of the restaurants were closing, but music and lights still spilled out of others. He observed them with detachment. He had grown up in this neighborhood, in a tiny rent-controlled apartment a few blocks from the ocean.

The air smelled the way he remembered, a hint of ocean salt mingled with the heavy scents of fried potatoes and meat and car exhaust. He had never felt a part of this neighborhood, and the smells and sounds held no nostalgia for him, although he did feel a pang when he thought about Nadia. His mother had been the only woman he had ever loved.

He tried hard not to think about her, to bury the hurt and rejection. Seeing Saul tonight had opened a wound Vlad had thought had healed over. He wouldn't call Nadia. He couldn't afford the distraction. He needed to stay focused. He had a mission, a goal, a promising future, and he wouldn't be derailed due to a twenty-year-old family drama.

A creepy feeling stole over him. He was being watched. An icy chill breathed over his skin. He felt the eyes of his assailants before he heard them. The tap of footsteps on concrete. Vlad didn't glance over his shoulder. If they knew he sensed them, he would lose an important advantage.

Vlad moved away from the buildings, closer to the street, where a row of cars—old and new, shiny and rusted, a manifestation of the rundown fortunes and great wealth living side by side in the neighborhood—were parallel parked. The streetlights shone down, and the harsh light cast reflections on the windshields and hoods.

The reflections off the doors of a black BMW gave him his first view of the two men behind him, dark figures in long coats. They crept close to the building, but hurried to keep up with his long strides. There were only two, not very stealthy. Not cops either. Their gold rings and heavy neck chains glittered, catching the light. Dressed for show, not serious business, he thought hopefully.

He couldn't tell what weapons his welcome party had. They didn't look like the macho types to depend on fists alone. Too bad for him. Guns were too much of an equalizer. Even a hack could do mortal damage with a lucky shot, and dead was dead.

The thought of death didn't scare him, not the way it should.

Vlad reached for his guns and turned to face the two. In his career in law enforcement, the difference between right and wrong had come down to a thin dividing line between legal and illegal, a hairsbreadth tightrope that didn't differentiate between good and evil or offer any assurance that he wasn't exactly the same kind of monster as his old man.

The law could be a shield for some truly terrible acts. Murder, for instance, was sanctioned if it was an act of self-defense.

He knew he needed to serve up some diplomacy, have a chat with the bling brothers, get the Georgians—he assumed that's who they were—to stand down. He almost hoped they'd give him an excuse to fire.

"Hands up, fellas."

Of course they didn't freeze or raise their hands. The shorter of the two, a squat man, ran at him full speed, head down as if preparing to gore him like an angry bull. The other, slim with shoulder-length black hair, held back, drew a gun.

There was nowhere to run, and an armed standoff was an impossibility with the human torpedo coming his way.

Vlad sidestepped, but the man corrected course and head-butted him. The blow hit him in the ribs and threw him against a car door. He winced at the wallop and the hard impact against the side of the car. In the moment he lost catching his breath, his attacker let his fists fly and tried to pummel Vlad against the passenger side of a black Mercedes.

The car's alarm sounded, a siren followed by steady beeps and then a swooping sound. Loud and irritating, the noise echoed off of the subway tracks above them, creating a ruckus that drowned the sound of their heavy breathing.

Perhaps immune to the noise or too frightened to stick their necks out, no one came running to the car's rescue. Or Vlad's. Not that he expected help. He had never received any, not when it mattered, anyway.

He was cornered against the car, almost pinned, without enough room to bring up his arms and block the blows. In the close space between them, Vlad used his pistols like fists and punched his attacker with a short, hard jab to the solar plexus. In a move that indicated he was not a trained fighter, the man staggered back with a gasp.

The extra distance gave Vlad the space he needed. He went on the offensive and hit hard with the barrels of his guns—shoulders, arms, face, neck, whatever he could get. Adrenaline shot through his system.

He was high on the physical violence and the sense of threat that gave him license to deliver a brutal beating.

With the car alarm blaring behind him, he didn't hear the crack of bone, but his attacker's right arm dropped limp at his side, and the man's face turned ashen with pain.

"Freeze!" Slim, who had been standing back, now aimed his gun at Vlad. Time to get scarce. Vlad slid across the hood of the nearest car and crouched behind it. He lifted his head enough to peer through the darkened windows.

A shot rang in his direction. Vlad ducked and the shot missed by a wide margin. The slug embedded itself in the hood of a red sedan. A warning shot or Slim's best shot?

"I said freeze," Slim said.

"Fuck you," Vlad said. He trained one pistol on his crumpling assailant and the other on the man's accomplice.

Slim laughed heartily, as if Vlad had told a dirty joke. "Ivan will be pleased," he said in a very heavy Russian accent, "*kogda ya yemu skazhu chto ti ne malenkaya devochka.*" *When I tell him you're not a little girl.*

"Is that what this is about? Ivan sent you to test me?" A strict adherent to the Thieves' Code, Ivan had never openly acknowledged Vlad as his son nor married Nadia—having a family was forbidden, at least at the time when Ivan had battled his way through the Siberian prison camps. He had never denied he might be Vlad's father, although there were many nights as a young boy when Vlad had wished he would.

Ivan had made clear he wouldn't abide any child who might possibly be his to be a sissy. He used to beat Vlad and forbid Nadia to comfort him—so that he would become tough, Ivan had claimed, while his mother urged him to see Ivan's bruises as a kindness, a lesson that would serve Vlad well.

Vlad hated his father, hated even more the little sting of pleasure he got from the thought that this minion might send his old man a favorable report.

"You waste my time," Vlad growled. His gaze moved back and forth between Slim and Torpedo, who cradled his broken arm against his middle and cupped his nose as blood dripped from his fingers. "Tell me why I shouldn't shoot you both where you stand," Vlad said.

"Your father has a message for you," Slim said with a shrug.

"You lie." Vlad kept his guns pointed at both men. "I have no father."

A smile spread slowly across Slim's face. "Perhaps not, but you're exactly like him."

Vlad didn't want to be anything like Ivan. Slim's comment, perhaps meant as a compliment to Vlad's toughness, resonated with the force of a curse. Vlad spit at the ground.

The specter of his father's brutality had shadowed Vlad most of his adult life, ready to claim his soul with every shot or swing he took, ready to trap him into addiction with every sweet drop of violence. He couldn't deny he loved the adrenaline rush, the ferocious power, when he let the savage in him take over.

Only a few slender threads of self-control, or perhaps self-deceit, kept him from being a brute like Ivan. Vlad had never hit a woman. Or a child. He had never hurt someone who had not attacked or threatened first.

"Ivan's watching you. He knows you used to be a Fed."

Vlad raised his hand, squeezed the trigger of his gun, and a bullet arced past Slim's shoulder. Slim ducked and then stared in his direction with a look of dumb surprise, as if he hadn't expected that Vlad would shoot.

"That was a warning," Vlad said. "Stop wasting my time."

"There's an agent in the field," Slim said. "Know anything about that?" There was a challenge in his words, but weaker now that a bullet had buzzed his ear.

"Yeah. Tell Ivan his intel's worthless."

"What do you mean, worthless?" Slim acted as if he had handed Vlad a priceless gem.

"The mole was a cop, not an agent. And now he's dead."

"You kill him?" Slim asked, prepared, it seemed, to be impressed.

"No. But the Georgians think Inna Koslovsky did. Tell Ivan there's a threat against her."

"Why would he care?" Slim challenged.

"If you don't know, then you don't need to know," Vlad said. "Just tell him."

"I don't take orders from you," Slim said.

"If you take them from Ivan, then you'll tell him."

"Or what?"

"Or you'll be dead," Vlad said simply, trusting it was true. He had seen the style in which his mother lived. Artur had taken care of her all of these years, just as he had sent Vlad to military school before Vlad had slipped Artur's radar. Vlad had no doubt that Ivan and Artur had pooled their resources into *obshak*, a common fund meant to be used, among other things, to support criminals' families. More importantly, Artur controlled that money, a clear sign of his importance, at least in Ivan's eyes. If their partnership was what Vlad suspected, then Inna's safety had to be, by agreement, as important to Ivan as Nadia's now was to Artur. If Ivan's underling failed to notify him of the threat, Vlad was willing to bet there would be deadly consequences.

Guns still trained on both opponents through the car's window, Vlad backed up slowly into the street, still crouching to use the cars as much as possible for cover. He wasn't sure where he stood with Ivan, although he hardly expected to be included in the man's circle of protection.

Vlad didn't have time to waste if he hoped to execute his plans. Ivan could be freed soon, and Vlad needed to deal with him from a position of strength. Ivan's appeal could be granted any day now, and Vlad aspired to be a key player in mob business before he arrived. So far, he had traded on the old connections, the automatic legitimacy and entry bought by being the son of a high-ranking *vor v zakone,* the closest thing the Russian mob had to royalty.

People knew Vlad had spent time with the FBI, but his ties to Ivan overrode what might otherwise be an impediment. His father had an almost mythical reputation, and the denizens of Brighton Beach, upon seeing how much Vlad favored his father, were willing to accept that his blood ran true. Some, like Artur, could even appreciate how well his training might serve them all now, especially on a night like tonight. Still, until Vlad proved himself, a word from Ivan could have him out on his ass, which was why Vlad intended to be occupying his father's old seat as an indispensable and central member of Artur's organization. From there, he could execute a takeover, with or without his father's approval, and hold the full operation in his own hands.

When he got to the curb in the middle of the street and Slim failed to take another shot, Vlad turned and ran. Behind him, he heard Slim laughing.

Vlad ran the rest of the way to Troika. The ocean wind slapped at his cheeks and battered his leather jacket, but he barely felt the chill. He had survived his latest test, and he felt alive.

He slowed when he reached the red carpet marking the entry to the club. The lights shined brightly under the black awning, but he saw only shadows behind the large double doors with their golden handles and the club's logo, three horsemen, stenciled in red. For a moment he wondered at the significance of the number three in the name. As best he knew, the club was owned by Aleksei Koslovsky and his brother-in-law, Jack Roseman. Was there a third owner, or had the nightclub merely adopted a common Russian icon?

Vlad rapped on the glass door, hoping that Svetlana would still be in the club. She knew the players here and was good at working out the angles. Her devious mind might pick through tonight's intrigue and see the relevant patterns. Even better, maybe she had seen something firsthand from her post at the bar.

As he waited, he glanced over his shoulder for signs of Slim or Torpedo or any new surprises, but the street corner was quiet. A minute or two passed. Maybe Sveta had gone home already. He decided to try his luck at the back entrance. At best, he might find her there. At worst, he might be able to make his way in and do some investigating on his own.

He ducked into the alley that led to the back of the club. When he reached the rear lot, he saw a police cruiser. Eager to avoid another encounter with NYPD's finest, he hung back in the shadows, watching.

The rear door opened and Sveta came out. Under her open coat, she wore the black bootie shorts and white low-cut blouse that were the skimpy uniform for all of the female servers at Troika. In her mid-forties, Sveta, with her showgirl legs and smart mouth, managed to hold her own among the waitresses, many of whom were in their early twenties, shy and timid, having recently arrived from the former Eastern block on seasonal visas.

Sveta stood under the floodlights and lit a cigarette. Vlad knew she didn't smoke, and he recognized her nicotine break for what it was: an excuse to come outside and look for him and a signal for him to draw closer.

"Psst," he whispered. She nodded, indicating she had heard him and nonchalantly crossed the dock to lean against the rail near the alley. She gripped the metal rail with her right hand, and Vlad noticed her fingernails had been chewed to the quick. He wanted to ask her what had caused her nail-biting anxiety, but now wasn't the time. Perhaps Troika was a series of pass-or-die trials, too, even though on the surface the nightclub had seemed the easier assignment.

"The police are inside," she said. "You need to stay out here. I don't want anyone to see us together." She ran her hands through her brown bob. She used to wear her hair slicked back in a tight no-nonsense ponytail, and Vlad was still adjusting to her new minx-like look, complete with sexy makeup and tousled hair. Her eyes seem rounded and more open. She appeared more winsome and flirtatious than harsh, but Vlad knew that, like himself, Sveta was a summa graduate of the school of hard knocks.

"Understood," Vlad agreed, keeping to the shadows. He wasn't about to blow her carefully devised cover. "The dead guy's a cop."

"Ah. That complicates things."

It certainly did. Their operation was risky enough as it was; they didn't need the cops crawling over it, too.

She tapped the cigarette against the rail and let the ash fall to the concrete. "Maybe that explains all the questions about drugs and drug dealing. Was he on a bust?"

"Don't know," Vlad said. "The police weren't in a sharing mood. I'd like to know who he was after—the crew at Troika or the Georgians."

Sveta nodded thoughtfully. "Could have been either, but the murder had to be an inside job. There's no surveillance in the back hall or offices or upstairs in the party rooms."

"Good to know," Vlad said. "I was thinking the Georgians wanted to get rid of the cop and shift suspicion onto Artur, but this suggests other possibilities. What I can't figure out is how Inna Koslovsky fits in."

"You're not laying odds on her as the killer?" she asked.

"Maybe if it were a simple rape case and she killed her attacker. Otherwise, what's the motive?"

Sveta shrugged. "Around here motive is the easy part. Everyone has a motive. *Pravda?* The only issue is opportunity." She turned to face him and propped a foot up on the lower rail. She wore fishnets and high stilettos, and he wondered how she stood all night at the bar serving drinks to the locals.

"Not everyone's a killer," he said.

"We all have the potential. It's human nature."

"You don't think there are good people in the world?"

"You, Vladik, are the closest thing I know," Sveta said. "The rest are a bunch of assholes."

"Sucks to be you, then," he said glibly, but he wasn't sure he knew any truly good people either. Even Saul Hersh had found his way to the devil on a road paved with good intentions.

"Ain't that the truth." She waved the cigarette in her hand and regarded it wistfully, as if she wanted very badly to take a smoke. "Koslovsky's sister's a pretty girl. She turn your head?"

"Maybe," Vlad admitted.

"I always wondered what your type was."

"Going to remind me to think with the big head and not the little one?" Vlad asked.

"Do I need to?"

"No."

"Good." Sveta huffed a laugh. "For what it's worth, I don't favor her as a cold-blooded killer, either. Her brother, on the other hand…"

"Wasn't here. He arrived after the police did."

"That doesn't mean his hands are clean. He got drunk off his ass tonight to avoid talking to the cops."

"A murder at his club can't be good for business," Vlad said.

"Which business?" Sveta asked. "The man owns pharmacies. I wouldn't be surprised to learn he's dealing prescription meds on the side."

"You think the cop was on to him?"

"Maybe. Or maybe he didn't even know the guy was a cop. Maybe Aleksei encroached on the Georgians' territory and didn't want to pay *krysha.*"

"You think all this—the rape and the murder—was a ploy to make Daddy step up and vaporize the competition," Vlad said, incredulous. "She's his sister."

"Weren't you listening to me? Pay attention! The world is full of assholes. Don't let wishful thinking blind you," she said. "When you let down your guard, that's when they sneak in and shit all over you." Sveta dropped the stubby cigarette to the concrete and ground it out with her shoe.

Behind her the metal door opened, and one of the waitresses stepped outside. Sveta swiftly bent down and fussed with her stockings. "Beat it before someone sees you," she whispered, and Vlad retreated farther into the shadows.

He needed to find Artur and let him know what was happening. Protecting Inna from the Georgians would be hard enough, but the real threat might be much closer to home.

MAYA

SITTING BESIDE ARTUR in the hospital waiting room, Maya fumed. Artur's calling Victor was entirely predictable. He had always turned to his associate before he turned to her, even back in the Soviet Union before they had come to America to start over. They had been free of Victor for a few glorious years, before Victor had joined them on this side of the Atlantic. For the past twenty years he had plagued her, the albatross around her neck with his knowing glances and the threat of blackmail that still held weight after all of these years.

She imagined her life would be so much better if Victor suddenly died, but she knew that wasn't true. However reluctantly, however unfairly, she and Victor were now a sort of team, and he was an integral part of their lives. She didn't have to like it or the fact that her husband maintained an emotional distance that she couldn't bridge—no matter what she did.

Tonight should have been different. She had expected more reaction from him, more closeness. The child they had raised together had been hurt. This should be a moment when they turned to each other, when their love burned brightly and helped them get through this dark moment.

"Mikhail… and Maya have everything under control," Victor said, adding insult to injury by making her an afterthought. She had been here before all of them. In Artur's life. In this emergency room. "Let's get a cup of coffee from the cafeteria," Victor suggested. He barely hid his anxiousness to pry Artur away from her, to get him alone and discuss their super secret business as if she were entirely in the dark about what they did, as if she believed her husband's bloody hands were clean, as if she couldn't be trusted with their secrets and schemes.

Little did they know she had a thriving business of her own.

"I'll keep her safe," Mikhail promised Artur, nodding, not toward Maya, but toward the closed double doors of the emergency room, but he positioned himself by Maya's shoulder, as if he would care for her, too.

"Come on, Artur. The kid knows what he's doing," Victor said.

Artur hesitated for a moment, studied Mikhail, who met his searing scrutiny with impressive equanimity. A weaker man would have flinched, but Mikhail held steady, earning Maya's grudging respect. It would be easy, she thought, to like him, to be wholly seduced by his good looks and ambition. He worked hard for Artur and, unwittingly, for her.

"Go!" she agreed. "You look like you need a coffee. I'm sure nothing will happen here while you're gone. Go ahead and discuss your business." She let the anger bleed through her words and noticed the way Artur recoiled. Did he feel guilty for leaving her here with his lackey for company? Or did he not want to be with her at all?

The niggling insecurity that had plagued her ever since she first met Artur made her body tighten with anxiety that, as usual, he did nothing to alleviate. He let Victor lead him away. The swift glance over his shoulder was not toward her, but toward the doors, toward Inna, and she resented the way their daughter had succeeded where she could not.

Inna had captured and held Artur's unconditional love. No matter what Inna did or said, he would stand steadfastly by her. For herself, Maya feared he would use any excuse to break their bond, and she wasn't about to give him one. She loved him.

Everything she had done, she had done out of love for him, to keep him and bind him to her, but she had no illusion that he truly shared her feelings. She survived on a shadow of what could have been, telling herself she was satisfied with the small shafts of sunlight he let shine in her direction. If Artur ever found out what Maya had done, he would cut her out of his life like a malignant tumor. He would stomp her into the ground and never look back. And so, he must never know.

Maya pretended not to notice Artur's indifference toward her or the freshly scrubbed man at her side who radiated heat and virility. She crossed her legs and picked up the magazine she'd been using earlier as a prop. She pretended to be absorbed with the outdated gossip about celebrities she couldn't care less about, but her foot bounced with agitation.

Mikhail touched her shoulder, and the light pressure of his fingers sent a jolt of desire through her. Her face heated with embarrassment, and she buried her nose in the magazine. She was old enough to be the man's mother, but she didn't pull away the way she knew she should. She never did, and she despised herself for this small weakness, for her inability to resist the temptations that he freely offered her.

Surely, the touch meant nothing to Mikhail, save perhaps a secret "screw you" to her husband. But the attention eased the aching hurt inside her, and she craved him like the worst addiction. She let her muscles relax under the light touch of Mikhail's hand. Why not take comfort where she could? It was getting difficult to pretend that Artur gave a damn. She was so sick of being ignored.

As soon as Artur and Victor turned down the hall toward the elevators, Mikhail dropped into the seat next to her. She felt almost deprived when he withdrew his hand and let it drape carelessly on the armrest behind them.

He sprawled his legs and leaned back languidly, but his dark eyes were bright and alert. He wasn't a big or tall man, but he filled the space with his presence, a kind of raw sexuality that was impossible for her to ignore. She shifted uncomfortably, and her mood soured further.

"It's not right the way he treats you," Mikhail said. His voice was husky, a rough caress over her skin.

The physical sensations he provoked gave him an unfair advantage, and her body heated with lust and temper. For this, as for many things, she blamed Artur. If he would pay more attention to her, she wouldn't find herself drawn to a young man the same age as her own son. She wouldn't be looking in his direction, or remembering the feel of his hands on her, or feeling the sting of knowing he couldn't possibly want her as much as she wanted him, no matter how prettily he might whisper in her ear.

"You're right," she said curtly and turned the page.

"Why do you put up with it?" Mikhail asked. When she again turned the page of the magazine and didn't answer, he shifted toward her and pulled the pages away from her face. "You're a beautiful woman," he said. "Artur should feel lucky to have you." He touched his palm to her jaw, leaned close as if preparing to kiss her. "Tell me, Maya. Why do you put up with him?"

His breath tickled her lips, and she wanted so badly for him to kiss her that she thought she was losing her mind. But she wouldn't debase herself by falling too swiftly into the well of his charm. She smiled condescendingly at him. "We all make our deals with the devil." She made herself sound worldly and bored. "Why do you put up with the way he treats you?"

"I don't know what you mean," Mikhail began to protest.

He wasn't nearly the accomplished liar that she was. This deception, though trivial, annoyed her. He shouldn't think he could keep any secrets from her now that they were having an affair.

"I'm going to see if there's any new information on Inna," she said and left him alone. She felt the smallest tick of satisfaction that his gaze lingered on her rather than returning immediately to the emergency room doors.

She had to wait in a short line at the nurse's station, while the woman competently triaged the newest arrival, a squat man with a squished nose covered with dried blood. The nose wasn't the worst of his problems, though. He cradled his arm, likely broken. He wore a track suit and gold chains and looked the part of the proverbial tough guy, but he howled like a baby when the nurse tried to examine his lame arm.

Maya suppressed her mirth. Men thought they were the stronger sex—tougher, superior. The men in her life constantly overestimated themselves and underestimated her—if they gave her any thought at all. They might never realize their mistake, but she would make them all regret it.

She waited patiently for the nurse. Patience, she knew, was one of her greatest assets. While Artur and Victor and her father were constantly in motion, constantly doing and running and evading, she had learned to wait quietly, to watch and to listen, to find the openings and opportunities to move stealthily and pilfer what she wanted. Like Mikhail's loyalty and affection.

The nurse returned to the desk, and Maya asked after Inna. "She's resting, and she's under observation," the nurse reported and couldn't or wouldn't share more.

"I'm so worried about her," Maya said and bit her lip. "My baby." The small show of anxiety won her sympathy.

The plump, kindly nurse patted her hand. "I'll let you know as soon as there's anything I can report," she said.

"Has she asked for me? She has to want her mother at a time like this," Maya said.

The nurse leaned closer, confided, "She had a hard time when she first came in, but she's sleeping now. I'm sure she'll ask for you when she wakes up."

Maya nodded, reassured, then asked. "Do you think they'll keep her for a while? She has medication that she takes." She lowered her voice as if imparting a secret of her own. "You know, for mental problems. She's so fragile. And now she's been through this horrible ordeal. I'm afraid of what's going to happen to her."

"I'll let the doctor know," the nurse said, taking down the information about Inna's medication. Maya made the appropriate expressions of gratitude and returned to Mikhail.

"What's the news?" he asked as his blue eyes scanned the waiting area.

"No news. She's sleeping. My guess is we won't get to see her until the morning."

"Do you think she'll remember anything that happened?" Mikhail asked.

"Will it matter if she does or doesn't?" Maya said. "What's done is done."

Mikhail took a breath as if to respond and then silenced himself. He straightened, and his face darkened perceptibly, as he focused on someone behind Maya.

She turned to see Vlad, Artur's new lackey. The two men, close in age, were rivals for Artur's good graces, or at least Mikhail felt that way. Vlad's blunt features were drawn in concentration. His leather jacket was draped over his right arm, hiding his hand, as if concealing a weapon, but she doubted even Artur's new head of security could get his guns into Coney Island Hospital. Still, he had an air of lethal danger. His flinty eyes flicked quickly over the waiting room before returning to her and Mikhail. He moved swiftly, with purpose and surprising grace.

"Where's Artur?" Vlad asked, all business. Mikhail rose to his feet before answering.

"Taking a much-needed break," Mikhail said. "Where the hell have you been?"

Vlad leaned toward Mikhail, perhaps trying to intimidate him with his height. His voice was a gravelly rumble that reminded her of a growl. "Chasing down leads."

Unflinching, Mikhail crossed his arms. "On what?"

"On who might have wanted the Georgian dead," Vlad said. He crossed his arms now, too, a sign he wouldn't divulge anything more.

His shirtsleeves were rolled up to his elbows to reveal impressive forearms that flexed with his movements. His jacket still concealed his right hand.

"Then you were wasting your time," Maya said and physically inserted herself before Mikhail foolishly provoked Vlad. He was still an unknown quantity, and Maya's own philosophy was to approach with caution until she learned more. Both men blinked at her as if surprised by her intrusion on their battle of wills.

"Inna killed him. Right?" she said. "That's what Artur said."

"That's what someone wants us all to think," Vlad said, and she noted with approval that he had curbed the aggression in his voice and stance to address her.

"And what do you think?" Maya asked.

"I think I need to talk to Artur," Vlad said.

"She's my daughter, too. I have a right to know what happened. And why."

His face softened, and the kindness there surprised Maya, raising him in her regard. "You do," he agreed. "And that's exactly what I'm trying to find out."

"He's in the cafeteria with Victor," Maya said. Vlad nodded in thanks, turned abruptly on his heel, and jogged away. He was unquestionably Artur's man.

"I hate that guy," Mikhail muttered under his breath.

"Do you? Why?" Maya asked, although she already recognized the signs of jealousy. She placed her hand on Mikhail's arm. She expected him to pull away or take back his words. Instead, he leaned closer, confided in her. Perhaps there was more affinity between them than she had credited.

"I was Artur's right-hand man," Mikhail said. "I used to get the key assignments, have a seat at the table, have access to all of the important information. And then Vlad came along. There was no warning. Artur didn't even make Vlad prove himself. He just brought him in as my replacement."

Sympathy pulled Maya closer to Mikhail. She had felt the scarring burn of betrayal, the internal poison of her own jealousy. Even though she had won Artur back, she had lost him irrevocably to another woman. As if that weren't hurt enough, the other woman was gone, but Maya was still second in Artur's affections, which he reserved entirely for Inna.

Daringly, she placed both of her hands on Mikhail's chest. She caressed her palm over his pecks, taut and firm under his button-down shirt. Emboldened when he neither laughed nor pulled away, she closed the small gap between them. "I know how that feels," she said. "And I know how to get revenge."

She bunched her hands in his shirt and pulled him toward her. His arms came around her in implied welcome, and the small spark from his embrace filled an empty space inside her, not enough to slake the gnawing hunger, but enough to abate it. If she could have more, then maybe she could forget the pain she constantly carried. She leaned into him, needing his kiss.

Their lips met for the briefest moment. Mikhail cast a wild glance around the waiting room and released her.

He sat down, as if feeling unsteady on his feet, and pulled her into the chair beside him. He didn't let go of her hand as he tilted his head toward hers. "Oh, Maya," he said. "If Artur finds out what we're doing, he'll kill me."

"Let's make sure he never finds out," she said.

"He might suspect," Mikhail said, but she silenced any further worry or protest with a finger to his lips.

"I know my husband. If he knew, you wouldn't be here right now standing watch over Inna and me," she said. Mikhail visibly relaxed. She ran the pad of her finger over his bottom lip, so full and ripe she wanted to take a little nibble. "Trust me," she said.

His blue eyes met hers, full of promise and a silent agreement.

VICTOR

EVEN WITH A hospital security guard and one of their own men babysitting the doors to the emergency room, Victor practically had to drag Artur away from the waiting area. They couldn't talk openly in front of Maya, who managed to regard Victor with a potent mix of beauty and venom.

She still hadn't forgiven Victor for his blackmail twenty-six years ago, even if it had given them both exactly what they wanted—Artur. Or maybe she had forgiven him but still guarded Artur jealously, as if she wanted to tell the world Artur belonged to her and her alone. Victor almost felt sorry for her. The only person Artur truly cared for was Inna, the great hero's Achilles' heel.

"I'm not waiting for Dato's crew to strike," Artur said. Victor sat across from Artur in the nearly empty hospital cafeteria with Styrofoam cups of coffee Victor had purchased from a vending machine. "It's time to be proactive."

"I agree about being proactive," Victor said in an attempt at diplomacy, "but, Artur, you can't just go in and kill them all." Right now was not the time to let his partner go renegade.

"Why not?" Artur challenged.

Victor took a moment to assess Artur before answering. Artur hadn't washed or slept. He had spent the night in vigil at the hospital. He was merely edgy now with adrenaline, Victor told himself. All Artur needed was a firm reminder about what was at stake to make him fall back into line.

"Why not? I'll tell you why not," Victor said. He leaned toward Artur, resting both hands on the gray Formica tabletop. "Because of the Directorate," he whispered.

"I don't give a damn about the Directorate," Artur confessed.

Victor choked on the sip of coffee in his mouth. Artur hadn't even bothered to lower his voice. The name of the secret organization that had cowed Artur in the past seemed to hold no special power for him now.

Not good. Not good at all.

"For all we know, they're behind what happened tonight. It's the kind of thing they would do. Isn't it? To keep us in line. To make us do the next deal," Artur said, his voice filled with disgust.

Victor had known Artur a long time. He'd had a front row seat to the dramas in the man's life. Losing Sofia had dampened the man's rebellious streak, had given Artur a taste of what could happen. "No, Artur. It's not what they would do. It's not their style. You know that. They don't play like this. If you defy them, they kill."

For more than twenty-five years, veiled threats against Inna had been more than enough to keep Artur on the straight and narrow, never deviating from orders. He might think those decades of threats had finally taken form. But the worst hadn't happened. Inna wasn't dead.

"That's where you're wrong," Artur said. "I've been thinking a lot about the Directorate tonight. About what they want. About how they control us. Inna's worth more to them alive than dead. If she dies, they have no way to make me do what they want. I'm out. Done. And they know it."

Victor silently kicked himself for not arriving sooner, for giving Artur so much time to ruminate.

"I made the deal for her, Victor. I came to this country and did their bidding for her. So she could have a good life. But they'll make her life hell. They'll terrorize her. Just to control me."

"So what are you saying?" Victor asked. Years of training kept the frisson of alarm from tightening his voice. Tonight's events should have made Artur more pliable, more compliant. Instead, they had pushed the man past his edge, introduced a feral quality. Artur was a brilliant man, and Victor had spent the better part of his career harnessing that genius to their mutual benefit, but now Artur threatened to slip the yoke.

"You can't go up against the Directorate. They'll crush you," Victor said.

Artur frowned down at his coffee cup, and Victor couldn't tell whether the frown was one of concentration or disappointment—in him. Age had been kind to Artur, kinder than it had been to Victor, who had grayed and let himself go soft in the middle. Younger than Victor, Artur was distinguished and fit. Time had only deepened his charisma, made people want to please him, to trust him. Even now, after all of these years, Victor felt the pull, understood how easy it would be to fall into Artur's orbit.

"Artur, step back from this. You're upset tonight. Don't let emotion push you to do something stupid," Victor said quickly. "You're my oldest friend. I don't want to see you hurt."

"We're all hurt," Artur said. He took a breath as if he were about to say more, but stopped. "Vlad!" he called and waved his hand in the air.

The hulk Artur had recently hired to manage security strode toward them. Vlad was large and imposing, conspicuous, the type of man a person would remember meeting and wouldn't want to cross.

"Artur. Victor." Vlad gave them each a curt nod. He was a man of few words, and Victor liked that about him. He preferred the muscle to be big and silent, seen and not heard. Problems started when the help started thinking for themselves.

"What did you learn?" Artur asked.

Vlad cut a glance in Victor's direction, as if he were asking Artur whether Victor could be trusted. Victor bristled. Artur and Victor were partners, but Victor suddenly saw how easily he could be marginalized, unimportant, replaced, the way he had been when Ivan was around—before Victor had managed to neutralize him.

It wouldn't do for Artur to have his own secrets or sources of intelligence, his own men loyal to him.

"The information's sensitive," Vlad said.

"There's no secrets between Artur and me," Victor said. "We're partners. And you work for both of us."

Vlad again looked to Artur for confirmation, and Victor resolved to spend some one-on-one time with Vlad to make sure the big dog answered to him as master. Artur granted his permission with a nod.

Vlad sat down in the empty chair at the square coffee table and bent his head in toward them. They both leaned forward. "Zviad wasn't a real member of the Georgian crew. He was an undercover cop," Vlad said.

Artur blew out a breath. "A cop? What was he doing with Inna?"

"And why at Troika, on the same night you were sure to be there?"

Artur tapped his fingers on the table. "You think it was a setup."

"Get rid of the cop and cast suspicion on us," Vlad said. "It's a possibility."

"But why would they do that to us? What about the... deal?" This time, Victor made the cutting glance toward Vlad, a reminder to Artur that their newest associate had not been fully briefed on their activities.

"The deal's off," Artur said with a decisive wave of his hand.

"You can't do that!" Panic rose up, and Victor couldn't stem the tide. A wave of protest spilled from his mouth unchecked. "What happened to Inna is nothing next to what they'll do. They'll kill us, Artur. Not just you. Both of us."

"Who'll kill you?" Vlad asked.

"The Georgians," Victor lied.

ARTUR

ACROSS THE CAFETERIA table from both men, Artur could tell Vlad sensed Victor's lie, although Vlad still hadn't sniffed out the truth. Victor and Artur both had too much sense of self-preservation to serve it up.

Artur was secretly glad of Vlad's suspicion. The kid might not be a great mastermind. Still, he picked up important nuances and had the right instincts for survival. He could be very valuable and, yet, he would have to be carefully watched and managed.

"Take a walk, Victor," Artur said in warning. Victor was too close to hysteria, too liable to slip up.

"No." Victor pushed away his coffee and gave Artur an affronted look. With his beak nose and flashing dark eyes, he reminded Artur of a hawk with ruffled feathers. "I'm fine. Maybe I'm the only one who's fine here. You're the one jumping to conclusions and making bad decisions—to go after the Georgians, to cancel the deal." Victor shifted in his chair, and tension vibrated off of him. "It's not like you, Artur, to trust whatever people say."

Artur himself was on the edge, but he was playing a deep game. Plots within plots. In light of what had happened tonight to Inna—or perhaps especially because of what had happened—he couldn't afford to lose focus. Keeping his edge was essential.

Well before tonight's events, he had realized he needed to outsmart and manipulate everyone, including his old friend, if he wanted to escape the Directorate's tyranny. His resolve was strengthened now, his timeline accelerated, but the plan was already in motion.

"How do you know the dead guy was a cop?" Victor demanded of Vlad.

"It's a long story," Vlad said. Evasive. Artur could tell Victor didn't like that. He could almost feel the brittle crackling of Victor's resentment, the same as Mikhail's. It couldn't be helped. Neither man could know who Vlad really was or why Artur had gone to lengths to make a place for him. The secret was crucial to all of his plans. So was Ivan's return.

"We have time," Victor said, his voice acid.

"It doesn't matter how he knows," Artur said. "He's right."

Vlad had to be right. The information explained so many oddities about the evening—why the police had treated him and Inna the way they had, why they had asked so many goddamn questions about drugs and drug dealing.

"Now you're going to tell me the Georgians set this all up. That's crazy," Victor said. "They wouldn't dare take on the Russian mob like that."

"They do whatever they damn well please. And now they're going to try to kill Inna," Artur said. He was heartily sick of Victor's mistaken bureaucrat's view of the Russian mob. Victor imagined that there was a big, cohesive group with a leader, a king in his mind, and treaties or agreements over turf and activities. Victor didn't grasp the reality, or else he didn't believe Artur whenever he tried to set Victor straight. At times Artur suspected Victor imagined him to be some kind of Mobster-in-Chief or mafia don, ruler over a kingdom of organized crime, capable of exacting hefty taxes or reaching into the kingdom's coffers to feed the Directorate's insatiable maw.

There was no umbrella organization, no distinguished crime families, only a bunch of people out for themselves, separate lawless crews that occasionally partnered for mutual profit.

"I'm not sure the Georgians knew Zviad was a cop," Vlad said. "If they did, there were a thousand quiet ways to make him disappear. This way, all they did was rile up the police and call attention."

"Someone else set this up," Artur said, embracing Vlad's logic. "Someone trying very hard to provoke me." Or to get Inna out of the way.

"So maybe someone else wants a war between us and the Georgians. If we fight each other, who gains?" Vlad asked.

"Another very good question."

With such a wide network of associations, even temporary ones, no one benefited if the authorities started taking a close look at anyone. There were only so many degrees of separation. A trail that led to one could easily lead to many.

Whoever had set Inna up was a novice or an outsider, someone who didn't understand the way things worked, or else someone with a serious vendetta, immune to concerns about provoking the other crews.

"So we'll go reason with the Georgians," Victor said with self-serving optimism. "We'll tell them how Inna did them a favor, and we'll salvage the deal."

Artur took a sip of scalding black coffee and regarded Victor carefully over the rim of his cup. Victor enjoyed thinking he was the smartest man in the room. His arrogance left him vulnerable to manipulation and dislike, and his misconceptions set him up for worse, but he was a fixture in Artur's life. They had been partners for a long time, practically since the beginning of Artur's career.

They had been an odd pairing in the beginning. Artur had been idealistic, filled with naïve ideas about the Communist party and the difference he might make in the world. Victor, likely from birth, had been jaded, hungry for power and ways to wield it, yet lacking the charm that would make it flow easily into his hand.

In meeting Maya, the daughter of a high-ranking Soviet politician, Artur had stumbled onto the fast track to advancement, and Victor had pushed him along, a fact for which Artur could easily resent his old comrade. Every time he had sold his soul, Victor had been at his side to help broker the deal, not as a loyal friend, although Victor tried to present himself that way. Rather, he was something more akin to an agent intent on collecting his commission on a sale. The sale of Artur.

This last deal, the one with the Directorate, the one that had made it possible for Artur to leave the Soviet Union in 1986 with his family, had gotten the better of both of them. The Directorate was more greedy and vicious than Victor could ever aspire to be, constantly pushing Artur and Victor to take more risks and dirty their hands.

Victor had come to the United States in the mid-1990s. He had missed the all-out violence of the previous decade when the criminals and Jews, all released together as Refuseniks in an attempt to best the Americans, had descended on Brighton Beach to build their businesses and homes.

Back then, the Russian mob had been little better than street thugs determined, it seemed, to make their names in blood. Their brutality had been noted in the papers, and the community had rejoiced in the notoriety of being more violent, more ruthless, than the Italians or Colombians. In those days, an infraction as small as looking at someone the wrong way could mean a bullet to the brain, and the Directorate had saddled Artur with orders to find a way in, to make himself one of them, to find ways to make money.

Artur had been canny and quick, but he hadn't known the rules of the street. His partnership with Ivan, a respected and high-ranking *vor v zakone* or Thief in Law, had made the difference between survival and death.

"What's your plan, Victor? That we sit down and talk things out?" Artur asked. Resentment churned in his gut.

"Yes, exactly. This deal's too important," Victor said. "We can't let it fall apart."

Artur and Ivan had fought Brighton Beach back to back. The man might have been a lousy father, but he had been a far better partner than Victor. Ivan understood loyalty and, in his own warped way, love. If he were here tonight, he would be plotting with Artur the best way to blow up the bastards who had hurt him and his, not cowering and whining about potential lost profits and the threat of the Directorate.

Ivan, with his tattoos and flash temper, would be an uneasy fit in this new age of quasi-legal enterprises, a liability when crime was committed with ledgers in boardrooms and not just guns and fists in back alleys, but Artur was nonetheless grateful Ivan would be back soon.

Victor was a bureaucrat and a businessman. He understood accounting in dollars and cents, not in blood and loyalty. What currency did Vlad understand?

"The only thing that's important to me is Inna. If they threaten her, they die. If they so much as look wrong in her direction, they die. *Ti ponymayesh?*" *Do you understand?* He directed the question to Vlad, who nodded once, decisively, no hesitation. Perhaps he was his father's son after all. Artur was counting on it.

EPISODE #2

INNA

WITH ALL OF the tests and the wait for a psychiatric evaluation and then the questions from the police, Inna's stay at the hospital lasted well into the evening following her "incident." So many people seemed to need to take a look at her that she was almost surprised when she was released—without a hospital admission or arrest.

When Inna was ready to leave the hospital, there were too many people waiting for her—her parents, her brother and sister-in-law, her father's associate. Now they invaded her apartment, hovered over her, offered their sympathies, inspected her.

They knew, she thought, tasting bile. They all knew what had happened to her, what she might have done. They probably even knew she didn't have any underwear beneath the scrubs the hospital had given her to wear home.

She didn't want sympathy. Nothing would comfort her. Nothing made any sense, least of all the crowd that had gathered to see her home.

"Go home," she told them all. "I'm fine. I just want to be alone." She wasn't fine. She might never be fine. But her misery didn't need any company.

Ribbons of anxiety, tautly strung from wrist to wrist, cinched tighter, bunching the muscles in her shoulders and neck. All she wanted was her next dose of anti-anxiety medication and a good long sleep.

She went into her bathroom and pulled the amber bottle from her medicine cabinet. Funny, there was only one pill left. She thought there had been more. Had someone stolen her pills? She shook off the silly thought. She was merely jittery, enervated by last night's terrible events, her usual anxiety skittering on the edge of paranoia. Fifteen minutes, she told herself. In fifteen minutes, the medicine would work its magic and she would feel fine, able to cope.

Inna filled the cup of water at the sink and swallowed the pill. It stuck in her throat. The tablet seemed somehow larger than she remembered, and she struggled to choke it down. She resented her dependence on the pills.

She splashed water on her face and studied her reflection in the mirror. The stress of the day had left its mark; dark smudges under her eyes and a wrinkle across her forehead, no color in her cheeks, no sparkle in her eyes. She had left her apartment feeling beautiful and confident in her bold red dress. Now, she felt old. She braced her hands against the white basin of the sink and bowed her head. Her hair formed a thick curtain around her face, and she wanted to pull it closed, hide, shut everything out.

When she had finally had her interview with the police, they had been frustrated by her lack of memory, and they had repeated and repeated questions as if in the hopes of tripping her up or getting a different story. They had pounded on her nerves until the small glue holding her together broke and crumbled, and she had started to cry. "I don't know what happened. I don't know if I killed him. I don't remember anything."

The doctor had intervened, had pulled the detectives aside, likely had explained to them what he had to her about the drug he had found in her blood. When they returned, their tone was different, softer and more careful, as if they had decided she was also a victim or that she was too fragile and might crack under more strain.

Then the questions had shifted. Did she have any enemies? Was there anyone who might want to hurt her—a jilted boyfriend, for example? How often did she go to Troika? How well did she and her brother get along? Did she know Jack, the other owner of the club? Were they involved in dealing drugs?

The questions sat uneasily with her, especially now with her family, her brother included, camped out in her living room. The direction of the questions was clear: How could this have happened to her at her own brother's nightclub?

Her thoughts circled and spun around that question. There was an implication hidden there; that Jack or Aleksei might have targeted her or caused this to happen, but neither had even been there. Jack had been at home with his wife and children, and Aleksei had been changing a flat tire somewhere on the Belt Parkway. Inna and Aleksei might not get along as well as Inna wished, but she couldn't imagine that her brother would ever hurt her. Not like this.

Inna felt like a rubber band pulled so tight it might snap. She could hear her father's voice rising in the living room, his frustration directed at Aleksei, demanding to know how he could let such a thing happen at his club.

"You can't blame Aleksei. He wasn't even there," Maya said, but Aleksei, Inna noticed, did not participate in his own defense. "Inna brought this on herself. If you have to blame someone, blame her."

The recrimination was no less than what Inna had told herself, but her mother's biting tone gave it more force. She wanted the earth to open up and swallow her.

"It's not Inna's fault," Katya said.

"She went to the club looking like a prostitute, and she got treated like one," Maya said.

"She was raped!" Katya said.

"We don't know that," Maya said. "We don't know what happened. She claims she doesn't remember. Isn't that convenient?"

"She can't remember because she was drugged," Katya answered. Katya, usually the family diplomat, wasn't the type to pick a fight, but she also didn't back away from the ones she thought needed to be fought. Inna wondered now at her sister-in-law's defense of her. Could she be right? Was Inna's anger focused in the wrong place?

Inna forced herself to return to the living room and face her family, but they were so intent on arguing about her that no one seemed to notice her return, save Mikhail, who edged around the room, coming toward her. She wished he would stay away. He made her nervous, although she couldn't say why.

"She asked for it," Maya said viciously.

Inna knew her mother's vitriol wasn't really aimed at Katya. The two might fight tonight, but they would be friends again tomorrow, despite the snip in Maya's tone. Katya didn't hold grudges, and Maya adored Katya, as if she were a special gift that Maya had never expected to receive, the daughter she had always wanted.

Katya looked more her mother's daughter than Inna did. They had the same coloring—light eyes, although Katya's were green rather than blue, creamy complexions, and thick blond hair. Maya was more delicate, Katya more curvaceous, but they both had classic hourglass figures. They could easily pass for mother and daughter, while Inna hardly resembled her mother. Dark-haired and dark-eyed with a slight olive tinge to her skin, she had none of her mother's porcelain qualities. Her eyes weren't round. They were almond-shaped. Aleksei used to tell her she was adopted, and she might have believed him had she not had the same high cheekbones and sharp nose as her brother and father.

Inna rubbed at the ache in her chest. She wasn't jealous of Katya. She just wished she could at least have a small portion of her own mother's love.

"You go too far!" Papa bellowed at Mama. His voice seemed to come from far away. The scene took on a hazy quality. Inna blinked her eyes, but couldn't quite bring everyone into focus. She swayed and bumped against the wall behind her.

Mikhail put his arm around her. His breath tickled her ear. "How are you holding up?"

Normally, she would have shied away from him, gone to lengths to avoid him. Now she melted toward him. The muscles that had been so tight before now felt loose, almost slack. A glowing sense of well-being washed over her, warm and soft. "I'm sleepy," she said. Her voice sounded thick to her own ears.

"Inna's tired. We should all go so she can rest," Mikhail said, surprisingly solicitous. Maybe he wasn't so bad, she thought foggily, as he ushered everyone to the door.

Katya caught her by the shoulders, and Inna felt wobbly in her grasp. "I'm so sorry this happened to you," she said, "and I keep thinking if only we'd arrived earlier, we would have stopped it."

"It's not your fault," Inna said, and the words floated out of her. She could almost see the bubble around them. She touched Katya's cheek.

Katya embraced Inna in a tight hold. "Let me know if you need anything. I can imagine how terrible this has all been."

Inna had never confided to anyone, except Dr. Shiffman, about what had happened that terrible night in college. She had hidden her shame to avoid her parents' disappointment, the disapproval that now telegraphed off of Maya in thick waves. Katya couldn't possibly imagine what it was like to carry this burden, to worry that her family might discover yet another reason to find her wanting, to crave their love while knowing deep down that she didn't truly deserve it.

None of that was important right now. Any anger or ugly thoughts bounced in her brain with little effect. The magic pill was making that all not matter so much. It was as though there were a shield around her and nothing bad could touch her. She even felt herself smiling. "I'm going to be fine," she said. "Don't worry about me."

It was the last thing she remembered that night.

ALEKSEI

AS ALEKSEI KISSED his baby sister on the cheek, he couldn't hide from the truth any longer. In hospital scrubs, face pale, hair matted, Inna looked ravaged, a shell of her already quiet self, despite her fragile smile and easy assurances that she was fine.

Aleksei steered Katya into the hallway. He didn't have time to stick around and do the extended hug-hug kiss-kiss thing. There was too much damage to control. What the hell had happened last night? Mikhail had some explaining to do.

Mikhail waited in the hallway by the elevator. Aleksei tried to catch his eye.

"Mikhail, what did you do at Troika last night?" Katya asked, as if reading his mind.

A practiced liar, Mikhail answered smoothly. "I wasn't at Troika last night."

As Aleksei's parents joined them to wait for the elevator, Aleksei silently willed Katya to be satisfied with Mikhail's answer and drop the matter.

The elevator arrived. Aleksei pulled open the outer door and held it as everyone filed in. Inna lived in a pre-war building, and the old-fashioned elevator was roughly the size of a coat closet.

They all squeezed into the tight space. When the inner door slid closed, Katya picked up her interrogation again.

"Aleksei said you were supposed to handle something at Troika last night," she persisted.

Mikhail darted a sharp look at Aleksei as if to say, *Control your woman.* What he actually said was, "I don't know what you mean."

Katya appealed to Aleksei. "When we arrived, you said, 'Mikhail said he had everything under control.'" She quoted his own words back to him. "What was he supposed to have under control?"

Artur turned to him with an expectant look. Aleksei shoved his hands into his pockets to keep from fidgeting. He couldn't afford to look the least bit guilty. The elevator cab was lined with mirrored tiles, and Aleksei felt slightly claustrophobic in the small space with multiple reflections of his father's scrutinizing gaze assessing him. The bell dinged at each floor, and the cab moved slowly to the next.

"When we arrived last night." Aleksei drew out the words as his mind reached for a plausible excuse. "The cops were everywhere. At first, I thought there had been another fight. The crowd's been rowdy lately." *Yes, good.* He picked up speed as the lie came more easily. "Mikhail said he would hook us up with a new bouncer to keep things calm. The guy was supposed to start last night. Keep everything under control."

"That's right," Mikhail agreed. "I asked a guy I know to take the job."

"Did he?" Katya asked. "I didn't notice a new bouncer when the detectives were questioning people. Where was he? Was he there?"

Katya asked too many damned questions.

"His name's Vitaliy. He's starting work tonight," Mikhail said, naming one of their friends.

"Oh." Katya didn't seem satisfied with the explanation.

The elevator stopped on the ground floor. Artur ducked his head out, blocking the others from leaving until he scanned the lobby. Beside the doorman, a man in a leather jacket nodded at him as the group spilled into the brightly lit lobby.

"You arranged extra security," Aleksei said.

"The cops said they'd keep an eye on the building, but I don't trust them to do enough."

"Who would want to hurt Inna?" Katya asked.

"The man who was killed..." Artur began.

"You mean the man Inna killed?" Maya interrupted, voice soft. Aleksei recognized the edge underneath his mother's sweet tone, the deliberateness to her words.

"She didn't kill him," Artur said. Maya took a step back as if his defense of Inna cut her. "Someone wanted it to look that way."

Blyad! Less than twenty-four hours and his father already knew the whole thing was a setup. Doubts and worries crowded him, while Mikhail stood with the assured ease of a man whose schemes were all going according to plan. A secret smile played on his lips. *Trust me. I'll handle the Georgians.*

Aleksei wanted to wipe the smile off of his friend's face.

"Who would do that? Why?" Katya asked.

"We don't know yet," Artur said.

They didn't know *yet.*

"I have Vlad chasing down a few leads. I want to get to the bottom of this."

"What leads?" Aleksei asked.

"I sent him to Troika to talk to the staff, see if anyone noticed anything suspicious. Take a look at the surveillance video."

"Why didn't you tell me? I should be there with him." Aleksei had viewed the video early this morning. He had satisfied himself that nothing incriminating had been caught on camera. But Vlad had been in the FBI. He might see something Aleksei had missed.

"Jack's there," Artur said. "I thought it was more important for you to be with your sister."

Aleksei saw the explanation for what it was—a lie. His father blamed him, whether or not he suspected Aleksei's involvement in the larger plot. *Where the hell were you? You were supposed to be with her.*

If anyone learned of his role in this mess, the cops would be the least of his worries. He needed to get to Troika and find out what his exposure was. Then he needed to deal with it.

Katya put a hand on his shoulder. "He's right. It was important to be with Inna tonight. She needs her family."

Her touch was reassuring. She didn't know or suspect, and he would keep it that way. He wrapped his arm around her, pulled her closer, and inhaled the light, clean scent of her perfume.

He scanned the street before exiting the apartment building. He knew the Brighton Beach folklore of the mobsters who had been gunned down in the street. Nothing so blatant had happened in years. Most people didn't walk around Brighton Beach thinking they might get sprayed with bullets.

Aleksei wasn't most people. Not anymore.

As they walked together through the small parking lot behind Inna's building, he shielded Katya as best he could. He tried not to be too obvious as he hustled her through the open space to his Ferrari. He didn't want to scare her.

He opened the door for her, and she slid into her seat.

"Mikhail's lying," she said.

"About what?"

"About being at Troika the other night. One of the waitresses saw him."

Aleksei slammed the door. He cursed silently as he rounded the car to the driver's seat. Katya had helped the detectives interview the staff last night, serving as translator. Who knew what she had heard?

"He's at Troika all the time," Aleksei said. "Maybe she was confused." He started the ignition.

"What if she wasn't? Do you think he could be involved?" she asked hesitantly.

For the first time, Aleksei saw his wife as truly dangerous. Would she turn him in if she knew his role? Would he need to silence her?

"*Goddamn it*, Katya. How could you even think that?" Aleksei exploded. He pounded his hands on the wheel in an exaggerated show. "Mikhail's my friend. My *best* friend. Do you actually think *my best friend* would do something like this to my own sister? Come on!" *His friend. His own sister.* The ugliness of it sank in. He clutched the steering wheel.

Katya opened her mouth as if to argue.

"We're talking about rape!" He bullied her into silence. She turned her head away from him and looked out the window. She didn't speak to him again for the rest of the ride to their home. In a mere five minutes, they had exited Brighton Beach and entered the tonier Manhattan Beach neighborhood with its pricey single-family homes on postage-stamp lots.

He pulled his Ferrari into the short driveway of their home, a recently constructed white stucco mini-mansion that boasted a waterfront view of Sheepshead Bay and a price tag that the average, honest, hardworking person could never afford.

So much could go wrong. If the scheme didn't work, he would lose everything. The nightclub, the car, the house … and Katya.

There were no cars on the street. No suspicious activity. He idled feet from the front door with its leaded glass and wrought iron ornaments.

Wordlessly, Katya slid out of her seat. She started up the marble steps. When he didn't follow, she doubled back. She knocked lightly on the glass, and he lowered the window. "Aleksei, come inside. It's cold out."

"I've got to stop by the club." It was time to plan his next move. He needed to stay a step ahead.

"Everyone will understand if you don't make a showing tonight."

Make a showing. She had such an innocent way of belittling his activities, as if he merely pranced around the nightclub and pretended to be important.

She didn't know about the rest. The other business that he ran from his office at the club. The one that had brought them all this trouble.

He hoped his father nuked the Georgians. Damn them.

"Please, Aleksei. Please stay with me," she pleaded.

The moonlight cast a halo around her golden hair. His Katya, his angel. She anchored him. She was the only part of his life that made any sense. For a brief moment, he wished he could lay the whole set of problems at her feet and have her help him solve them.

That wasn't what men did. Real men faced their problems and didn't involve their women. "I have to go."

Katya looked stricken. For a moment he feared she would tell him not to come back.

"I love you," he said. He reached through the car window and touched her cheek. Her eyes didn't soften for him the way they usually did. He offered her a concession. "I won't be late. I promise."

She didn't say anything. She turned away and headed toward the house. He waited while she unlocked the door and let herself inside, the whole time wishing she would look back at him. That he would see the loving look in her eyes.

She didn't.

He tore out of the driveway.

VLAD

VLAD FOLLOWED ALEKSEI'S business partner, Jack, to a room in the back of Troika. The tile was covered over with a muddy carpet runner, and the hallway led out to a loading dock.

Jack had his five-year-old daughter, Becca, with him. She climbed into his lap while he booted up the computer and opened the security files. Becca wrapped her arms around her father's neck and snuggled against his chest, a picture of innocent trust.

Vlad couldn't help being reminded of Inna as a little girl, sweet like this one. He could picture her so clearly at this age, remembering the day Saul Hersh had escorted him back to Artur's house after Vlad had nearly robbed a convenience store with some of Ivan's thugs. She had burst out the front door and scrambled down the steps of her home, her pigtails flying. "Where were you? The bad men took you. Did they hurt you?" *Bad men.* That's what she had called Ivan and his crew, seeing the world around her with surprising clarity. She had flung herself into his arms without any reservation, clearly not fearing that he had lost the battle of good and evil, and then when he had caught her and swung her up into the air, she had pressed a wet kiss on his cheek and clung tightly to his neck. "How do you know I'm not bad too?" Vlad had asked, unsure himself and ashamed—for having attempted the robbery, for having been caught, for causing trouble for Artur, who had taken him in. Inna had cupped her little hands around his cheeks and stared hard at him as if reading his soul. "Because I know."

"That poor, poor girl," Jack said. "I just don't understand how something like this could have happened here."

"Let's take a look at the security feed, and maybe we'll have our answer." Vlad certainly hoped so. Solving this mystery—about Inna, about the undercover cop—had become a personal obsession, one that had everything to do with why he was back in Brighton Beach working his way up in Artur's organization.

In his flight from Brighton Beach twenty years ago, Vlad had defected to the other side, desperate to claim a place as one of the good guys, pursuing a career in law enforcement, joining the FBI. His grand plan had been to escape his father's legacy of violence and protect the innocent.

That hadn't worked out so well.

In his line of work, truly good people had been few and far between, even at the Bureau. Serving faceless, distant masses who might possibly suffer the vague consequences of victimless crimes like drug dealing or prostitution had paid his bills, but it hadn't fed his soul.

Vlad hadn't saved or protected anyone—not directly, anyway. Following his few highly successful busts, the wheels of justice moved so slowly and with so many ruts and obstacles in the road that the whole machine veered off course. Technicalities. Loopholes. Appeals. Immunity. In his experience, official justice could take a long detour from right and wrong.

Truly, he understood why Saul Hersh had framed Ivan to get his bastard of a father off the streets. Vlad credited the detective with saving Nadia's life, if not his own. Ivan might well have beaten them both to death in between playing King of the Jungle in New York's vicious world of organized crime.

Sometimes taking the law into your own hands was the surest way to real justice—and the quickest way to the wrong side of the law. Vlad's own shoot-first-fuck-the-paperwork approach hadn't sat well with his supervisors.

Maybe it was no surprise he was now back where he had started, seeking his father's place as the biggest mafia motherfucker, the arbiter of justice, the one who ultimately got to decide whose eye would be taken in exchange for whose.

Along the way, he would extract a few eyeballs for Inna. But whose?

"What happened, Daddy?" Becca asked.

"A bad thing happened to Inna," Jack said.

"What? What happened?"

"I'll tell you when you're older."

Vlad silently applauded him for sparing his daughter the details of a darkness she was too young to understand.

Children should have a chance to be children.

Whether Jack was a good father or not, Vlad well knew a person could be a different man in family than in business. His own father had been a barbarian in every facet of his life, but Artur Koslovsky was exceedingly devoted to and gentle with his own daughter. How much did Inna know about what her dear Papa did for a living? Did she look at her father and see a good man or a bad man, and did the distinction even matter to her anymore? Maybe she was more central to Artur's mafia dealings than Vlad had initially allowed himself to think.

What did Jack do, for that matter? He was Aleksei's partner at the club, which could easily be a legitimate business—even if some of its accounting inhabited a gray area. He was also an outsider, an American, who had married a Russian. He wasn't nearly as plugged in to the Brighton Beach community as his brother-in-law, Aleksei, was, and he wouldn't be easily welcomed into any of the mafia circles.

Jack might have nothing to do with the criminal activities the Georgians claimed operated out of Troika. Or he could be complicit in the murder of the undercover cop and Inna's rape. So could Aleksei.

The more Vlad analyzed the events and motives of the previous evening, the more convinced he was that someone at Troika had been involved.

But who and to what end?

Jack clicked the mouse and opened a file. He turned the monitor sideways so that he and Vlad could both see it on their opposite sides of the desk. Jack ran his fingers through his daughter's tangled, curly hair. She smiled up at him adoringly.

"I watched the tapes earlier," Jack said. "Inna came in at seven-thirty, had a drink at the bar and then danced with one guy. The police asked about him, but I don't know who he is."

Jack fast-forwarded through the video from the night before, slowing when Inna arrived in her vivid, red dress.

"She looks so pretty." Becca pointed at the screen. "Doesn't she look pretty?"

Vlad's mouth went dry. Pretty didn't begin to cover Inna's appearance. For months, Vlad had unsuccessfully attempted to ignore her and focus on his goals. Still, Inna had managed to invade his thoughts, even in the drab garb she usually wore to work—too loose slacks and shirts, all in black, minimal makeup. The sensitive little girl who had crept past Vlad's self-destructive anger and loneliness with her crayon doodles and cuddles and whispered stories had grown into a woman he desired more than any he had met, but couldn't have.

Last night, she had dressed to impress. No camouflage. No hiding. She was dressed for seduction. Her tight red dress showcased her assets—her slim figure, the perfect round curve of her butt, and her long, long legs. She was a knockout. Katya's friend, the blind date, was one lucky lawyer.

Vlad hated him more than a little.

Inna's charms weren't lost on the men at the bar. They watched her, the tender lamb among the wolves, with hungry eyes and sly calculation, and Vlad's blood pulsed with the desire to do violence.

The video gave a panoramic view of the bar. At the far end, Vlad recognized two of the men, one stocky, one tall and lanky with hair hanging to his shoulders. His father's men, the ones who had accosted him last night after he left the police station. Torpedo and Slim.

Vlad didn't believe in coincidences. The men's presence at Troika last night was more than a little suspicious. What did Ivan and his *bratva* have to do with last night's events?

Inna took a drink straight from Svetlana, a gin and tonic. No chance the drink was drugged. Svetlana was the only one who handled it.

Inna sipped her drink slowly while glancing around the bar as if looking for someone. At one point, she checked her cell phone, frowned, and put down her drink as if preparing to leave.

As she crossed the club, a short man with curly hair and a large paunch intercepted her. There was no sound on the video, but he clearly seemed intent on detaining her. Somehow he coaxed her onto the dance floor.

Ivan's men seemed to be concentrating their attention in the other direction, watching the main entrance and the staircase to the upstairs party rooms, where Artur and Vlad would soon be meeting with the Georgians. Had they been waiting for Vlad?

"Maybe he drugged her?" Jack pointed to the screen where the man now held Inna tightly against him, one hand on her bottom and the other in the middle of her back as if he were holding her in place. He spun around with her, and the camera caught her vacant expression. She looked dazed.

"Looks like she was already gone when he pulled her onto the dance floor. He knew it, too," Vlad said with a growl. He leaned forward, watching intently as the man maneuvered Inna past the bar to the back door, studying every feature of the man's face, marking him for vengeance.

They disappeared from the feed. Vlad watched for a few more minutes. No one followed them out.

There were still too many missing pieces. How did Inna go from dancing with that man to getting horizontal with an undercover cop? Zviad hadn't even appeared on the video. And who had drugged her?

"We only have feed for the main dining room," Jack said.

Vlad thought he detected a note of apology in the man's voice.

"I found out today when the police requested the footage. I called the security company to make sure I wasn't missing something. Apparently Aleksei saw fit to cut a few corners," Jack said. "A mistake I'm planning to rectify."

It wasn't a mistake. No surveillance upstairs made for a high level of privacy, one clients like Artur would value highly. If they entered through the back of the club, there would be no record of their coming or going or who had joined them. Very discreet. Very convenient. Especially for clientele seeking drugs or prostitutes, assuming someone was dealing out of Troika as Dato had accused.

Whatever had happened had taken place off screen. Whoever had made the arrangements must have known about the spotty surveillance at Troika.

Becca yawned. Jack cleared his throat. "It's getting late. I've got to get this one home."

"I understand." Vlad rose. He wanted to like Jack, but right now everyone connected to Troika was suspect in his mind. He was cynical enough to wonder whether Jack had brought the kid along to deflect suspicion. "Thanks for your help."

"I hope they catch whoever did this," Jack said with exactly the right touch of earnestness. He was either sincere or the most dangerous kind of liar.

Vlad merely nodded. He hoped he would get a chance to serve up his own brand of bloody justice before the authorities got involved. *For Inna.*

There wouldn't be any vigilantism tonight. His next stop was Inna's apartment, where he would spend his next several hours on security detail, safeguarding her against the angry Georgian crew. They hadn't made a move in the almost twenty-four hours since their man—did they know he was an undercover cop?—was murdered, but they hadn't backed down, either.

Vlad headed to the loading dock and the railed enclosure where the kitchen staff liked to smoke. Cigarette butts littered the cement. The area smelled of rotten produce and ash. The smells undoubtedly carried to the customer entrance several yards to his left. Yet the party arriving in fur and Armani hardly seemed to notice. They filed under the black awning and disappeared into the nightclub, leaving the back lot eerily quiet.

Vlad jumped lightly down to the parking lot and headed for the alley to his right, which led to the street. Inna's apartment was only a few blocks away, and he hadn't brought his sorry excuse for a car, a boxy gray 1990 Honda Accord that his landlady in Miami, Mrs. Rodriguez, had left him when she died.

The car's engine wheezed whenever he pushed fifty miles an hour, but it only had twenty thousand miles. He would have preferred something sharp and sleek that promised speed at only a whisper, but he seldom had a need to drive around Brooklyn. Who was he going to impress anyway? He preferred to hoard his limited cash for the inevitable rainy day—should he be so lucky to survive until then.

Working for Artur was supposed to be lucrative. Artur had lured Vlad to leave Miami and join the operation in Brighton Beach with the promise of all sorts of profit-sharing and income. So far Artur supplied Vlad with only enough cash to fill his belly and keep a modest roof over his head. Another test among many. He knew better than to complain—for now.

When the time was right, he would demand his due. And more.

The nightclub might only be a few yards away, but the lot was empty of patrons now. Out of habit, Vlad kept his steps light and stuck to the shadows, ready for danger.

As he turned into the alleyway, the lights in the parking lot flickered and then went out. With the moon only a sliver in the sky, darkness engulfed the area.

On instinct, he reached for his Glock with his left hand. With his right, he felt along the wall of the building, using it as a guide through the alleyway.

"Good thinking, Dumbass. He can't see us, but we can't see him either."

The voice was close, only a few feet away. There was nowhere to go for cover. No dumpster or car to hide behind.

He guessed there were at least two men, Dumbass and his buddy. He couldn't see to be sure. The shadows from the two buildings flanking the narrow alley obscured everything in darkness. He blinked, willing his eyes to speed up their adjustment to the change and bring the dark into focus.

He slid his second gun from his holster and waited for his assailants to reveal themselves. Who were they? Georgians, looking for vengeance, or his father's men, seeking to test him again like they had last night?

Either way, they attacked, they died. Vlad's body tightened with the promise of a fight.

MAYA

THE CAR RIDE HOME from Inna's apartment was excruciating. Mikhail drove the Lincoln, while Maya and Artur sniped at each other in the backseat.

"I don't want to hear another word from you," Artur said, as if he could order her around, as if she deserved his censure. She resented that he yet again cast her as the villain in their family drama.

Why? Because she had dared to say something against Princess Inna. To think, Inna was the child who was supposed to save her marriage.

Maya drew her fur-lined collar closed and rubbed her cheek against the soft mink. She had only ever wanted to be a good mother to Inna. But how? Her daughter was strange and alien to her, with thoughts and feelings so different from her own, so unpredictable.

Maya hardly felt she knew her daughter. Meanwhile, Artur was always there, hovering, intervening, questioning Maya's methods and undermining her. Why would Inna ever turn to Maya when Artur always had approval shining in his eyes?

"You're not listening!" Maya's blood simmered with the intense heat of her own anger. Her skin felt prickly and tight, sun-burned from the inside. She hadn't meant to start a fight with Katya or with Artur. But couldn't they see? Inna wasn't the only victim here.

The scandal had broken at Aleksei's club. Undoubtedly, it would affect business. Worse, she could tell Artur held him responsible. The circumstances never mattered to her husband.

Inna had refused to listen to Maya's maternal advice. Maya had warned her not to wear that skimpy red dress on her date. Inna had made her own choice and ignored her mother. Now she would live with the consequences. But why should Aleksei suffer in his father's esteem?

"Aleksei wasn't even there last night. But Inna was. She showed up in a dress made for scandal, and scandal's exactly what she got."

Artur, infuriating man, didn't respond. He turned his head away from her and stared out the window. She would have preferred a fiery argument to his withdrawal. Then she might tell herself he still held some passion for her. She would be happy even with a fraction of what she held for him.

His silence ended their verbal sparring. What use was it to fight if he wouldn't listen? The words wouldn't make a difference, wouldn't help Aleksei or change Inna's fate, and would only widen the gap between them.

Artur had already made up his mind. The more she pushed, the more he pulled away, killing almost any chance of a passionate kiss-and-make-up. Or any closeness at all.

She well remembered Inna's last crisis, the paranoia and hallucinations, the need for an intervention. She and Artur had never been as close as when they had come together to help their daughter. Yet now it seemed they were on opposing sides.

She settled into the corner of her plush seat and carefully considered her next words. "Did you stop to think maybe Inna's behavior is a cry for help?"

Artur turned slowly to her, his hazel eyes sharp. "What do you mean?"

"She's been under so much pressure lately."

To Inna's credit, she'd had great success this past year, using the Russian and European imports that were Artur's specialty to decorate homes and businesses in the neighborhood. With her design sense and her surprising intuition for what her clients wanted, she had demonstrated a knack for feeding the community's nostalgia for a better Russia than the one they had actually come from. "You know, with all of the work she has now and the attention she's receiving. It takes a lot to maintain that degree of success. Maybe it's too much. Maybe her constitution's too delicate."

Until recently, Inna hadn't gone out with friends, didn't date, kept to herself. She had hung back, stood in the shadows. Sometimes people had hardly noticed she was there. Truthfully, it could be a little creepy. Then last year, something had changed. She had finally shown signs of embracing the world around her. Her designs were growing more glamorous and gaining recognition, and last month, she had surprised them all by announcing she wished to start dating.

Artur had been so pleased. Maya only wished she could share in the sense of achievement. Inna refused to tell them what had caused her problems or finally alleviated them, leaving her own mother in the dark. Suspicious about Inna's sudden transformation, Maya had resorted to her own detective work.

She had discovered that Inna was no longer seeing the psychiatrist Artur had handpicked for her, a doctor on his payroll, who had the right incentive to keep certain vital information quiet. Instead, Inna had found her own therapist, the unbending and independent-minded Dr. Shiffman.

Artur had had no choice but to convince the therapist that a precipitous retirement was in her best interest. Too bad she had been too dedicated and scrupled to enjoy it.

Patient confidentiality. Hmmph! Daughters shouldn't have secrets from their mothers.

"Maybe the stress of dating pushed Inna over the edge—especially now that Dr. Shiffman's gone," Maya said. "And her dress and the drug and the supposed rape are all a cry for attention. For help."

"*Dostatochno!* *Enough!* Artur cut the air with his hands. "What happened isn't her fault. I won't hear any more about it."

"But what if she needs our help? What if she's on the verge of another breakdown?" Her words hit home. "Artur, I'm worried." She reached out, squeezed his hand, was gratified when he didn't pull away.

The moment didn't last. As they pulled into the gated drive of their home, Artur's cell phone rang. Victor, damn his hide, interrupting their hard-won peace yet again.

Artur radiated tension as he listened to Victor, the line of his jaw taut. He got out of the car and slammed the door. Maya scrambled out from her side in time to hear him say, "He wants to meet now? Tonight?"

Artur marched into the house, leaving Mikhail and Maya to follow. Again, she was forgotten as Victor and their business took center stage. Without a word or a backward glance, Artur headed straight to his office and closed the door.

Standing in the two-story foyer, Maya felt small and insignificant, a stranger in her own home. What good were all of these stately rooms when all they provided were more places for him to hide from her? More doors for him to shut against her?

Mikhail stood near Maya. He didn't touch her. Yet she could feel the heat of him. His fingers bumped hers. When she glanced up at him, she saw the compassion in his dark blue eyes. Compassion, but not desire.

The way Mikhail had sidled up to Inna hadn't pleased her—even if he was merely playing the part of concerned employee in front of his boss. Maya had caught the flicker of interest in her lover's eyes, interest not directed at her. *Traitor.*

"Don't you dare feel sorry for me," she said.

"When I think of you, I feel anything but sorry."

"Prove it."

Mikhail darted a quick glance down the hall where Artur had disappeared. He caught her hand and pulled her into the small powder room. He backed her up against the wall.

She didn't dare turn her head or let her eyes dart to the mirror. She didn't want to see herself, to be reminded that she had wrinkles and sagging skin that obscured the exceptional beauty of her youth, to remember that they weren't equals and she was so much older than he. She closed her eyes.

Slowly, sensually, Mikhail slid his hands under her sweater. His fingers danced on her skin. He pushed against her, making plain the evidence of his arousal.

His murmur, his touch, the musky scent of him as he leaned down and nuzzled her ear chased away the cold, lingering emptiness, leaving heat and desire in its place.

She buried her fingers in his thick, dark hair, and he didn't disappoint. His lips blazed against hers in an urgent, open-mouthed kiss, a prelude to the intimacy she craved. As he deftly undid the button at her waist and yanked her slacks and panties down past her hips, she didn't have to pretend that he wanted this as much as she did.

She only wished he were Artur.

Their labored breaths echoed in the bathroom. Artur could come out of his office any moment. The risk of discovery only heightened her excitement. How would Artur react if he saw her lost in passion with his young associate?

Her thoughts seemed to summon her husband. She heard the creak of the door to his study.

"*Blyad!*" Mikhail swore and disentangled himself. "Fix yourself up. Take your time. I'll intercept him."

He was barely mussed, already zipped up, no sign of her kisses on his lips. He nudged her away from the door and slipped back into the foyer. Maya wondered if perhaps she had only imagined the passion between them.

She splashed water on her flaming cheeks, willed them to cool. She forced back the sickening tidal wave of guilt and emptiness that threatened to overtake her. If the tears started, she wouldn't be able to hold them back or quiet the wracking sobs building in her overstrung body. This wasn't the life or the marriage that she wanted. She loved only Artur, no matter how he neglected or ignored her. He stood outside the door, so near and yet so far out of reach.

"I want you to go back to Inna's apartment and keep watch." Artur's instructions lacked his usual calm. His words were clipped, almost panicked.

"Sure, no problem," Mikhail said.

"Be careful. Vlad was supposed to be back by now and hasn't checked in. I'm worried there's trouble with the Georgians."

"I need to get some supplies," Mikhail said with his usual cool. "Tell the guys I'll be there within the hour."

Maya waited until Mikhail left before coming out of the powder room. She found Artur slipping on his coat. "Where are you going?"

"Victor will be here soon. We have to go to a business meeting."

Worry seemed to age Artur before her eyes. The vertical crease deepened between his eyebrows. She suddenly noticed the dark circles under his eyes, the new hollowness to his cheeks. When had he last slept? Eaten? He had spent all of last night and then today in the hospital standing vigil and, she imagined, strategizing how to respond to this latest crisis.

"On Saturday night? Artur, are you sure about this? You haven't eaten. Haven't slept. You're in no shape to go out and do business."

"I don't have a choice," he said.

He never shared details with her. She knew better than to ask him what the meeting was or why he was compelled to go. But nothing could be so important. He needed to rest.

He was so powerful and independent. She sometimes forgot that he was only a man. A weary warrior who needed her love and support.

"Victor's not here yet. At least let me get you something to eat. And maybe a little cognac to settle you."

"Fine. Sure," he agreed. He let her send him back to his study, likely thinking he was appeasing her and avoiding a fight. She poured him a glass of cognac from the leaded crystal carafe on the sideboard.

She watched him take a long swallow of the amber liquid. She didn't tell him she had no intention of letting him leave. She wouldn't have to.

She left the study to make a sandwich for him. By the time she returned, her poor husband had fallen asleep at his desk. His head rested on his arm. His hair was silver now, but when she looked at him, she still saw the young man who had stolen her heart forever.

She remembered the night he'd come to her father's apartment for dinner. Her father had hand-chosen Artur to be his protégé. He was an up-and-comer, Semyon had claimed, with a promising political career ahead of him. Maya had become heartily sick of listening to her father sing Artur's praises. She hadn't joined him in Moscow only to be left alone and ignored while he invested his time and attention in his career and a surrogate son, who succeeded in the one way Maya never could— by being a man.

Then Artur had arrived. She had expected him to be cocky and arrogant, a boorish man who only cared about politics and the Communist Party.

He had stood in the doorway, awestruck, staring at her. "You're so beautiful," he had blurted. He had been so young then, twenty, only a little older than herself, and easily the most handsome man she had ever seen—not pretty, but powerful. He had an inexplicable charisma, the countenance of a leader that people would follow. She suddenly had understood her father's fascination. Even now, at fifty-five, he had the same magnetism.

She feathered her fingers through his hair and bent to kiss him.

"Sofia," he murmured as her lips whispered over his cheek.

The sound of that name—that name!—was a sharp slap. Maya recoiled with a gasp. All these years later, *that* woman still had a hold on him.

When would Maya find her way back to being first in Artur's heart?

She backed out of the study. Her cheeks burned with the sting of his rejection. But she was here, and Sofia was dead.

Maya would secretly punish Artur for all of the hurt he inflicted. And then she would make him love her again.

VICTOR

THE DIRECTORATE'S MOSCOW representative, Gennady Morozov, demanded a meeting. Tonight. Within the hour. Victor had been in the business long enough to know that nothing good ever came from emergency meetings with his bosses, or in this case their messenger.

Victor stopped at Artur's house first. The ride over would give them a chance to strategize and, more importantly, for Victor to remind the man what was at stake should he entertain thoughts of turning against his employer.

Maya met him at the door. A sharp scowl shaped her lovely features. "He's not coming with you tonight. I don't care how important you think it is."

"Maya," he scolded.

She raised her hand to silence him. "He's not a machine, Victor. You can't take and take and take from him and expect him to keep giving. He's not a superman."

"I know that."

"But you don't care!" She crossed her arms as if she would bar him entry. "I've never seen him this tightly wound. He hasn't slept in two days. He's not a young man anymore."

"I know you're worried for him," Victor said.

Her blue eyes flashed with anger. "Don't you dare patronize me. I'm not some little girl who'll be quieted with a lollipop and a pat on the head. He's *my husband*."

Victor quieted her tirade with a mere arch of his brow. They both knew Maya and Artur would no longer be together if not for Victor's timely interference twenty-five years ago and his continued silence on Maya's own indiscretions.

The two had made a pact long ago to share Artur.

Victor staked his claim. "Our bosses called a meeting."

"Tell them to wait."

Victor blinked with surprise at her refusal. Business was supposed to trump everything.

Victor decided he had stood politely on the stoop long enough. Now he pushed past Maya. She huffed with indignation as he brushed past.

"I won't tell them to wait."

"You'll have to," Maya said. "Artur won't be joining you."

Oh yes, he will. Victor would bring Artur along to meet the Directorate's messenger, even if he had to bind and gag Maya to get to him.

Victor marched to the study, Artur's headquarters, only to find the man slumped over his desk, fast asleep, a half-finished snifter of cognac beside him.

"He'll be asleep for at least a few hours," Maya said.

"You drugged him," Victor accused.

"What would make you say such a thing?" she demanded. Her cheeks blushed a pretty shade of pink. She was almost convincing.

"Have a sip of cognac," he challenged and gestured toward the glass.

"Get out," she said.

"He's talking rebellion," Victor said.

Artur suspected the Directorate might have been involved in Inna's rape, that it was staged to teach him a lesson and keep him in line. Victor highly doubted the Directorate had sullied its hands this time. If they had, surely Victor would have been informed.

What worried Victor was the spark of angry determination in Artur's eyes. For the first time in years, he feared Artur might actually try to break free, the way he had years ago. Then where would Victor be?

"Why should I care?" she asked. "Your business is no concern of mine."

"If he leaves me, how long before he leaves you?"

Maya swallowed. He watched the convulsive movement of her throat with grim satisfaction.

"He won't leave me," she said.

"Because he loves you?" Victor taunted.

He walked away without giving her a chance to retort. He might have had the last word, but the victory was hollow.

Victor still had to face Gennady. He would have to deliver the message to his bosses that there was trouble. Moscow was likely to shoot the messenger when he reported that Artur planned to renege on the deal with the Georgians.

Victor was no better off than Maya, dependent on the cooperation of a man who would bear him no love or loyalty if he ever learned the truth and who had already tried once to leave them both.

Victor's car was parked on the street. As he squeezed behind the wheel, he saw the curtain move and Maya's anxious face watching him from the window. Because she couldn't wait for him to leave, or because she now remembered how closely entwined their fortunes were? He doubted she felt any guilt for her actions.

Maya had never once shown any remorse.

KATYA

KATYA PACED BACK and forth in her kitchen. Her feet slapped against the cold limestone tile. Her chest blazed with the hot discomfort of too much acid. Perhaps because of her pregnancy. She feared the real cause might be her breaking heart.

Why hadn't he stayed with her tonight?

Aleksei claimed he loved her. He barely touched her. They spent almost no time together. Her pregnancy was a minor miracle. She had blamed herself for the distance between them. Maybe if she didn't work so much. Maybe if she tried a little harder to please him. She had hoped a baby would cement their bond, would provide a way to fix their marriage.

What if she couldn't fix it?

For a while now, she had suspected he was only going through the motions. Appeasing her. To be fair, concentrating too much on baby making could kill the heat in any relationship, but she was having trouble remembering when there had been any heat in hers. She suspected he was saving his passion for someone else.

Her cell phone rang. Nick was calling her. He had been trying to reach her all day. She couldn't bring herself to answer his calls. Nick had witnessed an ugliness last night that she would prefer not to remember. Her drunken husband had hit her and made her nose bleed.

She wanted so badly to believe it was an accident. He hadn't meant it. He loved her, right? It had been the alcohol, that was all.

An affair might be the least of their problems.

She opened the refrigerator. On the door shelf was a tall bottle of Grey Goose, relatively new, now almost empty. In a fit of pique, she yanked the bottle from the shelf, twisted off the top, and poured the remaining liquid down the drain.

She kicked the base cabinet open with her foot and ripped a new garbage bag from the roll under the sink. Snapping it in the air, she returned to the fridge on a mission.

She scouted every last beer bottle and threw it into her trash bag. The bottles made a satisfying clink as one hit the next.

She threw the bag of loot over her shoulder and marched to the den. She threw open the cabinet to the bar. The assorted bottles of liquor with the fine cut glass and oddly shaped tops were nearly empty. *Damn it, Aleksei.*

With one arm, she scooped the bottles into her garbage bag. Aleksei would complain. He liked the good stuff. She was probably throwing away hundreds of dollars of top-shelf liquor. It might be the only thing she'd done in weeks that he would notice.

She marched out the side door with her haul of bottles and yanked open the top of one of the metal garbage cans. The city wouldn't haul the trash for a couple of days, but at least the alcohol wouldn't be in the house.

Would that stop Aleskei or merely slow him down?

The evening air cooled the angry flush in her cheeks. She stood outside her home, forcing herself to take deep breaths. Before she could approximate anything approaching calm, a car she didn't recognize pulled into her driveway.

Two men in wrinkled suits got out. She recognized one, the detective who had questioned the staff at Troika last night. What was his name? Rodriguez? Ramirez? Rosales? She couldn't remember now.

She had sat beside him for the better part of last night helping to interview the Troika staff and marveling that a man with such impressive forearms and formidable shoulders could have such a gentle and coaxing demeanor. The waitresses had all been nervous to talk to the authorities, but they had all succumbed to the light in his chocolate-colored eyes and the dimples in his cheeks, subconsciously returning his encouraging smile and playing with their hair.

"Good evening, Mrs. Koslovsky. You might remember me. I'm Detective Rosales, and this is Detective Sharp. Is your husband here? We'd like to ask him a few questions."

"No, he's not."

"Do you know where we can find him?"

"He's at Troika."

"We were just at the nightclub. He wasn't there," Sharp said. He reminded her of a turtle with his large rounded nose and bulgy eyes.

"Oh," she said. "Then I don't know where he is." Where had Aleksei gone when he sped away from her?

"Are you sure?" Rosales asked, suspicious, perhaps with good reason. He had walked into the bar last night after Aleksei had hit her and heard her make an excuse for him. Shame heated her cheeks. Likely he thought she was covering for Aleksei ... again.

"He said he was going to Troika. If he's not there, I honestly don't know where he is." She made herself look him in the eye.

"Then maybe you could help us."

"Okay," she said uncertainly. "Do you want to come inside?"

The detectives exchanged what seemed like surprised glances and followed her through the side entrance of the house. "Can I get you anything? I could make some coffee."

"That's not necessary," Rosales said. He had a manilla folder in his hands. He opened it on the kitchen counter and pulled out a photograph. "Do you recognize this man?"

She studied the hazy picture, a shot of a portrait that seemed to have been cropped from a photo and blown up in size. She vaguely recognized the blunt features set in a round face, but the helmet of curly hair was distinctive. "Yes. His name's Stan. I don't remember his last name. He works for Aleksei. At the International Pharmacy on Brighton Beach Avenue. He's one of the pharmacists."

"He works for your husband?" Sharp asked. Rosales shot him a quelling look.

"Yes. Why?" She didn't particularly like Stan, but overly unctuous manners and the occasional leering look weren't crimes that would interest the police.

"The photo was taken last night at Troika," Rosales said. "We need to ask him a few questions."

Although she couldn't see how the pieces fit together, she couldn't shake the feeling that everything was somehow connected and kept circling back to Aleksei—his sister, his friend, his pharmacist, his nightclub. What did it all mean?

Rosales gently pulled the photo from her numb fingers and put it back into his folder. He pressed his card into her hand. "If you need anything, anything at all, please call."

He was offering her help. She wasn't sure what kind. The gesture made her nervous. What more was going on beneath the surface? What didn't she know?

"Do you want me to tell Aleksei you were looking for him?"

Sharp said, "It might be better if you don't mention we were here."

NICK

NICK WAS IN a somber mood as he made his way to the Salvatore family compound in Old Brookville. He had waited until the last possible moment to leave his office in midtown Manhattan, hoping to catch a moment with Katya. She reliably surfaced for several hours every Saturday, as all of the young law associates did. Not today, however.

Nick wasn't surprised, given the events of last night. He wondered how Katya was coping, what lies her husband was telling her to explain away last night's rape and murder, whether Aleksei was hitting the bottle again, whether he had hit her again.

He thought about calling her again but wasn't sure she would welcome his intrusion. She had been rather quick to defend her abuser, after all.

He tried to tell himself it didn't matter. She didn't matter. But he couldn't stop thinking about her, about the shame and anger in her face.

Maybe Katya would see the light and leave her no-good husband. A good thing for her, but a disaster for Nick.

If Nick had needed any confirmation that he had found the right family, he'd received it the other night in spades. He had no doubt that Katya's father-in-law, Artur Koslovsky, was the very same man he had been hunting all these years, Artur Gregorovich, the KGB agent who had seduced Nick's mother and then, tiring of the affair, persecuted and murdered most of Nick's family.

Katya was his best shot at getting close to Inna and getting inside the Koslovsky family. He could feel his plans unraveling, and the sensation made him uneasy, agitated. He had hoped to have made a little progress meeting Inna by now, an offering of hope on his mother's birthday.

Waiting for Katya had made him late. He missed his train and had
to take another to a different station out on Long Island and then call a
taxi to take him out to the Gold Coast mansion owned by his step-father
Paul.

Houses tended to be grandiose on this part of the North Shore of
Long Island. Nonetheless, the cabby whistled low as they pulled onto the
private lane and Nick directed him to the drive. The carriage house, at
the end of the long, tree-lined driveway, was big enough to be a four-
bedroom home for a bustling family. The mansion beside it was a
masterpiece, Paul's masterpiece.

Paul was a builder and a devoted family man, who subscribed to the
theory that the cobbler's family, far from having no shoes, should have
the best shoes.

The long driveway was filled with cars, not all of them from the clan.
Paul had disregarded Nick's advice to keep the party small. The man
imagined his wife longed for a large, elegant party, everyone there to
celebrate her birthday.

After twenty-five years, the poor man didn't know that today wasn't
her actual birthday.

The secret wasn't Nick's to tell. Lying didn't come naturally to him.
As a child, he had worried constantly that he would accidentally reveal
the truth and be ejected from his new home. He used to toss in his bed
at night as every word he'd uttered replayed itself, until he had
determined that silence was the simplest course.

Nonna, Paul's mother, threw open the door before Nick had
finished climbing the stairs. Had she been watching for him? She
welcomed him to the party, taking his face in her hands and kissing him
on both cheeks. Her large gold rings were warm on his skin. She had
always been warm and affectionate, even before Nick had become part of
the Salvatore brood. Her pudgy hands, soft with wrinkles and pebbled
with dark spots, shook slightly with age as she patted him on both
cheeks. "I don't see you enough," she chided.

He expected Nonna's customary scold about how he didn't make time for the important things, when Frankie cut in and bussed him on the cheek. "I don't see you enough either."

"We just had lunch in the City this week," Nick reminded her.

"After I stalked you for weeks," Frankie said. Her caramel-colored eyes sparkled with mischief, and her wide mouth, though pouting, twitched at the corners with a smile ready to burst forth. She had pulled her black curls back into a ponytail, but several springy spirals had escaped her attempts at order. She seemed to have too much life to be contained, one of the things he had always liked about her.

Frankie had always been something of an antidote to all of the death he had left behind him in Russia.

"You work too much," Nonna said.

"We all work too much," Nick said.

If anything could be said for Nick and the Salvatore clan, they had a mighty work ethic. Paul, the patriarch, ran a construction business and seemed to be on jobs 24/7. Nick's step-brothers, the twins, were computer programmers with their own start-up company, and they never seemed to leave their screens—even at the dinner table. Frankie, the baby of the family, ran a matchmaking service.

"Come say hello to Mimi." Mimi, a name that sounded like Mama, but wasn't. Frankie looped her arm through Nick's and pulled him with her to pay his respects to the "birthday girl."

Frankie didn't lead him very far into the house before they were waylaid by the twins, Marco and Roman, for a round of effusive shoulder slaps and fist-bumps. The twins resembled Frankie, with the same broad mouth and dark hair, which Marco tamed with hair product and Roman covered with hats. The hats were Roman's signature thing, the way he distinguished himself from his twin. Tonight he'd dressed up, trading his usual baseball cap for a hipster knit deal. In build, the twins favored Paul—broad shoulders, barrel chest, and a wide stance that made them seem grounded and confident, solid.

"So we heard you had a date," Marco said.

"One of Frankie's chicks?" Roman asked.

"I don't have chicks. I have clients." Frankie crossed her arms. "And she wasn't one of mine."

"No, but I asked your advice," Nick said.

"True." She was appeased. Frankie had wanted to fix Nick and her brothers up from the moment she'd opened her business. They all had yet to agree, claiming they were too busy for serious relationships. Nick could tell Frankie took the refusal personally. He hated to disappoint her. To soften the sting, Nick had invited Frankie to lunch and solicited her advice on dating in preparation for wooing Inna.

"You should have heard him." Frankie brightened as she related the story to the twins. "He wanted to know what to wear. Fussed over his hair. His cologne. Everything. He asked me to pick out his tie."

"How'd it go?" the twins asked in unison. The two were inseparable, finishing each other's thoughts and sentences. Nick had always felt a little on the outside around the pair. Likely Frankie did too.

"Did she fall in love with…your tie?" Frankie knocked Nick with her shoulder and ribbed him, the way only a little sister could.

He was sorry to have to tell her the date was a non-starter.

"I didn't get to meet her," Nick said. "We were running late. Traffic. Flat tire." He neglected to tell them how Inna's brother had delayed the meeting, as if on purpose. "When we got to the restaurant…" he paused. He realized he didn't want to tell Frankie and the twins about the rape and murder. Such ugly things had no place here among the marble and fine things, among the people with good hearts, people he cared about even if they weren't his real family. "It was pretty late, and she had to go to the hospital because she wasn't feeling well." He whitewashed the truth.

"That's too bad. Is she all right?" Frankie asked with genuine concern.

"I don't know. I've been trying to get hold of Katya to get the scoop, but she's not returning my calls."

"I could fix you up with someone else," Frankie offered.

"Yeah, right." The twins both coughed into their hands. Frankie cast them a dark look.

"I appreciate that. But I need to see this thing through with Inna," Nick said.

"She must be special," Frankie said. He could tell she was excited for him. She likely imagined he was about to embark on some hearts-and-flowers romance.

"Oh, she is," Nick agreed.

He didn't tell Frankie he'd never even met Inna or that he only wanted to date her so that he could get close to her father and destroy him.

Nick worried Inna would lose all interest in dating after what had happened to her the other night. Then how would he get close to her and, more importantly, Artur?

"Earth to Nicky." Frankie snapped her fingers in front of his face. "Come back to us. You're a million miles away."

"Something on your mind?" Marco sniggered.

"I'll tell you what's on his mind." Roman waggled his dark brows. They bumped their fists together and laughed. Frankie rolled her head back as if asking the heavens for strength to deal with her idiot brothers.

Nick threw his arm around Frankie's shoulders. "Let's go find Mimi."

"She's in the great room," Roman said. "Careful. She's in a sour mood."

"Never knew anyone who hated birthdays so much," Marco said. "Maybe seeing you will cheer her up. You always know how to handle her."

He didn't. He couldn't claim to be her favorite either. Frankie was everyone's favorite, and Mimi had always held him at arm's length.

Mimi stood beside Paul in the house's great room. Paul leaned against the white grand piano with a drink in one hand and his other draped over her shoulder. Mimi never moved far from Paul when he was around. She hovered, anticipated his needs, doted on him, whether from love or duty, Nick didn't know. Paul had given them security in this new country—a safe home and family. Although he was their hero, they had never reciprocated his trust and openness with their own.

At only forty-five, Mimi looked old enough to assume the full fifty-five years on her passport. Frown lines creased her mouth and chin, and worry lines pinched her eyes—as if she were afraid she would be sent back to Russia and all the horror they had never quite managed to leave behind.

Mimi didn't light up when she saw Nick, the way he imagined a mother would. Instead, her smile was tight and grim. She frowned at him, perhaps afraid that after all of these years of perfecting their lie, he would somehow give her away now.

The charade wore on them both, but Mimi had rejected every opportunity to come clean to Paul and the family. After all these years, she still didn't feel safe.

Nick kissed her gently on the cheek. "Happy birthday."

He slipped the gift-wrapped box from his pocket and handed it to Mimi.

"Go on. Open it," Paul urged. To the guests in the room, he said, "Sofia's not good at accepting presents."

Mimi pressed her lips together, enunciating the deepening grooves in her forehead and around her chin. She hated to be the center of attention, and now everyone in the room watched as she unwrapped her gift.

"I saw it in the jeweler's window. It reminded me of the one you used to have," Nick said. He waited, holding his breath, as she tore aside the wrapper and then opened the velvet box within. He always found pleasing her so difficult. He hoped she would like this gift.

Her eyes teared. She snapped the box closed. She puckered her mouth before speaking, as if pausing to censor any sentiments that might expose them.

"Oh, Kolya," she said, using his childhood nickname, "You shouldn't have."

Nick wasn't sure whether her sigh was grateful or reproving.

"What happened to the old ring?" Frankie asked.

"I pawned it," Mimi said, voice thick with emotion, "to pay bills." She shook her head sadly, perhaps remembering. "That was so many years ago, and you were so young. I'm surprised you remember."

"You did it to buy medicine for me," Nick said, remembering his own terrible guilt. He had grown up feeling like such a burden. She had sacrificed so much for him, again and again. "You cried all night."

"I didn't know you heard me. You shouldn't have heard me. You were so small."

"I can't get back everything we lost, but I want to make things as right as I can."

She moved in close for an unexpected hug. Mimi had never been one for spontaneous shows of affection. She was bony and angular in his arms, and he held her lightly. She was the strongest person he had ever met. Yet he feared he might break her.

"I've found Gregorovich," he murmured against her hair.

She gasped and then clutched him hard. Her fingers dug into his shoulders. "Nick, no!" She sounded so betrayed.

"I'm going to avenge our family," he whispered.

She switched into Russian and pleaded with him. "They're dead. All of them are dead. Leave this in the past. Please, Kolya," she implored. "*Pozhalsto*." The words flowed out of her in near hysteria. She started to cry.

"What's this about?" Paul interjected. "What did you say to upset her like this?" He gave Nick an accusing look.

The ghost of all of the lies Mimi had told over the years rattled their chains and crowded the room. Weeping, she turned her back on Nick and huddled in the shelter of Paul's arms. For his part, Nick reverted to the trusty silence of his childhood.

He wanted so badly to give her peace, to end the nightmare that had haunted them both and shaped the course of their lives. Now he was finally so close.

ALEKSEI

"WHERE THE HELL have you been? Why haven't you been answering my calls?" Aleksei demanded when Mikhail finally appeared at the secret apartment they kept over the tarot reader's shop.

"You sound like a needy girlfriend. Katya talk to you that way?" Mikhail asked. He smelled faintly of women's perfume.

Aleksei could easily guess how his buddy had been spending the last few hours when Aleksei had been desperate to reach him. He had been calling Mikhail continuously. And getting no answer.

The anger that had been building in Aleksei all night exploded out of him. He punched Mikhail in the jaw.

Mikhail's head whipped back. "What the hell?"

"That's for my sister, you miserable fuck." Aleksei threw another punch, but Mikhail blocked his arm.

He hit harder. Again and again. The better fighter by a mile, Mikhail caught his blows easily—until Aleksei got lucky and landed another punch on Mikhail's cheek.

"Hey, watch the face," Mikhail complained as if they were merely sparring. Aleksei's temper ignited. His friend wasn't taking him seriously. He punched him again, harder this time, and sent him stumbling back.

Aleksei stuck out his foot and tripped Mikhail. His would-be friend hit the floor with a hard thud.

"Hey!" Mikhail shouted.

"You lied to me!" Aleksei followed him down and straddled him. "You set her up!" He pounded Mikhail with each accusation. "You let that thug rape her."

Mikhail kicked and twisted. Suddenly, Aleksei was on his back, Mikhail astride him. Mikhail pinned him down with his body, and their chests heaved almost in sync. The anger in his blue eyes was riveting.

Struggling under Mikhail, Aleksei felt alive in a way he hadn't in a long time. He despised himself for the arousal that the violence and nearness to Mikhail incited.

"Cut the bullshit," Mikhail panted. "You knew exactly what was going to happen. Be a man and own it."

"She's my sister!"

"What choice did we have?"

"What choice? You let him rape her!"

"What else would be enough to force your father to make war on the Georgians?"

Aleksei had been desperate to get the Georgians off his back. They were a nasty bunch. They owned the drug trade on Brighton Beach and the prostitutes. When they had caught wind of the success at Troika and started to poke around asking questions, Aleksei had known he'd gotten in over his head. Dato, the leader of the Georgian crew, was famous for carving up his enemies with a long knife. Sick, bloodthirsty bastard.

Aleksei didn't have the muscle or the stomach to fight the Georgians. Instead, he'd opted to force his father's hand. Start a feud between his father and the Georgians. Make his big shot father step in and finish what the Georgians had started. Getting Artur involved had seemed the only sensible plan.

A coward's plan.

Mikhail worked closely with Artur. He had assured Aleksei he knew exactly how to motivate Artur to take care of Dato and his crew. He had arranged the meeting at Troika between Artur and the Georgians.

Mikhail had neglected to mention that his "fail-proof" plan involved Inna. Yet Aleksei could think of little else that would stir his father to violent action. Certainly he wouldn't entertain a war merely to help Aleksei.

As the truth penetrated, Aleksei hated himself all the more. He had known. Deep down. Of course, he had known. He just hadn't wanted to admit it.

"You done trying to pound me?" Mikhail asked, releasing him. He jumped lightly to his feet, but Aleksei remained prone on the floor. He covered his face with his hands.

His own complicity galled him. He had set up his own sister. She had been waiting for him and Katya while he had followed Mikhail's instructions to delay, delay, delay. She had sat alone at the bar, all dolled up to impress Katya's friend, never suspecting that anything bad could happen to her at her own brother's club.

"Cheer up," Mikhail said. He tapped Aleksei with his foot. When Aleksei removed his hands, Mikhail took one and hauled Aleksei to his feet. "The drugs did their trick. Inna won't remember anything. It'll be like it never happened."

Aleksei tried to take comfort in the words, to believe the happy ending Mikhail dangled in front of him. Inna wouldn't suffer for her sacrifice; his father would solve the Georgian problem; and no one would ever know what a fraud Aleksei was—on every count.

If he stayed the course, the plan could still work. As long as no one discovered the setup or Aleksei's involvement. As long as Artur decided to go to war.

But there were so many ways this plan could backfire.

"All Artur needs is a little prodding," Mikhail assured him. He slapped Aleksei on the shoulder in a half-embrace.

"I've got this covered," Mikhail said. "Just trust me. I need one more day. That's all."

"One more day," Aleksei agreed, trying to sound like he had some control. Who was he kidding? Aleksei had no idea what he would do if the plan didn't work.

MIKHAIL

WHEN ARTUR CHARGED Mikhail with guarding Inna for a few hours during the night, he undoubtedly expected him to sit outside in his parked car, stakeout style, and watch the building. Mikhail had other plans.

He nodded at the doorman, who recognized him as a fellow employee of Artur's, and let him pass without question. His natural confidence surged. He had no worries about getting caught, not when he had already gotten away with so much worse.

Sneaking behind Artur's back—to seduce Maya, to create the scene at Troika, to join Aleksei in the "other" Koslovsky business—had all been accomplished so easily. A secret visit to Inna was mere child's play in comparison.

If anyone later asked, Mikhail would claim he had been doing his job: He thought he had seen someone suspicious lurking around the building and came inside to investigate and assure himself she was safe.

He hadn't seen anyone, but the rest was true. He would ensure her safety—from the Georgians anyway.

Tonight Inna had been friendlier, looser than usual. She hadn't ducked away from him or found an excuse to be on the other side of the room. Attuned to the signs, Mikhail knew Inna had taken yet another special pill, not her usual medication, but one from the prescription bottle that had been swapped for hers and planted in her medicine cabinet.

Taking the pill, Inna had now unwittingly offered him the fantasy he had been forced to provide another man, one who didn't deserve her. Visiting her wasn't part of the original plan, but he couldn't resist.

He didn't bother knocking on Inna's door. He didn't expect she'd be fit to answer.

He pulled the key from his pocket and let himself inside, kicking the door shut behind him.

He found Inna passed out on the sofa. She lay on her back, eyes open and staring blankly at the ceiling, her hair an uncombed, matted tangle. She didn't come out of her trance when he snapped his fingers in front of her face. Good.

Growing up in a Russian orphanage, Mikhail's pretty face had been his saving grace. No one had adopted him and rescued him from that cinder-block hellhole, but he had been a favorite among the wardens. Treats and favors had all been his in a simple exchange that he had learned to turn to his advantage until sexual manipulation was as natural for him as breathing.

Tonight would be different. He wouldn't have to perform for her, wouldn't have to consider her enjoyment or pretend his own, wouldn't have to count out the steps in his head to reach his goal. Tonight was for him, for his pleasure.

He hadn't recognized how desirable Inna was, hadn't realized her potential, until he'd seen her the other night at Troika sitting in Zviad's lap.

Now, despite the faded hospital scrubs that draped her body, he easily imagined how she would look on his arm in a skimpy dress like the one she had worn last night. Leggy and fashionably thin, she had turned her share of heads, including Zviad's. Plenty of men would envy Mikhail for having her on his arm, never mind that she was the one that came with the Koslovsky fortune.

Artur's request for Mikhail to play bodyguard opened a new move on the chessboard. The lovely Inna was vulnerable now, in need of a hero.

Inna had always been skittish around Mikhail, seemingly repelled by the seductive charms he depended on to get his way. His fault. She had been away at college when he joined Artur's organization. He had made his move on her as soon as she came home, hoping to use her to cement his place in the closest thing to family he had ever known. Too eager, he hadn't watched her closely enough and hadn't paid sufficient attention to see what a puzzle she presented.

He had grossly misjudged her, imagining a college graduate would be more experienced and open to suggestion. He had cornered her in the office and whispered naughty suggestions that would have made other women, even virginal or prudish ones, weak in the knees.

Inna wasn't like other women. Instead, she had actively avoided him ever since, not giving him the chance to redeem himself and try again.

That was about to change. He had her number now.

Events would force her to stick close to him. She would undoubtedly feel grateful to the man who protected her from further harm and fall easily into his arms.

When he had thought he had Artur's loyalty, Mikhail had convinced himself Inna didn't matter to his goals. He had been content to leave her alone as long as he was secure in his place and got his due. Now that Artur had made the unforgivable mistake of relegating him to the sidelines, Mikhail planned to claim Artur's little princess.

If he could lay claim to Artur's greatest prize, the others would all be ripe for the taking. Getting a share was no longer enough, not when there was no loyalty and no family for him. Mikhail wanted everything he thought Artur had and possibly more. One way or another he would have it, all of it. Then he would crown himself king of Brighton Beach.

Tomorrow would be soon enough to start romancing Inna and put his newest plan in motion. Tonight, there was no reason to waste the effort on impressing her—or forego the opportunity that presented itself.

"Inna, princess, let me put you to bed." He scooped her into his arms. Her head flopped heavily over his arm. He navigated the hall and doorway to the bedroom with care not to bump her head into the wall or door frame.

Inna's bedroom was stark and modern, a platform bed and squared teak wood furniture, not what he would have expected from a designer who specialized in embellished interiors that harkened back to the Tsar's Winter Palace.

Mikhail didn't favor the simplicity of the design she'd chosen for herself. When they had a place together, he would insist she make it ornate, fit for a king and his queen.

Inna was entranced, sleepy and pliable, her expression vacant, maybe slightly pleasured. He slid off the green scrubs she'd worn home from the hospital and then straddled her and sat her up to remove her shirt. She wore the same lacy red bra she'd had on last night, the one that matched her thong and hinted at the naughty, naughty plans she might have made for her evening with Katya's lawyer friend.

"Slut," Mikhail said with a playful yank of her dark hair. Soon she'd be making those plans for him.

She turned her head and blinked at his forearm.

"Will you dream of me, Inna?" he asked as he bent to kiss her neck and worked his way down to her small, pert breasts. She lay still, not reacting at all when he suckled and then bit her nipple. He pinched the peak of the other between his fingers and twisted, hard enough to make most women gasp with pain, but Inna was far away in dreamland.

His erection pressed painfully against his zipper, and he ached for release as he nipped and squeezed at her, careful not to make a mark.

He couldn't leave any sign or clue that would send her running back to the police for another round of forensics. That still left him quite a few options. His blood pumped with excitement. He reveled in the unlimited power he wielded over her.

He could do anything to her, and she'd never remember. No one would ever know. And tomorrow he would convincingly play her hero.

VICTOR

VICTOR DROVE SLOWLY to *Secretnaya Banya*. There he would meet Gennady, the newest in a long line of Directorate emissaries.

In the old days, these meetings had never worried him. He had worked in the KGB alongside the Directorate's leadership, but there was a new regime now. The old guard, the ones Victor had slaved to impress or mollify or blackmail, had moved on, leaving Victor with a worthless account of debts and favors owed that could never be collected and a new set of Machiavellian bosses whose desired end wasn't power for the Motherland but profit, profit, profit.

Victor's power and influence had seemingly diminished overnight, leaving him with responsibility and no leverage. A dangerous position.

Secretnaya Banya was a secret club opened to the elite of the New York Russian community by special invitation only. For a hefty sum, members of the *banya* enjoyed traditional Russian baths, gourmet food, and privacy in a rarified environment that spoke to them both of their Russian roots and their fabulous success.

Yet the club was not a venue for displaying success to others. The building had a grimy, brick facade that gave no hint of the luxury inside. Visitors were stripped of all of the trappings of their position. All belongings, including cell phones, were left in the locker room. While at the club, everyone wore Turkish robes that had been specially designed with wide sleeves and no pockets, a uniform that made them all equal. Sort of.

Upon arriving in the United States, Gennady had immediately received an invitation. Victor never had.

Victor had loudly and openly complained about the "oversight." No doubt Gennady sought to rub Victor's nose in the slight. The Directorate operatives specialized in psychological warfare, even against each other.

Gennady waited in the lounge when Victor arrived. A man at ease, he sat in a leather armchair, reading a newspaper and indulging in buttered crackers with Beluga caviar. Victor assessed him, looking for weaknesses or signs of vice, finding nothing obvious—no bloodshot eyes or yellow-stained fingers or even extra weight around the middle. The man, in his early forties, if that, was a picture of robust good health and classic Russian handsomeness with his blue eyes and a full head of wavy blond hair.

"You're late." Gennady folded the newspaper and placed it on the side table. His eyes, a light blue, were unfriendly. Likely Gennady was keeping a tally sheet of all of Victor's and Artur's deficiencies, which he intended to bring back to Moscow to help his own advancement.

"Where's Artur?" he demanded.

"*Eezvenete.*" Victor was carefully polite. "There were pressing matters."

"I see." Gennady rose. He was taller than Victor, and he stood close as if using his height to intimidate him. "What is more pressing than meeting me?"

The question was rhetorical. The man's sense of superiority grated on Victor. Gennady seemed to think that since he was delivering orders, he was actually giving them. He forgot he was only a messenger.

Tempting as it was to remind the upstart of his true position, Victor pressed his lips together and remained silent. He treated Gennady with extreme caution.

Gennady had a key advantage. Stationed in Moscow, he had direct influence with his superiors, while Victor had none.

Still, Victor had his rank, and it was higher than Gennady's. He had his years of experience. He had Artur with his incredible charisma and penchant for strategy, both of which kept the money flowing.

What he didn't have right now were his favored tools of the trade. Victor had been forced to leave everything—his recording devices and his pills—in the locker room.

Now, he had no way to gain an advantage.

"*Davai.*" Gennady turned away and led Victor down a hallway to the Russian baths. Victor, no stranger to a visit to the *banya,* pulled his robe closer around him. Soon they would leave their robes behind, too.

The anteroom to the *banya* was empty. The area looked like a spa, with green glass tiles and simple carved wooden benches. Gennady disrobed without hesitation and hung his robe from the hook near the bench before removing his slippers.

Victor tried to hide his own hesitation, his sense of disadvantage. He was more than a decade older than Gennady, and he certainly didn't have the man's muscular physique.

The *banya* was deserted. There was no one to witness or comment on the differences between the two men, but Victor felt as if an arena full of spectators bore witness to his humiliation.

Gennady smiled slightly, as if he felt Victor gawking. He strode wordlessly to the wood and glass door of the bath and went inside. "Victor, *chto takoe?* Don't you like the *banya?*" he called over his shoulder.

Through the glass of the door, Victor watched as Gennady picked up the *venik,* a green pile of birch branches lying on the wooden bench inside the hot room. Gennady wielded the collection of branches, hitting different parts of his body with smooth and rhythmic swings, as if he were engaged in martial arts training.

Everything the man did, whether or not by design, showcased his vitality and physical power.

Victor felt his own power slipping through his fingers. He didn't know how to hold on.

He untied the plush robe and quickly placed it beside Gennady's. He looked straight ahead, refusing to let his gaze wander toward his gray chest hair and liver spots or the rolls of fat hugging his chest and abdomen. Inside he felt the weight of his years.

He was past his prime, no longer a competitor or a peer, merely an old man to be handled and ordered around.

He opened the door to the sauna, and the heat hit him full in the face and throat, along with a growing fear that he wouldn't be allowed to retire with dignity.

"Your shipment arrived last week, and you haven't yet sold the merchandise," Gennady said. "I hope you haven't decided to back out."

"No, of course not."

"Good."

Victor felt slightly nauseous in the hot room with sweat pouring down his face. His knees buckled, and he landed heavily on the bench. If the heat and humidity of the sauna hadn't made Victor break out into a sweat, Gennady's question would have.

There was no rebellion, no backing out, or changing your mind. Once you were a part of the Directorate, there was only one way out. Victor had no intention of following that path—or of letting Artur take that road to perdition.

"You should know there's a problem," Victor said.

"A problem?" Gennady lay the bundle of branches on the bench and sat down beside him. He gave Victor his full attention. "What problem?"

"Artur's daughter was raped last night."

"What does that have to do with business?"

"The Georgians are involved. Their man raped her and was murdered."

"That's unfortunate," Gennady said. No emotion inflected his words. Cold-hearted bastard. Victor would have admired him were he not such a threat.

"Artur wants to punish them. They hurt his daughter. He wants to call off the deal. He's talking about going to war."

"Unacceptable," Gennady said. "The risk is too great. You can't let him do anything that will call attention to us or jeopardize the deal."

"That's what I told him," Victor said.

"Tell him again. Make sure he understands. It's your job to control him, Victor. Don't tell me you can't handle your job anymore. I'd hate to have to terminate you."

Victor could taste the bitter edge of his own panic. For years, he had hoarded information and power. Now, his life's work could turn to dust overnight because personal revenge was more important to Artur than business.

Victor was not about to let Artur's selfish decisions leave him in the cold. Decades ago, if he had left the decisions to his friend, Artur would be living in the American suburbs with Sofia and a pack of brats and no imagination or riches, and Victor would be ... nowhere. Maybe rotting in Moscow in a dead end job and rubbing his worthless rubles together—if he had managed to keep his position now that his sponsors had moved on.

Then as now, Victor couldn't afford to lose Artur, his most valuable asset.

The secret to controlling Artur was to play into his favored myth of himself as a tortured hero. Artur clung staunchly to the fiction that beneath everything he was a good man, a good father.

A truly good man wouldn't descend to the depths of corruption Artur had—for any reason. He wouldn't go along, head down, performing greater and greater feats to appease his tormentors.

This latest venture was no mere white-collar crime. Initially, Artur had balked at the newest assignment from the Directorate. Yet with the proper pressure, he had brilliantly masterminded the newest deal.

At some point, a good man would turn on them, refuse, or try to escape. In a quarter century, Artur had done none of these things. He had even stayed with Maya, whose father, Semyon, was their last remaining link to power in Moscow.

Gennady exited the hot enclosure and plunged into the icy pool beyond the doors. Victor followed. The cold made him gasp and sputter.

Victor had no intention of getting trapped in a prison worse than the one he lived in now. Maybe Maya had done him a favor tonight. While Artur slept peacefully, Victor would take matters into his own hands. Artur made the right choice when he imagined he had none. Victor was a master at narrowing Artur's choices for him.

This time, as before, Inna was the key.

VLAD

"HE'S OVER THERE!" The suppressed *pop, pop, pop* of a fired handgun punctuated the words. With each shot, the silencer lost its power. The gunshots grew louder. The bullets sparked as they flew from the gun muzzle, briefly lighting the alleyway with a strobelike effect.

Vlad had two guns, fully loaded. But he wouldn't be able to reload. His attacker shot wildly, freely wasting bullets. Vlad took aim at the shadowy figure. One shot, unmuffled, louder than the rest exploded in the narrow space. The shots near the street stopped.

More shots rang, this time from the other end of the alley, near the parking lot. He pivoted, facing down flares from two separate muzzles. One shooter, like him with two guns, or two gunmen?

The scorched smell of gunpowder filled his nose. Bullets hit the wall a mere foot from Vlad's shoulder. Bricks shattered. The dust stung his eyes, scratched his throat. He couldn't hold back his cough.

"Over there!"

A bullet punched his shoulder and threw him back. His head hit the wall.

"Got him," someone crowed.

Vlad's knees buckled. He slid down the wall toward the ground, dizzy from the impact. The sudden blistering pain in his shoulder momentarily stunned him. A few more shots fired with no answering shot. Then silence.

"Did we get him?"

"Better make sure."

Vlad held himself still. He hardly dared to breathe. He still couldn't see well enough to take aim. He prayed his attackers were as blind as he was and that they wouldn't resort to spraying the ground with bullets in the hope of turning his battered body into Swiss cheese.

The moment he heard the tentative footsteps, the soft slap of fine leather soles on pavement, the flapping of a long trench coat, he fired a single shot. The body hit the ground with a satisfying thud.

"Vasya?" Vlad fired in the direction of the voice.

The recoil sent a throbbing reminder to his body of his latest wound. The hot bullet casing bounced off his leg and made a musical sound when it struck the ground.

Three down. Was it over? Were they dead? Were there more? He held his breath and waited.

Vlad gingerly touched his shoulder. No blood. There was a tear in his leather jacket, but his bulletproof vest had kept his skin intact. Fingering under his shirt, he winced at a raised welt the size of a golfball. The sucker would leave an impressive bruise, but he'd live.

After a string of tense minutes, Vlad reached into his pocket for his phone and texted Svetlana. "Trouble in alley outside Troika. Use caution." He trusted she would be able to assess any remaining threat and that any thugs lying in wait wouldn't rush to attack the bartender in her stilettos and bootie shorts if it seemed she was merely having a smoke in the back lot.

Within moments, Vlad heard a familiar whistle, his signal with Svetlana. He whistled back. A light appeared at the end of the alley near the parking lot. Vlad scrambled to his feet, guns at the ready as the flashlight beam stopped on each of the unmoving bodies in the alley. The men were light-skinned. He couldn't be sure, but he didn't think they were Georgian, especially not when one of them had such a classically Russian name as Vasya.

"Get their guns," Vlad said while he kept his weapons trained on the prone forms. She kicked a gun away from the first body and then prodded him with the point of her stiletto. No reaction. She moved to the second, only feet from the first.

Vlad covered her as she crossed the length of the alley to the side near the street. She inspected the third shooter. "Good and dead," she reported.

She returned to where he stood in the middle of the alley. "Busy night." She flashed the light over him. "You okay?"

"Nothing some frozen peas can't cure."

"Care to tell me what happened out here?"

"Fuck if I know," Vlad lied. He had a strong suspicion the men in the alley worked for Ivan. He didn't know what his father's game was, but telling Svetlana would only lead to questions Vlad didn't want to answer.

He didn't plan on telling her he was Ivan Chertoff's son. If she found out Vlad had a family connection to such a powerful member of the mafia, she'd suspect Vlad planned a double-cross—move into Artur's operation and then keep the whole thing for himself.

Svetlana had some serious trust issues. Vlad had committed a grave violation with his lie of omission. She might not forgive him when she finally learned the truth, even if he delivered what they both sought.

He didn't fool himself that they were friends. Svetlana could turn on him, and she would be a formidable adversary. With luck, he would already have achieved their goal by the time the truth came out.

Too bad Lady Luck had never been Vlad's friend either.

ALEKSEI

ALEKSEI HEADED HOME, feeling dejected. He found Katya asleep in their bed, and he felt relieved not to have to face her.

He told himself he would make it all up to her tomorrow. A bouquet of flowers and a romantic note. That usually did the trick.

Careful not to wake her, Aleksei tiptoed downstairs to their kitchen and straight to the fridge. He searched the shelf for his bottle of Grey Goose, but didn't see it. He moved around the takeout boxes and the home cooking his mother-in-law had delivered yesterday. He sighed with disgust. His vodka was gone. So was his beer.

He headed for the bar in the den in search of some other poison to dull the sharp edge of his failures. Empty.

He easily guessed Katya had gone on a rampage. She had cleared the house of alcohol—or so she might have thought.

Their reconciliation would require something fancier than flowers this time, he supposed.

He returned to the kitchen, and opened the cabinet next to the stove with all of the cookbooks. Katya never opened this one. She never cooked. His stash had to be safe here.

Sure enough, when he reached to the back of the cabinet behind the cookbooks, he found his hidden supply and pulled out an unopened bottle of vodka.

Aleksei didn't bother with a shot glass. He screwed open the top of the long-necked bottle and took a swig. *Ah*. The hot, familiar burn of the alcohol gave him an immediate sense of comfort.

He padded barefoot over the cold marble tiles of their gracious home to the living room, which his sister had decorated for them as a wedding gift. He swallowed another mouthful of vodka to banish the guilt he was feeling over Inna. And Katya.

She would never, never forgive him if she learned his role. She would never stay another second with a man who would use his own sister the way Aleksei had.

Aleksei would be lost if Katya left him.

He sat on the soft leather sofa and consoled himself with his favorite drink. She wouldn't leave. She wouldn't know. Mikhail had sworn he could fix everything.

Aleksei would buy Katya diamonds. Or maybe a fur coat. Something ridiculously extravagant and expensive to show her how much he loved her. That would satisfy her, smooth over their current difficulty. Right?

The front window lit up with a flash of lights. A car pulled into their driveway. Aleksei rose and headed to the window in time to see a portly figure with a fedora and overcoat exit the car. Stan!

What was the idiot doing coming to his house? And in the middle of the night?

Aleksei hurried over to the front door and threw it open before Stan could knock or ring the bell or make any loud sound that might awaken Katya and lead to more trouble between them.

"What are you doing here? I told you not to come to my house."

"This is serious." Stan pushed his way into the house. "We need to talk. The cops are asking questions."

"Keep it down," Aleksei warned. "I don't want to wake Katya."

Stan made a derisive sound. "Gangster wives do what they're told. What's the matter? Don't think you're man enough to control your woman?"

Aleksei grabbed Stan by the collar and yanked the man forward. "Be careful what you say. I'm your boss. I control you."

Stan's face reddened. "I don't think you fully understand the situation. How about I change my story for the cops and tell them how you conspired to commit murder?"

Aleksei released Stan and plunked down on the sofa. He motioned for him to sit. As head pharmacist, Stan's willingness to do *anything* if the money was good enough had been a huge asset to Aleksei's schemes, but his involvement could now be a liability if the man decided to turn him in.

Stan didn't sit. He stood in the middle of the living room. "The police came to my home tonight. To question me. They recognized me," he said. "From the cameras the other night at Troika. They can't prove squat, but the way I see it, I'm holding all the risk. If the Georgians don't take me down, the cops will."

Wishing for numbness, Aleksei nursed another swallow of vodka before saying, "You knew the risks when you made the deal."

"The deal's changing," Stan said. "We're renegotiating. You're going to pay me so that I don't suddenly remember details the cops would find interesting."

"You think so?" Aleksei asked.

"I know so," Stan said. "I want a million in cash. In twenty-four hours."

"You're crazy," Aleksei said. "I can't get you that kind of money so fast."

Stan gestured toward the vodka. "Crawl out of the bottle long enough to pay attention, *Boss*. I have the power here. Who do you think they'll go after if all this stuff comes to light? The lowly pharmacist or the boss with family connections to an even bigger mafia boss? Ask your Papa for the money. We both know he's got it."

"Oh, he's got it," Aleksei agreed. "But he won't give it to you." *Or to me.*

"Then maybe Mommy Dearest will make the transfer to keep your ass out of the slammer. I don't give a good goddamn who you ask or what you have to do. I want that money. You have twenty-four hours."

Stan turned his back on Aleksei and headed for the door.

"Don't turn your back on me," Aleksei said.

"Or what? You'll shoot me in the living room and leave a nice big bloodstain for Katya to find?" Stan chuckled at his own humor.

Aleksei clutched the neck of his vodka bottle so tightly he risked crushing it.

Stan opened the front door. Over his shoulder, he said, "You're a useless drunk. Stop pretending to be a big man and get me my money." He slammed the door on his way out.

Stop pretending. Stop pretending. Aleksei mimicked, growing angrier by the moment as the combined threats and insults penetrated and cut deep.

Stan was going to pay. And dearly.

KATYA

KATYA AWOKE WITH a start. The room was dark, but she couldn't roll over and go back to sleep. Aleksei was gone. Had he even come home?

She thought she heard voices in the house, and her imagination ran wild with scenarios. Who was here? In the middle of the night? Had something terrible happened?

She strained to listen. Yes, there were voices. Men talking low and with menace. Only a few words rose to her level of hearing: *Boss, man, money, twenty-four hours*. Not enough for her to be sure of the meaning of the conversation.

Adrenaline propelled her out of bed. On bare feet, she tiptoed from her room down the hall. She reached the top of the stairs and stopped short. Stan! The pharmacist the police had wanted for questioning stood in the front hall.

She hopped silently back into the shadows as Stan told her husband, "You're a useless drunk. Stop pretending to be a big man and get me my money."

Stan slammed the door. She heard what sounded like the crash of glass against the wall and tiptoed to the edge of the stairs. The floor didn't creak, but even if it had, Aleksei might not have noticed. He was muttering to himself and angry. So very angry.

Katya's heart beat with fear. Before last night, her natural response would have been to fly down the stairs, to check on her husband, to talk with him about what had just happened and how she might help. Before last night, Inna hadn't been drugged and raped; a man hadn't been murdered in Aleksei's nightclub; and Aleksei hadn't gotten himself falling-down drunk in front of Nick and the police. Before last night, her husband had never hit her. Before last night, the worst thing she could have imagined in their relationship was that Aleksei might be having an affair.

Katya stayed where she was and watched silently from the landing.

Aleksei cursed at the broken glass and the liquid that had sloshed the stone around the fireplace. She could guess what kind of bottle it had been and what the liquid was. She imagined he had stolen out of bed to drink, and she wondered how much he had imbibed before smashing the bottle. She pressed herself against the wall and chewed on her thumbnail as Aleksei bent to pick up the phone.

"I don't care where you are or what you're doing," he snapped into the cordless receiver. "Stan was just here. The asshole thinks he's got my nuts in a vice. Wants a million dollars in twenty-four hours."

Aleksei paced the living room. He was shirtless, and the moonlight cast a glow over his sinewy muscle and smooth skin. He raked a hand through his platinum hair, and the ends stuck up in spikes.

The moment was so surreal. He looked the same as he always had. Yet, she couldn't see him with the same eyes. Everything was different now.

"He can't do this to us," Aleksei said. Another pause. More listening. "No, listen. I have another plan," he responded to his partner. "Early retirement."

Early retirement. She imagined he meant something far more sinister than early job termination.

Bile rose in her throat, and this time she couldn't force it back down. She pressed her knuckles to her mouth. On shaking legs, she hurried quietly back to her bedroom. She rushed into the luxurious master bathroom, as large as a bedroom itself, and made it to the toilet with barely enough time to heave into the commode.

Footsteps pounded up the steps. Aleksei had heard her.

"You're up. How long have you been awake?" He stood with his arms braced against the doorway as if he planned to bar her from leaving. "What did you hear?"

The implied accusation frightened her. What had she heard? And what would he do about it?

For the first time in her married life, she felt afraid of her husband. She couldn't let him know she had heard anything. She needed to pretend everything was normal, that nothing had happened. Without answering him, she turned her head back toward the toilet and retched again.

She hoped the sight of her doubled over the commode would make him forget the possibility she might have heard something.

Her throat was raw, and her eyes burned with tears. "I'm pregnant."

"You're having my baby?" He came to her, his mood changing in a flash. The face that had been dark with anger only a moment before now gazed at her with an almost angelic wonder.

The tears came now, hot and fast. Big fat teardrops slid down her face. She wiped them away with the back of her hand, but the flow didn't stop.

"Hey! What's wrong?" His voice held the kind of tenderness and care that had lured her into falling in love with him. He wrapped his arms around her.

"I'm scared," she admitted. How could she raise a baby with this man?

"Don't be scared. I'm always going to take care of you. You and the baby. We're going to have a wonderful life together."

He kissed her hands. She closed her eyes and wished hard that his words were true. Maybe all of this was a terrible misunderstanding.

ARTUR

ARTUR LEFT THE KGB headquarters in Lubyanka Square and breathed in the fresh air. His pockets were heavy with gifts. For Kolya, the boy, a deck of cards to keep him busy on the plane, and for the baby and Sofia, a rattle with diamonds hidden inside—all the wealth he owned. He would give Sofia the world.

He had a spring in his step as he made his way to Ilyinskiye Vorota, the park where he and Sofia met in secret. They could do little more than exchange longing glances or letters, but that was all about to change.

Sofia and the children were headed to Israel on Refusenik visas. After he saw them off, he would board a plane to Hungary for a business trip. They would meet in Italy and head together to America.

He planned to leave everything behind him—the State intrigue and the dirty dealings that weren't part of Soviet doctrine but were part and parcel of Soviet politics and espionage; his wife who was by turns clinging and cold-hearted; and the oppression of knowing his actions and words were being observed and scrutinized. At the KGB, Artur pretended to walk the Party line. While he doted in public on his wife, he secretly made his plans to run away with Sofia and the children and start anew.

He felt a niggle of guilt about Aleksei, his own son. He didn't want to leave without him, but he wouldn't take the boy from his mother. He hadn't said good-bye or explained. He couldn't take the risk that someone would discover his plans and try to stop him—again.

Artur scanned the park for Sofia. She had lunch here almost every day, bringing Kolya and little Ilana to the park for fresh air and exposure to the few patches of green to be had in Moscow. He didn't see the checkered *blanket or the stroller, the woman with the dark eyes and hair who made him believe in souls and destiny.*

He walked past their favorite spots, then circled back, but there was no sign of them.

He sat on a park bench and waited. And waited. Twenty minutes passed. He checked his watch, walked around the park, searched the brick walkways and green lawn for them.

He checked his watch again. A whole hour had passed. He could hear his heart beating in his ears.

He should be getting back to his office. He didn't want anyone to suspect. Yet, he couldn't shake the feeling that something was very wrong.

Sofia had told him she loved him, had given him no reason to doubt. So where was she?

She wouldn't miss meeting him in the park on this, their last day in Moscow, unless something had happened.

He knew he shouldn't risk it, but his instinct screamed at him to check her home. He hurried from the park, jogged a mile in his neat pinstripe suit and loafers to the cement block building where Sofia lived.

He hadn't been here for months, not since the baby was born, staying away to allay suspicion, resigning himself to stolen glances in the park and a clandestine exchange of notes—love letters or instructions. Now he raced to her apartment, heedless of who might see.

Leaving today. Leaving today. Leaving today. *His heart beat hard in his chest. In just a few hours, she would be outside the Soviet Union. Safe.*

Why hadn't she come to meet him?

He pushed the button to call the elevator, but it didn't light up. Out again. The damn thing never worked.

He jogged seven flights up the stairway, taking the stairs two at a time. He was panting when he reached the dim hallway on her floor.

Her door was slightly ajar. He imagined her behind it, urging Kolya into his jacket and buckling the baby into the stroller. But there was no sound, no voices.

He pushed open the door to the apartment. The room was unusually dark, the shades drawn.

And then he saw her.

Artur awoke with a start. There were tears in his eyes. He dashed them away. He stood and stretched, trying to shake off the haunting dream of the past, of the worst day of his life.

He didn't remember falling asleep at his desk. The grandfather clock in the hallway chimed. Three o'clock in the morning.

He padded to the kitchen, slid open the glass door to the deck and stood by the rail, staring out to the ocean. The waves were foamy and gray in the moonlight. They reminded him of a black and white film, and the rolling motion of the tide pulled his thoughts to the past and then back to the present. To Sofia. To Inna.

He couldn't lose Inna, too.

It was only a matter of time before the Georgians lashed out in retribution over the dead man. They may have already tried to take their wrath out on Vlad. No matter how many Artur stopped or killed, there would only be more to take their place. A never-ending cycle of violence.

Artur was only one man. He would willingly fight the world for his daughter, but he knew he couldn't win. Not with brute force.

There had to be another way. There was always another way.

The Georgians weren't the only ones he needed to consider. Someone else had hurt Inna, had set her up to be raped and then blamed for a murder she most likely hadn't committed. Who? Why?

Victor had been quick to absolve the Directorate of any wrongdoing, but Artur wasn't so sure. The new deal they had in play was audacious and sat uneasily with Artur's conscience, despite the crimes he had committed for them in the past.

He had voiced his reservations and then had stalled and delayed. Could the Directorate now be sending him a warning? *We see. We know. We own you. We will hurt the people you care about if you defy us or try to escape.* Was it the same message yet again?

The prepaid cell phone he used to receive Ivan's calls rang in his pocket. In prison, a cell phone was contraband, but with the right connections and enough money, anything could be smuggled in. Ivan risked calling only when he had an important matter for Artur to handle and the expectation of a few stolen moments of privacy. His favorite time to call was the middle of the night, when he could slide the cell phone into his pillow case and, if necessary, pretend he was talking in his sleep.

Ivan crowed in Russian. *"Malchick xorosho zdelal."* *The boy did well.* "The boy" was how Ivan referred to Vlad.

"On ubil tree cheloveka dlya menya." *He killed three men for me.* "Vasya and his cousins. Singlehandedly! Nice and neat. You'll arrange payment."

"Konechno." *Of course.* Artur's throat constricted with anger—at himself, at Ivan, at Vlad.

Artur had pulled Vlad into his schemes for his own purposes. Tonight Artur had relied on him to investigate the murder at Troika and, most immediately, the threat to Inna. Instead, Vlad had been playing Ivan's assassin, reporting trouble at Troika to cover up his other assignment and explain his temporary absence.

Artur had made a gross miscalculation at a time when he couldn't afford mistakes. Vlad's relationship with Ivan had initially been a blessing: No one questioned why Artur would overlook Vlad's past in law enforcement and elevate him so quickly upon discovering him in Miami when he was the son of Artur's former partner, a *vor* still active in organized crime even from prison. Now it was also a curse.

"I'm telling you, Artur, he will make an excellent addition to the *bratva*. We will make him a *brigadier*."

This was a new side of Ivan. Twenty years in prison had made him sentimental. Although Ivan never said so, Artur supposed the *vor* now regretted the family he had never built with Nadia. The son Ivan had refused to claim as blood, he now hoped to claim in brotherhood. By making him a murderer.

Vlad was supposed to be Artur's man.

Long after the call ended, Artur stood at the railing and pondered his options. The waves crashed onto the shore then receded, back and forth, attack and retreat. Artur had planned to keep a tight rein on Vlad. He hadn't anticipated this opportunity for Vlad to climb so high so fast, this competition for the younger man's loyalty.

"You can't sleep either." Maya joined him on the porch and brushed his cheek with her hand. He supposed they appeared an idyllic picture, a handsome middle-aged couple, standing side by side and staring out at an ocean view in the gray light of morning.

"I had a bad dream," Maya said.

Artur turned and paid close attention. He wasn't a superstitious man, but there was something of the witch in his wife. Her dreams and pronouncements had an eerie level of prophetic accuracy. "It was about Inna."

"Tell me." The air suddenly felt charged with danger.

"I dreamed she was in trouble, but she didn't want our help. She said she could take care of herself. Then she went home and locked her door and wouldn't let anyone in, not even us. You yelled and screamed, and she wouldn't answer, and so you knocked the door down. But when we went inside, she was dead."

Maya turned her body toward him. Her voice dropped as if the words pained her. "Artur, she had swallowed a bunch of pills and killed herself."

Artur couldn't speak. The scene Maya described was too much like Sofia's murder.

The weight of his failures bore down on him. He wouldn't let history repeat itself. A long game like this one was about strategy, not reactivity. This time, he had laid a careful plan to escape, more audacious and crafty than any of his life, a plan that had taken years to ripen. He would extricate himself and Inna—from the Directorate, from the mafia underworld, from Brighton Beach.

Events forced him to accelerate his timeline. Artur no longer had the luxury of testing and priming. Ripe or not, perfect plan or not, the time had come to act.

It was time to bring Vlad fully into play.

INNA

INNA'S CHEST TIGHTENED with a familiar and unwelcome anxiety, almost panic, but her limbs moved slowly, as if weighted. Her heart pounded, and still it was difficult to lever herself off of the bed. She was naked, but she had no memory of removing her clothes, or really of anything from last evening. When had everyone left?

She had a sense of lost time, a new hole in her memory. Perhaps the residual effect of whatever drug her attacker had given her.

The clothes from yesterday were in a pile at the bedside as if she had tossed them there, her lacy red bra on top. The sight of it made her slightly sick to her stomach as unpleasant memories rushed up to meet her. She'd had such high hopes for herself, and look what had happened.

Standing by the edge of the bed, she noticed that both pillows had deep indentations, hers with a wet spot of drool. How could they both be indented? Had someone been there? She imagined she detected a musky scent in the air.

Unsteady and frightened, heart beating wildly, she careened toward the closet and grabbed her robe. She wrapped the soft, bulky terrycloth around her, and cinched the belt tightly as if it were the only thing holding her together.

She had felt this way once before. The medication was supposed to keep her from falling back into the hellish pit of her own anxiety.

She headed toward the shower. She wanted to scrub away the dirt and grime of the last couple of days, wash herself clean. She turned the tap on, waited for the water to heat and the steam to rise, and stepped into the shower stall.

She had slept deeply, but she didn't feel at all rested. Her body ached as if she had wrestled and tossed all night. She leaned her head against the cold white tiles and let the hot water pour over her and ease the tension.

Strange images flashed behind her eyes, brilliantly clear, but also disconnected. They teased and tormented her.

She couldn't call the images at will, couldn't quite catch them. She wasn't sure she wanted to. Would she recover if she truly knew what horrible thing had happened the other night at Troika?

As it was, a growing sense of doom pressed down on her. She couldn't remember the previous evening after her family left her apartment at all. Her instincts fired with a vague but urgent warning of imminent danger. A strong desire to bolt and hide—from what?—thrummed in her pulse.

She turned off the water. As she toweled herself dry, she battled her body's warning signals. She dressed quickly in jeans and a baggy sweater and pulled her hair back into a ponytail.

She had worked hard in the past to control and override the fear, the rampant anxiety that seemed to be building in her now. She could feel a lump of it congealing in her chest and preventing her from breathing deeply. If the fear got too much bigger, it would overwhelm her.

She needed help.

She rifled through her drawer for the card with Dr. Shiffman's number. Dr. Shiffman had precipitously left her Psychology practice in Brooklyn to retire to Florida, but Inna hoped the doctor she had been seeing for the past year would take an emergency call from her.

She didn't know how to process what had happened, and she didn't want her life to take another detour through the dark place she had worked so hard to escape.

It was still early for a Sunday morning, earlier than politeness allowed for a call of this nature, but she couldn't wait any longer. She thought she might jump out of her skin. She dialed the number, only to find it was no longer in service. She vaguely remembered Dr. Shiffman mentioning a grandchild in Miami Beach.

She pulled out her laptop and searched the web for a Marjorie Shiffman in Florida. She found several and decided to call each one.

There was a slight tremor in her fingers as she dialed. This small sign of anxiety fed on itself. It was already happening. She was sliding back.

The first three calls yielded nothing. On the fourth, a woman answered the phone. A baby cried in the background. Inna felt sure she must have the right house.

"May I speak to Marjorie Shiffman?"

"Whatever you're selling, I'm not interested," the woman said.

"No, wait! I'm looking for Dr. Shiffman. I'm one of her patients." Inna found herself pleading. "Please. I need to talk with her. Something terrible has happened."

There was a deep sigh on the other end. "I'm sorry," the woman said. "Haven't you heard? My mom ... She died a week ago."

"Oh. My um ... my condolences," Inna said, numb with shock.

The call ended, and Inna sat dumbfounded. Over the past year, she had poured her heart out to Dr. Shiffman. She had laid all of the broken pieces of herself out and held nothing back. She had found healing and acceptance in the therapist's office, where for the first time in her adult life she felt safe talking honestly about her life and family and the people around her. There had been no judgment or knee-jerk conclusion that her observations were clouded by paranoia, that she was mentally unstable, or that she needed a new or stronger dose of medication to erase her concerns.

The sudden retirement had been an emotional blow, but this news was so final. The world wasn't a safe place, and she had just lost her most stalwart ally. Permanently.

The phone rang in Inna's hand. The doorman informed her Detective Hersh was here to see her. Inna instructed him to send her visitor up. Why not? Her whole world was crashing down.

She paced the floor in her entryway as she waited for the detective. Would she be arrested now? Would the detective handcuff her and take her to jail?

Inna rubbed sweaty hands on her jeans, tucked her hair behind her ears, and opened the door to her apartment just as the detective was about to knock.

"Are you here to arrest me?" Inna blurted. Her own impulsivity frightened her. She was losing control.

"I'm here to ask you a few questions," Detective Hersh said. His answer didn't rule out an arrest. "May I come in?"

The detective was taller than she, but on the short side for a man. He had gray hair, but a young face. His wire-rimmed glasses made him look scholarly rather than tough.

Inna moved out of the doorway and let the detective enter. He walked a few steps into the apartment and stopped. His eyes scanned the open floor plan, and Inna caught a perplexed look on the detective's face. He tapped a manilla folder against his thigh.

"What's the matter?"

"Nothing. This just isn't what I expected."

"What do you mean? What did you expect?"

He gave her an abashed look. "Something fancier. Full of Russian imports."

Inna supposed she knew what he meant. As an interior designer, she furnished houses and businesses in the area with *matryoshka* dolls, heavy oil paintings in gilded frames, and lacquered knickknacks that fed her clients' nostalgia for all things Russian and that showcased their wealth and success. For herself, she preferred clean lines and little clutter, a controlled environment with as much sense of calm as she could create.

The detective didn't need to know that. He didn't need to know how much she had suffered with anxiety in the past or the lengths she had gone to gain control of herself, a control that now seemed to be slipping. She stuffed her hands in her pockets and tried not to fidget. She forced a smile and then retracted it.

Detective Hersh wasn't going to be won over with a strong dose of Koslovsky charm. He considered her a murder suspect.

Maybe Inna was a murderer.

"You were pretty distraught yesterday. I was hoping maybe now that you're calmer, you could tell me something else about what happened the other night."

Calmer, ha!

"I don't remember." She closed her eyes, shook her head with disgust.

Detective Hersh slid a photograph from the folder. "Maybe this will jog your memory. The photo came from the security video at Troika. Do you remember dancing with this man?"

The bushy-haired man in the picture looked slightly familiar. She couldn't immediately place him, but she felt as if she had met him before. She had absolutely no recollection of seeing him at Troika.

She released a frustrated sigh, and then the images teased her again. An ornate chandelier. The square face and thick dark hair of a man with a hungry gaze. His dark hand on her thigh.

"She's totally compliant. Willing. You can do anything to her. Any naughty, dirty fantasy. She won't tell. She won't even remember." A voice and a snicker behind her.

The man hesitated, and another voice behind her nudged him. "Look at her. She's sex on a stick. What's the matter? You a cop? A prude? Gay? Married?"

"No."

"So sample the merchandise. Then we'll talk business."

Inna opened her eyes and met the detective's curious gaze.

"You remember something."

"It's hazy. And doesn't make much sense to me."

"Tell me whatever you can."

"Men talking. I was sitting in one's lap—not the man from the photo, the other one. The other one ... who died."

"What else?"

"I remember the chandelier; so maybe it was in the ballroom at Troika. There were two men behind me. They said something about 'sampling the merchandise' and 'talking business.'"

"So three men. And a deal," the detective said.

"I guess. Maybe," Inna said. "But I think I was the merchandise." She shuddered.

"Do you remember anything else?"

She closed her eyes, reached for the memory, but it was gone now. "No. Nothing. What's going to happen to me?" she asked.

"My hope is that you'll get past this and live a long and happy life," Detective Hersh said. His words felt like a benediction.

"Sooner or later we're going to catch the guys who did this to you," he said. "We usually do." He handed her his card. "Call me if you remember anything else. No matter how trivial it seems."

VLAD

Cleaning up the mess in the alley outside of Troika had taken a solid chunk of the night. Removing the bodies, collecting the bullet casings, washing away the blood. Vlad hadn't tried to fix the shattered brick, but he'd erased the other signs of a skirmish, no easy task working in the near-dark with a stiff shoulder.

Afterward, he returned to his shithole of an apartment, stripped away his bloodstained clothes and threw them in the incinerator, and then cleaned and reloaded his guns.

He fell into a dead sleep on top of his bed, with his two dependable friends, Glock and Sig, within easy reach.

He startled to a sound and awoke with both guns at the ready. Overkill for a ringing cell phone. He almost laughed at himself.

The call was from Artur. The man didn't sound happy. "Come to Koslovsky Imports right away."

"What's happened?"

"There's something you failed to tell me." Artur ended the call, leaving Vlad to wonder what Artur had discovered and how badly the information would set him back. Vlad was keeping so many secrets. Which one had been exposed?

Vlad shuffled to the bathroom and showered, washing off the remaining grime from last night's adventures. He didn't wait for the water to heat. Under a lukewarm spray, he soaped, rinsed, and finished quickly. Afterward, he didn't feel clean.

He inspected himself in the mirror. The swelling near his shoulder had mostly dissipated, leaving him with a black and blue mark, roughly the same size and position of the *Vory* star tattoos on his father's shoulders. His resemblance to his old man jolted him.

He had taken three lives last night. In self-defense, yes. Yet, he didn't feel the stalking remorse he imagined should follow taking another life. He had never felt it.

He supposed he shared this similarity with Ivan, along with his near-addiction to violence and the high it gave him. Amidst all his secrets and lies, one thing was certain: embracing his birthright as Ivan's son, he was more himself than he had ever been, a fact that didn't make him proud.

He was genetically hard-wired to be a monster. His biological destiny stalked him constantly. Despite all of the promises he made himself, all of the distinctions he made between himself and Ivan, he feared he couldn't outrun it.

Artur's call suggested a certain level of dress might be in order—button-down, tie, and his bullet-proof vest, now compromised where the bullet had lodged in the right shoulder, but still serviceable. Although the vest bulked him up, it wasn't easily visible under his clothes.

Vlad doubted Artur meant to shoot him but couldn't be sure. What exactly had Artur learned? Vlad's fate might depend on how smoothly he talked his way around this newest challenge.

Pass or die.

When Vlad arrived at Koslovsky Imports, the storefront wasn't opened yet. He peered in the front window, but saw nothing. Lights off. No movement. Although he had the key to open the locked metal gate around the front entrance, he headed around to the building's rear door instead. His eyes scanned the area. He preferred not to walk into another ambush.

He found Artur in the workroom, a large stark office with desks and fluorescent lights where Artur's employees wrote orders that Vlad and others filled.

For the past few months, Vlad's work had consisted mainly of delivering imported empty vases, garish canvases, and gaudy light fixtures—all at a very high markup—to Artur and Victor's wealthy Russian clients all over Brighton and Manhattan Beach. Determined to ferret out Artur's secrets, Vlad paid close attention, watched who came and who went, who bought and who sold, who was a player and who a mere nuisance.

He couldn't make out a pattern yet, couldn't see the larger enterprise, didn't have the knowledge he needed to take over. Artur carefully controlled the flow of information. While he had been including Vlad in more meetings lately, Vlad sensed he still stood on the outside looking in—with the most limited of views.

Artur withheld his trust. Smart man.

Artur paced back and forth between the tables. He held a bulky envelope in his hands. When he saw Vlad, he tossed the package at him.

"What's this?"

"Your money," Artur said flatly.

"For what?" Vlad wondered if this was the payment for all of his work and now he was being dismissed.

"The hit you did for Ivan." Artur's words were carefully modulated. Vlad admired Artur's self-control. If he hadn't seen the man's pacing, he'd never have suspected the depth of his agitation.

"What hit? I don't know what you're talking about."

"Don't play stupid with me. Four men walked into an alley, and one came out. Sound familiar?"

Vlad almost chuckled. The situation was so messed up it was almost funny. The father he hadn't seen in years had most likely sent men after Vlad with orders to kill. Now that Vlad had prevailed, Ivan made a show of sending money, as if the shots in the dark had been agreed to and contracted beforehand. Clearly Ivan wanted people, his business partner in particular, to know that Vlad had successfully and intentionally committed murder. Why?

"He's very pleased with you, by the way."

"Ask me if I care." The burn of anger in the back of Vlad's throat lent acid to his words.

"You should care. He's a very powerful man—even in prison. You handled a problem for him. Quietly. Discreetly. He thinks you'll make an excellent addition to his *bratva.*"

Artur's mildness didn't fool Vlad. He detected the challenge in the man's words.

"I didn't come to New York to work for Ivan."

Artur continued as if Vlad hadn't spoken. "Go if you want. No hard feelings. Go play tough guy for Ivan. He thinks you have the makings of a *brigadier,* a full-fledged member of the *Vory.* Isn't that what you want?"

"No." Vlad didn't want to be a Thief in Law like Ivan. Nor did he aspire to be his father's underling and certainly not his contract killer. His ambitions reached so much higher than that. He planned to take his father's place, to usurp him and Artur both as the leader of their operation.

"Don't lie to me. You think I don't know why you're here? What you want?"

How much did Artur know or suspect? The fear that he had been exposed rippled through him, drew a cold bead of sweat down his back, made his breaths quicken.

Vlad ruthlessly quashed the fear. Weakness like that would only give him away.

Artur couldn't possibly know the full truth. Vlad forced himself to breathe slowly, through his nose. "It's the truth. I don't want to work *for* Ivan."

"But you want his power," Artur surmised. "To be a big man like him."

Vlad saw no need to deny it. "Yes."

In a swift move, Artur grabbed Vlad by the tie and yanked, as if he held Vlad in a noose. With surprising strength, he pulled Vlad, taller and larger, down toward him until their eyes met. "Then listen very closely."

Vlad gulped against the tightening knot.

"Last night, you were working for me. But instead, I hear you were out playing hired killer for your father."

"It wasn't like that."

"I'm not interested in your excuses." Artur jerked the tie and cinched it tighter around Vlad's neck.

After months of watching a gentleman with an almost placid demeanor, Vlad had finally caught a glimpse of the true man beneath the thick veneer of respectability, the mob boss who had brought the worst of thugs, including Vlad's own father, to heel.

Though strong and agile, Artur was also older and smaller than Vlad. There could be no doubt as to who would win a physical contest. Assuming Artur played fair.

Men didn't achieve Artur's reputation—or Ivan's respect—by playing fair.

"Understand what it means if you stay. You work for me. You answer to me. Me. Not Ivan. Not Victor. Me!" Artur's dark eyes glittered with emotion. Vlad imagined he detected a yearning that belied the tough-guy diatribe.

"You do what I tell you. If you cross me, I will cut you where you stand. I don't care whose son you are." Artur wound his hand in the tie, tightened the chokehold. "Your first loyalty is to me. *Ti ponymayesh?* Do you understand?*

Vlad managed a nod. He could feel his face reddening with the effort of drawing the barest breath. Still, he didn't fight back.

"The only thing that matters ... is keeping Inna safe."

Vlad had fully expected to have his loyalty questioned at any point as he attempted to infiltrate Artur's operation. He had expected challenges and tests at every turn. He had expected to be pushed to dirty his hands with tasks akin to the hit Ivan had supposedly commissioned.

Yet protecting Inna was not an assignment Vlad had ever in his wildest dreams anticipated, especially when Artur had seemed so set on keeping him away from her.

"You want power? You'll have it. You want money. I'll pay you. I'll bathe you in money." Artur released Vlad and pushed him away as if disgusted. "You can have whatever you want. Whatever I have. Name your price. I don't care. None of it means anything." He raked his hands through his silver hair. "Just help me keep her safe."

There was a pleading in the man's tone, a desperation. Vlad realized suddenly that he had the upper hand. Artur was a man on the edge. He needed Vlad.

A father's love. Who knew that admirable trait would provide the vulnerability Vlad could leverage to gain control? His own father had tried to kill him, as recently as last night.

After all of his months of scheming and watching, Vlad had won. Artur was handing him exactly what he wanted. His trust.

So why didn't it feel like a victory?

INNA

AFTER DETECTIVE HERSH left, Inna sat at her kitchen table, head in her hands. She felt lost. She wished again that she could speak with Dr. Shiffman.

What would Dr. Shiffman have advised her? She imagined she sat again in the soft chair in the doctor's office, describing the terrible thing that had happened and the anxiety she felt now.

She easily conjured her doctor sitting across from her, yellow notepad on her lap. "You have to make a choice," the doctor would tell her, had told her.

Inna had chosen life. She had chosen to jump in and stop letting everything pass her by. She had chosen to be a full participant, not a shadow.

This was a setback. That was all. She had conquered the other fears, the other trauma. She would conquer this one, too.

She decided to reach for normalcy. Small steps. She would go to work.

In moments she was outside in the cold, brisk air. The sky was gray, the air heavy with an impending storm. Anxiety stole her confidence. She turned up a narrow side street that led to the main drag of Brighton Beach Avenue and caught a glimpse out of the corner of her eye of a man behind her.

Inna quickened her steps, tossed a quick glance over her shoulder as she hurried down the busy street. She saw no menacing stalker following behind her, only an old grandma, babushka tied around her chin, pulling an empty cart for groceries.

It was early still, a good hour before most businesses opened their doors to welcome the Sunday hustle and bustle of Brighton Beach Avenue and the voracious appetites of its varied immigrant community. Junk and pawn shops stood beside expensive jewelers, rag shops beside the furriers, all with their windows barred, a reminder that Brooklyn's Little Odessa was not truly safe.

The small coffee joints, bakeries, and *aptekas*—the Russian pharmacies—with signs lettered in both English and Cyrillic already did brisk business. Their storefronts cast a deceivingly warm light, a false invitation to comfort and security.

Inna's heart pounded erratically, fast and skipping and then doubling beats. She dodged and darted past the shoppers, frustrated by the way their steady march and window-shopping slowed her. They seemed to pay her no mind as they stalled and blocked her, shuffling along the sidewalk and pulling their wool coats and jackets tighter around them to ward off the salty cold.

The ocean wind whipped their hair and screamed of the coming storm, one Inna felt stalked immediately behind her, the danger near at hand. She paused at the crosswalk in front of a blinking neon sign for a psychic. She didn't need a tarot reading to know she was in danger. She felt the predatory eyes on her, sensed her pursuer closing in. But who would be following her? And why?

She hadn't caught a full glimpse of anyone behind her and couldn't identify the shadowy figure she felt certain had tailed her since leaving her apartment. She worried she was falling prey to paranoia. Her own fear chilled her, leached through her bones the way the coldest wind never could.

She supposed she could stop and confront the shadow that she suspected was creeping along behind her, if indeed he would stop hiding and show himself. Or perhaps he didn't really exist.

She was too afraid to stop and investigate.

The pedestrian light blinked an orange hand, but she plowed into the crosswalk, desperate to get to her family's import-export business. To safety. To normalcy. Three more blocks.

Above her, a monstrous subway car roared over the tracks, casting dark shadows around her. It belched and gasped to a stop inside the station. The sound rang in her ears, made her dizzy. Here in the middle of Brighton Beach Avenue, in the familiar heart of Little Odessa, where she had lived most of her life, she had a strange sense of disorientation, as if she were moving through a nightmare, as if all of the usual smells and sights and sounds had taken on a blurry and sinister quality.

A car screeched to a halt mere inches from her hip. The driver blared the horn and shouted at her in Russian. "*Chto ti delayesh?*" *What are you doing?* "Watch where you're going."

She paused and blinked stupidly at him. Out of the corner of her eye, she thought she saw a flash of black, but she didn't turn to look, didn't pause. *Keep moving.* She broke into a run. A cold sweat dripped down her back inside her sweater.

She ran the rest of the way across the street, jumped nimbly over the sour puddle running toward the sewer from the grocer's stall. Her breath came fast and shallow, and she couldn't swallow enough air.

Fear squeezed the air from her lungs, made her short of breath, made her throat and chest burn with raw cold.

She powered through the discomfort. She measured her momentum with the quick, steady tap of her heels, her steps regular as the beat of a metronome despite the unevenness of her pulse and her shortness of breath. She caught sight of the black and gold awning that signaled safety—Koslovsky Imports—and sprinted to the storefront with a burst of speed.

She wrenched the door open and pressed herself against the wall beside it, struggled to catch her breath as she both hid and surveyed the street. There! There he was! A tall, dark man in a black trench coat swiveled his head side to side as he searched the street.

Inna's breath came in sparing gasps. *Not paranoid. Not paranoid.*

His gaze paused on the glass of her door. She doubted he could see her pressed against the wall, but he smiled menacingly in her direction as if he knew she was watching. He tipped his fingers at her in a salute.

A hand clamped down on her shoulder, and she jumped with a shriek.

"What's wrong?"

She whirled around. Vlad. Scowling and far too imposing. Too muscled. Too big.

She clutched at her chest, but she had no power to calm her unsteady heartbeat, no control over her racing pulse or thoughts. Instinctively, she shrank from him, backed away, pressed herself tighter against the wall.

"Inna? *Devushka, chto takoe?*" Her father hurried to her side, asked her what was wrong.

She pointed toward the street, toward the man outside. She fought to breathe, to speak. "Followed," she managed. "I'm being followed."

Wait! The sidewalk where he had stood only moments ago was empty. Where had he gone? Her body shook, but with a chill that had nothing to do with the sudden cold snap.

Vlad muscled past her and raced into the street. He jogged in the direction she had pointed, stopped and peered into the alleyways.

"*Tixo.*" Quiet. Her father pulled her against his side and stroked her hair as he studied the street outside the shop window.

She sank against him and rubbed at her tired eyes. With dismay, she watched Vlad circle back, jog in the opposite direction. Moments later, he returned to Inna and her father, grey eyes fierce and alert. His features were chiseled and hard.

"I didn't see anyone suspicious," he said as he came through the door on a blast of bitter wind. If the chill in the air had touched him, he showed no sign, no telltale shiver. He reminded her of a rock wall, an impenetrable slab.

Once she had been on the other side of that wall. She remembered the gentle boy who had accepted her scribbled drawings like they were great gifts, who had hung on her words as if they were important, even though she was only a child and he had stood on the cusp of adulthood. There was no trace of that boy now.

She inched closer to her father, who gazed down at her with increasing concern. He scrubbed his hand over his face, over the high, angular cheekbones, and pinched his chin, the way he did when truly distressed.

"I'm not paranoid!" she protested.

"No, you're not." Her father's agreement gave her a token of reassurance but didn't stay the anxiety nipping at her.

"Maybe she saw Mikhail." Vlad positioned himself near the wall by the window, as she had before, and surveyed the street.

"Why would I have seen Mikhail?"

"I asked him to guard you," her father said.

Her chest tightened. She supposed she should be grateful for the protection after her attack. Yet somehow she didn't feel any safer. Despite his good looks and the ease with which he charmed their customers, there was something cold and calculating in Mikhail's gaze, as if an essential spark were missing.

"I don't want you to worry." Her father took her hand. Only when he started to chafe it between his did she realize she had been fluttering her fingers in agitation. "But we can't be too careful. Someone hurt you," his voice cracked, "and murdered a man at Troika."

Maybe normalcy was out of her reach. A true threat couldn't be overcome by deep breathing exercises and a commitment to forward momentum.

"So you assigned Mikhail to be my bodyguard," she finished before he felt compelled to provide more detail. "And are hoping I mistook him for a stalker."

When they both regarded her silently, she said, "It wasn't Mikhail."

"Tell me what you saw," Vlad demanded, eyes still trained on the street.

When she described the man in the trench coat, Vlad and her father looked at each other and seemed to communicate without speaking. She didn't fully understand the secret message, but she didn't need to be a genius to intercept the meaning: Something was very wrong.

"I never saw Mikhail. Where is he?"

Vlad's voice was a low growl. "Good question."

MIKHAIL

"SHE'S NOT ALONE," Vitaliy said. "Vlad and her father are there."

Mikhail was a block away from Koslovsky Imports and running hard. He held his cell phone to his ear and cursed viciously. No one was supposed to be at Koslovsky Imports this morning. Inna was supposed to make a narrow escape and then be waiting alone for Mikhail, afraid and needing his protection.

"Tell me what they're doing now."

"Vlad's standing near the window keeping watch," Vitaliy said. "Artur's with them. It looks like she's telling them about her big bad wolf. I spooked her good."

"*Molodetz.*" *Excellent.* At least that part of the plan had worked. Mikhail ended the call and shoved his phone into his pocket.

So far, Vitaliy had been an asset. He wasn't Georgian, but he looked the part with his dark skin and hair. Mikhail had dressed him up in a trench coat and instructed him to act menacing. His performance at the hospital the other night had been noteworthy enough for Artur to call for backup. Mikhail could only imagine how his boss would react when he heard the same suspect had shown up this morning in pursuit of Inna.

If only Artur had arrived to find Mikhail there protecting her.

Turning the corner, Mikhail added a limp to his run. He needed to make this extra convincing now that he had a larger and more savvy audience. He sprinted the half block to the import-export storefront. When he reached the door, he was panting as if he had been in an Olympic heat.

"Inna! Inna, are you okay?" he demanded as he opened the door and pushed past Vlad to get to her. "He didn't hurt you. Did he?"

"What happened to you?" Inna asked. She didn't rush to him and fuss over him as he had hoped. What did he expect? She didn't remember the intimacies she'd shared with him last night, and she had other protectors huddled around her.

She hung back, as usual. Yet, her voice held the proper note of concern as she studied his bruised face—the black and blue courtesy of Aleksei's punches.

"I was waiting for you." He could have caught his breath, but he preferred to milk the drama. He let himself gasp loudly between phrases and followed the script he had planned earlier. "And then some *podonok* in a trench coat—one of the Georgian crew— jumped me." Mikhail dropped his head as if ashamed. "He got the upper hand. Landed a few punches." He touched his hand gingerly to the darkened bruise on his jaw to draw their eyes to his embellished wound. Instead of covering them up, Mikhail had enhanced them slightly to make it look like he had been attacked.

"That's a pretty dark bruise," Vlad said. His voice was flat, and Mikhail couldn't read whether he'd impressed him or not. His resentment for Vlad flared.

Mikhail used to think he was rising quickly in Artur's ranks, that Artur and Victor had special plans for him. He had imagined partnership with them was in his future, that he was already a trusted member of their operation, a key member of the inner circle, part of the family.

Then Vlad had arrived.

Vlad had appeared out of nowhere and somehow conned Artur into bringing him into the heart of the operation. Without making Vlad prove himself first, Artur had bumped Mikhail from his position as Artur's right hand—despite his years working with Artur and Victor.

Mikhail wouldn't sit idly by waiting for Artur to remember him.

The one lesson life had taught him was to take what he wanted. Otherwise, the world would never give him what he truly deserved.

In asking him to play bodyguard, Artur had, perhaps unwittingly, given Mikhail the job most likely to secure his advancement. Even if Artur chose to promote Vlad and not Mikhail, Inna was heir to Koslovsky Imports. If Mikhail won Inna, he could have everything— whether or not Artur wanted him to have it.

"How bad is it?" Mikhail rubbed his sore jaw. Aleksei hadn't pulled any punches last night. "I haven't seen it yet," he lied. "I got knocked out. When I came to, the guy was gone. And so was Inna."

"You got lucky," Vlad said. "That he only roughed you up."

"And didn't get Inna," Artur added. Instead of approval and admiration, there was censure in his tone. He turned to his daughter. "Vlad's going to be your bodyguard from now on."

In a single moment, Artur destroyed Mikhail's plan, giving everything to Vlad. "What? Why Vlad and not me?" Mikhail protested.

"You really have to ask?"

"But…"

"Not another word," Artur threatened.

"Papa, he did his best." Inna's quiet defense made Mikhail imagine she was softening toward him. At least this part of his plan was working.

"His best wasn't good enough. He failed," Artur said.

"Hey! I held him off long enough for Inna to get the head start she needed. She got here safely."

"Go clean yourself up. Then go home and get some rest," Artur said.

Mikhail got the distinct feeling he was being dismissed. He didn't like it one bit.

"Vlad's your bodyguard now," Artur told Inna. "You're not to go anywhere without him."

Mikhail could see she wanted to protest, that she didn't like the idea of having Vlad as her bodyguard. Instead, she whispered a reluctant, "*Spasibo, Papa.*"

Thanking her father, she kissed him on his cheek and then ducked away. In her haste to put as much distance between herself and her new bodyguard as possible, she nearly knocked over the antique table behind her. The white-and-gold China tea set displayed atop the lace tablecloth shook and rattled. Inna steadied the table. She held herself unnaturally stiff and straight as if clutching to a dignity that threatened to flee.

She headed with brittle grace to the back office, while Vlad watched her with an almost pathetic longing. As if she felt his gaze, she cast a hunted glance in his direction and then cut her gaze away.

Mikhail almost snickered. Inna was afraid of Vlad. Bodyguard or not, the brute didn't have a chance with her, no matter how badly he might like one. He wouldn't be able to hold Artur's approval, either, once Mikhail was done with him.

All wasn't lost.

MAYA

Maya had hardly been able to credit Mikhail's call. Inna had actually gone to work today? She had expected her daughter to crawl back into her shell, perhaps to sulk and wallow in her misfortune, maybe to backslide into her problems with anxiety.

She had expected Inna to need her mother.

Instead, Inna had gone to work. She hadn't called to talk. She hadn't called for help.

Inna sat at the mahogany desk in her plush office at Koslovsky Imports. Maya lowered herself into the chair across the desk from her daughter. A Tiffany lamp cast a soft light onto the desktop, spilling a warm glow onto the fine Oriental rug.

Inna was bent over a thick catalogue, making a note on a yellow sticky with the name of a client. Her fingers were long and slim. She had graceful wrists, and Maya watched the fluid stroke of her pen.

Inna had her father's elegance, and Maya's heart brimmed with both love and pain while she watched her work.

"Do you need something?" Inna's tone was the slightest bit harsh.

"Is that any way to talk to your mother?" Maya asked, affronted.

Inna and Artur had furnished the office together. Inna had wanted something modern and sleek to suit her own taste, but she had capitulated when Artur insisted her office reflect the image of the business they had started together. Together, just father and daughter. They hadn't invited Maya or Aleksei to join them.

It had always been that way, father and daughter thick as thieves, never letting anyone else get close. And now that Maya had taken the step of visiting, Inna didn't seem particularly pleased by this motherly show of concern.

Children! Maya could never predict how they would behave.

Artur spoiled Inna terribly. She had no reason to try her independence or strike out on her own, not when her father anticipated her every need, gave her whatever she might want before she could even think to ask.

"I'm only here to check on you. Because I care about you."

Inna grumbled under her breath.

"Inna," Maya chided.

"Don't 'Inna' me," she said without looking up. She pretended to be absorbed in her catalogue and flipped another page. "You think I deserve what happened to me. And now you're waiting to see if I'll go crazy again."

"What a horrible thing to say!" Maya pulled the catalog out of her daughter's hands to force Inna to look at her. "I'm your mother! Is it a crime to worry?"

"There's no reason to worry. I'm fine," Inna said. "I'm going to be fine." Her pronouncement had the quality of a mantra.

"Who are you trying to convince?"

Inna pressed her lips together. Holding back her angry words made her tremble, but the effort pleased Maya.

"I don't want to fight with you," Inna said finally.

Maya counted the exchange a victory, a small step closer. She had despised her own mother. Was it so much to want Inna to love her?

"You look terrible," Maya said, studying her. She fretted over the dark smudges under Inna's eyes. "Maybe you should make an appointment with your psychiatrist."

Inna's gaze slid away from Maya back to the catalogue. She smoothed the page, one of a gold-crusted Fabergé egg. Maya could feel the furrows in her forehead deepening. Her child aged her so.

"I don't want to discuss this with you." Inna crossed her arms over her chest. Her elbows created sharp points that pulled and thinned the fabric of her sweater. So thin, so fragile, and yet she still mustered the will to defy her mother.

Maya might have admired her daughter's resilience if it didn't present such an obstacle.

Inna refused to confide in Maya—no matter how much Maya had fretted and worried and tried to help. With Dr. Shiffman permanently removed as confidante, Maya should finally stand a chance. Yet, Inna insisted on shutting her out.

Inna's gaze shifted to the door. Maya turned her head to see what had caught her eye. Artur stood in the doorway. Maya held her breath, waiting for her husband to scold her for questioning Inna.

"You should see your doctor," Artur echoed.

Inside, Maya smiled, gratified. So seldom did he take her side. Maybe they were turning their latest corner.

"You've been under a lot of stress," Maya said. "This isn't the time to play games with your care."

"You remember what it was like before," Artur said.

Inna flinched, likely remembering the episodes that had required she visit a shrink in the first place.

"Please, Inna. Don't make me worry," Artur said. "You need to take care of yourself."

"I am taking care of myself, Papa."

"She hasn't seen Dr. Kasporov in months," Maya said.

"How do you know that? I didn't tell you that," Inna said.

"He asked after you when I saw him at the grocery store," Maya said at the same time that Artur asked, "Are you seeing someone else? A different therapist?"

"No," Inna said. "I don't need him."

"Are you sure? Look at the way her hands are shaking," Maya told Artur. His tight nod confirmed that he also saw the danger signal.

Finally, after months of growing distance and disagreements, they were in accord. They were a team.

"Inna, are you taking your medicine?" Artur asked.

"Yes. Of course." Inna tucked her hands in her lap. "I'm not a child. You need to trust me to handle my own problems."

Predictably, Inna didn't want help, not even from Artur. The weight of the awful premonition Maya had described this morning hung in the room. She knew it haunted Artur, and she savored her power over him as the seed she had planted blossomed into distrust and worry.

"You will make an appointment with Dr. Kasporov," Artur decided.

How gratifying when a plan started to come together!

NICK

NICK'S PLAN WAS simple: bring Inna flowers, tell her he was sorry about what happened and that he felt responsible. Maybe she would agree to get a cup of coffee with him and talk about it. Maybe he could ease her into a tentative friendship.

Nick found Inna's number easily enough in the directory, but she didn't answer his call. Maybe she wasn't home. Maybe she had gone to work. Or maybe she didn't want to talk to him.

He stopped at the florist anyway and bought a modest mix of colorful flowers—nothing too romantic or over the top. This was a small gesture, an invitation.

She might not accept.

Katya had told him that Inna was a designer working out of Koslovsky Imports. Nick took the subway to Brighton Beach. As he walked the main drag, he passed a number of brightly colored shop fronts and more than a few pharmacies, including International Pharmacy. Wasn't that one of the businesses that Aleksei owned? The place was clean and brightly lit, a typical storefront with neatly stacked boxes of toiletries and vitamins.

Koslovsky Imports itself, another block down, was also rather unremarkable. In fact, Nick walked right past it the first time. It fit into the neighborhood, another shop with Russian-style trinkets made in China and "genuine" Fabergé eggs in the window. He supposed he shouldn't be surprised. Artur Gregorovich had been a KGB spy. He would specialize in fooling people that he fit in.

The bell rang when Nick opened the door, but no one appeared. The store seemed to be empty. He walked toward the back, past wooden tables and nostalgic oil paintings of horse-drawn sleds and churches with colorful onion domes.

As he neared the register, he heard voices.

"Inna, please. Don't make me worry."

Nick crept past the register and slipped through the door to the private offices. He followed the voices into a short corridor, passed an open office with desks and overhead fluorescent lights, and paused by another door, this one only slightly ajar.

He peered inside and found a scene so painfully familiar: Artur, older now, more distinguished, pleading with a dark-haired woman with almond-shaped eyes.

Suddenly he was eight years old again, hiding in the one bedroom in his mother's apartment while Artur by turn argued and wheedled with his mother. Some nights their arguments had ended in passionate kisses and others with his mother folded on the living room carpet, sobbing.

Then he had been only a child, too young to understand the argument, too small to take up his mother's cause.

Nick had wanted to hate Artur for making his mother cry. Yet, the man's sweet lies had turned in his direction. "We'll be a family, Kolya. Would you like that? We'll go to America together. I'll be your father."

At eight years old, he had been so hungry for affection. His grandparents had died in Siberia—thanks, he learned later, to Artur. Nick had missed his grandfather, his surrogate father, terribly.

Aunt Vera had been the only one to see through the lies, had known how Artur had already betrayed the family, how he merely toyed with Sofia, and how he would never leave his wife or keep his promises.

Artur had promised his mother the world—had promised them both the world—and delivered only death and loss.

Over the last twenty-five years, Nick had imagined Artur over and over. What he was doing. How Nick would bring him to justice.

Finally, he had found him. The man who killed his grandparents. Killed his mother. Killed his baby sister. Destroyed Nick's family.

He clenched his fists, almost crushing the flower stems in his hand.

Artur cupped the woman's face in his hands and bent so that his forehead touched hers. "Please, Inna. For me," he wheedled. "I love you beyond reason. Don't make me worry."

"I love you too, Papa."

Fury unfurled in Nick's chest. The man had stripped him of everyone he loved, even while soliciting Nick's affection. Nick had lost everyone. Everyone. Yet here was Artur all these years later, prosperous and doting on a daughter he adored, one who obviously loved him back. Inna couldn't be so much different in age than Nick's own baby sister would be now—had she lived.

KGB spy. Adulterer. Liar. Sociopath. Artur Gregorovich would pay for his crimes against Nick's family. Nick would find a way to expose him and strip him of all of the things he cared about.

"Step away from the door and put your hands up."

Nick did as instructed. He turned around to face a hulk of a man with a gun and an angry glare.

"Now tell me. Who the hell are you? And what are you doing back here?"

"I'm Nick Salvatore," he said. He stared at the gun. He hadn't expected one, but should have. Artur might seem on the surface like a successful businessman, but Nick had glimpsed the true monster underneath, a beast that might change its country but not its stripes. Of course Artur would be surrounded by guns and violence. Who was this man with the gun? Mafia? A spy?

Nick was only a lawyer. No match for physical force. No match for bullets. Maybe he was in over his head.

Rage and raw determination overrode fear or caution. Facing down the barrel of the gun, he forged ahead with his plan. "I'm here to see Inna."

The guy with the gun gave him a critical once over. His eyes lingered on the bouquet. "Do you have an appointment?"

"No," Nick said. "I'm not a client. Could you tell Inna that Nick's here?"

"Nick?" The dark-eyed woman promptly appeared in the hallway. Inna.

"What are you doing here?" she asked. Self-consciously, she ran her hands through her hair, tucked some loose strands behind her ear.

"I came to see how you were doing."

She seemed almost unearthly with her inky, wavy hair in its long ponytail and her pale skin and solemn eyes, so large in her delicate face. She was prettier than he had expected and somehow very familiar.

He wasn't a particularly spiritual man, but he had the sense their souls had met before.

Unprepared for the immediate emotional pull she had on him, he thrust the bouquet at her. She took the flowers as if they were precious. Her dark eyes seemed to drink him in. The mix of apprehension and hope he saw there made his heart stutter.

He suddenly wished he had something more to offer her than a bunch of wilting flowers wrapped in green cellophane.

"Who are you? How do you know Inna?" Artur joined them in the hallway and regarded Nick with edgy wariness. A blond woman with ice blue eyes peered at him from behind Artur's shoulder.

"This is Katya's friend," Inna said. She swallowed hard. "The one I was supposed to meet the other night at Troika."

"The blind date," the blond supplied.

"Ah," Artur said. There was an awkward pause. The guard crowded nearer, his gun in his hand, as if Inna needed protection from Nick and his flowers.

Inna's gaze darted to the gun. Nick caught the quick flicker of fear in her eyes. "Do you need to point that at him?"

Only when Artur nodded did the guard lower his weapon. He didn't holster it.

Inna licked her lips nervously and hugged her arms around herself as if she were cold. Every move she made spoke to Nick of fear and vulnerability.

"I heard about what happened... I was worried for you," he said.

"Thanks." Her eyes slid away, the momentary connection between them broken. The loss hit him like a physical ache.

Nick had no business being here or offering condolences, especially when all he wanted was to destroy Inna's father.

Yet this moment between them held the weight of destiny.

A fierce protectiveness surged in him. He recognized Inna as a good soul, an innocent victim like his mother, caught in Artur's machinations, tangled up in the sticky web of what Artur termed "love."

His resolve faltered. He couldn't use her, not the way he had planned, not at all. Nor could he let his family go unavenged. He couldn't abandon this vendetta that was so much a part of who he had become. To do so would be like cutting off his own arm or leg.

He wasn't ready to walk away—from her or from his revenge. Never in his life had he felt so conflicted and confused.

"Do you think we could talk?" Nick ventured. "Alone."

"No." The thug glowered at him. "Not alone."

Inna turned to Artur. "Papa, we're in the shop. It's safe here. Isn't it? Nick and I can talk in my office. With Vlad right outside. What could happen?"

Artur bent and kissed her temple, his affection for Inna evident and infuriating. "You're right."

VLAD

WITH ARTUR'S BLESSING, Inna ducked into her office with Nick. They left the door open a crack in deference to Vlad's role as bodyguard or perhaps, and more likely, to Artur's concerns for her safety.

"I'm taking Maya home," Artur said, code for he didn't want his wife out alone given the potential threat. "I'll be back in an hour. In the meantime, we'll close the shop."

Artur put up the closed sign and helped Maya into her coat. "I almost forgot. Igor said he has a delivery for us this afternoon."

Vlad could only guess at the nature of the delivery. Maybe this time he'd get a look inside the boxes Artur's contact delivered every weekend, usually when Vlad was away.

Artur and Maya left together. Vlad stationed himself by the door of Inna's office. He had no qualms about eavesdropping.

He didn't like the look of Inna's suitor or his timing. Nick had to be the same age as Vlad himself, several years older than Inna. Robbing the cradle—although Inna didn't seem to mind the age difference.

Age might be the only thing the two men had in common. Nick was fancy, a lawyer, who sat at a desk all day. His wavy hair had been cut at a salon, not buzzed at the barber's. His hands were soft and manicured, his fingertips unmarked by the stain of gunpowder. He had a cashmere coat and elegant Italian loafers that hadn't sloshed through blood while dragging dead bodies through darkened alleys.

A heavy feeling settled in Vlad's chest. He had nothing to offer Inna. Other than his guns. She deserved so much more than the violence and deception he brought in his wake.

Not for me. Not for me.

Inna didn't want Vlad around. She clearly didn't relish the idea of having a bodyguard, and she liked his guns even less.

Regardless of what or whom she wanted, he would do his best to keep her safe. Both of their futures depended on it.

Becoming Inna's bodyguard for the foreseeable future represented its own kind of torture. Vlad wanted her, had wanted her from the moment he'd seen her three months ago, all grown up and working at Koslovsky Imports, a hint of interest in her eyes. He'd shut down her shy advance, knowing it was the right thing to do. His fascination with her was inappropriate on so many levels. Yet, she regularly invaded his thoughts when they were apart—and Artur often kept them apart.

Now they would be spending so much time together. Every waking minute. Night and day.

He leaned his head back against the wall and stifled a groan. He couldn't lie to himself. He wasn't noble or a gentleman. If those brown eyes so much as looked with any spark of interest in his direction again, he wouldn't resist, wouldn't show restraint, wouldn't make himself step aside for her own good—even if being with her violated every rule.

Even a threat from Artur wouldn't be enough to hold back his instinct to fight, win, and claim.

Lucky for her, she wasn't interested anymore. Not even a little.

Vlad didn't deserve her. Nick didn't either. There was something duplicitous about Nick. Vlad could tell the man had another agenda. His gaze on Inna was too intense. He wanted something. What?

Listening to their conversation yielded little information. Stops and starts. Awkward pauses. Not an auspicious start to a romance. Perhaps not a start at all.

"So, um, could I... Do you think you would like..." Romeo had lost command of his silver tongue. "What I mean is that... Do you think we could get together—coffee or dinner? Your choice."

Inna politely demurred, and for a moment, Vlad wanted to crow, even though he had no call to gloat. Nick had exchanged more words with Inna in these few minutes than Vlad had in a few months, and she hadn't agreed to coffee or dinner with Vlad, either. Not that he had asked. Not that she gave any indication she would accept—after three months of his giving her the cold shoulder.

"No pressure," Nick said. "I know the timing's bad. But it's just… I'd really like to get to know you. I feel like we have a connection. Like this could be important."

The words could have come from Vlad's own mouth, except that he would never have promised not to pressure her. He only lied when he had to.

Vlad didn't hear Inna's response. Nick came out of the office a moment later, his expression wistful and slightly bemused. Had she agreed to meet him again?

"The door's locked. I'll see you out," Vlad said.

He led Nick to the front of the store, did a quick check of the street, and then unlocked the door to let him out, hoping he, and especially Inna, would never see the fancy lawyer again. He watched Nick stroll out of the store as if in a daze and locked the door behind him.

When he turned around, he found Inna standing behind the register, her elbow on the counter, chin in her hand.

"Are you going to see him again?" To his own ears, he sounded like his father, jealous and possessive. Inna merely shrugged, but Vlad sensed a restless energy in her.

"Who knows? Kind of hard to date when a girl has a bodyguard."

"I'm not trying to make your life difficult."

"Didn't say you were."

There was a rap at the front door. Vlad turned to see a man in black slacks and a black polo shirt. He held a large cardboard box in his hands. His cap was pulled down so that Vlad couldn't see the man's eyes. "You recognize him?" he asked Inna.

"You can let him in. That's Igor. He usually makes deliveries on Sundays."

Vlad approached the door cautiously, hand on his gun.

"Not everyone's a threat," she scolded, sweetly naive.

She hadn't seen the things that Vlad had.

He paused at the door. The name sewn onto the deliveryman's breast read "Igor." Inna seemed to know him. The delivery was expected. The man raised his head, met Vlad's gaze, frowned impatiently as if the box he held were heavy.

Vlad unlocked the door. The man turned sideways to bring the box inside and tripped over the threshold. He lost his grip of the box and fumbled to recover it. Reflexively, Vlad reached out to catch it.

That's when he felt the jolt on his arm. A stun gun. The buzzing zap knocked him off his feet.

He fell face down on the box. The deliveryman followed him down, giving him a long dose of voltage. His entire body erupted with pain, a thousand needles pricking his skin, as he lost control of his limbs. He spasmed uncontrollably.

"Vlad!" Inna shouted.

"Run!" he wanted to yell, but he couldn't even speak.

EPISODE #3

MAYA

EARLY RETIREMENT? ALEKSEI'S plan for his sleazy head pharmacist had merit, Maya admitted, except for one significant detail: Murder required a certain finesse and skill that Aleksei lacked.

Her son was no killer.

She zipped the backpack, careful not to touch the neatly bound stacks of money it contained. Certainly Aleksei would be upset that she was interfering, but what choice did she have?

Her conscience gave no objection—not that she expected one. After all, she couldn't sit by and do nothing. Stan would surely go running to the police with everything he knew, every damning bit of information, if he wasn't silenced—one way or another.

It was a mother's prerogative—wasn't it?—to keep her children safe and protect her own interests, too.

She hefted the backpack onto one shoulder and sneaked out the back door from the basement. Through the back window, she could see the light in Artur's study.

As usual, her cautious husband stood away from the window. She couldn't see him, but she imagined him in his office with Victor, absorbed, as always, in Directorate business.

It wasn't the first or the last time she would sneak out under the cover of his distraction. She knew about his double life, but he had no clue about hers.

He could never know.

The wet wind whipped her blond hair, and she pushed it out of her face with gloved hands. She wouldn't remove the gloves until after the money had been safely delivered and received.

Adept at evading Artur's surveillance cameras, Maya stuck to the shadows. Keeping close to the bushes, she darted across the yard to the front of the property and then slipped into the side door of the garage. She pulled the drape from the sleek, black Ducati that Aleksei stored there.

Aleksei's helmet hung from the front handle of the motorcycle. Maya curled her hair around her fist, stuffed it into the helmet, and secured the buckle under her chin. The front visor covered her face. She pulled his leather jacket from the peg nearby and zipped it up to the collar.

Covered in black, she might pass for a man. She wasn't sure. But it didn't matter so long as no one recognized her.

Who would? No one expected Maya with her perfect lipstick, her neatly combed hair, her ladylike chain of pearls, and her fur collars to ride around town on a crotch rocket.

People only saw what they expected to see and looked no further.

She rolled the Ducati out of the garage, careful not to make a sound that might alert Artur. The events of the past few days had made him cautious and overly protective, not only of Inna, but also of her. He worried the Georgians were out for blood. He didn't want them going out alone.

She had no need of his gilded cage. Georgians or no Georgians, she could take care of herself.

She carefully scanned the area. Seeing no signs of anyone watching her house, she walked the motorcycle to the next yard and then mounted with a practiced motion. She eased both arms into the straps of the backpack.

The bag was lighter than she would have liked. There weren't nearly enough bills to meet the entire blackmail demand, but she had added plenty of sweetener to this pot—enough, she hoped, to satisfy Stan for good.

Men's natures were greedy. If you gave them something, they only came back asking for more and then even more, until they milked you dry or you got the upper hand. With Stan, she would get the upper hand.

The wind picked up and tossed droplets of rain at her. They penetrated the legs of her jeans, making her skin cold.

She checked her mirrors. Twilight cast the street in gray and shadows. She looked hard into them, but she didn't discern any unusual shapes or, perhaps more importantly, movement. She listened to her senses, trusting in the sharply honed instincts that had aided her schemes so far.

No pings of warning came to her. No gooseflesh on her arms. No one was following her. Or watching.

She revved the motorcycle. Excitement pulsed through her veins, compounded by the aggressive rumble of the bike between her thighs. Her own unadulterated sense of power gave her a heady sensation.

Tonight she had a perfect plan, and she fully expected to get away with murder.

She left her ritzy street with the big houses that looked out onto the water and headed across town to the grittier neighborhood, full of dirty apartment buildings and post-war houses dressed in worn vinyl siding.

The neighborhood here could be a little rough. She stayed alert. If anyone discovered she had a backpack stuffed with cash, she'd be an open target.

Maya wasn't worried. She was the biggest threat here.

She parked the Ducati across the street from Stan's house, a small blue cape with chipped siding. The drizzle continued unabated. She kept the helmet on and hurried across the street. Despite the weight of the backpack, she ran lightly up Stan's sunken front stairs and rang the doorbell.

The wood on his porch was peeling and warped, and the front knocker was speckled with rust. If the drug trade had been good for

Stan, his house certainly didn't show it. Stan was smart that way. It was
the only thing she admired about him. Yet, his little nugget of
intelligence hadn't been enough to prevent his latest stupidity.

Did he really think he could blackmail a Koslovsky and get away
with it?

Faintly, she heard the sound of heavy footsteps. She knew Stan had
arrived behind the door. She rapped with the rusted knocker.

Stan was likely staring through the peephole and trying to discern
who was there. She wore Aleksei's helmet, but she was too petite to pass
for her son.

She waited with an almost giddy sense of excitement. Everything
would go according to plan. She was fully in control.

Finally, the door swung open to reveal a meaty arm and a gun.
"What do you want?"

"It's raining. Can I come in? I've got your money," she said.

"Maya?" His surprise turned quickly to what sounded like gloating.
"So the tough guy went crying to Mommy after all."

He stepped aside to let her in but didn't lower his gun. He was a vile
man with a halo of frizzy hair and pointy yellow teeth. His belly strained
the buttons on his shirt.

She stepped into the dark hallway of his home. Stan shut and locked
the door behind her. He took care to turn the deadbolt and fasten the
chain across the door, oblivious to the danger she presented.

As her eyes adjusted to the dark, she noticed two large suitcases in
the hallway. So Stan was serious about leaving town, after all.

She would make sure he never came back.

"Let's see what you've got." He nudged her with the point of his gun
down the hall.

"There's no need for that. I brought what you asked for," she said.

"We'll see." He jabbed the gun into her side. Perhaps he wasn't so
oblivious, after all.

He pushed her roughly into his kitchen, a dated room with chipped and crooked dark wood cabinets and a scratched and faded yellow and white linoleum floor. The stale air stank of cigar smoke.

He yanked the backpack from her shoulder and hefted it in his hand. Then he snorted with disgust. "Do I look like I was born yesterday?"

He dropped the backpack on the table with a loud thunk. "No way there's a million dollars in there."

"Open it," she invited, almost breathless with anticipation. "There's more than cash inside."

She clasped her gloved hands together. She could see in her mind how the whole scene would play out. In but a moment, he would tear open the backpack and start counting the money, holding the wads of cash in his greedy hands, touching each individual bill.

"Yeah?" He tugged at the zipper with one hand.

When the bag didn't open immediately, Stan laid his pistol on the table. Maya felt the slow, satisfying burn of contempt as he surrendered his weapon to his own greed and impatience.

Men were so predictable.

Using both hands now, Stan ripped the zipper open. Maya held her breath as he pulled the first stack of neatly bundled bills from the backpack.

He held the money in his hand for the briefest moment, not nearly long enough. Then he tossed the stack aside. He grabbed another and then another.

Stan pawed through the bag, piling the money on the table. Soon he grew impatient and dumped the entire contents out.

He was too quick to discard and dismiss her offering. He didn't hold the money for any significant length of time or rifle through it the way she had imagined.

The velvet jeweler's cases she'd packed at the bottom of the sack tumbled out. He snatched one of the boxes, opened it, and scowled at the necklace inside. "Did you think you could trick me? Where's the rest?"

"That's a valuable piece," she said. "Four carats."

"Was this Aleksei's idea or yours? You think you don't need to take me seriously? I'm serious as a heart attack. I'll tell the cops everything."

"Most of the value's in the diamonds," she said quickly and held her hands up, not wanting his anger to escalate and provoke him to something stupid like calling the cops.

She needed a little more time for her plan to come to fruition. He hadn't succumbed to her enticement yet, but she had faith he would.

"Between the bills and the value of the diamonds, there's more than a million dollars there," she said. She could tell he wanted to believe her. "Count it."

Touch the money. Just touch the damn money.

"If you're lying to me, I'll make sure the cops learn your part in all of this." He picked up one of the wads of cash, and Maya almost sighed with relief as he began counting bills.

In mere moments, Stan would be dead before he could tell anyone anything.

"It's all there. Just like you asked." She soothed him with the words she thought he wanted to hear. "I just want you to leave us alone. I want this whole thing to be over."

Suddenly, two men burst into the kitchen from the back door. Before Stan could react, one of the intruders threw a knife. The long blade arced through the air. It sliced through the back of Stan's fleshy hand, wedged into the wooden tabletop, and pinned his hand to the table next to his handgun.

Stan howled wildly with pain. Maya sprinted for the hallway and escape.

She flew to the front door and threw the deadbolt. Before she could work the chain, one of the men grabbed her by the arm. He twisted it behind her back. He jabbed her in the back with a blunt, heavy object. A gun, no doubt.

She glanced back at him. He had an eyepatch and a long nasty scar on his cheek. He didn't speak or threaten. The gun at her back did that well enough. He hustled her back into the kitchen.

"Got her," he told his associate, and she had her first good look at the man with the knives.

Dressed in a leather overcoat and tall boots, he looked rough and wild. His curly hair hung to his shoulders. He sneered at her, revealing a mouth full of even, gold teeth. He pointed his second long blade at her. "What have we got here?"

She knew who he was by reputation. Dato Dzugashvili, the head of the Georgian mafia in Brighton Beach, a boogeyman whose name her son would only whisper, a man famous for carving his victims to pieces.

His knife glinted in the kitchen's yellow light as he limped toward her. She could scarcely breathe. He was so much more terrifying than she had credited.

The gunman's grip on her arm tightened as if he imagined she might bolt, but she couldn't run, couldn't move. His hold on her arm was the only thing keeping her upright.

Dato grabbed her chin in his hand. He pressed the cold metal of the knife against her skin and caressed her neck with the flat side. She whimpered—or maybe that was Stan.

She shut her eyes and braced herself for a slash of pain. There was a pause, but the cut didn't come.

She opened her eyes again to find Dato appraising her. He flicked the knife and cut the strap of her helmet. He pulled it roughly from her head and dropped it to the floor.

"Ah," he said as her hair tumbled out and fell around her shoulders. "Mrs. Koslovsky. I did not expect to make your acquaintance…here."

He smiled with malice, and a cold, slithering fear coiled around her. "It's going to be a good night for vengeance."

He turned toward Stan and slashed the air with his knife. Stan moaned. A dark, wet splotch spread out across the front of his slacks. The sickly scent of urine wafted from him.

"A very good night," Dato laughed.

INNA

DEPRESSION SETTLED OVER Inna as she said good-bye to Nick. He pressed his lips together, saying nothing but speaking plenty with his large, soulful eyes. *Don't do this. Give me a chance.* He had the restraint, or perhaps the self-respect, not to ask her again. With deliberate care, he negotiated a path past the ornate displays of antique tables with delicate tea sets and figurines. He kept glancing at her over his shoulder, as if he couldn't get enough of seeing her, as if he were truly interested despite the events of the past few days, as if she might call him back and change her mind.

She was sorely tempted. He seemed genuinely kind and caring, with his gentle manner and his low voice, a "good one", like Katya had promised. She liked the look of him too, the dark wavy hair and boldly ethnic features, the rangy athlete's body.

She dared wonder how things might be different if he had been on time for their date, if they had managed to meet and talk, if Vlad weren't now standing in the front of the store with his hand on his gun.

Vlad locked the door as soon as Nick was through—locking Nick out or locking her in?

Through the shop's glass door, her gaze lingered on him, on the possibilities she had rejected. Nick's cashmere coat flapped in the growing wind as he crossed the street, putting distance between himself and her. *Run!* She wanted to warn him to get as far away from her as fast as possible, to go and not look back.

She wanted to get away herself.

Her father just happened to have an employee—two, if she counted Mikhail—who could be called upon to play bodyguard for her at a moment's notice. Vlad just happened to be armed and ready with a gun and willing to use it on anyone without hesitation. What kind of business was her father involved in? Was that the reason someone was out to get her?

No. Don't go there. Don't even think it.

Paranoid thoughts buzzed through her brain, and she tried to swat them away. She'd listened to those thoughts and been stung on more than one occasion.

The anxiety would subside. She wouldn't slide into that awful, dark place. She could let the frightened feelings pass, observe the nervous thoughts, and let them go. She shouldn't credit them, shouldn't give them any power. Not like she had before.

She leaned heavily on the wooden counter behind the cash register. She pressed herself against the solid surface and hoped it would absorb the nervous tremors that hadn't stopped surging through her body since she'd awakened this morning.

Breathe in. Breathe out. Breathe in. Breathe out.

She'd been through an ordeal the last few days. This shaking was perfectly normal for someone in her situation. Right?

Vlad spun around. His face was impassive, but she imagined she could feel the heat in his gaze.

Her heart beat even faster as she observed him. Big and imposing, he bore hardly any resemblance to the sensitive and scrawny man-boy she'd worshipped as a child. He was all man now.

She had definitely noticed. She couldn't help but notice, much as she tried not to. She'd had such a crush on him when she was a little girl. When he'd suddenly reappeared in Brighton Beach, the small tug on her heart was still there. The feeling had surprised her. She never thought about romance. She had no desire to date or have a boyfriend—not after what had happened to her in college.

But Vlad's return had awakened a spark she hadn't known was there. Sometimes she thought she saw the same spark—maybe even more than a spark—of interest in his eyes. But that wasn't possible.

He had rejected her soundly. He had greeted her invitation to dinner with three little words enunciated in a way that still cut to the core. "Sorry. Not interested."

Still, the magic had happened. She had feelings she hadn't expected. Maybe, just maybe, after a long dormancy, she was finally ready to move forward with the next phase of her life. Finding a man. Starting a family.

Nick was supposed to be the answer to that prayer.

"Are you going to see him again?" Vlad asked.

To her ears, he sounded jealous. She doubted her senses. She imagined she felt the flame of his attraction for her. Even now, when she knew it was impossible. Even now, when the tightness of her nerves should have shut off any fantasies of them together.

"Who knows?" Her voice didn't crack. It sounded strong, not reedy. Emboldened by her acting achievement, she added, "Kind of hard to date when a girl has a bodyguard."

"I'm not trying to make your life difficult."

"Didn't say you were," she said with pitch-perfect nonchalance.

A tap on the glass startled her. A sense of impending disaster grabbed her by the throat. Something terrible was about to happen. They were about to be attacked.

Breathe in. Breathe out.

The worries weren't real. None of it was real.

It was a normal, blustery evening in Brighton Beach, nearly dark now. The streetlights fought the glowing gloom. The deliveryman stood under the awning to the shop with a large cardboard box in his hand.

She shouldn't be so fearful, but her heart pounded now as if she were being pursued.

"You recognize him?" Vlad asked.

For a moment, she considered voicing her fear. But it made no sense. She couldn't see Igor's face under his baseball cap, but she recognized his solid build, his uniform with the black collared shirt, the white truck parked out front behind him. It was the right time. The right day.

She had to let go of her fear. She couldn't let Vlad see what a wreck she was. Not when Dr. Shiffman was dead and her parents were colluding to send her back to Dr. Kasparov, whose answer to everything was pills that dulled her senses and stole her sense of self.

"You can let him in. That's Igor. He usually makes deliveries on Sundays."

Vlad hesitated. Igor shifted from foot to foot as if the box he held were heavy in his arms, but she imagined something was off. Where was the puff of his breath in the cold air? The stooped strain in his shoulders? Why was he standing in the middle of the doorway and not balancing the box against the wall while he waited? Her instinct, which she'd learned not to trust at all, told her the box couldn't possibly be that heavy.

She'd been so wrong about so many things before. *Papa wasn't a spy.*

"Not everyone's a threat," she said, scolding herself, even as her anxiety ratcheted up another notch.

Vlad moved with deliberate caution, one hand hovering over his gun, as he opened the door. She waited for Igor's hearty salute, but it didn't come.

Why didn't Igor say anything? Was the package really so heavy this time? He was usually chatty, greeting her warmly and sharing a joke or silly story about one of his kids. She had put aside a bottle of Georgian wine, after learning last time that it was his favorite. She should go and get it for him now.

She clutched the counter, immobilized by her irrational fear. She pressed her eyes closed against the icy wave of doom crashing over her. *Breathe in. Breathe out.*

There was an unexpected buzzing sound. Her eyes flew open in time to see Igor drop the box and prod Vlad with a small black device.

Vlad's body jolted.

"Vlad!" she shouted. His body jerked and spasmed. He fell face down on the box, which collapsed beneath his weight.

Empty. The box was empty!

The deliveryman's hat had been pulled low over his face, but when he looked in her direction, she could see he wasn't Igor.

She wasn't paranoid or hallucinating. Not now anyway.

The deliveryman stepped over Vlad's twitching body and advanced toward her. The tables and displays in the small shop blocked his path and created an obstacle course that bought her a few extra seconds at most.

He held what looked like a cell phone, but Inna had just witnessed the way the small device had dropped a big man like Vlad to the floor.

Trembling, she kicked the panic button under the counter with her foot. How long would it take the police to arrive? Five minutes? Ten?

They'd never had a problem in the store before, but Olga, who worked the floor during the week, believed in caution. She claimed she kept a gun hidden underneath the register. Inna blindly felt her hand along the shelf.

Sweat beaded on her forehead. No amount of anti-anxiety medication would make this latest problem disappear.

Maybe she had never really been paranoid.

Her intruder closed in quickly. She couldn't let him get close enough to zap her. Where was the damn gun? Olga would have put it somewhere in easy reach. Inna pictured the heavyset woman with her enormous glasses taped together at the bridge and the silver duct-tape handbag she proudly carried everywhere. Olga had a crazy love affair with duct tape, which she claimed could be used to fix or make almost anything. *Duct tape!*

Inna patted her hand along the wooden shelf and then turned her palm over and skimmed her hand along the underside of the counter. There!

Olga, the duct-tape McGyver, had secured the gun to the counter with a criss-cross of durable sticky stuff. Inna yanked on the gun. The tape reluctantly tore away from the counter. The bands of tape hung from the gun's barrel, but Inna didn't strip them away. She had no time. He was too close.

"Stay where you are!" she yelled. She struggled to hold the gun in her unsteady hands. The sight of the gun brought the man up short. He paused only a foot from the counter.

"Put zat down and I von't hurt you." He spoke with a heavy Russian accent.

"What do you want?" *Keep him talking.* Less than a minute had passed since he had disabled Vlad. Four more seemed like an eternity for stalling him. "Where's Igor?"

She knew nothing about guns. She had touched one, held it in her hand, for the first time two nights ago, when this whole nightmare had started. Until that moment, guns had been part of a different world— crime dramas on TV and action films—that had nothing to do with her real life.

She had never shot anyone, at least not that she remembered. She still didn't know whether she was responsible for killing the man who had raped her, although Detective Hersh clearly hadn't thought so.

She didn't know if the gun was loaded. Or if she could hit a target even if she tried.

"I von't hurt you," he said again. "We just go for leettle ride." He took a step forward.

"Stay where you are!"

By the door, Vlad groaned. Her eyes darted in his direction, and in that moment the intruder rushed toward her. She squeezed the trigger.

A loud explosion shot from the gun, and an antique chandelier over one of the display tables shattered.

The recoil threw her back. The gun pinched her thumb and sent a surprising shock of pain into her hand. She fumbled the pistol and dropped it.

The intruder rushed around the counter.

She scrambled, grabbed the gun, and squeezed the trigger. Her heart beat wildly in her chest. She snapped the trigger again and again in quick succession until a bullet hit his leg and he stumbled and fell down.

His cell-phone stun gun dropped from his hand and skittered across the floor.

"You fucking beetch," he swore. He cradled his leg, and she kept the gun trained on him.

"Drop gun!" a new voice yelled from the doorway.

Another Russian man, also dressed in a black delivery uniform, entered the shop. This one had a gun. Inna bet he was a much better shot than she.

The second intruder pointed his gun at Vlad's prone body. Vlad groaned again. She could barely swallow against her fear for him. He was vulnerable, utterly defenseless. She wasn't a good enough shot to fight both intruders off with whatever bullets were left and save Vlad.

Knowing he had her attention, the man said, "Put down gun and come vit me, or I shoot him dead."

She believed him.

Hands shaking and cold, she slid her gun onto the counter.

NICK

NICK SAT IN the coffee shop across the street from Koslovsky Imports and struggled to regroup and recover from the tangle of emotions Inna evoked, the deep yearning, the bone-deep conflict.

He didn't understand the immediate connection he felt with her, a connection he had no business feeling.

Nick's whole life had been molded by Artur's betrayal. He had grown up in the shadow of loss, a grieving that never ended for the family he had lost and a childhood crippled by the gnawing fear that Mimi and he would be sent back to Russia if anyone discovered their deception.

He had finally found Artur Gregorovich after all of these years. Justice was in his reach. He would see Artur exposed for the monster he was and brought to justice in the country that had unknowingly embraced the man and his pretty lies, as Nick's mother had.

But what about Inna? With only one look, she had slipped past all of his defenses and touched his soul.

He couldn't use her to ruin her own father. He couldn't walk away from her either.

She had tried, politely, to send him away. *Thank you, but ...* But what? Surely she couldn't have looked into his eyes and found him wanting. Not when his feelings for her were so strong and overwhelming. Didn't she feel their connection, too?

Inna had been through a lot in the last few days. A better man would respect her wishes, give her space. Yet, his whole heart rebelled at the thought of abandoning her to her evil father and the menacing goon with a gun.

Did Inna have any clue who her father really was or how he ruined innocent lives?

Nick didn't have to stretch his imagination to think that what had happened to Inna the other night at the nightclub was related to her father's crimes. She was the latest casualty, another good person hurt in the wake of Gregorovich's deceit.

I love you, too, Papa, he had heard her say. How could she love such a monster? She couldn't possibly know the truth. Gregorovich undoubtedly kept her in the dark, deceiving her the way he'd deceived Nick's mother.

He glanced in the direction of Koslovsky Imports, his thoughts full of Inna and her beautiful dark hair and soulful eyes. And there she was. In the street. In the drizzling rain without a coat. Without her formidable bodyguard.

She was walking to the back of a delivery truck next to a man in a black uniform. He couldn't see what was happening clearly, but the scene struck him as wrong. He couldn't say how, but he knew. With every fiber of his being, he knew. Inna was in trouble. Not sparing the time to grab his coat, he dashed for the door.

"Call the police," he instructed the cashier. Then he sprinted into the street, dodging past cars.

He saw the gun in the man's hand as he approached.

Nick was fit, but from running, not body building. He had never been a fighter, not physically anyway. The kidnapper outweighed him by a good thirty pounds.

None of that mattered or gave Nick a moment's pause. There was no room for doubt, only one thought in his head—*save her!*

He launched himself at the man from behind and jumped onto his back. He wrapped one arm around the man's neck in a chokehold. Inna tried to pull away from her kidnapper, but the man jerked her arm hard. She gasped as her kidnapper pulled her up against him.

Trying to throw Nick off, the man raised his gun. Nick grabbed the barrel and wrestled for control of the weapon.

Spectators huddled together under the shop awnings on the street. No one rushed to their aid. He supposed that was the way among the Russians. No one had helped his grandparents in their time of need, either.

Inna jabbed her captor with her elbow. She kicked and flailed. The man couldn't fight them both, and she wrestled herself free.

"Run!" Nick yelled.

The kidnapper fired in his direction, but missed. The car window behind Nick shattered.

Nick clamped his hand even tighter around the gun, determined to keep the man from taking aim again.

Inna didn't run. She came into close range.

"Run!" he shouted at her again. But she didn't run.

She screamed for help that didn't come and added her hands to the fight for the gun. Nick's heart pounded with fear for her.

The kidnapper kicked at Inna. She grunted with pain but only tried harder to wrench the gun free.

Nick refused to suffer another loss on Artur's doorstep. He squeezed his forearm against the kidnapper's throat, ready to snap his spinal column or cut off his air supply. Ready to kill with his bare hands.

Drizzled rain poked like little needles onto his back and shoulders as they struggled with the kidnapper to gain control of the gun. He could feel the muscles in the man's throat straining against his forearm as he squeezed. Their hands were slick from the rain, and the assailant's grip was weakening. Still, the bastard clung to his pistol.

Inna kneed the kidnapper in the groin. The man's body folded as he curled inward from the blow with Nick still on his back.

He had his first glimmer of hope. The bad guy was going down. They'd get the gun. Inna would be safe.

There was a loud pop as the gun fired unexpectedly. Pain exploded in Nick's shoulder. Inna screamed his name.

Another set of hands grabbed him. Ripped him from the kidnapper's back. Threw him to the ground. The impact as his head hit the wet cement blinded him with pain.

"Nick!" Inna screamed. Her terror sliced him to the bone. He had to do something. He had to save her. He struggled to get up, and the world went black.

VLAD

THE STUN GUN hadn't dampened Vlad's awareness. His body rioted with pain that dissipated slowly. He heard the gunshots in the shop and the threats designed to gain Inna's compliance.

Vlad couldn't control his muscles enough to crane his neck so that he could see Inna, but he heard the *thunk* of her gun as she placed it on the counter and the soft sound of her footsteps. She walked straight into the arms of a kidnapper to save him.

Get up. Get up! Don't let him hurt her.

Vlad struggled to gain his feet and failed. The shock from the stun gun had scrambled his muscle control. He couldn't make his hands and legs move.

"Be a good girl. That's right," the kidnapper said.

Vlad raged against his own helplessness. Time seemed to warp, and he was back in another scene, twenty years ago, the past and the present in an eerie sympathy with one another.

"Be a good girl, Nadia. Tell me," Ivan said, voice low and threatening. When she didn't answer immediately, he backed her up against the wall, the steps to their passionate dance familiar and achingly wrong.

No matter how many times Ivan hurt her and Vlad or how many months passed, she always took him back, inviting him into the apartment, into her arms, into her bed.

Vlad hated Ivan.

Ivan's bare arms caged her. Dark tattoos of daggers and crosses flexed as he leaned in close. "Who was he? Who was that man you were talking to?"

"No one. He was no one," Nadia said quietly.

Maybe she thought she could placate Ivan, but Vlad knew better. He had seen the devil in his father's eyes tonight and caught the unmistakable scent of liquor on his breath, long before Ivan had starting pouring shots for himself from the bottle on the table.

"Leave her alone." Vlad's voice started with the power of a man's and ended with the sound of a squeaky child's. Ivan didn't even spare him a glance.

"Who was he?" Ivan grabbed Nadia by the shoulders and shook her hard. "Tell me. Tell me!" When she didn't answer, Ivan smacked her across the cheek.

Vlad felt the blow in his own body. "Get your hands off of her!"

He charged Ivan. He threw himself against his father with all of his strength.

Ivan flicked him off as if the whole of his weight and anger were a mere nuisance. With the barest flex of his arm, Ivan threw him flying across the small room.

Vlad landed hard on his back and jumped to his feet.

"I'm sorry," Nadia sobbed. Was she apologizing for herself or for Vlad? She cowered against the wall, arms raised in a hopeless attempt to fend Ivan off.

"I'll make you sorry." Ivan rained blows on her small body. "You talk to no one. No other man. Only me. Only me!"

"Leave her alone!" Vlad was going to make the bastard stop, make him pay. He looked around for something—anything—harder than his fists.

"Say it!" Ivan demanded, ignoring him.

"Only you," she choked.

He grabbed a wooden chair and rushed Ivan.

"Vlad, no!" Nadia pleaded. Pleaded with him, not with his abusive old man. "He'll kill you!"

He couldn't stop. Wouldn't stop. They'd suffered too much at Ivan's hands. Tonight, it would end one way or another.

He swung the chair with all his might and landed a blow that only made Ivan grunt.

Not hard enough. Not strong enough.

With one hand, Ivan snapped the leg off of the chair and swung. Vlad ducked and blocked the blows with the chair until Ivan cracked the leg against his knuckles and wrested the broken chair out of his grip.

Ivan pounded him hard with the chair leg. He slammed it against Vlad's legs and knocked him off balance.

"You worthless weakling." Ivan hit him on all sides with the stick, until he couldn't stand, until he could hardly breathe for the pain in his ribs. Ivan smacked him hard across the head. The chair leg broke in Ivan's hand.

"Hard-headed like me." He heard Ivan laugh. His father's voice sounded far away. "Get this lesson through your hard head. When you take on the Devil, be sure you can win."

Unconsciousness beckoned. Vlad refused to close his eyes and give in.

"Please, Ivan. Leave him alone," Nadia begged.

"I'll kill anyone who tries to take you from me. Even your son." Ivan kicked him in the side with his steel-toe boot.

"I love you, Ivan. Only you."

"That's right. Tell him he's nothing." Ivan crossed the room, returning to Nadia in a matter of steps, like loud drumbeats. "You're mine. You'll always be mine. Only mine. Say it!"

He couldn't let Ivan hurt his mother. Tonight, between the alcohol and the jealousy, Ivan might kill her, especially if Ivan learned the man she'd gone to see was a detective with the Brooklyn police.

He rolled onto his stomach. Each breath was agony. He panted with the effort to draw his knees beneath him.

He crawled closer to the table. Wincing with pain, he reached for the coffee table to lever himself up.

His hand encountered the vodka bottle, lying on its side. He closed his fist around the cool glass and cracked it against the table. The end broke away, leaving a jagged weapon in his hand.

Using the coffee table for support, Vlad struggled to push himself up. Half-blind with pain and desperation, he commanded his limbs into position, told them to stand.

They refused to obey. The salty taste of blood filled his mouth.

Nadia shrieked as Ivan grabbed her by the arms and shook her. The sound of her suffering tapped some reserve deep inside of Vlad.

Then, as now, Vlad climbed to his feet.

He heard a single shot and staggered to the door, his movements jerky and uncoordinated. *Please don't let her be hurt. Please don't let it be too late.*

"Nick!" Inna yelled, as if in answer to his prayer. She was alive.

Vlad's vision sharpened. Through the glass, he saw the two intruders forcing her into the back of the delivery truck. He reached for one of his guns.

Though the move should have been smooth after so many years of practice, his disorientation made him falter. He pulled the gun from its holster with a jerky motion. A wave of dizziness threatened to take him down again.

He balanced himself against the wall, borrowing its steadiness as he opened the door. The overhead bell tinkled, but the kidnappers, intent on forcing Inna into the truck, didn't seem to notice.

He pointed at his target but took a long, deep breath before squeezing the trigger. He hadn't recovered yet from the scramble to his senses. He couldn't afford to miss and hit Inna.

He couldn't let those men take her either.

ARTUR

VICTOR WAS WAITING in their driveway when Artur returned home with Maya. Judging by the pile of butts at his feet, he had been here a while, leaning on the hood of his car and chain smoking. Artur braced himself for bad news.

Victor didn't say a word. He'd given a surly nod to Maya and then closeted himself with Artur in the study. Artur watched his friend pace back and forth over the silk Oriental.

"What is it, Victor?" he prodded. The sooner he got rid of Victor, the sooner he could attend to his own business. He had told Vlad he would return to Koslovsky Imports within the hour, and he still had several more arrangements to make.

Victor checked his watch and frowned. Was he stalling? Or was he in a hurry?

"I met with the messenger," Victor said.

By "messenger," Victor no doubt meant the emissary from the Directorate, although Artur wouldn't have risked the assumption that their bosses had sent a mere errand boy to oversee the latest operation. There was far too much at stake if their dealings were exposed—a fact Artur was counting on.

The Directorate was full of clever men. Someone else had surely seen the vulnerability in this newest operation and sought to contain it.

"He doesn't want any trouble with the Georgians."

"Too late for that," Artur said. "Did he also say he wanted world peace and an end to global warming? Do I look like a miracle worker?"

"You don't have to go after them."

"What do you think this is, Victor? A meeting of the Politburo? How do you think things work in Brighton Beach?"

"There are bigger things to consider than your dispute."

"My dispute?" Artur snorted with disgust. He had humored Victor's stubborn naivete long enough. The man's deliberate tone deafness was fast becoming a liability. Victor insisted on clinging to the old rules, despite living in a new country and with a new world order. He refused to understand that power didn't flow the same way without a government monopoly or that his rank in a secret government organization wasn't enough to make people revere him the way they had in the former Soviet police state.

Artur rose. He braced his hands on his desk and leaned, looking down at Victor, his supposed superior in the Directorate.

"Listen to me, Victor. There is only one rule here. One rule that matters: If anyone strikes at you, you strike back twice as hard. That's how you get power. That's how you keep it."

"What are you saying? You're declaring war on them?"

By "them" Victor undoubtedly meant the Georgians, but Artur had other potential targets. The Directorate for one. His own son for another.

"They declared war when they tried to hurt Inna. They tried to kidnap her this morning."

"This morning?" Victor asked, surprised. "Are you sure it was the Georgians?"

No, he wasn't sure, and he didn't like the list of suspect parties he was accumulating. He would unravel this whole mess, the overlapping plots he sensed at work, and soon. In the meantime, he was taking precautions and calling in reinforcements.

His old partner, Ivan, understood everything that Victor didn't, and Artur was ready to cash in his chips for the *vor's* assistance. He knew with total certainty that he wouldn't have to ask twice. He need only say the word and the bonds of loyalty would launch Ivan into action, marshaling fire power and feet on the ground even from his prison cell.

"If the Georgians didn't do this, they'll do something else," Artur said. "They think they've been wronged, and they won't rest until they feel they've been avenged."

"They're not the biggest threat here," Victor said. "What do you think the Directorate will do if you won't follow orders?"

"What exactly were the orders?" he asked, but he already knew. He'd missed the meeting with the Directorate's new representative, but he had accessed the recordings of Victor and Gennady's conversations at *Secretnaya Banya*, the exclusive Russian bathhouse that was supposedly a safe haven for conducting sensitive business.

"You can't do anything to call attention to us or jeopardize the deal," Victor said.

"The fucking deal. You think it's not already in jeopardy? You think the Georgians are going to go on with business as usual now that their man's been killed? Let's not forget he was an undercover cop. You think the cops aren't paying attention to every move we make?"

"Don't rock the boat," Victor said.

"You live in a dream world."

Victor didn't reply. He made another telltale glance at his watch. Artur had an uneasy feeling. Why did Victor keep looking at the time? Was something about to happen? What did Victor know? "I notice you keep checking your watch."

"Morozov is waiting for me tonight at Troika," Victor said. "We're meeting with the Georgians. To go finish the deal. You need to come with me. To show the Directorate we're on top of things."

"No," Artur said. "I don't."

"Don't do this to me, Artur. Don't ignore me. They're watching Inna," Victor warned. "I wouldn't want them to grab her themselves, just to prove a point."

"They'll be very sorry if they try to prove that point," Artur said.

"Save your bravado. Remember what happened to Sofia."

"You think I could forget?" Artur said. The ache of his loss haunted him every day. He wouldn't make the same mistakes again. He would protect Inna and wrest her free of the Directorate's looming menace, the way he hadn't managed with Sofia. "Don't threaten me, Victor. I'm not the same man I was."

"What's that supposed to mean?"

"It means you can tell our bosses that when anyone strikes at me and mine, I will strike back twice as hard."

MAYA

DATO'S MAN HELD Maya captive, his gun pressing into her side, while Dato advanced on Stan. Dato slashed his second knife through the air. "You've been a busy man. Talking to the police."

Stan wheezed and whined. "I'll tell you everything I told them."

"Don't bother." Dato dug the tip of his knife into Stan's chin and drew a large red drop of blood. "I want the truth."

He carved a thin line down the column of Stan's neck on one side and then the other, as if preparing to dissect him. Blood outlined the cuts in an angry, dripping red. "Who killed Zviad? Was it you?"

Stan's skin had a greenish cast. Maya felt a flicker of hope as she recognized the symptom, her own plan working after all. Not long now.

But not soon enough.

"No. No, it wasn't me. I didn't do it." Stan was near hysterical. Blood oozed from the knife cuts and soaked the collar of his shirt.

"Who did?"

Dato pulled the knife on the table from Stan's hand and backed up a step, letting Stan believe that fingering someone else would save him.

Stan gasped and clutched his bloody hand to his chest. He didn't hesitate, didn't consider that he might be killed no matter what he said. "It was Mikhail!"

"Mikhail." Dato repeated as if memorizing her lover's name and marking it for violence.

"Yes. He lured your man to the p-p-party room. P-p-promised him a pretty woman and drugs. And then shot him."

"Why?" Dato crossed his knives at Stan's neck and marched the pharmacist to the wall. Stan's curly hair pressed against the worn wallpaper with its faded pattern of blue roosters.

Maya's stomach curled into a tight knot. In his current state, Stan would surely spill the whole plot, sentencing not only Mikhail, but also Aleksei, if not herself, to a horrible death at the point of Dato's blade.

Stan made a strange gurgling sound. He clutched at his chest. His eyes rolled up in his head. He surrendered to the poison Maya had painted on the blackmail money and collapsed. Slumping forward, he sliced his neck on Dato's crossed knives.

"What a fucking mess." Dato jumped back with a hiss as blood poured freely from Stan's neck. Stan's body hit the linoleum floor with a dull, sickening thud.

No stranger to violence or even to death, Maya nonetheless shuddered. These men did not know the art of a quiet kill, and, worse, she was now at their mercy—a mercy she knew better than to expect.

JACK

DOUBT CLUTCHED AT Jack's gut as he glanced nervously at the back door. Aleksei could arrive any moment. Or one of the waitresses. Or the bartender. Someone might come out for a smoke and notice Jack breaking into Aleksei's office with a teddy bear under his arm.

He glanced once more at Becca. She sat at his desk, busy with an assortment of pens and paper. He wished he hadn't had to bring her with him tonight, but Lena had insisted. They didn't have a babysitter on the weekends, and his wife had a deadline and needed the relief from Becca's constant questions and five-year-old need for attention.

Jack didn't have a key to Aleksei's private sanctuary. He took two paper clips from his pocket and unbent the metal until it was straight.

He hoped the lock would yield as easily as the flimsy one on the bathroom at home. He'd mastered the trick of unlocking that one when Becca had accidentally locked herself in, claiming she needed "piracy."

Prepared to jigger the paper clips in the lock, he closed his eyes against the shame of what he was doing, or perhaps against the pain of feeling driven to it.

Jack had suspicions that he didn't want to name. Six months was too long to hide from the truth. He didn't trust Aleksei anymore.

The lock snicked easily—more easily than he had expected, so easily that guilt niggled at him. There was no high security here, no locking up of secrets.

Jack had always thought his Russian friends were joking when they said, "You want him dead? I know a guy in Brooklyn." The notion that he might actually know someone in the Russian mob had always been laughable. In his mind, real people, the people he knew, would never do such things. They didn't cheat, or lie, or kill. It was all stereotypes. Right?

But now a man had been murdered and a woman had been raped. In Jack's nightclub.

He crossed the room in a couple of steps and tucked the small bear behind a crystal-framed wedding picture of Aleksei and Katya. The camera would have an unobscured view of the desk and anyone who came into the office. The stuffed animal was out of place if anyone looked closely, but Jack hoped it would hardly be noticed amidst the crowded collection of family pictures.

He heard the door from the loading dock open and froze to the spot. Someone was coming. Someone might catch him.

Heart racing, he tiptoed to the door. He leaned his head against the frame and prayed that whoever had come in would walk right past, that they wouldn't notice that the door was slightly ajar.

"Uncle Aleksei!" his daughter squealed with delight.

"Masinka!" Cutie.

"Want to see what I made?" Becca asked.

"Of course," Aleksei said.

"This is my mommy and my daddy," Becca explained.

With any luck, Aleksei was across the hall in Jack's office and bent over Becca's picture. Taking his chance, Jack eased the door open and slipped out.

Luck was in short supply. Aleksei stood in the hallway, looking in on Becca and pretending to admire her scribbles from afar.

"Do you have candy for me?" Becca asked as Jack shut the door behind him. The soft click made him jump. Had Aleksei heard? The last thing he wanted was for his brother-in-law to catch him sneaking around.

"Let's go to my office," Aleksei said and turned.

Jack's paperclips still poked out of the keyhole. He tried to palm them, but fumbled the move and dropped the slim wires to the floor. He stepped on them, hiding them with his shoe.

"You're here," Jack said.

"You sound surprised."

"I was looking for you, that's all." But he was surprised. Aleksei was hardly a partner. He strolled in casually, whenever it suited him, in his ridiculous leather pants and partially opened silk shirt, dressed for partying and not for working. He drank more than his share of vodka. He took for granted that Jack would do all of the real work—manage the menu and the deliveries and the waitstaff schedules—and then acted as if he were doing Jack a favor by letting him be his business partner.

"I wanted to talk with you about what happened the other night."

"Come into my office," Aleksei said, his usual affable self. How could he be so sunny when his own sister had been raped upstairs? "I promised Becca candy. That's okay, isn't it?" He looked guilty. Because of the sweet or because of what had happened?

Jack dragged his foot along the floor as he moved aside so that Aleksei could unlock the door. He didn't manage to move the paperclips with him, though, and the unbent metal gleamed accusingly in the hall light.

"Your father's security guy came by last night," Jack said. If he kept talking, maybe Aleksei would be too distracted to notice Jack's makeshift lock pick winking at them from the dark carpet runner.

"You mean Vlad." Aleksei paused with the key in his hand.

"Yeah, him," Jack said. "He asked about the security cameras." He felt like a child about to get caught at some mischief. But why should he feel guilty?

Jack and Aleksei had agreed to have security cameras installed throughout the club. Now, when the cameras would have been most useful, after a rape and murder in the ballroom, Jack learned his brother-in-law had skimped on surveillance.

Surely not because of the money.

"What about them?"

Before Jack could formulate his question, Becca inserted herself between them. She rubbed her little hands together. "I love candy!" she said and danced with the enthusiasm of a small child.

"How could I forget?" Aleksei tossed her in the air and caught her in one arm. Holding her like a shield, Jack thought uncharitably.

Aleksei opened the door to his office. He perched Becca on his desk and opened a crystal dish there with chocolate candies, giving her one.

Aleksei unwrapped the candy for her, showing such affection and attentiveness that Jack suddenly doubted himself.

Guilt compelled him to turn his head and glance at Katya and Aleksei's wedding picture. He and Aleksei were drinking buddies, friends, business partners. Aleksei was the uncle to Jack's children. Jack had come so close to getting caught moments ago. He would have ruined all of that and for what?

Jack was merely shaken because of the crime that had taken place. He was letting his imagination get the best of him. He had no evidence, only suspicions that fear blew out of proportion.

The crimes the other night were merely a stroke of bad luck, a once in a lifetime event. The odds of another crime like that one happening here at the nightclub were infinitesimally small. Right?

What about the rest? Whether or not Aleksei was wrapped up in the crimes the other night, Jack couldn't forget the weight of his other suspicions.

Aleksei might be a good uncle, but Jack's brother-in-law was hardly the partner Jack had expected.

When Jack's own restaurant venture had gone belly up last year, he hadn't thought twice before jumping on Aleksei's offer to open up a place together. His brother-in-law seemed to have a Midas touch with his own businesses. After all, Aleksei and Katya lived in a wealthy neighborhood in Manhattan Beach in a large house with a view of the ocean, full of the newest gadgets and luxurious gizmos. Aleksei spent money as if he printed it.

Katya came from the same penny-pinching, cost-conscious background as Jack's wife, Lena. She might make a very decent salary as an attorney, but she would never abide such frivolous spending unless Aleksei hit the numbers.

Believing in Aleksei's business acumen, Jack had conceded to him on every decision. If Aleksei wanted the waitresses to wear bootie shorts instead of slacks, that's what they did. If Aleksei thought they should have scantily clad live entertainment, they did that too. They did everything Aleksei wanted until the party center Jack had envisioned, the kind of family place a person could come to celebrate birthdays and anniversaries, had become the sort of sexed-up establishment where a rape could happen.

Worse still, something in the business did not add up. How could they keep hiring waitresses and turn a profit when they had a straggly flow of customers and few events in the fancy party rooms in which they had invested so much capital?

The uneasy feeling that had compelled him to plant the camera in Aleksei's office didn't ease, no matter how Jack tried to rationalize away his fears about his brother-in-law. He struggled not to look in the direction of the camera recording everything from its hiding place on the bookshelf, but he couldn't help himself. His eyes flitted nervously past the teddy bear and fixed on the wedding picture hiding it. Katya beamed up at her new husband, her face radiant with love and excitement.

Jack hadn't seen his wife's sister that happy in a long time. Last week, Katya had come to visit, had held the baby in her arms, and then suddenly burst into shoulder-wracking sobs. She wanted a baby, she had said, but she suspected Aleksei was having an affair. He was so secretive, and he was hardly ever home.

Of course, his in-laws had told her she was crazy. They always discussed Aleksei in hushed, awe-inspired tones, as if he were the perfect man, the perfect husband, the opposite of Jack. How could Katya question Aleksei? Why, just look at how generous he had been with Jack, the American, the outsider.

Sometimes Jack imagined a special place was reserved in Hell for his in-laws. Perhaps for Aleksei as well.

Katya deserved so much better. Hell, so did Jack, when it came down to it.

"Why don't we have security cameras in the ballroom and the back hallway?" Jack blurted. "I thought that was the plan."

Aleksei hesitated, and Jack braced himself for one whopper of a lie.

The lie didn't come from Aleksei, though. Instead it came from his friend Mikhail. Jack hadn't heard Mikhail enter, perhaps because he hadn't been as attuned to his surroundings as he had been when he'd been worried about getting caught.

"An oversight," Mikhail said smoothly, jumping in to support Aleksei. He was dressed in the high style the Russians favored—fabric with an expensive sheen, pointed shoes made of fine leather, a thick gold chain at his neck, his hair sleekly styled but not oily, and a little too much cologne.

"He told me everything was done, and I didn't realize until…well, I didn't realize that he'd taken the money but hadn't done all of the work." Although the excuse slithered easily from his tongue, the bruises darkening his jaw and cheek seemed to call his carefully orchestrated smoothness into question.

"You don't work here," Jack said, not quite calling him out.

Mikhail was here almost as much as Aleksei, constantly tempting him away from responsibilities. Aleksei did nothing all day other than hang out in his office playing cards with Mikhail and their buddies, ogling the waitresses, and smoking cigars. If Jack ever questioned or challenged him, he shrugged his shoulders and said he was working. What was Jack's problem? Wasn't there money in the till?

There was. There was always money, enough at least to cover basic expenses. But where did it come from?

His brother-in-law had a practiced line, a smooth excuse for every pretty waitress hired and every bookkeeping oddity. Jack had wanted to believe him. Now, he wondered if he'd willfully let himself be blind.

Jack wasn't the type to wallow in denial. His wife might accuse him at times of acting no better than a big kid, but he faced his problems like a man. He refused to be ruled by suspicions, doubt, or perhaps even unadulterated jealousy of a man who was easily successful when Jack struggled.

"Don't blame Aleksei. It was my fault. I recommended the contractor," Mihail said. He plastered a small, self-deprecating smile on his face. Jack had seen that same expression before on the married men who hit on his waitresses and then apologized for being overcome by their charms. He wanted to gag.

Just like that, all the guilt he harbored over spying on Aleksei and his friends solidified into a hard resolve. In this, he had done the right thing.

"What did you bring?" Becca asked. Jack noticed then that Mikhail was holding a black plastic case in one hand. What was in it? Money? Gambling chips?

"Is it a present? I love presents," his daughter said with flirtatious innocence.

"It is a present," Mikhail said, "but I'm sorry. This one's not for you, sweetheart. I'll bring you something next time."

"Really?" Her eyes lit up.

"Really." Mikhail chucked her on her chin, and she fell easily under his spell. She clasped her hands to her heart in a romantic gesture Jack had seen only in cartoons. *Don't fall for his tricks.* His resentment and suspicion burgeoned to a rolling boil.

"You should have told me about the security problem," Jack said sharply. He directed his comment to Aleksei and ignored Mikhail.

"We'll have to have someone else in to install the cameras. Obviously, we need them. I'll make a few calls."

"I didn't want to disappoint you," Aleksei said.

True or false? It almost didn't matter. In that moment, Aleksei seemed to believe his own words. He hunched his shoulders in apology and looked at Jack with such a boyish expectation of forgiveness. Was that how he made a woman like Katya forgive him again and again?

"Too late for that." Jack couldn't hide his bitterness. Aleksei nodded as if to say he understood and there would be no hard feelings.

"Here. Take some more candy for later," Aleksei said to Becca, perhaps reaching for the approval and affection Jack had just denied him.

"Thank you. Thank you. Thank you," she sing-songed. She shoved a handful of candies into her pocket and then raised her plump little arms up to hug her uncle. Aleksei bent to her, and she gave him a big, wet kiss on his cheek. He gave her a brilliant smile and then surreptitiously wiped his wet skin with his hand.

"Now run along. Mikhail and I have business we need to discuss," Aleksei said to her.

Jack bristled at the dismissal. He had wanted to discuss business with Aleksei, but his "funny business" with Mikhail always seemed to come first.

Jack knew better than to protest. He scooped Becca into his arms, happy to be distancing her from the two charmers. He wasn't going to get the answers he needed, not from Aleksei and certainly not from Mikhail.

But maybe his hidden camera would.

ALEKSEI

AS SOON AS Jack left with his daughter, Mikhail pulled the door to Aleksei's office closed. "Your brother-in-law asks too many questions."

Aleksei merely grunted. What could he say? Jack was his business partner and part of his family. Jack was also a far better man than Aleksei could ever claim to be. Jack's disappointment in him left a bitter taste.

"You okay?" Mikhail asked, but Aleksei knew that wasn't his real question. What he really wanted to know was whether Aleksei had the balls to follow through on his plans to silence his head pharmacist.

Stan had been caught on Troika's surveillance video manhandling Inna and disappearing with her. Off camera, he had dragged her, drugged and compliant, to a meeting room upstairs at Troika, using her as bait for a member of the Georgian crew.

The cops couldn't possibly prove Stan had done anything wrong, especially since he hadn't drugged Inna himself nor pulled the trigger on the Georgian. Nothing, other than his groping her, had been caught on camera. Yet, the cops had questioned him last night, and Stan had suddenly become nervous.

Now he wanted to skip town. Not a problem, except for the blackmail.

If Aleksei didn't hush him with a million dollars, which he didn't have and couldn't possibly raise in the twenty-four hours Stan had given him, then Stan would tell the cops everything.

By everything, Stan meant *everything*. The murder of the Georgian was only the tip of the iceberg.

Stan would get nothing, provided Aleksei could find the fortitude to do what needed to be done.

How hard could it be to shoot a gun?

"I'm fine. You're the one who looks like hell," Aleksei said.

"No thanks to you." Mikhail fingered the dark bruises on his cheek and jaw.

"Sorry about that," Aleskei gave the expected responses. Yet, the bruises gave him an odd sense of satisfaction. He had left a mark of his anger, of his aggression. He had, he felt, claimed a small part of Mikhail in the process.

"Yeah, well, it might have worked out for the best. Inna slipped past Vitaliy this morning. She made it to the shop before he could grab her. But I put on a good show for your father. Told him I'd been jumped and had held off her attacker long enough to let her escape."

"And you had the battle scars to prove it."

"Exactly."

"You don't think he's suspicious? That he knows something?" He knew his father already suspected a setup at Troika. Despite Mikhail's bravado, Aleksei worried that they were rank amateurs compared to Artur.

Here they were, after all, hoping Artur would save them from their latest scrape, since they couldn't save themselves. They had made the Georgian problem Artur's problem by compromising Inna, and now they hoped they could provoke him to war so that he would neutralize the threat and save them from Dato and his infamous knives.

"I predict he'll take action soon," Mikhail said.

Aleksei noticed the evasion, as well as the tentative statement, so different from Mikhail's previous over-assured confidence. "What's happened?"

"Nothing." Mikhail plopped down in the chair across the desk from him. "Except he fired me as Inna's bodyguard and gave the job to Vlad."

"So?" What difference did that make? The important thing was that his father recognized a threat against Inna, one that might motivate him to move against the Georgians, and that Inna had protection in case the Georgians really did lash out against her.

He couldn't stand the idea that his little sister might suffer for his mistakes. Mikhail had promised him that the drugs she'd taken would keep her from remembering what had happened and assured him she hadn't suffered, even with the rape. But she'd been a shadow of herself the other night at her home, and he couldn't deny she was indeed suffering.

"I brought this for you." Mikhail plunked a black case onto Aleksei's desk. Aleksei didn't need to open it to know what was inside. He supposed Mikhail sensed his weakness and didn't want to give him any excuse to back out.

Both their necks were on the line.

"I have a gun," Aleksei said with empty bravado. He had a gun, but he had never shot it, except at the practice range.

Mikhail hitched his shoulder. "This one's unmarked. The police won't be able to trace it to you."

"Oh, that's good." Inside he felt cold. He wished for a finger of vodka, for the warmth or maybe for the courage it would give him. The plan he had hatched last night when angry and half-drunk didn't seem quite so brilliant or simple now.

"Don't forget to wear your gloves. You don't want to leave any fingerprints."

"Right. Right. I'll do that." Aleksei had never killed anyone. He wasn't sure he could do it tonight, despite how much was at stake.

He couldn't meet Mikhail's eye. Mikhail had already killed to protect their schemes. If Aleksei couldn't pull the trigger when it mattered, Mikhail would know the truth.

"You're not having second thoughts, are you?"

Did Mikhail know the rest? Did he know how his chiseled body invaded Aleksei's dreams with dirty images no real man would tolerate?

Yet, Aleksei, despite his shame, would close his eyes and relive the tangle of limbs in those dreams, the clutching, grabbing, thrusting urgency—even when he was with Katya.

Especially when he was with Katya.

More than the drug trade he ran from his pharmacies and Troika, this was his most closely guarded secret. No one—not his wife, not his best friend, not his parents—would abide this weakness, this affinity that proved he wasn't a real man.

Sure, Hollywood made it seem normal. But he didn't live his life in Hollywood or even in metrosexual Manhattan. He lived in Brighton Beach with his feet firmly planted in the mafia world.

Stop pretending to be a big man and get me my money. Stan's taunts and threats replayed in his head, rekindled the anger that had set him on this course.

Aleksei pushed to his feet and grabbed Mikhail's black box. Time to face his next rite of passage. Stan would get exactly what he deserved.

SVETLANA

EVERYONE AT TROIKA was a poser.

Svetlana watched the couple at the table in the window with disgust.
Poor little Anya had gone to wait on the impossible pair. The wife was a
complainer: this on the table wasn't good enough; that was too cold; the
drink didn't have enough alcohol. She criticized in a whining voice and
then turned her head to the window. Svetlana already knew they
wouldn't leave a tip.

The balding husband ordered a drink and then surreptitiously
pinched Anya's bottom, hard enough to make Anya wince. *Lecher!* His
wife, with her big diamond ring, pretended not to notice.

Svetlana snapped her dishrag and scrubbed harder at the counter in
front of her. Despite an i.d. card that claimed she was twenty-three,
Anya could not possibly be old enough to serve alcohol let alone drink it.
Much as Svetlana would like to intercede on the girl's behalf, she
couldn't risk upsetting the customers and losing her job. Anya had
tolerated the abuse with exceeding politeness—something neither her
bosses nor her miserly customers deserved.

Attendance at Troika had been anemic at best, limited to a new-
money crowd willing to pay the inflated prices and desiring others to
notice. The coatroom was occupied by fur coats, even when the weather
was merely brisk instead of Arctic cold.

The fancy décor, courtesy of Koslovsky Imports, certainly made the
place seem swanky. While the sweet, young, and foreign waitresses all
clad in tight little outfits didn't exactly up-class the place, they did
contribute to the novelty and perhaps to an illusion of high service. Still,
the band and live entertainment were third rate, and the food, despite its

high sticker price, was basically the same chow every other Russian restaurant in the area served.

How they stayed in business was a mystery—unless the nightclub was a front for a much more lucrative business venture, as Svetlana and Vlad both suspected.

Jack regularly tried to upgrade the menu and get the surly cook staff to cooperate. Everyone nodded and smiled and then pretended not to understand English and did whatever they wanted. He was American. So what did they care?

They might be singing a different tune if anyone ever got fired. So far no one had. Most of them weren't on an official payroll anyway. They were in the country illegally, and Aleksei paid them in cash. Not the waitresses, though.

The gaggle of nubile young women, recently arrived on seasonal visas from Odessa and the former Eastern bloc countries, had all of their paperwork in order. They received official paychecks. Their employment was exceedingly legal, even if their documents were full of lies. They claimed to be in their twenties, but Svetlana guessed Anya and several of the others were closer to seventeen.

Svetlana surveyed the club. She had expected only a few stragglers tonight. Who would want to drink or have dinner downstairs from where a man had been murdered? But tonight, for once, the place was packed.

Murder seemed to stimulate the Brighton Beach economy.

She had caught more than one customer sneaking up the spiral staircase to gawk at the yellow crime tape sectioning off the ballroom. She directed the bouncer to guard the steps. He stood now at the foot of the stairs, arms crossed. He looked formidable, but Svetlana bet he would let anyone pass for a little green. Everyone in Brighton Beach, herself included, was an ambitious entrepreneur.

The patron at the end of the bar tapped his bejeweled fingers on the counter. "Vodka, straight up," he commanded. His accent sounded

English, which likely meant he had come straight from the mother country. Troika was not an international tourist destination, unless said tourists hailed from Russia.

Was he a member of the mafia? She inspected the loose cut of his jacket. He could be packing.

She guessed him to be her age, early forties. He attracted his share of glances from the giggling waitresses. Because of his playboy good looks—broad shoulders, dark blond hair, eyes a Russian blue—or the Rolex gracing his wrist?

Money could make any man attractive, but this one was beautiful to start.

She placed the shot glass in front of him. He cast only the briefest, wordless glance in her direction, as if she were barely human and completely beneath his notice.

His contempt hurt her pride. She realized she was old enough to be the mother of most of the girls working the floor tonight, but she didn't appreciate the way his eyes slid over her as if her age had left her a wrinkled old hag.

She rocked the damn bootie shorts and stilettos Aleksei forced her to wear, damn it!

But she was no longer seventeen. Or twenty-three. Or even close to thirty.

She expelled her frustration with a harsh breath that blew the wispy hair out of her face. What did she care what the man at the bar thought of her? Her job didn't depend on his approval—unless Aleksei and Jack suddenly decided the bar would be more profitable with a younger, sexier bartender.

She had already been cast aside once. Nothing to stop the same thing from happening again.

While she didn't depend on this job for her livelihood, she couldn't afford to lose it. As it was, she could barely make ends meet, even with her main employment.

She knew whose fault that was. Her ex-husband with his young wifey. The newer, shinier model had been picked from the ranks, just as Svetlana had been, and now enjoyed the executive-level job that should have been hers. Would have been hers if her husband hadn't cheated on her, abandoned her, and then saddled her with caring for Philip all on her own.

Her ex lived a fancy life—exotic trips and shiny new foreign cars and a housekeeper—while she scraped by with what little she could cobble together after she paid the fees to Philip's facility. She couldn't even pay those anymore, not when the costs of care rose faster than her earnings.

Past due. The group home had sent a notice that her payments were past due and issued a warning. If she didn't settle her account soon, Phillip wouldn't be allowed to stay.

She plunked the glasses harder on the counter than she should have as she filled drink orders. One day she would have enough money to make sure her son got everything he needed—whether his father wanted to pay or not. One day soon, provided her project with Vlad reaped the promised rewards.

Role-playing at Troika was a means to an end. Vlad had exceeded all expectation and danced them straight to the center of intrigue in Little Odessa. Now she watched and waited like a spider patiently spinning its web.

Anya came up to the bar with the happy couple's newest request, vodka for the husband and something complicated—hold this, extra that, tell the bartender not to be stingy with the gin, and just a twist of lemon—for the wife.

Anya delivered the order in her quiet voice and with a shrug of apology. She was a good girl, too good for this place. And too young.

Anya with her sparkling eyes reminded Svetlana of the woman she had been—before life had knocked her around.

"Have you seen Mr. Victor?" Anya asked shyly.

"No. Not tonight."

"Oh." The disappointment was palpable and distressing.

"Why?" Svetlana asked as she poured the drinks for the couple.

"He said he would come talk to me this weekend. About getting married."

"Victor can't marry you. He's already married," Svetlana said, but knew the warning was useless.

"Not to him," Anya giggled. She leaned over the counter and whispered, "To someone else. A citizen. So I can get a green card. And make more money."

Svetlana nodded. She had expected something like this, but confronted with it, she felt sick to her stomach. Anya couldn't possibly know what awaited her.

"He told me he found someone. We're supposed to sign papers." Anya had a guileless excitement, like a puppy wagging its tail and begging to play, not suspecting she was about to get beaten with a stick. She would never be the same.

"Do you know who this man is? Or what job you'll get? Victor makes things sound easy, but they're not. Maybe you should go back to Odessa." Before the words were out of her mouth, she knew they were a mistake.

The girl's face hardened with determination. "I can't go back. I have to make money. For my family. For my son."

"You have a child?" The information surprised Svetlana, who was so seldom surprised. She should have known little Anya wouldn't be waiting tables in bootie shorts at Troika if the world had offered her a better option. Neither of them would.

VICTOR

PAUSING AT THE entrance to the nightclub, Victor squared his shoulders and prepared for his next round with Gennady Morozov, the Directorate's representative. Around him the buzz and hum of the dinner crowd would create an excellent cover to their business. His prospective buyers could inspect the merchandise while Gennady watched the deal go off without a hitch.

This meeting would go differently than their first. There would be no ignominious repeat of the encounter at *Secretnaya Banya*. Tonight Victor was prepared. Almost.

He checked his watch one last time before entering the bar. He hadn't received confirmation yet that everything he needed was in place. There was no reason to think his plan had gone awry. It was still early. Possibly, the help he'd hired had forgotten their directive to call him immediately with news.

Gennady spotted Victor and moved from the bar to a table at the back. Victor read the implicit command in his motions and went to join him. Blond-haired and blue-eyed, fit and lean, virile and relatively young, the Directorate's new representative was a perfect specimen of Russian manhood, something Victor couldn't help adding to all of the reasons to resent him.

Gennady scowled at him when he pulled the chair out for himself. "Where's Artur?"

"He'll be along shortly," Victor promised, even though he didn't have the means in hand to make Artur jump to do his bidding. Not yet. He checked his watch again. Any minute now.

"I trust you've gotten him in line."

"*Konechno*," Victor said with borrowed confidence. Soon he would get the notification that the men he'd hired had Inna under lock and key. Then he would have Artur firmly under his thumb, despite all of Artur's posturing and threats.

After all, Victor had broken Artur before—with Sofia.

Victor didn't want to hurt Inna, but he *would* do whatever was necessary to keep Artur under control and prove his worth to the Directorate. This deal with the Georgians would move forward, no matter what twinges of conscience Artur might feel or how badly he opposed working with the Georgians themselves.

"The Georgians are meeting us here tonight. For a private showing. Artur will arrive later to close the deal," Victor said.

"Ah," Gennady said. The one syllable contained a world of inscrutable meaning. Gennady fixed his cold gaze on Victor.

Victor found himself struggling not to squirm under the younger man's icy scrutiny. He was losing his touch. He used to be the one to lift an eyebrow and set others on edge. Indignation with his own lack of self-control made him straighten and return a stare just as hard and cold as the one Gennady leveled at him.

"The showing is for your benefit, too," Victor said. "So you can run back and make your little report."

Gennady blinked. For a moment Victor thought his aim had struck true, and he had finally bested this upstart who acted as though he had the mantel of power when in truth he was a mere underling. But no.

"My little report," Gennady echoed. His lips tipped up at the corners with the hint of a calculated smile. "Is that what they told you? That I'm a messenger? An observer?"

Wasn't he? What else could Gennady be doing here? Victor schooled his outward expression, mimicking the condescension in Gennady's eyes. The man was trying to play him, but it wouldn't work.

Victor outranked him. His connection with Moscow wasn't what it once was, but Gennady didn't need to know that. Two could play the intimidation game, and Victor had had far more years of practice.

Gennady was only a lowly, junior member of the Directorate, an errand boy, a messenger, no matter how impressive a picture he might try to paint with his posturing and innuendo. Wasn't he?

There was nothing else the man could be. Surely, a meteoric rise would have come to his attention, even with the trickle of information he now got from the few informants he had left. Power shifts and threats never went unremarked. Gennady hadn't been mentioned in connection with any of the big names—the old-timers or the newcomers in power. He was no one's protégé so far as Victor knew.

"I'm sure they told you otherwise," Victor said in his most patronizing tone.

"What they told me is irrelevant," Gennady said, leaving Victor to wonder whether the man across the table from him was secretly empowered or whether he had ambitions to grab for more than what he currently had. "We both have our assignments. The only question tonight is how well you're doing yours. Frankly, I have my doubts."

"What doubts?"

"You can't guess?" Gennady said with something that sounded like pity. "You really are losing your edge."

Who thought he was losing his edge? Was that the word on him in Moscow? Once, no one would have dared say such a thing.

Maybe no one was saying it now either. He had to credit Gennady. The man excelled at mind games, but Victor had dealt with far more formidable rivals and emerged victorious.

Victor checked his watch again, impatient for the news that would bring Artur to heel.

Every man had his weakness. He already knew Artur's. Now he only needed to learn Gennady's.

Anya, Victor's favorite new waitress, approached their table to take their order. Victor had already imagined every way she might express gratitude when he helped her secure a green card. His body tightened as his favorite fantasy replayed in his mind—the lovely Anya on her knees, her hair in a luscious cascade down her bare back, her breasts pressed against his leg as she coaxed him to ecstasy with her soft lips and pink tongue.

That pink tongue darted out across those pillowy lips now. "Mr. Victor," she said, "I was hoping you'd be here tonight. Have you found a husband for me?"

She cast a sidelong look at Gennady, as if she hoped he were her candidate. Gennady watched them both with a shuttered look.

"Soon. We'll talk in a little while. I'm meeting some candidates tonight," Victor assured her. "In the meantime, I'll have a vodka straight up."

"Yes, of course," she said, an intoxicating combination of demureness and excitement all at once.

"Anything for you?" She glanced sidelong at Gennady. The bright flirtation in her voice rankled. Victor had promised her a future. All Gennady had done was sit in his chair and scowl.

"No." Gennady's firmness seemed a rejection of anything Anya might offer him.

She turned back to the bar. Her bootie shorts hugged her pert little bottom. Victor would have given her a slap if Gennady hadn't been there, sitting in disapproving judgment.

Despite his supposed lack of interest, Gennady followed Anya with his ice-blue eyes and watched her give the order to the bartender. A brief, tense moment between the two women ensued, although Victor could not hear the argument between them.

"Tell me about the bartender," Gennady said. "She's been watching us."

"Svetlana?" Victor harrumphed. "She probably has the hots for you. That's all."

"Yes, that's probably it," Gennady agreed. He brushed his fingers through his thick blond hair. "She was overly attentive toward me at the bar." He tapped his chin thoughtfully and watched Svetlana for another few moments as if contemplating his own level of interest.

"You're doing the showing here?" Gennady asked, finally returning his gaze to Victor. "I'm surprised the Georgians agreed to this venue, given the murder of their man upstairs."

"Actually, they requested it." Dato himself had taken Victor's call and suggested they meet here.

"Curious. Don't you think?" Gennady said.

Victor almost laughed at this ineffectual attempt to unsettle him. Gennady wasn't nearly as good as he supposed. "The Georgians know what's in their best interest. They're showing that they're willing to put the feud aside. Business, after all, is business."

"And Artur?"

Victor checked his watch again. Too much time had passed. The men he'd hired hadn't checked in. Had they failed?

He didn't dare consider failure. No, he decided, they had merely forgotten to adhere to the strict schedule Victor had given them. What else could he expect from hiring locals? These weren't the professionals he would have commanded in Moscow.

Even so, they couldn't possibly have failed. Inna was such an easy target, anxious and easily cowed.

"Artur understands what needs to be done," Victor improvised. He would continue on as if he had already attained the winning hand.

He noticed a swarthy man enter the club. The man hadn't checked his trench coat at the door. He stood at the entrance and surveyed the crowd, and Victor recognized him as one of Dato's men.

"Ah, there." Victor waved to him to join them. Here, at last, was some confirmation that his schemes were working. The Georgians had shown tonight, as promised.

Soon, he'd have Inna in his custody, and the deal would move forward as planned, no matter what Artur thought or wanted.

INNA

"NICK!" INNA SCREAMED as he fell to the ground. An angry red splotch started to spread out on his shoulder. He wasn't moving. Was he dead? Without thinking, she rushed toward him.

The man Inna had shot earlier, Fake Igor, grabbed her arm and stopped her short. He wagged Olga's gun at her. "Get in truck. Now."

He gave her a shove toward the back of Igor's delivery truck. The other man, the one Nick had been wrestling, grabbed her gruffly by the arm and dragged her toward the back of their waiting vehicle. Fake Igor rolled up the back door, and his comrade hoisted her by the waist and shoved her inside.

She landed on her hands and knees. Briefly, she saw neat stacks of cardboard boxes and what looked like a man slumped in the corner. Then her captors pulled down the door, shutting out all of the light. She couldn't see a thing.

"Igor?" she whispered and crawled in what she thought was the man's direction. "Igor, is that you?"

He didn't answer.

Her hand brushed something rubbery—the sole of his steel-toed work boot. "Igor, it's me, Inna," she said.

He didn't respond.

Maybe he'd been zapped the way Vlad had. Maybe he couldn't respond for now. She traced her hand up his leg until she found his hand. His skin was cool to the touch. She clasped his fingers and gave them a squeeze, thinking to reassure him. She was going to get them both out of here, although she hadn't the faintest idea how.

Igor didn't make any sound that she could hear over her freight train heartbeat. She pressed her fingers to his wrist.

No pulse.

No, no, no! He couldn't be dead. She'd find his pulse at his neck. She moved her hand up his arm to his shoulder. He was shirtless. Her hand skimmed over a tuft of soft hair on his shoulder. She pressed her fingers firmly against his neck.

Still, no pulse.

She searched frantically for signs of life—anything. She pressed her ear to his chest. No heartbeat. She put her hand over his mouth. No faint warm breath.

Oh, God. Those men had killed Igor. They'd stripped his shirt and stolen the van. To get to her. They'd planned everything. To get to her. Why?

Please let me be paranoid. Let this all be a horrible hallucination.

It felt too real. All of it felt too real. She squeezed Igor's lifeless hand. Her own breath came in quick little gasps. Not enough air. She couldn't breathe. She was going to suffocate. She was going to die in here from lack of oxygen. Maybe that's what had happened to Igor.

Or maybe those men had murdered him.

She closed her eyes and focused, as Dr. Shiffman had taught her, on her breathing. *In, out. In, out.*

Outside, she heard gunfire. She couldn't ward off the certain knowledge that someone else was going to die tonight.

Dr. Shiffman had told her that at some point soon, she wouldn't need her medication anymore. She wished that moment were now. She craved the amber bottle in her medicine cabinet at home, the magic pill that would calm her shattered nerves and put the world back to rights. But last night she had taken the last one. She would get no relief from the pressure squeezing her lungs, even if she could magically get home and open her medicine chest.

What pill could help her now anyway?

Someone was out to get her, would kill people to get to her. Why? She'd never harmed anyone. *Let it all be in my mind. Another paranoid delusion. Like the time I thought Papa was a spy for the Russian government.*

She had to be crazy. Or maybe the truth was staring her in the face.

Igor was dead. Nick might be, too. And then there was the man at the club. The body count was getting too high to ignore. Who else was going to die? And for what?

She clutched Igor's hand. *I'm sorry. I'm so sorry.*

In the darkness, she made a silent vow. She wouldn't look away. Wouldn't doubt her senses. She would look frankly at the world around her and confront it. Even if it meant another prolonged stay at the hospital or worse, a strait jacket.

It was time to face her worst fears.

No more medication. No more numbness. No matter what her parents said. No matter what Dr. Kasparov prescribed or how hard he threatened to send her to an institution.

She refused to be passive in her own life.

She'd been suppressing her own senses, ignoring the signs all around her for far too long, and people, good people, were dying. No more. This time, she'd be brave. This time, she wouldn't back down. She wouldn't look to medical experts to explain the mysteries unraveling right in front of her.

If she survived the night.

She felt her way along the boxes and scrambled back to the door. She clawed at the opening. She dug her slender fingers under the edge of the door, expecting it to open only enough to let in a sliver of light and the promise of more air to breathe.

The door opened easily. They hadn't locked her in. Surprised, she poked her head out in time to see Vlad take a bullet to the chest.

"No!" she screamed.

Heedless of the danger, she scrambled out of the back of the truck and rushed to his aid.

VLAD

ON A PRAYER, Vlad pulled the trigger, forcing Inna's kidnappers to duck for cover. His reflexes were slower than usual thanks to the zap he'd received from the stun gun, but his shots robbed the men of their opportunity to secure the door of the truck and take off.

Both men were armed with guns. The prudent action, the strategic action, the action the FBI had trained him to take, would be to stop but not to kill her kidnappers. Disable them. Keep them for questioning. Who were they? What did they want with Inna?

On a normal day, Vlad would have disabled both targets easily.

Today wasn't a normal day. They'd caught him off guard and taken Inna. This was personal.

Vlad wasn't in strategy mode. He was mad as hell, and these fuckers were going to pay for what they'd done.

Shooting to kill, he easily picked off the first man, the one with the limp. The second kidnapper dove behind the truck to the driver's side. No way was he letting the bastard get in and drive away with Inna.

I'll kill anyone who tries to take you from me. He recognized the echo of his old man as he pulled the trigger and missed.

Movement at the back of the truck caught his eye. Inna stood, holding the rolled up door over her head.

In the split second that he paused his fire and registered her standing there about to get free, the kidnapper got off a single shot.

The bullet hit Vlad square in the chest and knocked him off his feet. He slammed into the concrete-encased light post behind him.

"No!" Inna screamed. Out of the corner of his eye he saw her launch herself from the truck and into the middle of danger.

The full body blow made him feel like he'd been hit with the mother of all hammers. His eyes watered, but he stayed focused on his target.

He wouldn't fail Inna now.

With effort, he pulled himself upright and shot again. *Mine! Again. Mine!* He shot twice more in rapid succession—*mine, damn it, mine!*—until there were no more answering shots.

"You were hit!" Inna cried out. Her hands roamed over his torso as she checked him over. Her eyes, feverish in their intensity, were wide with concern for him.

"I'm wearing a vest." He craned his head to get a clearer view of the driver's side of the van and confirm his kill. His latest victim stared up at him, half of his head blown off.

It was over.

Inna followed his gaze, gasped at the grisly sight, and then threw herself against him. She buried her face against his chest and clung to him. Even through his bulletproof vest, he could feel her trembling.

"Hey, you're okay," he soothed. He stroked her head, secretly savoring the silkiness of her damp hair and the faint scent of strawberries, the knowledge that she was safe and in his arms.

"You were shot. They could've killed you." She wrapped her arms tighter around his waist and squeezed.

His throat closed. He hadn't been hugged in years. He suspected Inna, when she was small, might have been the last person to do so.

He reminded himself that this sudden closeness meant nothing. She merely wanted comfort. She'd had a scare. This was a natural response. He represented safety and security. He was, after all, her bodyguard.

She didn't know why he was really insinuating himself with her father. She wouldn't be pressed against him like this if she did. *Not for me,* he reminded himself. *Not for me.*

"Don't worry about me," he said gruffly. "Danger's part of the job. You're what matters."

"Don't be an idiot," she said. "You matter to me. You've always mattered." She looked up at him then, and what he saw undid him.

He had no right to her. No right at all. But he wanted—no, needed—her more than air.

How could he ever let her go? He knew in that moment that he wouldn't. Couldn't. No matter the cost. No matter what rules he had to break. *Mine. Only mine.*

She pulled away abruptly. "Nick," she said.

He hated the sound of another man's name on her lips.

"We have to help Nick."

NICK

NICK STRUGGLED TO sit up. Distantly he heard Inna call, "Nick! Ohmigod, Nick, are you okay?"

Was he okay? Nick lay on the hard ground. His head throbbed. His shoulder stung like a sonofabitch. He touched it with his hand. Wet.

"He was shot, too." Inna hurried to his side. She pulled his hand away from his wounded shoulder. His palm was slick with blood. "Vlad, he's losing so much blood."

Her bodyguard leaned in close over her shoulder. "It's not bleeding that badly," Vlad said. "He'll live. Take off his shirt and use it to apply pressure to his shoulder."

Inna's hands shook as she peeled his shirt from his shoulders. He winced at the pain. "Sorry," she said. "I'm so sorry."

"Don't be sorry."

"You're hurt because of me. Because you tried to save me," she said.

"Yeah, he's a regular hero," Vlad said, gun still at the ready and pointed at him. The bodyguard seemed to target him with murder in his eyes. Couldn't he see that Nick wasn't a threat to Inna?

She pushed a damp hank of hair out of his face. As she did so, Nick caught a glimpse of her wrist.

"What's that—on your wrist?"

"Are you hurt?" Vlad crowded her, and there was no mistaking a protectiveness that went beyond any paid duties. So the bodyguard was interested in her, too.

Vlad took her hand and inspected her wrist, pushing back the wide sleeve of her sweater and giving Nick a clearer view of a berry-colored mark shaped like a wing. The mark seemed somehow significant, but pain kept Nick from focusing.

Inna laughed nervously. "Me? A few bruises and scrapes maybe. This is just a birthmark."

She pulled her hand out of Vlad's with a determined tug. Dare Nick hope she had no interest in the other man?

She turned her full attention to applying pressure to Nick's wound. He drank her in with his eyes, as if she were the nourishment he'd been craving all of his life. She was here with him and safe. For the briefest moment his world seemed right—despite the intense pain in his shoulder and the gangster and his gun hovering over them.

Sirens sounded around them. "Took them long enough," Inna muttered under her breath.

"You called them?" Vlad asked.

"I hit the panic button under the counter."

"Good thinking," Vlad said.

"Some good it did." Her mouth fixed in a grim line. She pressed his shirt against Nick's bleeding shoulder with renewed determination, and he gritted his teeth to keep from gasping with pain. He could feel the shaking of her hands. "You could've gotten killed. Both of you could've gotten killed. And they'd be too late."

"We're both okay," he said, even as the pain in his shoulder threatened to drown out everything around him. He struggled to keep his eyes open, to fill his eyes and heart with Inna.

"I think he's about to pass out," Inna said, and her voice was far away. She shook him gently. "Nick, stay with me," she urged.

"Always," he mumbled.

MAYA

"LET'S MOVE," DATO'S sidekick said. "We don't want to be here should the cops show up."

Dato turned to Maya. He waved his knives, smeared with Stan's blood, in front of her face. His eyes glittered with menace. "You," he said, "are going to come quietly. Understood?"

She closed her eyes—against the fear, against the insulting sense of helplessness, against the glorious moment stolen from her and now crushed beneath Dato's leather boot—and nodded.

His companion snatched up the backpack and scooped the pile of money inside with his sleeve. He didn't make prolonged contact with the tainted cash, and Dato didn't touch it at all.

Without her poison, her wits were no match for Dato's knives.

What terrible fate awaited her? She swallowed, and the sound was loud in her ears.

Maya scanned for escape routes, seeing none. Lights were on in the neighboring houses. Someone might see her being hustled down the driveway. Would anyone come to her aid if she screamed?

By the time they did, she might be dead.

At the end of the driveway, a black SUV with tinted windows waited. "Get in," Dato said. He brandished his long knife. The metal was stained red with Stan's blood.

She shook with what she guessed was terror. She'd never been gripped by this particular emotion. She felt stripped to her very essence, raw and achingly vulnerable. This man could hurt her irreparably, and there was precious little she could do to protect herself.

She complied with his request. What other choice did she have? She slid silently across the seat and shrunk as far away from her captor as she could. Dato climbed in beside her. He placed a bloodied hand on her knee and smiled at her with a predatory gleam.

Artur wouldn't even know she was missing until it was too late.

More alone than ever, she had no clever trick to get herself out of the mess she'd blithely helped to create.

Dato didn't restrain or gag her. He relied on the force of his own menace to keep her in check, and it did. She wasn't brazen enough to cross or confront him.

She didn't say a word. The car sped away from Stan's house and the mutilated body Dato and his man had left there in its own pool of blood.

The image of those knives cutting cleanly through Stan's jugular wouldn't stop playing behind her eyes. Her natural confidence bled away.

Stan's murder was supposed to have been nice and neat, designed to look like a heart attack, a common tragedy that wouldn't arouse questions. But this Georgian barbarian had barged in, ready to eviscerate anything and anyone, and left a scene the police would mine for easy clues.

Dato obviously didn't care. He didn't prize subtlety. He didn't pretend to be something he was not.

All her life, Maya had thought her secrets gave her power. She had held her own with her quiet manipulations and potions, using stealth and patience to shape her world to her liking. Now, she realized, men like Dato had true power. They did what they liked, took what they wanted when they wanted it, and they didn't hide; not like her, not like Artur.

Could Artur really win a war against this man? She had bet on her husband's power and tactical genius. Maybe she'd been wrong.

The car sped down side streets. On a Sunday night, few pedestrians were out. With unease, she noticed they were leaving behind the rundown apartment buildings and humble single-family homes of Stan's neighborhood and moving into a more familiar part of town. Mini mansions dominated nearly every inch of lot after lot.

"Where are we going?" Her voice was embarrassingly tremulous. She thought she had already guessed the answer.

Surely, Dato would take her home so that he could confront Artur. With his knives.

She hadn't confided in Artur nor consulted him, instead seeking solace in her secrets and choosing to manipulate him as punishment for his neglect. Another tactical error?

With her as prisoner, Dato would be able to make all kinds of unreasonable demands, provided he took Artur by surprise and that her husband cared enough about her to make concessions.

Fear ripped through her mind and heart, until all she could feel was the raw, animalistic clenching and tremors of her own body.

She had lost Artur's love. She'd never be able to win him back or punish him. No, she was going to die, a victim of his apathy toward her.

Dato was talking. She barely made out his words as she sank deeper and deeper into her own despair.

"...pay a visit to your son's nightclub," he said.

"My son?" she gasped. The fear took on new dimensions. Would Dato kill Aleksei the way he had Stan?

Icy premonition crept from the tips of her fingers up her arms, raising gooseflesh. Jagged shards of desperation stabbed her belly. She pressed her lips together, determined not to say another word and to pretend her usual mastery over her emotions. She couldn't let Dato see her appalling weakness.

"I have a busy night planned. Starting with cocktails at Troika." He bared his teeth. The gold across his bridge caught the light and set off his malevolence. "Molotov cocktails."

His evil grin widened as if he had amused himself with his own cleverness. When she didn't react, he asked, "You do know what a Molotov cocktail is. Don't you, Mrs. Koslovsky?"

He reached over the front seat and grabbed a dark amber bottle. It looked like a beer bottle, except for the stopper and wick at the top. "Highly flammable liquid that explodes in a fire ball when lit," he said. "Cheap and very deadly."

Her heart momentarily seized as she imagined this monster lighting her gorgeous son on fire. She had already seen the kind of carnage the man wreaked with his perilously sharp blade. She could scarcely contemplate what he might do with a blunt weapon designed for maximum destruction.

"Troika will burn to a crisp. I'll put it out of business for weeks. Maybe months." He seemed to relish torturing her with a clear picture of the violence he planned.

She could no longer control her breathing. Fear choked her until her breath came in almost sobbing gasps.

Dato touched her cheek. His brown eyes glowed with a demonic light. Then he mocked her. "And here I thought you were an ice queen. Nothing and no one touches you."

His hand trailed down her neck and over her collarbone. She forced herself to endure his touch, knowing she had to if she hoped to survive, but she shriveled inside with each stroke of his fingers.

He wrapped his hand around her throat and applied the gentlest of pressure, deliberately letting her know that he could choke her or snap her neck...or kiss her. Armed with his knives and firebombs, holding her prisoner, he could do whatever he liked, and she would be forced to bear witness to the destruction or suffer it herself as it pleased him.

Her soul cried out for Artur.

In this, her darkest moment, she doubted he would come for her. She doubted he would care. An icy wave of fear crashed over her and threatened to pull her under.

Artur didn't know her or see her. He would never imagine that she was here in danger. Needing him in a way she never had before, she hated him more than ever, feeling the biting double edge of her unrequited love.

The car turned onto Brighton Beach Avenue. It moved at a leisurely pace under the overhead train tracks, stopping at the lights. The windshield wipers swished softly, pushing away the clinging bits of drizzle that blew onto the glass. There seemed to be no hurry, but she found no solace in the slow progress toward Troika. She had no way to warn Aleksei of the impending threat.

The car pulled to a stop, double parking along the curb outside the nightclub, along with two similar vehicles with tinted windows. Dato cupped the back of her head with his palm and forcibly turned her head. He pressed her face to the window. "You will watch."

A man got out of the car behind them and strolled to the double glass doors of the club. No one on the street seemed to take any notice of him. Once she lost sight of him, Dato pressed on the back of her head. He shifted her so that she was forced to view the large picture window at the front of the restaurant. As Dato's driver rolled down his window, she spotted Victor at one of the tables in front.

The damp night air and the familiar smells of the street might have been soothing, but she could hardly breathe them in.

Another man got out of the car in front of them and hurled a brick at the glass window. She flinched as the glass broke with a loud crack and fell away in large chunks. Behind her, Dato laughed at her reflex, likely enjoying her distress.

Inside, patrons jumped way from the window and ducked for cover—for all the good it would do them.

She heard the click of a lighter. Then Dato's driver hurled a burning bottle through the broken window. People screamed. A man caught fire and transformed into a moving fireball.

Flames exploded everywhere. The man who'd thrown the brick lobbed a second Molotov cocktail into the frenzied crowd. The heat of the fire and the rising smoke made her eyes water. She prayed Aleksei was nowhere near the club at this moment.

She couldn't tell what was happening inside. She imagined Victor, survivor that he was, trampling people to get to the exit, but no one emerged.

Finally, Dato's man appeared at the door alone.

She became aware of the sounds of her breath, small panicked huffs. Behind her, Dato pinched her neck, almost lovingly, and chuckled. "Ah, Mrs. Koslovsky, I couldn't ask for a better companion this evening. And the night is still so young."

SVETLANA

THERE WAS A loud crack. Shattered glass. Svetlana spun around as the front tables near the window burst into flame.

Outside, three black SUVs idled in front of the club. A hand reached out from one of the drivers' windows and lobbed a flaming bottle through the decimated pane.

People started screaming and running toward the door, the grabby man and his wife at the front of the pack. Someone blocked the exit and threw down another flaming bottle. The two caught the brunt. They lit up, engulfed by fire, human torches.

Behind her, someone screamed. A waiter burst from the back hallway, a fireball at his back.

Svetlana grabbed the fire extinguisher and vaulted over the bar. Her stiletto heel cracked as she landed. Grabbing Anya, she limped away from the bar with its collection of flammable bottles. She pulled her toward the fires near the front door, the most likely route to safety.

Before them, the flames rose higher, feeding off of the accelerant from the bottles, creating a wall of fire between them and the exit. The heat licked at her. The air took on a wavy quality, as if reality were melting.

Determined to open an exit for them, Svetlana pulled the pin on the extinguisher and sprayed the worst of the flames. Through the raging fire, she watched the fire bomber, eyes intent on the bar, reach into his trench coat. How she wished for her gun!

He pulled out yet another Molotov cocktail and flicked his lighter. If the fire hit the liquor, the whole place would go up like a bomb had hit.

Everything seemed to move in slow motion as he raised his lighter to the Molotov cocktail.

Svetlana didn't have a gun. The only thing she had on hand was the fire extinguisher. The foreign patron from the bar stood behind her. She couldn't waste time wondering whether he had a gun and would use it. She needed to act.

With all of her strength, she hurled the extinguisher at the bomber. The red projectile caught him square in the chest. His eyes flashed with surprise as he stumbled backward and dropped the bottle.

The Molotov cocktail rolled toward the fire. Accelerant leaked out and fed the flames fanning all around them while the bomber scrambled to his feet and then raced for the door.

Now what? The small opening Svetlana had managed to create closed with flame. There was no exit this way. They were trapped.

She heard a hissing sound. The sprinklers! The fire hissed and spat as the spray from the ceiling doused the fire.

The mob in the bar pushed forward toward the door with Svetlana now at the lead, limping in her broken shoe.

Her foot slipped in the wetness on the floor. Her ankle turned painfully, and she flailed as she fell. She had a fleeting image of what would inevitably happen next: the panicked crowd would trample her.

Strong arms caught her, righted her, lifted her. The patron who earlier hadn't deigned to glance in her direction swept her into his arms, one hand at her back, the other under her knees, as if she were the heroine in a tawdry romance novel.

She wasn't too proud to accept his help. With grudging respect, she noticed that he didn't seem to lose stride with the horde, despite how heavy she must be.

He crossed the threshold where the door used to be. The evening air was raw and wet with a steady drizzle. She couldn't suppress a shiver.

He dumped her unceremoniously on the sidewalk. Leaving her hopping on one foot, he strode away as if he couldn't put distance between them fast enough. She hadn't even had the chance to thank him.

Sirens surrounded them. Fire trucks and police cars crowded in front of the club.

Svetlana scanned the throng for Anya.

"She is there. With her friends," an accented voice said. She turned to see the patron, returning to her, a full-length sable coat in his hands. He draped the fur over her shoulders like a cape.

"What's this?"

"A coat," he said. His full lips twitched with humor.

"Whose?"

"Yours."

The heavy coat held her like a hug, folding her in immediate warmth. The satin lining stuck to her wet skin.

"What's your name?" he asked as he came to face her.

"Svetlana."

"Svetlana. *Krasivaya*. I'm Gennady." The syllables rolled off his tongue with a melodic cadence. He straightened the collar on the coat and fastened the clasp at the neck. The scent of expensive cologne tickled her nose. Was the coat his?

Gennady regarded her steadily, his blue eyes almost hypnotic. The sudden solicitousness and the naked interest in his eyes contradicted his earlier dismissive attitude toward her.

Had she given herself away? Was that the reason for his sudden intense interest in her? Brighton Beach wouldn't be a safe place for her if someone here figured out her true identity.

She wouldn't second-guess herself. The sight of those human torches would haunt her for a long time. What if it had been Anya or one of the girls or Jack? A few more minutes, and it could have been any of them, all of them. She had done the right thing by springing into action at the bar.

He smoothed the wet hair out of her face. His brief touch sent a wave of heat through her body. "You saved everyone in the bar."

"No. I didn't..." She began to protest, but he pressed his finger to her lips and said, "You saved me."

Ah, so that was it. He felt grateful. She almost sighed with relief and disappointment. Gratitude wouldn't bust her cover. It also wasn't the same as interest in her. Not by a mile.

The last thing she needed right now was any kind of personal entanglement. Someone had tried to blow up the club. She should be focused on that, on solving this latest puzzle and how it related to the Koslovskys and her scheme with Vlad.

Yet, standing in the shadow of death, all she could think about for the moment was how it would feel to drop the subterfuge and gnawing worry, grab onto life with both hands, and kiss Gennady with his cold good looks and warm skin.

Even if all he felt was gratitude.

GENNADY

IF ONLY GENNADY had understood the depth of Victor's incompetence last night at the meeting at *Secretnaya Banya,* he could have been more proactive and averted this crisis.

He silently cursed Victor as the police made their rounds through the survivors of the fire bombing and tried to keep people from fleeing the scene. With an inbred wariness of authority, the Russians at the nightclub weren't eager to stick around and answer questions.

Gennady debated sneaking away, too. Attention was precisely what he didn't want. For himself. For this operation.

Svetlana, the bartender, stood before him, draped in the fur he had rescued from the coat check. "Go if you want to," she said, far too perceptive for her own good.

"Come with me." He needed to find out what she might know. She had been watching him far too intently at the bar.

"I can't. I have to stay here. The cops will know I was working the bar and will want to talk to me."

The ambulance-chasing news crews from the local stations jockeyed into position, putting their camera eyes everywhere. Gennady might attract more unwanted attention if someone caught him leaving the scene.

"I'll stay with you," he said.

"Suit yourself."

Despite the nonchalance of her words, she stared at him, her lips parted, an unspoken invitation shimmering in the charged air between them, one he accepted without hesitation.

He tugged on the fur he had wrapped her in, pulling her into his arms, and dragged his lips over hers.

The kiss had barely gotten started when they were interrupted.

"I need to ask you a few questions." A fresh-faced cop cleared his throat.

Gennady glared at him, but the timing couldn't have possibly been better. He now had an excuse for giving surly and miserly responses, and he could let Svetlana do the talking for both of them.

Indeed, she offered her name and address with no prodding and then launched into her account of the evening's events. "Three cars pulled up in front. Cadillac Escalades."

"How did you notice that?" Gennady asked. "I don't remember seeing any cars." A lie, but he couldn't have her suspecting him more than she already might.

"It's what my ex drives," she said with just the right amount of bitterness. A plausible explanation, and she sounded so convincing, but he wasn't fooled. "The difference was that these had gold rims."

The young cop in front of them scribbled furiously on his notepad as Svetlana relayed her observations, including a detailed description of the bomber who had entered the club.

"How did you remember all of that about him?" Gennady pretended to be impressed, but he would have been disappointed if she had recalled any less detail. "You were busy pouring drinks."

"I watch everyone," she said. "It pays to know who's likely to tip and who isn't. Who might cause trouble or try to rob the place. You get used to keeping your eyes open."

Another plausible explanation for how observant she was, but he recognized the signs of special training like his.

He had noticed the way her eyes constantly scanned the nightclub. Her active awareness of her surroundings had been his first clue.

When Victor had passed over his questions about her, dismissing her interest in him, Gennady hadn't needed any more evidence that the man was a complete and total idiot, unqualified to perform the job that had been given him. How often had Victor blundered into conducting sensitive business under such watchful eyes?

Gennady's second clue had come when Svetlana had reacted so swiftly to the threat from the firebombs, reacting the way only a person who had been specially trained would.

While the civilians had run and screamed, she had acted. She had jumped over the bar with the grace of a gymnast and the fierceness of a battle-hardened warrior, a Valkyrie in stilettos. Armed only with a fire extinguisher, she had taken out the attacker in the restaurant, buying all of them time until the sprinklers could put out the fire.

She had to be the American agent his sources had warned him was in the field.

Svetlana finished her account. The young cop looked at Gennady expectantly. "I have nothing to add," Gennady said. "I hope we're finished. This lovely lady needs medical attention and has been too polite to request it."

"The medics are busy with the burn victims," she said.

"That's no reason for you to suffer. Perhaps we can leave now and at least get some ice?" He appealed to the officer.

In exchange for a few details about himself, namely the information on his passport and the hotel where he was staying, they got permission to leave. He hadn't had to reveal anything even remotely sensitive. Still, he would have preferred to stay off of the American's radar entirely.

"I'll take you home," he said. Perhaps, if he could appear to be besotted with Troika's bartender, no one would suspect him of being a high-ranking Russian spy.

"That's not necessary."

"No? How will you get there? You can't plan to walk." He gestured to her ruined shoes and her swelling ankle. "Do you think it's broken?"

"Just sprained," she said. "But I'll take a taxi. I don't live far."

"Nonsense. I have a limo at my command. You will ride in style."

She opened her mouth as if she would argue, and he pressed a finger to her lips to silence her.

He would treat her like a queen, trail her like a love-starved stray, seduce her into revealing her secrets. "A woman like you should be draped in furs and ride in limos."

"Like me?" She cocked her head as if he had tripped her bullshit detector. The bright spark of intelligence in her brown eyes was inconvenient, but he welcomed the challenge. Who was she? CIA? FBI?

"You are magnificent," he said.

She squared her shoulders. "You didn't seem to think so before. When you were sitting at the bar."

"What do you mean?" he asked.

"You wouldn't look at me."

"You were watching me." He puffed his chest like a proud peacock. Did she suspect who he was? Or had she merely felt an attraction to him?

"I watch everyone," she huffed.

He threaded his fingers into her cropped hair and cupped her head, and she stayed exactly where she was, more affected by him than she would admit.

"I was blind to what was in front of me," he said, his face only inches from hers.

"And now you see?" Her question came out satisfyingly husky and inviting.

"Now I will always see."

He swept her into his arms and finished the kiss he had started earlier. Her mouth was soft but aggressively responsive, the chemistry between them the kind that couldn't be faked. Perfect.

He would enjoy using her.

In twenty-five years as an operative in America, Artur had not been caught or come under suspicion from the American authorities, despite generating substantial revenue for the Directorate and then laundering the money to a clinical grade of cleanliness.

Unfortunately, the trail from Troika was likely to lead to Artur, unless Gennady intervened. The Directorate couldn't afford to lose the man now.

While Gennady couldn't control whether Artur fell under investigation, he could ensure that the American authorities learned only what he wanted them to learn.

He would stay close to Svetlana, pretend he was in love with her, and then he would provide her with a trail of bread crumbs.

What she learned would undoubtedly trickle to the right ears. Misinformation could be a potent weapon, and the lovely Svetlana—if that was indeed her real name—would be a valuable asset in this war.

ALEKSEI

STAN LIVED LESS than half a mile away from Troika. Aleksei parked his silver Ferrari a couple of blocks away and then ran the rest of the way there. He slowed when he got to Stan's driveway. He glanced around him. Was anyone watching? Would they remember he was here?

The house was dark, no lights on inside, no lights on the porch. He pulled the gun from his waistband and rang the doorbell impatiently, imagining Stan would open the door and…pop. The pharmacist would be dead, and his latest set of problems would be solved.

Stan made him wait. As he stood on the front porch, he felt a prickle on his neck. Someone was watching him.

Blyad! He hadn't given a moment's thought to how this all might look—a man in leather pants taking a nighttime jog through a residential neighborhood and then pulling a gun.

He held the gun against his thigh. Maybe whoever was watching wouldn't see. Maybe they'd turn away.

The streetlights lit up the street, but Aleksei stood in the shadows of the house. Maybe whoever was watching couldn't really see him.

What if he got caught?

He hadn't thought this through, hadn't thought any of it through. Stan needed to be silenced. That was certain. But if Aleksei botched the hit, there would be a ripple of consequences.

The cops might come after him anyway, this time for murder. Inevitably, once they discovered his motive, they'd link him back to the murder at Troika, despite Mikhail's "foolproof" planning.

He'd watched his share of detective shows on TV, knew how they collected forensic evidence and DNA samples. Sure, Mikhail had procured an unmarked gun for him, but was that enough insurance that the authorities wouldn't be able to trace a bullet back to him?

The detectives on the shows were smart, almost always smarter than the criminals, certainly smarter than Aleksei.

But that was TV. A good bribe, he reminded himself, could make even the smartest man change sides and suddenly turn stupid or accidentally lose damning evidence or even a witness.

He didn't have to do this perfectly. He just needed to shell out enough money to cover his tracks.

He would have paid Stan if he'd had a prayer of collecting a million dollars by the ridiculous deadline and if he actually believed Stan wouldn't plague him for more.

What was taking Stan so long to answer? Aleksei rang the doorbell again. Didn't the asshole want his money?

If Stan was peeping at him through the window, he would see that Aleksei didn't have a briefcase or anything that might possibly hold the cash he'd demanded. And he hadn't pulled up in a car; so there wasn't even the possibility it was in the trunk.

Aleksei grabbed the handle of the door, not sure what he would do, but prepared to force his way in. He was surprised when it opened easily.

He stepped into the house, where he would be shielded from any watchful eyes on the block. The wood in the hallway creaked under his steps. He tried to walk on tiptoe, but his pointy-toe shoes weren't designed for stealth.

He stayed alert, trying to see everything all at once, looking this way and that, prepared for a sneak attack.

With all the aplomb of a drunken teenager sneaking home after curfew, he bumped his hip on the hall table and sent a vase crashing to the floor.

He froze and gripped his gun with both hands. The living room and dining room were both dark, but he could see light spilling from the doorway farther down the hall, presumably to the kitchen.

Stop pretending to be a big man. Stop pretending. Stop pretending.

His palms grew sweaty inside his gloves. He told himself that when the time came, he would pull the trigger. At close enough range, he couldn't possibly miss.

He would stop Stan's taunting voice forever.

He crossed the threshold into the kitchen and froze. The linoleum floor was covered with blood, and the scent was thick in the air.

Dizziness overtook him. He felt his body sway. *Bozhe moy!* He had seen dead bodies before, but few like this one—nearly decapitated, soaked in a bath of its own blood. He reached for the table to steady himself.

He recognized the handiwork by reputation. The carving and bloodletting were Dato's signature.

Stan wouldn't have a chance to go to the police now, but what had he told the Georgians? Would they be coming for Aleksei next?

KATYA

KATYA'S PHONE STARTED ringing. Feeling too low to talk to anyone, she ignored it. The ringing stopped and then started again. Katya glanced at the caller i.d. and finally picked up.

Jack, her sister's husband, was trying to reach her. Urgently.

"What's wrong?"

"You need to turn on the news." Usually calm and collected, Jack sounded shaken.

With a sense of dread, Katya picked up the remote from the large glass and chrome coffee table and turned to the local news station.

The announcer stood outside a broken picture window at a restaurant. The brick front of the establishment was charred, the remaining glass of the window in sharp, jagged points. Blue and red lights flashed on the announcer's face, and the camera panned to ambulances and police cars on a familiar stretch of Brighton Beach Avenue.

The black awning hung in shreds from the front door of her husband's nightclub. The stenciled horses on the doors were gone, the glass shattered.

"*Bozhe moy!*" Katya gasped and shuddered. Reflexively, she placed a hand protectively over her belly, over the baby growing inside.

"Eyewitnesses say the assailants were throwing Molotov cocktails," the announcer said. "Three people are dead and many more injured."

"I'm fine. So's Becca. Shaken. But fine," he said.

"Aleksei," Katya whimpered.

"I don't know where he is. I saw him with Mikhail not long before the fire."

Jack's tone was brusque, and she felt a surge of unease.

"The police want to talk to him. He's not answering his phone. I don't know where the hell he is. Do you?" Jack was angry at Aleksei. Why?

"He hasn't called me. I don't know where he is," she said, fighting panic. Had the culprits grabbed him and taken him somewhere else? Someone capable of throwing Molotov cocktails in a nightclub had no scruples, could do anything to anyone.

Aleksei could be in real trouble. He could be hurt. Her heart thumped heavily in her chest. She loved him, worried for him, even if he wasn't the man she thought she had married.

This couldn't be a coincidence. A murder a few nights ago. A blackmail threat last night. A fire tonight. No, not a fire, an attack, and all too close to home.

"The police are looking for him." The statement sounded like a rebuke. Did Jack blame Aleksei for the attack?

Katya herself suspected Aleksei's involvement in a world she didn't want to know, in activities she couldn't condone, ones completely at odds with her values and her profession as a lawyer.

But she couldn't turn her heart on and off like a tap. Love still flowed, whether or not he deserved it. And he would always be the father of her baby.

"Did they say why?" Katya asked. She was still willing to hear the evidence, still hoping that she could somehow try her husband and find him not guilty, still hoping that the things she had heard the other night were all a misunderstanding.

From the living room, she noticed the shiny black SUVs idling in front of her house. With dark tinted windows and gold rims, they didn't look anything like cop cars.

A man in a trench coat with a bottle in one hand and a brick in the other strode up her front walk. *Molotov cocktails.*

"Ohmigod. Jack, call 9-1-1 and send them to my house." She raced for the kitchen and the back door. She could run through the yard and make an escape.

"What? Why?"

"Just do it! Someone's here." She hung up the phone. She took a precious moment to disable the alarm—better not to have it go off and announce her escape.

She grabbed the knob to the back door, but something in the window caught her eye. A shadowy figure moved toward her from the side of the house. She backed away from the door. She couldn't get out, not without whoever was out there seeing her.

Where could she hide if they entered the house? Where would she be safe if they threw a firebomb?

She threw open the basement door. Hoping the man out back didn't glimpse her through the kitchen window, she closed the door behind her and fled down the steps. She hurried down the darkened staircase and across the finished part of the basement. With only the dimmest light shining through the high rectangular windows, she found the storage room door at the back.

Once she slipped through the door and closed it behind her, she was surrounded by thick darkness. She fumbled around, feeling her way to the back wall. She didn't dare turn on a light that would give any seekers a clue to where she might have gone.

Finally, she found the crawl space. The rough cinder blocks scratched her skin as she hoisted herself up into the unfinished space that she used as a deep shelf.

There was nothing in here, only some old suitcases. She crawled behind the largest one. It might hide her if someone thought to peer back here. With no light, the space around her felt desolate and a little spooky.

She pulled her knees to her chest. She placed a hand over her belly and promised her baby she would do everything she could to keep them both safe.

MAYA

MAYA PRESSED HER fingers to the glass of the car window. She watched in horror as Dato's henchman marched up Aleksei's driveway and shattered the leaded glass framing the grand double door of Aleksei's house.

Maya expected he would next let himself in. Maybe loot the place or search for Aleksei and Katya. Instead, he hurled a brick through the front picture window, leaving a large, jagged hole.

Then the man lit the bottle he was holding and lobbed it through the hole he'd made near the door. The glass that was still intact glittered with orange flame.

He pulled another bottle from his trench coat, lit that one, and pitched it into Aleksei's living room. In moments, smoke billowed from both points of entry, and Maya could only imagine the damage inside.

All the nice things Aleksei and Katya had accumulated, the signs of their success and prosperity, would be destroyed.

She watched for signs of Katya or Aleksei. So far, no one had come out of the house. The devastation to their home would be awful, but what if they were home and trapped inside the fireball?

Behind her, Dato laughed. "Your son brought this on himself," he said as if reading her thoughts and reveling in them. "If he's home, we'll smoke him out—or fry him."

How long would it take the whole house to burn to the ground? She closed her eyes. She couldn't watch.

Dato gripped her chin in his hand and turned her face toward him, forcing her to open her eyes and look at him. "No one fucks with me and mine," he said.

"What do you plan to do?" Fear made her words a stuttering whisper. She could hardly swallow past the lump in her throat.

"Whatever I want."

He placed his large, olive hand on her thigh. Her heartbeat quickened. Her chest felt so tight that she didn't dare take the gasping breath she badly wanted.

She tried to shift away from him, but his grip tightened until she did gasp. The sound made him smile. His gold teeth glittered in the moonlight. He moved his face closer to hers, and she involuntarily reared her head back until she bumped against the headrest.

He bore down on her knee and thigh, letting her know he could touch her however he liked, however intimately he wanted, and that he'd give her no quarter. She squeezed her eyes shut again rather than look at him.

His breath was warm on her face. He smelled of lemons and aftershave—a surprisingly clean and pleasant smell, but not enough to cover the stench of blood on him or to overcome her absolute revulsion.

He caught her lower lip in his teeth and tugged almost gently. The he bit her hard.

She could taste the trickle of blood in her mouth. Never in her life had she been so powerless. This man was a barbarian who gloried in destruction.

Dato pulled back and laughed. "I enjoyed that more than I expected," he said. "When I'm done with you, maybe I'll even send you back to your husband—as a lasting reminder of who truly rules Brighton Beach."

Bile filled her throat. If she were a heroine in a movie, now would be the moment when she lifted her chin and told the Georgian villain that her husband would finish him if he hurt a hair on her head. But she feared Artur might be relieved if she came home in a body bag.

So she lifted her chin and kept quiet. This wasn't a movie, and no one would ever have cast her as the leading lady. Not anymore. Her time in the spotlight had been all too brief.

Dato gripped her chin again and steered her gaze back to Aleksei's house. The drapes caught fire. The inside of her son's dream house glowed brightly as the furniture and cabinets and light fixtures were swallowed in bright flames.

In a few minutes, the whole structure would be nothing but ash and the stones from the fireplace.

"You like that?" Dato crooned in her ear, as if he were a solicitious lover. "We'll hit your son's pharmacies next."

All of Aleksei's hard work, his hopes and ambitions, the dream life he'd finally started to achieve—Dato was destroying everything. Even if Aleksei survived, what would he have left? She felt a mother's pain for her child's loss.

"Why?"

"An eye for an eye," Dato said. "He stole from my business and killed my man. He thought he'd get away with it, but he won't. I'll take everything from him. His business. His home. His family."

"It wasn't Aleksei," she said, pleaded. "He didn't do anything to you."

"No? Who did, then? Tell me what you know, Mrs. Koslovsky." He squeezed her jaw with his long fingers.

"No answer? We'll collect your whore of a daughter next," he threatened.

"It was me," she said. "All of it was me. I'm the mastermind. I made the drugs for him and told him where and how to sell them."

Dato let go of her and then slapped her hard across the cheek. Her skin smarted, but she didn't dare feel the spot with her hands. His dark eyes burned through her. "I don't like liars. Do it again, and I'll cut out your tongue."

She snapped her mouth shut. In the rearview mirror, she caught sight of the driver watching her and Dato with his good eye. She couldn't read his emotions—whether he also thought she was lying, whether he felt sympathy for her, whether he wanted to revel in destruction the way his boss did.

Yet, through the separation between the front driver's and passenger's seat, she saw him fumble with her backpack. He sneaked a hand inside and stole a wad of the poisoned cash. Human nature was so dependably consistent.

Maybe all wasn't lost.

INNA

WHEN INNA FINALLY arrived at the precinct and was seated in an
"interview" room, her clothes stuck to her skin. The dampness wasn't
from the rain and drizzle outside, but her own sweat.

Her palms and forehead were slick with a sheen of perspiration, no
matter how often she tried to wipe it away, and her mouth was
unbearably dry. She had a tremor in her hands.

Her own weakness, her body's betrayal, galled her. She had come so
far, survived so much. She had even managed to get herself to work this
morning.

And now she could hardly cope, could hardly breathe.

Falling apart. She was simply falling apart. She couldn't handle the
stress of all of this. She was going to die—if not at the hands of whoever
was stalking her, then from the strain.

Detective Hersh entered the interrogation room and gave her a
pitying glance. "Do you need something? Maybe a cup of coffee?"

"Water," she croaked, breath coming fast, as if she were running.
Her chest burned. Her mind sent the right signals to calm down, to
breathe. But her body had other ideas. The panic she'd almost banished
now took over her involuntary functions.

She needed a pill and peace and quiet. She needed to go home and
lock her door and wrap herself in her down comforter and tell herself she
was safe.

That tactic had worked in the past, when she could dismiss her
imaginings about the intrigue around her as fantasy. But she couldn't
imagine away the horrible, violent things that had happened in the past

few days. Those things had really happened. There were witnesses and evidence.

And victims. Vlad and Nick had both been shot. Igor was dead.

No one patted her soothingly and told her she was imagining things now, least of all Detective Hersh.

"Have you heard what happened at Troika tonight?" the detective asked.

She shook her head, not trusting herself to speak.

"Someone decided to throw a few Molotov cocktails and light up the place."

"What?" She blinked at him. Surely she was hearing things.

"Firebombs. At the nightclub. Three people are dead, and more seriously injured." He explained, as if he were almost reluctant to break the news to her.

"Is Aleksei okay?" she asked. "And Jack? Were they there?"

"We're looking for your brother. We need to question him," Hersh said. "But we don't think he was there. Jack is fine. Any idea why someone would try to catch their nightclub on fire? Or target you?"

"No. None."

"What do you know about your brother's business?"

"You mean the nightclub? Or the pharmacies?"

"Does he work with your father?"

"No. They had a falling out. Papa wanted him to make it on his own."

"But your father let you join the business."

She thought she detected the slightest challenge in his words, a hint of doubt.

"Sort of," she said. "I run my design business out of the import-export office, and I order furniture and decorative items through the company that I think will appeal to our clients. He's my partner in that, but the rest is his show."

"The rest?"

"The alcohol and packaged goods." And the mysterious deliveries she had previously refused to consider. She took a sip of the water, almost spilling it from the Styrofoam cup with the shaking in her hands.

"The question makes you nervous?" He perched on the corner of the table and leaned toward her. He smelled of Old Spice and spearmint gum.

"What? No." His questions didn't make her nervous. The true answers to them did. What kind of business were her father and brother really involved in?

"Do you have any idea who your father or brother might have upset? Or who their competitors are?"

"Is that what you think this is all about? Some business competition?" She took another sip of water.

"No, Inna. It's not what I think it's about. It's not what you think it's about either. Is it?"

The events of the day were taking their toll. Tonight was a hell of a night to stop her medicine cold turkey. She gripped the empty cup under the edge of the table, holding on so tightly to her slipping control that she crushed the cup in her hands.

"Your family's involved in organized crime."

She inhaled sharply at the idea and choked on the water in her mouth. She coughed and sputtered. "You mean, the mafia? That's not possible," she said reflexively.

Once, she had imagined the very same thing, only to reject the notion. Her papa, the honorable and distinguished man she knew him to be, couldn't possibly be a white collar criminal. Instead, she had latched onto the idea that he might be a spy, a theory terrifying in its own right, but one that elevated him above the criminal element. She recognized the romanticism now.

Organized crime? She thought about Igor, dead in the back of his own delivery truck. Maybe it was possible. She had vowed to consider the possibilities. To look at what was in front of her.

Detective Hersh cocked his head. She could feel him studying her, eyeing her sweaty face and shaking hands. She imagined she looked like a junkie in detox, not at all credible. Mentally unstable, Dr. Kasparov had said. Paranoid.

If she truly considered the possibility of her family's involvement in organized crime, was she now lucid, seeing clearly? Or was she sliding into the rabbit hole of fear and suspicion that would ultimately land her in an asylum, where white was the new black and no one cared if you drooled out of the side of your mouth?

She shuddered at the thought. The threat of institutionalization had always snapped her back to reality and motivated her to bury her unfounded suspicions.

But maybe they hadn't been unfounded.

"Are you okay?" the detective asked.

"No," she said as the repressed memories bubbled up—snatches of conversation that quickly ended when she entered the room, an expired Russian passport with her father's picture and a different name printed on it, and the lucrative warehouse almost empty of supplies. Puzzle pieces that together had seemed so damning.

A lot of nothing, Dr. Kasparov had told her. An overactive imagination. Paranoia that latched onto conspiracy theories. Hallucinations. With each new sliver of evidence she presented, Dr. Kasparov had told her that she was clinically delusional and needed her medication adjusted.

She hadn't broached this particular topic with Dr. Shiffman, too afraid of opening the Pandora's box of fear and illness. She wanted to get better. She wanted a normal life.

Hersh took off his glasses. He took his time cleaning the lenses with a cloth that he pulled from his pocket. Her hands shook harder as he waited for her to speak, as if a demon locked inside of her rattled its cage to get out.

She wasn't ready to voice any suspicions *again*. Perhaps it was enough, for now, to acknowledge them to herself.

Finally, he put the glasses back on and let out a deep sigh. "You've had a rough day. A rough couple of days. How about I send you home, and I'll stop by tomorrow to talk with you?" He once again shone his compassion on her and treated her kindly.

She nodded, not trusting herself to speak and dreading their next encounter.

He walked her out to the front of the precinct. Mikhail was waiting on a wooden bench, and he rose when he saw her. "I came to take you home."

He laid his hand on her shoulder, and she almost flinched at the contact. While she was grateful for his efforts to protect her this morning, she didn't want him touching her. She remembered all too clearly the horrific pass he'd made at her, when he'd promised to grab her hair, rip her panties, and make her scream for mercy. To be fair, he didn't know what had happened to her in college, but he creeped her out all the same.

He might be her brother's friend and maybe she should forgive him for the off comment he'd made, but her instincts screamed to stay away from him.

Hadn't she promised herself not to ignore her intuition?

He was too smooth, and he stood too close. She imagined other women found him attractive. Perhaps they even liked his straightforward offer of rough sex, but she didn't. She dodged him by turning toward Detective Hersh. "What about Vlad? I promised I'd wait for him."

"We have more questions for him. It might be a while."

"See?" Mikhail said. "No reason you should cool your heels here. Look at you. You're exhausted. And shaking. Have you even eaten anything?" He grabbed her hand and started pulling her toward the door.

Inna supposed she must look a wreck. Should she struggle? Cause a scene? She didn't want to go with him, but maybe he was right. Maybe she needed to go home, eat something, rest up.

She glanced back at Detective Hersh. He didn't seem alarmed at all by the prospect of her leaving with Mikhail. Were her fears unreasonable?

"I'll let Vlad know that you went home," Detective Hersh said, as if he agreed with Mikhail's course of action.

She let Mikhail lead her away, but she stayed wary.

MIKHAIL

"COME ON, INNA," Mikhail coaxed. "Look at you. You need to eat something."

"I'm really not hungry," she protested.

He caught her hand and felt the tremor in her fingers. He stepped closer, into her space. She was seated at the kitchen table in her stark industrial-style kitchen with its polished concrete countertops and stainless steel appliances. The rough wood table was covered with the fast food feast he'd insisted on buying for her, but she hadn't touched any of it. Not even a salty french fry.

Didn't matter. He didn't care what she ate so long as she took a few good long gulps of her milkshake.

"Please, Inna." He caressed her with his voice while he held her hand. Her eyes widened, but she looked more ready to bolt than swoon.

He wanted to kiss her, to see her eyes widen even more, perhaps even to shock her with the force of his passion for her. He held back, careful of frightening her just now, but imagining how he would like to take her here, now, on the floor of her spotless kitchen.

He wondered how long it would be before she relaxed and warmed in his presence. How long before he no longer needed to alter her state to get what he wanted from her?

When she was out, he could do whatever he wanted to her, but he thought he might like her participation. He'd like to override her resistance.

He would overpower her, overwhelm her, throw her down hard against the cold tiles, make her writhe under him, and beg for anything and everything. For release. For him to stop. For him to take her harder and faster. It didn't matter, really, so long as she eventually gave him her total submission.

He relished the vision of Artur's little princess kneeling at his feet and begging him to dirty her up or let her suck him off.

Abruptly he cut off this line of thinking. Now was too soon to act on even a fraction of his impulses. She was too skittish, too likely to scream and call for help.

A dose of the newest cocktail he and Aleksei were selling, even a small one, would fix that.

This new drug would lower Inna's inhibitions and make her more susceptible to Mikhail's expert seduction. Once she stopped being so skittish, the right words and the right touch would light her up.

"At least drink some of the milkshake," he urged. "It's vanilla. Your favorite. Right? I remembered," he said. "Drink a little. Just a sip even. Your father won't forgive me if you pass out from hunger. And he's already angry at me as it is for the scare you had this morning." He infused his request with the lies most likely to guilt her into compliance.

Her father had no idea Mikhail was here with her now. Artur hadn't called him. His boss wouldn't, not after the abrupt dismissal he'd given Mikhail this morning. But Inna didn't know that.

She also didn't know that the man he'd hired to chase her this morning had been spying on her all day, waiting for her to leave Koslovsky Imports to make another grab for her and steal her away from Vlad, giving Mikhail another opportunity to play hero. Neither he nor Vitaliy had expected another set of kidnappers to show up.

"Fine. I don't want you to get in trouble." She sighed, and he had to hide his smile at her capitulation, all the sweeter since her surrender was tied to concern for him. "But honestly I'm fine. Just tired."

He placed a hand on her shoulder. She pulled back, and he clamped his hand tighter. "Drink," he ordered. He pushed the straw into her mouth, but gently.

Her lips were plump and moist, and he imagined how he would lick and bite her, how she would welcome his advances once she succumbed to the influence of the tasteless, odorless drug he'd concealed in the frothy shake. He watched the movement of her mouth and throat as she sucked and swallowed.

"Again," he said, his voice thickening with lust. Soon, so soon. "Please, let me take care of you." His words, or maybe the silken quality of his voice, affected her. She blushed prettily, but then she ducked out of his hold.

For a brief moment, he was tempted to grab her, to pull her head back by her hair, and pour the milkshake down her throat.

He quashed the impulse. That wasn't the way to win her, and, even if he could rush things along in the bedroom with a push of enhancers now and again, he needed to win her devotion. He needed her to be his even when her father disapproved.

He watched her carefully, waiting for the moment he could finally make a move without her drawing away. He touched her shoulder again. This time, she didn't make her usual sidestep, but she maintained too much distance.

Just a few more minutes. That was all he needed. Then she would want him.

This time, she would want everything, remember everything. Tomorrow morning when she awakened in his arms, she would finally know she was his.

"You should go," she said. She headed for the door, determined to send him away.

Hadn't she drunk enough? Why was she being so difficult? His anger swelled, but he controlled it. "I'm here to protect you."

"I'm sure I'm perfectly safe in my home," she said, but he noticed the lack of conviction. "I'll lock the door behind you."

"Are you sure you'll feel safe? I thought you'd want someone nearby."

"I just want to be alone in my space," she said.

"Vlad crowded you today?" He took a guess. He couldn't resist casting Artur's favorite in a negative light, lest Inna start to admire the man and his firepower.

"No," she said. Then, to his immense relief, she immediately retracted. "Well, yes, actually. If I'm honest. You don't like him. Do you?"

He was touched that she had noticed. "No, princess. Can't say I do."

"Princess?" She crossed her arms as if she didn't approve of his chosen term of endearment.

"Should I call you something else? Darling? Baby?"

"No—"

"I've always had a thing for you." He cut her off before she could protest the newfound familiarity he wished to impose on her. "I'm just more aware of it now after all of the close calls you've had the last few days." He pushed a lank strand of hair out of her face, and she didn't shrink away from his touch.

That's right. Just a little longer. A few more minutes, and you'll be all mine.

VLAD

SHE'S SAFE. SHE'S safe. She's safe. Vlad repeated the mantra over and over. The cops had left him in lockup, separated from Inna. He didn't know where she was right now or what she was doing. He had to hope the precinct was one of the safest places she could be, provided she had actually arrived in one piece and that she didn't leave without him.

She had said she'd wait. What if she didn't?

The cops had clapped him in handcuffs and dragged him in here. He couldn't blame them for that. After all, they had found him with a smoking gun and two dead bodies. But once they got his statement—and Inna's and Nick's—they should have let him go. The gun he'd used was registered, and he'd stopped those men from abducting Inna.

He'd killed them, but that didn't mean whoever had sent them wouldn't try again.

He folded his hands behind his neck and dropped his head down. At this rate, he'd go insane worrying over her.

Why was he still here? The cops had taken his statement and then put him back in lockup. Surely they couldn't be thinking they would press homicide charges.

He was feeling rather homicidal at the moment. God help them if they didn't reunite him with Inna soon.

The vein throbbed at Vlad's temple. It seemed like hours before someone came to get him. Detective Sharp.

The choice of interrogator could only mean someone liked to fuck with him. He could easily guess who that was.

Sharp led him, handcuffed, to an interrogation room, as if he were the most dangerous of criminals. Once they were seated in the cinder block room with its viewing mirror, Detective Sharp said, "I have a witness who says you took money for a hit from Ivan."

"Your witness is lying," Vlad said.

"Did you do a hit?"

"No."

Vlad knew exactly what the cop was referring to—the men he'd killed in the alley outside Troika. Ivan had later claimed it was a sanctioned hit, but that was not what had really happened.

This was all a useless bluff on the cop's part. They couldn't possibly have any evidence, certainly not enough to waste a trial trying to get a conviction. He had no motive, and he'd sanitized the scene. Sure, the buildings on either side of the alley where he'd been ambushed by Ivan's men had pockmarks now from the spray of bullets, but he'd disposed of the essentials.

No bodies. No smoking gun. No conviction.

Still, they could make his life hell with an investigation. His usefulness to Artur would be dubious at best if he had Homicide constantly breathing down his neck. Murder charges wouldn't possibly stick, but Vlad had most definitely tampered with a potential crime scene—a very serious infraction with charges of its own if anyone found out.

It had to be a bluff, he reassured himself yet again. The only way Vlad could be tied definitively to the deaths outside Troika was if Svetlana had suddenly had a turn of conscience.

Fat chance. She hadn't left her son for months on end to have their careful plans scorched because some of Ivan's men had decided to take shots at him and paid the price. If they got yanked from this assignment now, when he was so close to proving himself... Such a failure didn't bear contemplating.

And he wasn't ready to leave Inna. Not yet. Probably not ever. *Mine. Only mine.*

"Did you take money from Ivan?"

"No."

The detective's slow-blinking eyes made Vlad tap his foot with impatience. *Hurry up. Get this over with. Let me get back to Inna.* But he knew Sharp would belabor the same points over and over, as if asking the same question would eventually get him a different answer, one he liked better, one that was a confession of guilt.

Sharp could go to Hell. Vlad hadn't committed a hit for his father, even if Artur had tossed a wad of cash at him and claimed it was compensation for the self-defense shootings outside Troika. He certainly wasn't going to tell Sharp about any of it.

The real question was, who had? Vlad and Artur had been alone in the shop this morning. Had someone been eavesdropping? Had they been bugged?

Maybe Ivan's man, Slim, had been onto something with his warning that there was an agent in the field. Maybe the cop who'd been undercover with the Georgians had a partner, someone with the DEA or a joint task force. Or maybe there was a confidential informant. Could there be someone planted in Ivan's organization, someone who'd heard about Ivan's plans?

Vlad didn't have enough information. He didn't know how far Ivan reached from his prison cell, how many men he commanded, what kinds of resources he had at his disposal.

All he really knew was that the once powerful *vor* and Artur kept in touch and still did business together, even if that business was no more than Artur's disbursing funds to pay for Nadia's apartment or for Ivan's hits.

"Did Ivan talk to you about killing someone?"

"I don't know what you're talking about," Vlad lied. He knew Ivan had boasted after the fact about commissioning him to do a hit, but said commission had never been discussed while the bodies in question were warm. Rather, Ivan had sent his men after Vlad, likely with orders to kill, and then chosen to tell a different tale when Vlad had been the only one to emerge from the alleyway without his own body bag.

"I also have this," Detective Sharp said. He slid a piece of paper, the size of a cigarette wrapper, across the table. "Recognize this?"

Vlad leaned down to inspect it. He recognized Ivan's clumsy handwriting: *$300,000 commission to Vladimr for Vasya and his brothers.* "What the hell is it?"

"A commission for you from Ivan." Sharp smiled thinly. He looked like a turtle that had just snapped its beak over a tasty morsel.

"Bullshit," Vlad said. He had to wonder why his father would send him a secret message printed in English, unless the message wasn't meant for him or to be secret. "How do you know it's from Ivan? Or that it's for me?"

"I won't reveal my sources," Sharp said.

"Fine." Vlad sat back in his seat and crossed his arms. "I want to talk to Detective Hersh," he said. When Detective Sharp looked like he might balk, Vlad added, "I'll only talk to him."

But he had no intention of telling old Hershey anything either.

Hersh arrived a few minutes later.

"Where's Inna?" Vlad demanded.

"On her way home."

"You let her leave?"

"She's not currently under investigation."

"I told her to wait for me," Vlad said. The muscle in his jaw twitched and tightened beyond comfort.

"We told her you'd be a while."

"Are you an idiot? She's in danger."

"We sent her home with Artur's other man."

"His other man? You mean Mikhail?" Vlad pounded his fist on the table. The scrap of paper with Ivan's supposedly incriminating bounty notice bounced off the table and floated momentarily in the air.

Mikhail. Vlad didn't trust the blue-eyed pretty boy. He didn't like the predatory way the man's eyes tracked and catalogued Inna's every move or how close he stood to her whenever he had the opportunity.

Did Inna like Mikhail? Was that why she hadn't waited for Vlad?

Maybe that spontaneous embrace earlier today had been nothing more than shock and leftover affection from their childhood.

Whatever the moment had meant to Inna, he knew what it meant to him. He wouldn't let a blue-eyed Casanova or anyone else get between them. *Mine. Only mine.*

"The sooner you cooperate, the sooner we get you back to her," Hersh said as if he had a valuable bargaining chip.

Vlad's temper threatened to break free of his tenuous hold. His head throbbed.

Hersh slid the small slip of paper in front of Vlad again. "Tell me about this."

"Your man Sharp thinks this is proof I killed someone," Vlad said. "But you and I both know you can't possibly have much of a case if this is all you've got."

"But you did kill someone," Hersh said.

"I've killed lots of people. Usually with the full blessing of this fine country."

"Ever in cold blood? Ever since you left the Bureau?"

Vlad's eyes narrowed. "Why?"

"Seems to me Ivan wants to ensure you've made a clean break from law enforcement—a public one so that he can promote you."

"Is that what he wants?" Vlad made the question sound like a taunt, but his mind raced, pulling puzzle pieces together. Suddenly, the ambush and Artur's sudden anger at him all made a certain logical sense.

He hadn't, not in his wildest dreams, expected his father's support. He'd thought he'd have to pledge himself to Artur and make his play before Ivan was freed from prison. But now...

For whatever reason, Ivan was paving the way for him to join the highest ranks of the brotherhood. What better method than to let everyone know he had blood—blood Ivan wanted—on his hands and then to promise even more?

There might not be any spies in Ivan's organization, other than the ones Ivan himself controlled.

"He'll be out of prison soon," Hersh said.

"And?"

"And it would be helpful to have someone on the inside."

Vlad pounded his fists on the table again. "I don't fucking believe it. You dragged me in here to ask me to be your narc?"

"Make no mistake. We'll get someone in there eventually," Hersh said.

Did that mean they'd already tried unsuccessfully to break into Ivan's organization? If they had planted someone with the Georgians, Vlad couldn't be surprised they'd also made a play to get close to Ivan or Artur.

"Might as well be you," Hersh said.

"Still trying to save my soul for God?" Vlad taunted.

Hersh didn't even blink. His quiet faith slipped like the sharpest knife beneath Vlad's skin and poked at his hidden doubts and fears.

He didn't want to be a monster. Not like Ivan.

But he knew what he had to do. Sometimes slaying a monster required being one. And he didn't need Hersh or anyone else getting in his way.

"Say I agreed. What then?"

"Immunity," Hersh offered.

Vlad barked out a laugh. "That all you got? Fuck you."

"Money?" Hersh asked tentatively, as if reluctant to believe the mighty dollar could be a motivating factor for Vlad. "Is that what this is about?"

"We're done talking," Vlad said.

He had no recourse but the tough guy routine. Even if Vlad felt swayed, it wasn't safe to say so in the interrogation room, where anyone might be listening in from the other side of the mirrored glass. Marano was Artur's man. Vlad would bet there were others here, taking bribes from one crew or another.

"We're not done 'til I say we're done. And you're not leaving here until I give the all clear. I have nothing better to do than sit and chat with you. All. Night. Long." Hersh raised a bushy eyebrow in challenge.

Vlad sat back in his folding metal chair, lips pressed firmly together, letting Hersh know what he thought of his pronouncement.

"I've got dead bodies piling up," Hersh said. "Firebombs at Troika, International Pharmacy, and Aleksei Koslovsky's house; an attempted kidnapping and a gripe between Artur Koslovsky and the Georgians. Seems to me there's a full-on mafia war."

"They firebombed Aleksei's house and businesses?"

A sense of imminent danger socked Vlad in the chest. A fear he hadn't known before gripped him. Mikhail might be the least of his worries. He had to get to Inna and fast.

"I looked up your record," Hersh said. "The most recent court proceedings from one of your cases. It took me a while, but I found what I was looking for. Hard to believe you'd testify with such conviction and then suddenly decide to play for the other team."

"I don't care what you believe."

"Time might come when you need a friend." Hersh's voice was low. Did he know there were ears in this place?

Vlad tried to read the subtext, the emotional undercurrent. Was Hersh merely trying to reach the decent man he hoped was hiding deep down inside Vlad, or did he know something he shouldn't?

"If I'm right about you, you'll help us when the time comes."

"And if you're wrong?" Vlad tried to imbue his words with smugness.

"I'm not the only one watching you. You might appreciate knowing there are agents in the field. This is bigger than both of us."

"They won't last long if you announce their presence all over town," Vlad said.

"Not just FBI," Hersh said, in a way that emphasized he suspected strongly that Vlad was still with the Bureau. "CIA, too."

Vlad knew about the feds, but the CIA? He had suspected they might be involved, but he hadn't known for sure. Hersh had done him a favor, confirming a strong suspicion. If the CIA were watching, then whatever secret deal Artur and Victor were planning involved players and people from far beyond this little corner of Brooklyn.

If the CIA were interested enough to plant their own agent, then one, if not all, of Vlad's suspicions had to be right: international money laundering, espionage and arms dealing, or human trafficking. He hadn't ruled out the first two, but he was increasingly favoring the third as a real possibility.

Maybe this was why Artur had sought him out in the first place, luring him away from a similar operation out of a strip club in Miami.

He recalled the conversation with Victor and Artur, with Victor's veiled references to the mysterious "merchandise," his concerns about the time-sensitivity of the new deal, and finally the need to involve the Georgians. The Georgian crew in Brighton Beach dealt in drugs and prostitutes and had ties to Las Vegas and other flesh hot spots.

Vlad bet Artur and Victor needed the Georgians' networks to distribute their "imports." He knew what he should be looking for, but he hadn't yet found it.

Should he demand a piece of the action? Just this morning, Artur had promised him anything he wanted—money, power, *anything*—so long as he kept Inna safe.

She's safe. She's safe. She's safe. He quickly recited the mantra again, but he didn't believe the words. Artur wouldn't have sent Mikhail to fetch her, not after the debacle this morning.

He needed to end the interview with Hersh and get to her. And whatever he did, he couldn't let anyone—not Artur, not Hersh, not even Inna—guess what he was really after.

He wasn't about to let a boneheaded move, like confiding to Hersh or pushing Artur too soon, undermine everything he and Svetlana had worked for.

"Why are you telling me this?"

"Consider that I'm paying you forward. Someday you'll return the favor."

"Your intel would have to be a helluva lot better than that for me to owe you one," Vlad said.

"So you already know," Hersh said in an obvious attempt to fish for information.

"I'm sure I'm not the only one," Vlad hedged. The question was, who else knew, and how much trouble would the information cause?

"But I'll pay you back right now," he said. "If you're as smart as you think you are, you'll disappear before Ivan gets out of prison and hunts you down. You're at the top of his list."

"No one ever said I was smart," Hersh said. "You can tell Ivan I'm ready for him."

"Are we done yet?" Vlad asked, growing impatient. "You've got nothing. And your days are clearly numbered."

"You're right." Hersh gave a mild shrug, as if to say he had tried. "We can't hold you. We don't have enough to charge you with—yet."

KATYA

FROM HER PERCH in the basement crawl space, Katya listened intently for footsteps. Were those men coming for her? Would they find her?

She didn't hear anyone coming, but she smelled smoke. *Molotov cocktails.*

The house was on fire. Oh God, the house was on fire, and she was hiding in the basement.

The basement was an excellent hiding place, but not if the house was on fire. No one would find her—if help even arrived in time, if they even thought to look for her in a burning house.

She had to get out. She pushed aside the suitcases and slid herself to the floor in the basement storage room.

The smoke-tainted air was thick down here. She raced from her windowless closet.

No flames in the finished basement. *Sla va Bogu!* She ran for the stairs.

Then there was a sharp crack. In front of her, a floor beam crashed through the dropped ceiling and lit the carpet on fire. Flaming ceiling tiles dropped around her.

She shrieked and backed away from the flames and billowing smoke. A wall of roaring flames blocked her escape.

The fire seemed to chase her across the carpet. She ran to the farthest high window, the one above the sofa. Her eyes watered from the heat and smoke as she hopped onto the sofa and struggled to open the window. The frame was swollen and warped, and she didn't know if she even could.

She pushed harder. Her feet sank deep into the foam sofa cushions, but the window didn't budge. She tried again, pushing with all her might, even as the air around her grew thicker and threatened to suffocate her.

She could feel the heat of the fire at her back, but she didn't dare spare a moment to check its progress. She had to get out, and this window was her only option.

She thought of the baby growing inside her and found a strength she didn't know she had. She pushed on the window again. Her muscles strained.

Mercifully, the window groaned and the pane pushed outward.

The outside air was cold and wet, and she took a greedy, gasping, sputtering breath. She poked her head and torso through the window. Awkwardly, she shimmied through the narrow opening and into the window well outside.

She crouched behind the shield of corrugated metal that surrounded the window, trying to hide behind the sparse shrubbery at the side of the house while she surveyed the area for signs of the men she had seen earlier. Had they tried to smoke her out? Or had they lit the fire and then left?

If they were here, they'd be on her as soon as she showed herself, but she couldn't stay in this hiding spot much longer, not with the flames and smoke building behind her. She couldn't hold back her choking cough.

She momentarily closed her eyes and prayed as hard as she had ever prayed in her life.

She promised she would be brave. She would walk away from Aleksei if that's what was required. She would do anything she had to do to protect her child. *Please let us survive this.*

Seemingly in answer, she heard sirens in the distance. Then closer. Coming for her. And she knew they would both be safe.

ALEKSEI

ALEKSEI STUMBLED THE few blocks to his car. His stomach roiled. The brutal scene in the kitchen—all that blood—seemed tattooed on his eyelids. No matter how much he blinked, he saw Stan, face down in a still pool of his own blood.

The smell of blood seemed to stick to him. To follow him. He hadn't killed Stan. Yet, he thought he might never wash the blood off of himself.

He hadn't had to pull the trigger. *Sla va Bogu.* He wasn't sure he would have been able to do it, especially now. Now that he'd seen the body up close. Now that he understood the aftermath. The violent permanence.

What had he been thinking?

Woodenly, he got in his car. Peeled off his gloves. Fumbled with the seatbelt.

Sirens blared from every direction. He clutched the wheel, suddenly afraid. They were coming for him. They knew what he'd done. He'd be arrested. Thrown in prison. His life would be over.

Police. Fire. Ambulance. The vehicles streaked past him.

They weren't coming for him. They were responding to an emergency. See? Nothing to do with him. He exhaled and relaxed his muscles.

He could have lost everything, but he hadn't. Wouldn't. It was over now.

A sapling of true optimism began to take root, a tight bud of hope born amidst all the blood.

Stan was gone now, just as he and Mikhail had planned. If this plan had worked out, then the others could, too. Even better, a dead man had big shoulders. If there were any questions from his father or the Georgians or the police, they could blame the dead pharmacist for everything.

He started the engine and drove slowly away from Stan's neighborhood, even though he could hardly wait to put as much distance between himself and Stan's corpse as possible.

In a few minutes, he'd be home with Katya. Maybe he could pretend, even with all of the horrors of the night, that everything was fine. She would hold him. He would put his hand on her belly and imagine the baby growing there.

Stan, face down in blood that Aleksei had promised to shed. The image invaded, wouldn't leave him. He could smell the blood as if it were on him, all around him. Would Katya scent it, too?

What if she asked questions? Would she believe the lies he would have to tell her?

He turned onto his street with an urgent sense of foreboding. Maybe he shouldn't go home just now. Maybe he should wait a little, have a drink, and settle his nerves first. He didn't want her to be suspicious.

He thought about turning around and heading to Troika, but then he saw the emergency vehicles—the ones that had passed him only a few minutes before—now gathered in front of his house.

Katya!

He parked in his neighbor's driveway and ran toward his home, where a team of firefighters aimed a hose at his burning house.

He ran up the driveway, but someone grabbed him, pulled him to a stop. "My wife," he said. "Let me through. I live here. I have to find my wife."

Then he saw her near the ambulance and tore away to be by her side. She was sitting on a gurney in the back of an ambulance, an oxygen mask over her face. He climbed in beside her. "Katya. *Bozhe moi!* Katya, are you all right?"

She nodded, but she was in an ambulance getting treated for smoke inhalation. How all right could she be?

"Mr. Koslovsky?" A cop poked his head into the ambulance. "We'd like to ask you a few questions."

"What the hell happened?" Aleksei demanded, as if this nightmare was someone else's fault.

"Your brother-in-law called it in. Intruders. Firebomb. Same thing happened at your nightclub earlier."

"My nightclub?" The Georgians had done this? He didn't know what to say. He couldn't gather his thoughts. They'd come after him with far more violence than he had ever imagined, despite his cautious fear of Dato and his vicious knives.

Katya could have been killed.

"I should have been here," Aleksei said. "I should have been here to protect you."

"Where were you?" Her voice was scratchy, almost unrecognizable.

"Don't try to talk," the EMT told her.

Her gaze seemed to pierce him. He could plainly read the accusation in her wide green eyes. He felt all of his inadequacies and knew he deserved her sharpest indictment. He hadn't protected her.

The oxygen mask covered her expression, but she stared hard at Aleksei as if she could see inside him, read his every thought and flaw.

He wasn't a real man. Maybe she knew it.

She squeezed his hand, with enough pressure to make him believe she would forgive him for tonight, so long as she never learned the whole truth.

"I was on my way home from Troika," he said. "I guess it was before the bombing." He reached for the first convenient lie to flit into his head. "Then I got a flat tire and stopped to fix it."

Katya squeezed her eyes shut. A tear slid down her cheek.

"Hey, I'm here now," he tried to soothe her.

Too late, he realized he'd already used the flat-tire excuse the night they were supposed to meet Inna, the night the violence began. And Nick had been the one to change the flat, because Aleksei had pretended not to know how.

"Mr. Koslovsky, would you mind coming with me? I need to ask you some questions."

Quietly, he followed the cop. He had survived tonight, but he might still lose everything anyway.

VLAD

A BLACK CAR with tinted windows rolled to a stop in front of the precinct when Vlad came out. He jumped back as the window rolled down. Torpedo, the portly Russian who'd attacked him the other night in the street, greeted him with a leer. "Get in car," he said in broken English.

"Fuck you," Vlad said. He didn't have time for his father's men and their bullshit. He needed to get to Inna.

The driver's door swung open, and Slim got out. "The *Pakhan* sent us."

That title. Had Ivan really risen so high in the ranks of the *vor v zakone* that he was now a godfather?

"What the hell for?"

"To deal with the Georgians," Slim said. "Inna Koslovsky is under our protection as you requested. We have men watching her building. The Georgians won't get near there."

Of course they wouldn't. Not when Nadia lived in the same apartment building. Likely Ivan and his men had heard about the firebombing and weren't taking any chances in protecting Ivan's woman. Yet, Slim presented the information as if Inna's protection were a favor from Ivan to Vlad.

What was his father's game? This seemed like yet another test, and once again he wasn't sure of the rules or where he stood.

"Good," Vlad said as if he were in charge and they had obeyed his command. In a sense they had. The two men must have taken his warning about the danger to Inna to Ivan. "Take me to her."

He opened the back door of the sedan and got in, fully aware of the risk he was taking in going with them but unable to come up with a better alternative.

Pass or die.

Slim tore through traffic and bobbed through lanes like he was on a NASCAR track. They pulled up in front of the apartment building less than two minutes later.

They arrived as three Cadillac Escalades pulled onto the street in front of Inna's pre-war apartment building. The doormen pulled out guns and trained them on the idling cars.

"The Georgians," Slim said.

"I thought you said they weren't getting anywhere near here."

"They're not." Men filed out of the building and blocked the door. How many were there? Twenty? Thirty? Certainly, there were more than the crew of eight that Vlad remembered. How many men did Ivan have at his command now?

"Come with me," Slim told Vlad. Gun in hand, he walked with an easy gait toward the line. Vlad fell into step beside him, wishing he still had his own guns. Why would Slim want him, unarmed, by his side?

He squared his shoulders and faced his newest test.

The second SUV rolled down its rear window. In the passenger seat, Vlad made out an olive-skinned man with gold front teeth and almost black, curly hair. Dato, the head of the Georgian crew.

Slim walked toward Dato as if there were no threat, as if he were stopping to help a stranger with directions. His easy manner didn't dissipate the tension. Ivan's men all had their weapons in their hands. This could get very ugly very fast.

"You need to move on," Slim said with the calmness of someone who expected to be obeyed.

"We have a claim," Dato said.

"None here," Slim said. "Inna Koslovsky is under the *Pakhan's* protection."

Dato pointed with his knife at Vlad. "Then we'll take him. He was there that night. He'll do in her place."

Was that why Slim had brought him over here? Was he now to be traded? He should have known better than to expect any help from Ivan.

"No," Slim said before Vlad could act on the anger and betrayal burning through his soul. "He is Ivan's son."

"I see," Dato said with a deferential nod in Vlad's direction. He rolled up his window, and the three cars drove away.

"What the hell was that about?" Vlad demanded. He couldn't imagine his father getting sentimental over the son he had never acknowledged but had tried to kill on multiple occasions.

"I told you already. Inna's under our protection. They can't touch her."

"Not that. The 'son' bullshit. We both know Ivan is never going to acknowledge any family tie."

"Not the family one. No," Slim agreed. "The older *vory* have no families, and Ivan holds to the old ways." He paused as if his words explained everything. When Vlad didn't react, Slim added, "He plans to name you Son in the *bratva*."

"Bullshit." Vlad couldn't imagine his father promoting him to his right hand, giving him control over various crews. "He tried to have me killed last night."

Slim shrugged. "You survived."

"So he's promoting me?" Ivan dangled what Vlad most wanted. His way would be clear. Having such access, so much power, would be a momentous victory. This had to be a cruel lie.

"No," Slim said. "You have to prove your loyalty and kill a man in cold blood first."

"I have to kill a man in cold blood," Vlad repeated, incredulous.

"How else will we know for sure that you're not undercover?"

Right. Because a federal agent couldn't kill someone in cold blood, especially not if he planned to bring anyone to justice.

Ivan was calling his bluff.

He didn't see a simple solution to this new predicament, no obvious move on the chessboard.

"I choose who and when," Vlad said finally, as if he were accepting the challenge and taking charge.

There was no way he could pass this test, though. He'd already broken a lot of rules and was about to break a few more, but not this one. He wasn't a stone-cold killer like his father. He wasn't prone to senseless violence.

He turned on his heel and headed toward the door of the apartment building, where Ivan's men stood watching him.

"Where are you going?"

"To see my woman," Vlad said, knowing he sounded exactly like Ivan, down to the growl in his voice.

Around him, Ivan's men chuckled. He flipped them the bird, giving them the same gesture Ivan would. He'd leave them remembering he was truly Ivan's son in all the ways that mattered.

He only wondered how long he could pretend to be the beast before he actually became one.

MAYA

DATO PRESSED MAYA'S face into his lap. His erection pressed against her cheek. He'd moved his knife away when he'd opened the window, but the threat was ever present, a warning not to call attention or cry out for help.

She listened intently to the conversation. Inna was under the mafia's protection. Why wasn't Maya?

When the conversation ended and the car began moving again, Dato let her sit up. "How do you know I'm not under their protection, too?"

"I don't. But then, they don't know I have you." His eyes glittered with menace. He squeezed her thigh hard enough to bruise. "Don't ask. Don't tell."

She heard the driver chuckle at Dato's pathetic witticism. None of this was funny. Not in the least.

He said something to the driver and then pulled out his cell phone. She didn't understand the language, but she understood the tone. He was giving his men orders.

They turned onto the ramp for the Belt Parkway going east, away from Brooklyn. Where was he taking her? The traffic was light, just a few cars out. She looked out the window behind them, but the other cars in their procession were nowhere to be seen.

The driver stayed in the right lane and let other cars pass, driving slowly, most likely to avoid unwanted attention from the police.

"I do wonder, Mrs. Koslovsky, what you were doing *alone* at the pharmacist's house with a backpack of money. Care to tell me?"

"No," she whispered.

"I was hoping you'd say that. I'll enjoy uncovering all of your secrets." He leaned down and slid his knife from his boot. Before she could react, he sliced her leather jacket with a clean cut from collar to waist. The two sides fell away. He leaned in close and caressed the flat of his knife over her shirt. "I'll start with your clothes. Then your skin."

She pressed her lips together, determined not to feed his sadistic enjoyment by showing him how much he scared her.

He flicked his knife, cut open her shirt, and then laid his knife against her bare skin. He meant to carve her up. Slowly. She couldn't hold back her terrified whimper.

"That's right. Scream for me."

The car put on an unexpected burst of acceleration. She darted a swift glance at the driver. He was slumped over the wheel. Dead?

The car listed to the left, cutting across the lane. Another driver bore down on the horn as he swerved around them to pass on the right. They bumped against the safety barrier dividing the highway.

The impact bounced her against her seatbelt. Dato's knife bit into the tender skin above her breast. She yelped at the pain.

"Later," Dato promised her. Moving quickly, he sliced his own seatbelt and levered himself to climb into the front.

The driver fell across the seat, pulling the wheel with him. The car careened across the lanes. As Dato reached for the wheel, breaks screeched. A car in the right lane plowed into them.

There was a thundering impact. The crunch of metal. Maya screamed. Her seatbelt jerked. An airbag punched her back into her seat and into silence.

There was a second collision as the car barreled into the barrier at the right side of the road. The wheels spun, but the barrier held fast. Her nose filled with the pungent smell of burning rubber.

She undid her seatbelt. She ached where the airbag had hit her. Blood dripped from the cut Dato had made in her skin. Otherwise, miraculously, she was unharmed.

Dato's side of the car had taken the full impact of the crash. He lay crumpled on his back, his head against the mangled side of the car. He made no sound or movement. She hoped the bastard was dead, but she didn't waste time finding out.

Seeing her escape, she pushed open her door. Crouching, hoping that no one might see her, she sneaked along the side of the car and darted, head down, to the barrier that separated the road from a slim span of empty beach.

She climbed over and walked away.

No one would know she had been at Stan's. No one would know of her ride with Dato. Most likely no one even knew she had left her house tonight.

Drizzled sparkled around her. The wetness kissed her face, and she savored the invigorating sting of tiny droplets against her skin. She opened her hands, lifted her face, and laughed with the joy of the gift she'd just been given.

The angels were indeed smiling on her, the way they always had, granting her their blessings. She had doubted tonight, but she needn't have.

She had indeed gotten away with murder...again.

INNA

"I CARE ABOUT you," Mikhail said again.

Inna looked down shyly and broke the potential connection. "Thanks?"

She didn't know how to respond to him. She didn't want his attention. She liked it better when he didn't notice her.

She could feel her body letting go of the strain she'd carried now that the horrors of the evening were behind her. She might even be able to relax, if only Mikhail would take the hint and finally leave.

"You should go," she said. She didn't feel like being polite, but she tried. After all, it wasn't Mikhail's fault that the weekend's events had opened her eyes and everything around her looked menacing and different, including him. "I'd like to get some rest."

"You should drink some more," he said.

She'd managed a few sips earlier, but she had no appetite. She had played with the straw and pretended to drink, just to get him to stop bothering her about eating.

Now he was on her case again, waving the plastic cup at her. Was it her imagination, or was he obsessed with this milkshake that she didn't even want?

Maybe Mikhail had put drugs in it.

Paranoid much? She was silly to entertain any of her suspicions. Wasn't she? Yesterday's Inna would have thought so, but today she couldn't ignore her instincts. Someone had drugged her the other night at Troika, after all.

"Just drink a little more first, so I can tell your father."

Her father? What did he care whether or not she drank a milkshake? He only cared whether or not she took her medication. Would he go so far as to ask his employee to lace her milkshake with her medicine if he thought she'd stopped taking it?

"A little more, and then I'll go." His cajoling only heightened her suspicions.

Something was off, even if she didn't know precisely what.

She took the plastic cup from him and took a long pull on the straw. The thick liquid touched her tongue, but she only pretended to swallow. Mikhail watched her with unsettling intensity.

"Happy?" she asked.

"No, you can't even call that a sip. Drink a little more."

Definitely off.

She took longer this time, pretending several more swallows. The cup was opaque. He would never realize that the level of the liquid wasn't changing.

What exactly did he do for her father when he wasn't playing bodyguard? She had never wondered before, but now she did.

"Satisfied?" she asked.

"Very. Thank you." He made a production of tying his scarf around his neck, stalling. Why wouldn't he just leave? Was he waiting for some reaction to the drink? She put the offending cup on the hall table.

He reached out to touch her cheek. She didn't exactly flinch, but she hop-stepped away from him and opened her apartment door. He was getting too familiar, making moves that weren't about concern for her well-being, but another agenda entirely.

He needed to leave. Now.

"Goodnight. And thanks for everything."

To her dismay, he came up behind her and pushed the door closed.

"Do you feel safe here on your own? I'm worried about you. Maybe I shouldn't leave you." He stood behind her and whispered in her ear.

She couldn't mistake the invitation in his voice. He obviously wanted to stay. He wanted to do more than watch over her.

She tried not to shudder.

He definitely needed to go. She made a move to open the door again, but his hand closed over hers on the knob.

She fought her urge to jerk away from him and instead slid her hand out from under his. She didn't want to let on that she was starting to panic. What if he had drugged her milkshake and started to realize she hadn't had any?

Extricating herself from what could have become an embrace, she turned to face him. "Where did you stay last night when you guarded me?"

"I made rounds," he said. "Your hall. The lobby. The street outside. You know."

No, she didn't know. It didn't make sense that he would make a circuit of her building for hours with no breaks and no backup. But what did she know about the bodyguard business?

"And then those men jumped you." She examined his bruised cheek, but she didn't touch him.

She remembered that Vlad and her father had looked askance at him when he'd claimed he was jumped. At the time, she had thought they blamed him unfairly for failing to best her would-be kidnappers. What if there was another reason?

Mikhail had said he'd been jumped from behind. Shouldn't he have a bump on his head or something? Maybe marks on his neck if they'd grabbed him. The bruises were on his face and jaw.

"It was nothing," he said.

Maybe it had been nothing. Could he have made the whole thing up? After the highly orchestrated kidnapping attempt tonight, it seemed hard to believe that the same people would bungle disabling Mikhail and grabbing her, unsuspecting, off the street.

She didn't have enough information, only quickly multiplying suspicions that might seem ludicrous after a good night's sleep.

There was no way for her to sort any of this out, but she was getting frightened. She needed him gone. Needed the deadbolt and chain between them.

"I'm tired. It's been a long day for both of us. I need to go to bed." He didn't budge.

Banging on her door made them both jump. "Who's there?" she started to call out, but he clamped his hand over her mouth.

"Shhh!" He pulled her up against his body, as if he were taking her hostage. "You don't want whoever it is to hear you. It could be anyone. The doorman didn't call up."

He pulled her back with him into the apartment. He kept his hand over her mouth and pulled her so close that she would feel his arousal.

The pounding grew louder. "Inna, open the damn door now."

Vlad! The sound of his voice gave her such profound relief. Whatever he might be up to with her father, she instinctively trusted him. She'd watched him risk his life to save her.

"Hush," he warned and stroked his hand up her ribcage. She struggled in his grasp, and he held on tighter. "They'll go away if we ignore them."

She yanked Mikhail's hand from her mouth. "Let go of me!"

"I'm only keeping you safe," he murmured against her ear. He pulled her tighter against him, one arm at her waist, the other hand caressing her throat.

"I mean it. Let me go!" She elbowed him in the ribs. He grunted, but didn't release her.

"Who's in there with you? I'm coming in. I'll break down the damn door if I have to."

"It's open," she yelled before Mikhail could try to quiet her again.

Vlad threw the door open. He hurled himself at Mikhail and pinned him to the wall. "Did he hurt you?" Vlad demanded. He pressed his forearm against Mikhail's windpipe, cutting off his air.

"No. I'm okay," she said. She didn't want to contemplate what might have happened if Vlad hadn't come to the rescue.

"Why are you here?" Vlad demanded.

"You should be thanking me. I'm the one who's been doing *your* job while you were under arrest."

"Artur and I made other arrangements. You're not needed." Vlad nodded toward the hallway, and for the first time she noticed the two other men who'd followed him in from the hallway, their eyes and guns trained on Mikhail.

Had Mikhail lied when he claimed her father sent him? Maybe her father knew nothing of Mikhail's clumsy attempts at seduction or his tainted milkshake.

She stood behind Vlad. Close to Vlad. Feeling truly safe for the first time since she'd left the precinct.

"Inna needs her rest," Mikhail said. "Come on, big guy. We should let the lady get her beauty sleep."

"Right," Vlad said. He motioned to the men in the hallway, and they backed off, moving toward opposite ends of the hall. He took a step and knocked Mikhail with his shoulder, giving him an ungentle shove toward the door.

Mikhail looked back at Inna. "Inna, princess, if you need anything—anything at all—call me."

"She won't." Vlad pushed him again and then slammed the door in his face.

Inna could have applauded as Vlad locked the deadbolt and secured the chain. All the pent-up tension and fear from Mikhail's visit rushed out of her on a noisy exhale.

Vlad spun around to face her. "Before you scold me for being rude, yes, that was absolutely necessary."

"I wasn't—" she started to protest.

"He's not your bodyguard. I am." Vlad crossed his arms and took a wide stance in a show of authority. She might have been intimidated were it not for the small wince he made.

Her gaze flitted to the hole in the fabric at the center of his chest, too near his heart.

"You're in pain." He wore a plain suit and tie—not cheap, but definitely not custom. It was a mark of difference among the men she'd seen working for her father, who either didn't wear suits or, like Mikhail, wore the very best that money could buy.

What did Vlad do for her father?

"I'm fine," he said. He held up his hand as if to ward her away.

"Suit yourself." She wouldn't argue with him or even vilify him, not with the poignant reminder that he had been shot in the chest while trying to rescue her.

She wondered what he looked like under his ruined shirt and bulletproof vest. Did he have a wound? A bruise? Certainly, he would have muscles. She'd had months of fantasies about that. And now they were alone.

She felt the heat of another kind of danger, the lick of a flame, so close it could burn her up if she drew closer. Her fingers seemed to have a mind of their own, wanting to reach out and touch him, to feel the dark stubble on his jaw under her fingertips, to run along the impressive width of his shoulders, to trail over the muscular hills and valleys that must be hiding under his layers of clothes.

She clasped her hands behind her back and stayed where she was. He had made it clear to her that he didn't want her.

He gave her another look, one she couldn't read, and then cleared his throat. "You were supposed to wait for me at the precinct," he said. "You promised."

"But Mikhail—" She began to tell him that Mikhail had come for her at the precinct and pretended her father had sent him, but Vlad didn't give her the chance.

"Mikhail," he repeated. He stalked toward her, closing the small distance between them. His gaze seemed to bore through her. She backed up one step and then another. She could feel the dark intensity of his anger.

"I'm sorry," she whispered.

He glided his knuckles against her cheek in the softest of caresses. In that unexpected gentleness, she felt the echo of the boy she used to know. "Don't be afraid of me. *Never* be afraid of me. I will never hurt you."

"I know." She couldn't explain why she trusted him. She just knew that she did.

His eyes weren't flinty and unreadable tonight. No. Instead of a lack of emotion, there seemed to be too much—a rising storm that could either savage her or wash her clean.

His voice shook with a barely contained threat. "Tell me you didn't want him to stay."

"You mean Mikhail?"

"You said you'd wait. You left me for him." His eyes flashed with the lightning that heralded a storm. He took another step toward her, and she backed up until she hit the wall, bracing herself for the violent roll of thunder. Welcoming it.

He caged her with his hands, but didn't touch her. She could feel his breath against her skin. He smelled of rain, and she felt as if the wind were picking up all around them.

She couldn't look away. She was locked in his gaze, saw herself reflected in his pupils. Only her, as if she were the center of his world.

He lowered his head, and she hoped he would kiss her.

Yet, he paused, a hairsbreadth between them, as if he were giving her the chance to push him away, to stop him, as if she could snap her fingers and end the storm chasing her.

Or maybe he was having second thoughts. Maybe he still didn't want her.

"Vlad," she said. A whisper. A prayer. A plea.

His hand cupped her neck. His fingers massaged her collarbone, and the world shrank to his touches, to the lightning in his eyes, to the promise of the kiss she'd craved for months.

She wanted his kiss, like she'd never wanted anything before. She couldn't remember any of the reasons this had been forbidden before, couldn't comprehend why she hadn't had a taste of what she wanted, couldn't imagine any obstacles in her way or risks, couldn't abide a moment's more delay.

He could have been killed today. This moment could have been stolen from her forever.

"Tell me you want me," he said. "Only me."

She reached up and kissed him.

The kiss wasn't gentle. It was a wild, untamed thing she unleashed on him, as powerful as the storm she glimpsed in his soul.

She threw herself deeper into their maelstrom of a kiss—climbing him, riding the storm, claiming everything he offered—and everything he didn't. Everything that had ever been denied her. All of it. She wanted. She wanted everything. Not only a kiss, but more.

So much more.

VLAD

VLAD AWOKE IN a room he didn't immediately recognize. Inna was tucked against him. A very naked Inna.

Mine. His arm curled possessively around her as the events of last night assaulted him in an erotic rush.

She had seemed afraid of him at first, and the fear had seriously pissed him off. He had gotten up in her space even though she'd flinched, or maybe *because* she had flinched—just so he could prove to both of them that he wasn't a monster, not like Ivan.

That was the last semi-rational thought he'd had before she'd kissed him and turned his world upside down. Inna hadn't been gentle or shy or any of the things he'd expected. Not fragile and vulnerable; not his woman.

Inna was a wild force of nature, and she had ripped him to bits, shredding his every last defense. He had fantasized about claiming her, but the reality was better than fantasy.

She had claimed him with more pent-up, desperate passion than he ever could have imagined.

This wasn't supposed to happen. It put everything he and Svetlana had worked for in jeopardy. Yet he was unrepentant.

Whatever this was between them, he wasn't going to give it up.

"You awake?" she murmured. She stroked his chest, touching the deep bruises from the impact of the bullets his vest had caught. The mark on his shoulder from the men in the alley and the one square in the chest, courtesy of her kidnappers.

"Does it hurt?" she asked.

"Not when you're touching me."

"Is that an invitation?"

"A little late for that," he said. "You stormed in and took possession."

"Oh." Her face heated. She drew away. Sitting up, she took part of the sheet with her to cover up. "I'm so, so sorry." She started to scoot off the bed.

"Sorry?" He didn't like her withdrawal or the shame he sensed in her. Did she think this was a mistake? He wanted her more than he'd ever wanted anyone or anything in his life, and she was about to pull the plug and retreat.

"You didn't want this." Her slender fingers clutched the sheet around her, as if there could be any secrets after the night they'd shared.

"What the hell are you talking about?"

She flinched at his harsh tone. He tried to soften his voice, to reach for the words that would entice her back to him. But damn it, soft words and flowery emotions weren't his thing.

He had no practice. None. His whole life had been comprised of harsh truths and jagged edges.

"You were doing your job. And I...I crossed the line. I jumped you."

Her words stunned him. "Is that what you think happened?"

She wouldn't meet his eye.

He groped for the right words, but they were slow in coming. She started talking before he had the chance to set her straight.

"This is never going to work." She took a deep breath and lifted her chin. "You're fired." The slight tremor in her fingers belied her air of command.

"You can't fire me."

"You're fired," she repeated. "I don't want you as my bodyguard."

"You're firing me because we slept together?" Something dark and ugly rose up in him in response to her rejection. "I don't accept that."

He couldn't abide the thought of anyone else this close to her, sharing her days and nights, sharing her bed. He lunged across the mattress and grabbed her wrist, making her tumble toward him.

She fought his grip and smacked him hard on the shoulder. "Tough. I refuse to be your job."

"You're more than a job to me, Inna."

She tore out of his grasp. "You don't understand."

No, he didn't understand. How could she boot him out? She grabbed up her clothes and stalked out of the room to her bathroom. He watched in bemusement. What had he said? What had he done? Why didn't she want him?

He scrubbed his hands over his face and bounced out of the bed. This wasn't over. He yanked on his boxers and suit pants and parked himself outside the bathroom door.

"No, I don't understand. Who's going to protect you?" His attempt to reason with her sounded more like shouting than a rational argument, especially when she shouted back, "Who's going to protect *you?*"

"I don't need anyone to protect me," he said.

"Right. That's why you keep getting shot."

"You think I can't do my job?"

"I don't want you hurt. I don't want you risking your life for me," she said from the other side of the door—a near declaration of love or, at least, the closest thing to it he had ever received.

"Firing me won't change anything," he said. "I care about you too much to let anything happen to you. Even if that means risking my life."

She opened the door then. "You're insane."

Maybe she was right. Love was its own kind of insanity.

He ended the whole ridiculous argument with a kiss. His lips moved feverishly on hers with the soul-bearing truth of his need and desire for her. She made a startled gasp, and then, miraculously, yielded and opened to him.

He clutched her to him. His whole life might be wrapped in deception, but this much—this passion, this intensity—was absolutely real and couldn't be denied.

With his kiss, he told her everything she wasn't ready to hear, all the true and loving words he couldn't say when everything else about him was a carefully constructed lie.

THANK YOU

Thanks so much for reading. I hope you:

Leave a review. Your reviews help authors like me get discovered by readers. So if you liked what you've read, please spread the word.

Read the rest of the *Kings of Brighton Beach Series.* The gang will be back in *Mobbed Up*, to be released in 2017. Visit dbshuster.com for more information about the series and characters.

Sign up for my newsletter at dbshuster.com for information about new releases, sneak peeks, contests, and special offers.

Check out my humorous and sexy *Neurotica Series* for thrills of another kind. There's an excerpt after this.

NEUROTICA SERIES

"A wicked romp through the hallowed halls of academia!" Laugh out loud at these clever and sexy tales. Academia has never been so naughty!

The university men in Professor Melanie Stevenson's life pressure her to take her proper place—under them. While the proper professor indulges in daring daydreams of…submitting to their will, her "evil" twin, Violet, takes on the role of academic avenger and cracks the whip, so to speak, to work out the kinks in higher education.

Written by a college professor, this witty series takes a darkly funny look at the neurotic people and politics of higher education. These eight consecutive short stories tell a larger tale with rich characters, escalating stakes, and steamy action.

What Readers are Saying

"Timid Professors, evil twins and a good dose of slightly naughty will have you chuckling over the office water cooler."

"Love this series! Smart, funny, and sexy. Great brain candy!"

"Hot and hillarious!"

""Funny, sexy, and intelligent."

EXCERPT FROM PLEASING PROFESSOR

HE WANTED THINGS his way, on his terms, and he would crush or damage anything that got in his way. Melanie would have been quaking in her sober pumps from fear ... and lust.

Too bad for him she wasn't Melanie. Or maybe that would be good for him... and for her. She would be more than happy to play professor and teach the haughty Hunter a thing or too.

"This is a bullshit course, and everyone knows it," he said.

"Then why'd you take it?"

"Because it was supposed to be easy. I already know everything I need to know about sex."

"Do you? Close the door."

He glanced at her with surprise, perhaps because he expected Melanie's Sesame Street voice and sweetness, or perhaps because he thought he was in charge and this interview was going better than he'd hoped.

He pulled the door shut. "I'm willing to show you—in exchange for a better grade."

"Oooh. The ultimate sacrifice," she said.

He stalked toward her and pulled her out of her chair. "I know you want me. I've seen how you look at me. I'm willing to give you what you want."

"I bet that's what you tell all the girls."

"Only the hot ones," he said.

"I bet they line up for the honor."

"They do," he said, with the confidence of someone surrounded at all times by sycophantic admirers. "I'm a sex expert."

"Who told you that? The inexperienced college girls you fumble in the dark? Forgive me if I'm unimpressed."

"I'll make it good for you," he said.

She didn't need a doctorate to read the raw desire in his eyes. What would he do if his professor gave him *exactly* what he wanted?

"How's this supposed to go?" she asked. "Am I supposed to say, 'Oh, yes, Hunter, I want you'?" She mimicked Melanie's sweetest, squeakiest muppet voice. She slipped out of his hold and perched on her desk. "Take me, Hunter. Right here. Right now. Brighten my miserable life with your godlike touch. Oh, oh, Hunter, I *crave* you. I'm incomplete without your golden hands kneading my skin." She leaned back on her elbows, spread out on the desk, her legs falling open. "Take me. Take me now. Give me the orgasm I've never had, and I'll give you the A you want."

He moved toward her as if her invitation were real. *Seriously?*

ABOUT THE AUTHOR

D. B. Shuster is married to a Russian man, who regularly assures her he is not a member of the mob. By day, she is a professor of Sociology, and her research keeps her busy with facts and numbers. By night, she lets her imagination run free with dark and twisted tales of crime and intrigue. Sometimes she sleeps. She lives in New York with her family.

I love to hear from readers. Here are some ways to connect with me:

Email: dbshuster@gmail.com
Website: http://dbshuster.com
Twitter: @DBShuster
Facebook: http://facebook.com/dbshuster/
Pinterest: http://www.pinterest.com/dbshuster/

CHARACTER LIST

Aleksei. Aleksei Koslovsky. Katya's husband. Son of Artur and Maya. Inna's brother.

Anya. Young waitress at Troika.

Artur. Artur Koslovsky. Maya's husband. Father of Inna and Aleksei. Ivan's former partner. A powerful figure in the Russian mob.

Dato. Dato Dzhugashvili. Head of Georgian crew.

Dr. Kasporov. Psychiatrist on Artur's payroll who used to treat Inna.

Dr. Shiffman. Marjorie Shiffman. Inna's therapist.

Frankie. Francesca Salvatore. Nick's stepsister.

Gennady. Gennady Morozov. Representative of the Directorate.

Goga. Dato's bodyguard. Member of the Georgian crew.

Gregorovich. Artur Gregorovich. KGB agent who Nick believes murdered his family and now goes by the alias Artur Koslovsky.

Hershey. Saul Hersh. Homicide detective who sent Ivan to prison on trumped up charges.

Inna. Inna Koslovsky. Daughter of Artur and Maya Koslovsky. Aleksei's sister.

Ivan. Ivan Chertoff. Vlad's father. Notorious vor v zakone, currently in prison for murder.

Jack. Jack Roseman. Co-owner of Troika with Aleksei. Katya's brother-in-law.

Katya. Katya Koslovsky. Aleksei's wife.

Kolya. Nikolai Salvatore. Kolya is the Russian diminutive of Nicholai and Nick's Russian nickname.

Marano. Tony Marano. Police officer on Artur's payroll.

Marco. Marco Salvatore. Nick's stepbrother. Roman is his twin.

Maya. Maya Koslovsky. Artur's wife. Mother of Inna and Aleksei.

Mikhail. Mikhail Gorki. Aleksei's best friend. Member of Artur and Victor's crew. Maya's lover.

Mimi. Sofia Salvatore. Nick's mother. Paul's wife. Frankie, Roman, and Marco's stepmother.

Nadia. Nadia Ambramovich. Vlad's estranged mother. Ivan's lover.

Nick. Nikolai Salvatore. Katya's co-worker. Believes Artur is the KGB agent who destroyed his family.

Nonna. Nick's step-grandmother. Paul's mother.

Paul. Paul Salvatore. Nick's stepfather.

Philip. Svetlana's son.

Roman. Roman Salvatore. Nick's stepbrother. Roman is his twin.

Rosales. Detective from Brooklyn Police Department.

Saul. Saul Hersh. Homicide detective who sent Ivan to prison on trumped up charges.

Sharp. Detective from Brooklyn Police Department.

Slim. A member of Ivan's crew.

Sofia. Sofia Reitman. Artur's lover. Nick's mother. Artur suspects the Directorate of her murder.

Stan. Pharmacist who works for Aleksei.

Sveta. Svetlana Timoshenko. Bartender at Troika.

Svetlana. Svetlana Timoshenko. Bartender at Troika.

Torpedo. A member of Ivan's crew.

Victor. Victor Zhirov. Artur's partner in his work for the Directorate.

Vitaliy. Mikhail's friend and co-conspirator.

Vlad. Vladimr Abramovich. Son of Ivan and Nadia. Handles security for Artur's operation.

Zviad. Member of the Georgian crew found murdered at Troika.

Made in the USA
Middletown, DE
19 April 2023